Escape for escape.

It was a fair exchange. Helplessly Sarah stood, hugging herself, uncertain of what she should do. Sinister sounds of approaching marauders were absorbed by the whispered crunch of boots upon leaves, creaking leather accompanied by the muted jangle of spurs, and the agitated snorting of animals eager to move. The jagged current of danger crackled invisibly in the darkness . . .

Once again the peculiar sensation that life would never again be the same blunted her thoughts. The time had come. From this moment on there would be no turning back.

Ballad in Blue

Linda Shaw

BALLANTINE BOOKS • NEW YORK

To Bennett

Ballad in
Blue

August 1863
THE LEGACY

THE TWO FURIOUSLY GALLOPING RIDERS were illuminated by a late summer full moon as they rounded the final bend in the road and pulled up before the tiny cabin, their horses lathered and panting. One rider, a blond man in filthy Confederate rags, dismounted even before his poor beast had stopped, and ran to the door.

Terror had gripped the cabin's lone occupant when hoofbeats awakened her, and she stood rigid now, not daring to breathe. The door was flung open and she wavered, stifling a sob, before throwing herself at the shadow of a man who stood before her. The whisper of small, bare feet moving across the rough floors broke the silence. Cries escaped both their lips as they embraced one another, clinging as hard as they could.

The other rider had the decency to keep his distance, but the moonbeams intruded, as moonbeams will, filtering easily through the little place, lighting the lovers' way to bed. Curiously, their coming together was not an act of lust but a bond of promise. In his desperation, the kind of desperation only war can bring about, the man offered nothing but his own need. The woman gave her husband what comfort she could, along with her love, and her promise for the future.

Her acceptance of his seed into her body was a ceremonial act and had little to do with sex: there wasn't time for ordinary human needs. And so the child who began growing inside her was a kind of exchange. Its

1

life was what his parents were given instead of a future together.

When the moon rose full the next time, it witnessed the bloody death of the blond Confederate. The man's child had taken a firmer hold on life, was a month closer to its birth, and the exchange had been made.

⣷ Chapter I

April 1865
TENNESSEE

"I'LL SEE YOU PAY for your wickedness!" shrieked the gnarled old woman. Her impossibly high voice reverberated painfully in the tiny mountain cabin, disturbing the sleeping baby no less than his fair, slender mother. She rocked him, soothing the boy back to sleep, her wide brown eyes searching the little room for something to focus on—anything but the pinched old face moving before her.

A bony figure poked close to Sarah's face, and she tossed back her thick, long brown waves with a nervous gesture. Would Rachel never stop? Could she endure yet another evening of the woman's ranting? *Oh, Charles,* she mourned silently. *How did everything become so terrible? And why am I so alone?*

"If it hadn't been for you, Sarah High-and-Mighty," the peevish voice resumed, "Charles would be home with me and servin' the South as a commissioned officer, as Langston Bradley's son should have. Enlistin' as a common foot soldier! I still can't believe it. Disgraceful! The whole affair has been disgraceful from beginnin' to end!"

Sarah's thick lashes all but hid her stormy eyes, yet she occasionally glimpsed Rachel's witch face, the cruel, pinched mouth and ceaseless tongue.

"How the two of you thought you could come here and live in this dream world is beyond me." Rachel clicked her teeth together, a mannerism that often provoked Sarah nearly to the screaming point. "If you,

3

missey, had spent half the time doin' somethin' practical that you spent playin' music or readin' books, you and Charles would've had somethin' by now, instead of his leavin' you destitute. Justin Fowler was a damn fool for ever givin' Charles this land to begin with. Charles certainly married beneath himself when he picked you! Charles *had* to marry for love. Well, you see where love got him!" she sneered, brushing out her hand as if to cast a disgusting insect from her face. "Charles could have finished his education and taken the practice his father built for him. I would've even paid you to keep your hands off him. Did you know that? Eh? Yes, I'd have paid you. Now Charles is dead and whose fault is it? Do you think you're not accountable for that? I'll burn in hell before I let you walk away from that without payin'! You can put it down in your book, Sarah Catherine Bradley. You'll pay all right!"

"You can't do anything to me except plague me to death, Mrs. Bradley," sighed Sarah. A strained silence finally began descending on the darkening room. The last rays of a sun as spent as she was created orange patches upon the freshly laundered curtain. Sarah's rocker creaked its weariness of Rachel's nightly lecture. "Why not go to bed? I'm quite tired, and I need rest."

Fully expecting a retort, Sarah listened thankfully as Rachel's scuffing slippers receded to the makeshift sleeping quarters that Sarah had arranged for her nearly a year ago. Had she dreamed that informing Rachel about the nearing birth of Charles' baby would have resulted in such a prolonged stay, she would have kept it a secret.

Charles Bradley had been a dreamer. She didn't deny that. And in one last, rash attempt to remove himself from the suffocating dominance of his grandmother, he had impulsively turned his back upon his preparations for the bar and brought his beautiful new

4

bride westward to this tiny mountain cottage in the Cumberland Mountains of Tennessee. Sarah's lips formed a faint smile, a memory of Charles in an old yellow sweater and tweed trousers shaping itself in her mind. She could almost smell his pipe tobacco.

"Ah, love," he had naively predicted, his gentle eyes sweeping to encompass the heavens, "we will live off the summer people. We will lie in the sun and eat wild strawberries. And I will make a baby grow in your beautiful belly."

But that had been before the war, before Charles had been killed by the sabre of a blue-clad Yankee, before Peter had cried his first, and before Rachel Bradley had come to fill Sarah's life with endless torment. Now Charles was gone, the summer people no longer came, and the fatherless baby lay slumbering in her arms.

"Well," she breathed, "I suppose I may as well bed you down, my beautiful little man." For the thousandth time Sarah searched the small face for the traces of a man now gone. Bending to inhale the sweet baby freshness that soothed her troubled spirit, Sarah cradled Peter and padded across the braided rug to their small bedroom. She lowered Peter softly onto his homemade cot, an arm's length from the larger bed she and Charles had shared.

As Sarah tucked the cover beneath his chin Peter roused slightly, adorable sucking noises puckering his rosy mouth. Abruptly, a devastating wave of pity for the child overwhelmed her. The seeming hopelessness of their future stretched so eternally before her that great tears spilled from her eyes. Dropping her tousled head into her worn hands, Sarah's slender body shook with great, heaving shudders.

"Trapped. I'm trapped." The truth struck home once more as hot tears cascaded down her cheeks. "Charles has died cruelly in a war with which he had no issue, and Rachel is slowly bleeding me to death—

5

living here and refusing to use a penny of her wealth to keep us from starving to death. *Why* doesn't she go home? Oh, lord, how much longer will I be able to keep three people alive in this place?"

In a tireless battle with the soil she grew potatoes and cowpeas, corn and turnips. The trick was the stratagem of growing it where it would not be found by scavenging hands and then hiding it carefully after it was harvested. Large clans of Confederate deserters scoured the countryside, plundering foodstuffs and horses. Sarah had rarely seen any deserters, but she knew when they had been there, for during winter snows she saw footprints weaving around the house site.

The Northern troops found little booty on the mountain and generally kept well to the valley for food supplies. Occasionally blue troops traversed the ridge from Chattanooga to McMinnville or Tracy City and back, in their unending struggle to keep the Nashville & Chattanooga Railroad running.

"It's a disgrace to see my great-grandson livin' like a darkie. Where I come from, people call your kind white trash!"

Sarah whirled—long tresses billowing from her tear-stained face. "Is there nothing sacred to you?" she hissed. Rachel was like a consuming malignancy, forcing its roots into every detail of her existence and greedily gobbling every shred of life force she possessed. Sarah gritted her teeth. "Please, please, won't you just go to bed and *leave me alone!*"

Rachel's high-pitched laugh cackled eerily, and Sarah shivered. Then suddenly Rachel turned and hobbled to her room. How could her tender, gentle-spoken Charles have been related to such a woman?

Absently, Sarah stroked the ridge of hard calluses spreading the width of her palm. Her hands, more than any other part of her body, spoke of her struggle against starvation.

Sarah was not a tall woman. But suffering had served to stiffen her back, lifting her fair head in defiance. Her facial features were delicate, and though tanned and a trifle drawn, they still did not acknowledge her twenty-one years. Her teeth were beautiful. Fine brows accentuated incredibly deep, brown eyes that could swiftly reflect smouldering anger or velvet warmth. Once Sarah's thick brown tresses had been a thing of beauty, but she had long ago accustomed herself to winding them into a plain knot behind her head, as they worried her when she toiled in the outdoors. When Sarah attired herself in her one remaining gown, severely simple, the trimness of its bodice pronouncing the gentle swell of her breasts and the slenderness of her waist, she was not unaware of her charm.

In defiance of Rachel's clamorous objections, Sarah had unpacked Charles' clothes and altered them to fit herself, her few dresses having suffered an exhausted demise, one after another. The snug-fitting breeches had served her well against the bitter Tennessee winters. Sarah created quite an alluring picture as she tromped about the mountain, attacking masculine chores with determination.

The resounding explosion caught Sarah so unaware that she stumbled forward in reaction, catching herself squarely against the bedpost. For a fleeting moment she needed to retch. Gunshots had frightened Sarah before, but since Sherman's march through South Carolina this past spring, Sarah and her mountain neighbors had found themselves lulled into a false sense of peace.

"Sa*rahh!*" Rachel's screech startled Sarah almost as badly as the explosion had, and the old woman thumped into the front room, her grey hair spraying out from her bobbing head like an alarmed porcupine.

Sputtering, shifting back and forth before the window, Rachel stopped jerkily, pushing her pinched old face against the glass. In vain she searched for the source of the explosion, grasping the curtain to rub at the windowpane, then peering again. She clicked her teeth again and again.

"It's too dark now, Mrs. Bradley, and too far away. You could never see it," Sarah sighed, tugging a fresh log from its box at the end of the raised hearth. Attempting to ignore the provoking woman, Sarah half-heartedly stirred about in the fire with a blackened poker, the flames responding as they greedily gobbled at the dry wood, forcing Sarah to recede from the heat. She turned her back, exposing slender calves to the warmth by raising the hem of her gown.

"Will you quit fussin' with that infernal fire and get out there on the porch! See if you can hear anything."

"Mrs. Bradley," Sarah began, "there is nothing I can do. If it is Yankees, we will be more or less at their mercy. And I doubt that anyone else would come to the house. I beg of you to settle down for the night. It's getting late and—"

"You witless baggage!" Rachel shrieked. Anger set Sarah's jaw, for she foresaw the elder Bradley continuing the railing she had commenced earlier. Her temper soared. In two strides Sarah stood before Rachel, burying bruising fingers into the loosely fleshed arms. Rachel's jaw dropped in astonishment.

"Mrs. Bradley," rasped Sarah between tightly clinched teeth, "if you say one more word, I think I'll strike you. Will you *please* go to bed? I can't stand anymore tonight."

Rachel found half her voice, at least. "Don't you touch me! Who do you think you are?" Calculating eyes squinted. Rachel raked the reckless younger woman through narrowed slits, and Sarah retreated several paces.

"How dare you speak to me like that? You need to

learn respect for your betters, you high-handed nobody! What you need is a hard lesson in humility. Don't you even have the sense to know when you're licked? Your fancy plans to marry money are ruined, my dear girl. You'll never get a cent when I die. Not one cent, do you hear?"

Sarah stammered, dumbfounded. "I never wanted money. Ch-Charles never wanted. . . ."

"Don't demean yourself by denying it," sneered Rachel.

"Well, deny it I will! As heaven is my witness, I will! I never wanted your miserable money, and neither did Charles. Charles couldn't tolerate the way you manipulated his life, Mrs. Bradley. Don't you think the man even had the right to an opinion about the repulsive engagements you tried to foist—"

"Wicked! Wicked! What do you think you gave him? Quality? Silas Hartman was a good-for-nothin' lumberjack. And no more pride than to desert his only child. For nothin'—everything was for nothin'. Cracker white trash! That's all your daddy was, an' that's all you'll ever be. No property, workin' like some field hand, lettin' yourself get brown as a darkie. No self-respectin' family would let you set foot in their house! Charles threw away a good life and a fortune when he married you!"

For too many months, Sarah had dammed the flood. And now, finally, the dam burst.

"You!" she cried, whirling, a damning finger pointing straight between Rachel's eyes. "Charles hated you, Mrs. Bradley. He was a fine, sensitive man, and you stepped on him until he felt the life breath crushed from his body. How many times did he say to me that he would never be free until you were in your grave? How many times?"

Sarah's mouth blanched ashen, and her hands shook, but the words had waited too long. She could not stop them now. "Do you have any idea what it's

9

like to live each day in a desperation so absolute that you can't even form the words to say how much you despise life? Well, Charles did. And you did that to him. You—with that strangling dominance that allows no way but your own."

Rachel's breath whistled past her teeth, but the torrent began in controlled quietness, rapidly increasing in rancor until Sarah doubted that the old woman could have stopped herself.

"When I get through with you, Sarah Bradley, there won't be enough of you left to mop the floor with," she said calmly. "Right now, at this very moment, two of the best legal minds in th' entire state of South Carolina are travelin' to Tennessee. Yes, to this hovel! You see, we're goin' to take that child from you, Sarah. You can't support him. Look at you, livin' like a darkie. Charles would have wanted me to give Peter the life he deserves. He's the last of my blood, and I mean to have him. You aren't fit to raise a Bradley. Why do you think I've stayed in this slovenly place, livin' like some nigger sharecropper? Because I will *have that child*. And there's not one damn thing you can do about it. I have more power than you dream possible. Now, smart girl," she snarled, "I suggest you put a civil tongue in your head."

Assured that she had the girl where she wanted her, Rachel subsided. She had not meant to disclose her plans so soon, but the creature drove her to distraction. Nothing was lost, for Sarah's well-deserved punishment would only be the keener during the dreadful waiting. This would be a good lesson in humility for the proud bitch! Rachel at last turned toward her quarters and a perceptive calm settled upon the dark cottage.

Sarah slowly discerned that she had sunk to the cold floor. Time had passed—how much she didn't know. The flames still crackled.

Flee—she must flee! Morning must not find them in the cottage. But go where? If worst came to worst, they could hide in the forest, but the first and immediate concern was to get out of this house! But as she frantically organized the steps she must take, a new fear threatened. What about Jackson?

Jackson was an old grey mule Charles had brought home one afternoon before the war began. Of the few possessions Sarah owned, the old mule was most important. The miracle of their survival was due in a large degree to Jackson, and she guarded him jealously. Every day, even in winter, he was moved to one of several hiding places deep in the many hollows of the Cumberland Mountains, and Sarah brought him out of seclusion only when very heavy work demanded it. Somehow, with an enormous amount of caution and a bit of luck, Sarah had managed to keep the old animal from being stolen.

"Why did I take Jackson toward the bluff, tonight of all nights?" she mourned, the bluff being well over a half mile's trek from the cottage. Without the mule, escape was impossible. So her first step was to fetch him. But that had been complicated by the explosion they had heard earlier. The question of who was moving about on the bluff was of the greatest importance.

Sarah felt a wave of nervous energy surge through her slight frame. Suddenly she became mobile. Her small feet flew to her bedroom, and her trembling hands were the only betrayal of her fear. Stripping off the nightgown, she hastily donned a pair of rough breeches and a shabby pullover sweater. Her naked flesh gleamed, innocently beautiful in the faint moonlight, and her full breasts grew gooseflesh in the chilled room. A swift glance at the slumbering Peter quickened her as she yanked on small, worn boots.

"They will not take you, my love," she silently promised.

Peter was oblivious to her quivering kiss, and Sarah sped to Charles's old brown jacket hanging on a peg near the front door. Rachel must be sleeping, for there

11

was no sound besides her steady breathing. Sarah had no idea how, but she never doubted that everything would come to pass exactly as Rachel had promised. From incidents Charles had disclosed, Sarah well understood Rachel to be a woman of considerable power, no matter how senile and incapable she might appear on the surface.

Flicking a last glance about the stark but orderly house, the house where she and Charles had kissed the last kiss nearly two years before, the house where Peter had been born, Sarah slipped the old jacket over her slender shoulders, bunching her long locks down underneath the back. Her life here was over, changed in a few minutes. How fragile life was, Sarah reflected despondently as the door closed softly behind her. A sigh of sorrow escaped her.

As Sarah turned up the collar on the old jacket and sped across the yard, a certain courage born of positive action began to renew her. With certain steps she began to penetrate the forest undergrowth of the ridge itself. Beech trees and chestnuts, so immense that two men could hardly encompass them, towered above her. Clumps of sumac and angry briers as thick as one's thumb tangled with creeping vines, furiously resisting her intrusion. She understood very well why the mountain defied army activities.

A narrow path, worn by her dragging of firewood from the forest depths, lay open for a major portion of the distance she traveled to reach Jackson. Her path lay parallel to the wagon road, and close enough that she could ascertain any activity taking place on the road. Her intuition told her that she was in no danger from whoever had caused the explosion.

"Whoever it was must surely have moved on down toward the valley, or I would have heard some sound, or seen something by now," she panted, her breasts rising and falling rapidly as a tiny cloud of vapor streamed from her lips. Her brief trek through the thick growth had been deftly accomplished with little betraying noise, for she knew the path well and slipped through the brambles as delicately as a wraith. She was aware, however, that the path ended just beyond her. Precautions must be increased, for the forested terrain would make a sudden dip toward the wagon road before it spilled into the creek. Every step must be calculated carefully. So intense was Sarah's concentration that she nearly collided with the reined-up saddle horse before she heard his warning snort.

At that precise moment, also, her ears detected muffled groans from some point just ahead. She froze where she stood, behind a tangle of vines. As she stood, she became aware of the muted rumbling of a deep voice. Rapidly it grew nearer, more distinct, and was suddenly just before her face. Sarah could discern his features, even in the darkness, and she saw that he was quite tall and broad-shouldered. Dark hair escaped from under his wide-brimmed hat, wisps of it blending with the stubble on his lean jaw. What prevented him from staring straight into her eyes Sarah didn't know. She almost screamed, he was so close.

She quickly detected the tightly controlled rage of the man as he growled under his breath. For interminable seconds he stood, gathering items from his saddlebags, with an impatient movement of his blue-sleeved arm he swept a rolled blanket from behind his saddle. With great relief, Sarah watched him turn away. But her relief was short-lived. In dismay she saw two mounted men, their horses stomping laboriously through the underbrush just beyond.

Full force, the impact of her state struck her—inadvertently she had stumbled on a small Yankee division of which one member was evidently injured, one extremely angry and to all appearances quite dangerous. Two more were scouring the terrain from horseback. God only knew what else there was besides.

"Reacher!" barked the tall man, unfolding himself from over the dark form on the ground. "Get some light over here."

The absence of the familiar Southern drawl startled Sarah, and the self-assured, easy command warned her—this man was certainly not one to trifle with.

"Comin' up, sir." Reacher was a slight, bearded figure, somewhat older than his superior, and his voice possessed an eerie quality, a combination of hoarseness and whisper. In less than a minute he had fished out a lantern from what Sarah now realized was a shattered wagon. Bright fingers of light were soon clawing their way through the thick forest walls.

"Davidson. Anything?" Standing, the commander allowed the rays to strike him squarely. He was thirty, and his blue Federal uniform carried captain's markings. His pants hugged slender, muscled legs, and a dusty jacket was belted securely over narrow hips and a flat belly. A holstered handgun rode at his waist.

"No, sir. Two of them are dead, sir, but the other three just disappeared. We looked around for about a half mile, but . . . no good, sir." The blond youth shrugged, his nineteen or so years underscoring the hesitancy in his reply. Alighting before the captain he tugged at the bill of a crumpled blue cap and swung his arm in a wide gesture toward the road.

"We can take the road a bit farther east, if you say so, Captain," he offered.

"Blasted deserters," gritted the officer. He stood for several seconds, removing his hat and running long fingers through his dark locks. Jamming his hat back on impatiently, he began to issue orders.

"Reacher, salvage what food you can from the wagon. If there's any ammunition left, bury it. The vipers could easily come back, and more besides. Davidson, unhitch the mules and help Reacher pack 'em with what's left. Go over Matt's horse for injuries, and I mean thoroughly. Matt has a head wound, but

14

I think otherwise he's fit. We'll have to tie him to the saddle if he doesn't come to in a few minutes."

They worked in silence, as Sarah remained crouched in her tiny huddle. Her legs were becoming stiff, and she wished terribly that she could move, but she didn't dare. Frowning, Sarah considered the gamble. The sounds of their movement were exactly the cover she needed, and a few seconds would see her safely out of danger. She heard the captain's fragmentary command as he made some movement with the two mules and, seeing her chance, Sarah rose and slipped soundlessly into the darkness.

She forced herself not to run. She moved quickly but carefully, arms outstretched slightly. She had no warning when he came up behind her.

"Hold it," was all he said, but his tone was lethal, and Sarah felt Death caress her with a breathless kiss. She dared not move.

He moved slowly, and in a moment she could smell him. The odors of leather, sweat, and the acrid stench of burned gunpowder assailed her as his boots whispered in the leaves behind her. Without deliberation Sarah knew that the barrel of his rifle was aiming squarely into her back. Then she gasped with pain as it jammed up hard below her ribs. At the same instant she felt the powerful clap of his hand about the calves of her legs, across her buttocks, and up her back. His left knee drove up into her left thigh, thrusting her forward, and as he reached around her the heat of his breath burned against her ear. With a swift movement his free hand swept up her abdomen and harshly clapped down across her breasts. Sarah's bewildered mind was aware of three things at once—the quick release of her breast, the sudden stiffening of his body, and her long strangling gasp for air.

His surprised "I'll be damned" seemed spoken by a phantom swirling somewhere in the chilly night. The phantom spoke to her, but she could not comprehend its meaning. It spoke again, this time more harshly, tightening bruising fingers into the flesh of her arm.

"Who are you?" The cut of the harsh Yankee voice brought Sarah into reality. A scream shattered the night and some seconds passed before she comprehended that it had come from her own throat. She lost control, and threw herself from the Yankee as strenuously as she could. He tossed the gun aside with a disgusted snort, and Sarah felt them both falling as his arms closed like a vise about her knees.

He subdued her. In only seconds the weight of his big body pinned her to the ground. They both breathed raggedly. When at last Sarah focused on his face in the moonlight, her brown eyes flared wide. Furiously he glared back, and his voice grated.

"You stupid little wildcat! You want to die young?" The crushing weight of his chest upon her breasts as he panted, the feel of his belly pressing almost painfully upon hers, the man-smell of his warm body, the humiliating intimacy of his thigh pinned deeply between her parted legs as his face hovered angrily, inches above her own—all subdued her, totally. Sarah could not reply.

"Good lord, sir! It's a woman!" his young companion choked, nervously rubbing a blond moustache and staring in disbelief.

"It would appear to be," growled the officer, standing up.

Nathaniel Garrett was exceedingly vexed at this dismal turn of events. An annoyed, rasping whistle broke the silence as his blue eyes raked the beautifully rumpled young woman before him. What had begun as a simple materials trade, ammunition and medicine for oats and corn to a small group of pro-Unionist families, now threatened to end in calamity. With a wounded man and the danger of returning scavengers pressing in on him, this female had turned up to worry him further.

16

"Oh, blast! Davidson, have Matt on his horse by the time I get there, in the saddle or over it. Take my horse with you and pull over near the road. Tell Reacher to see if he can find any remains of the medical supplies."

"If Matt comes to before I get there, give him some whiskey," he called over his shoulder. "And leave me the lantern."

His lips were wide without being thick, and his narrow nose tapered cleanly into black brows. Beneath the grime was a strikingly handsome face, the face of an aristocrat, a leader of men. Which this one indeed was, Sarah realized. It was he whom she would have to deal with. His hair was black, and the equally dark brows made a startling frame for the bold blue of his eyes. Was this beautiful man going to be her executioner? Would those eyes turn to ice? Or did she glimpse decency in their depths?

Nathaniel searched about for a convenient branch upon which to hang the lantern. Finding one, he then proceeded to find a small, half-rotted log which he nudged nearer to the light with the toe of his boot. From beneath lowered eyelids Sarah observed his legs, lean legs flexing beneath snug, dirty trousers.

"Your name!" he demanded succinctly. Finding just the right niche for his boot, the dusty captain leaned a negligent arm across his knee.

"I asked your name."

"Sarah." The word came out all cracked and trembly, and Sarah could have kicked herself. She had lived through too much to go to pieces in front of some Yankee—handsome or not! Feigning a great deal more courage than she felt, she smoothed her disarrayed hair, drew herself erect, and stared deliberately into his cold blue eyes.

"Sarah Bradley."

"Well come, come, Sarah Bradley. I'm pressed for time," he snapped. "Where do you live, Sarah?"

"Less than one mile away, Captain, in a small house with my husband's grandmother."

"Oh. You have a husband, then?"

"Yes. Well, I mean. . . ." Sarah shrugged, careful to look at a point just past his head with the most innocent expression she could muster, "He's not here *now*, of course. But I expect him! Very . . . soon."

"I see," he replied pleasantly. Swiftly his words lashed, and Sarah jumped. "I suppose your husband's one of the scurvy bastards that waylaid us back on the road. Or perhaps he's one of those lying there in the brush!"

With the unexpected viciousness of a cat-o'-nine-tails, sinewy fingers wrapped about one of her wrists. Sarah thrashed about for some object to prevent her from being dragged toward the irate figure.

"Oh, no!" her hoarse protest was to no avail. "No, you . . . Charles would never have done . . . Let me go! Don't!" Sarah clawed at his fingers, striking at his forearm with her free hand.

Nathaniel Garrett pried open her fingers under the lantern's rays. A fingertip traced its way across the rows of calluses, and then he heaved a weary sigh.

"Your jacket, Sarah," the deep voice was even more frightening when it was calm. "And your pants." The captain clucked his tongue gravely and shook his head in disappointment. "Your hands, Sarah."

Sarah kept her thickly lashed eyes downward. She was so stupid! He had easily seen through her flimsy lie, and now what would he do to her for lying to him? Brutally it occurred to her that the war was no longer a matter of hide-and-seek with an old grey mule and an assortment of food supplies. This soldier very possibly saw her as part of an attempt on his life. For the first time since the war's beginning, Sarah saw herself as an active participant in the battle rather than a secondary casualty. She was paralyzed with terror.

Harshly, Nathaniel jerked her against the length of his body. He towered above her.

"Mrs. Bradley," he began in earnest. "I am Nathaniel Garrett, presently stationed at Chattanooga with Colonel Michael Yarborough. Through no choice of my own I find I have been in these woods far too long. My intentions are to take this detail to your farm to care for my injured man and see to our damages."

Sarah's head raised sharply, her distress genuine. "But you can't do that! It's just a tiny house. There's a child—a small child. No room. And we don't have any food."

"I'm sure it will be sufficient, Sarah."

"But I'm afraid you don't understand, sir," Sarah tried. *"There's no food."*

"Enough, Mrs. Bradley! Everything will be all right. Come along. Time is short."

And so Sarah found herself on the road . . . without Jackson, and in the grasp of a Yankee officer. She couldn't match his long strides, and she felt like a punished child resisting his hand.

"Take your hands off me, you Yankee vulture!" she spat.

"War is war, madam," he growled hoarsely. Nathaniel bent his dark head until his breath fell against Sarah's mouth, and all she could see was the angry curve of his lips as they parted. Was this the kind of man who had robbed Peter of his father? This man, whose fingers moved so easily about her neck?

"Murderer!" she whispered, the shock of her rashness freeing one thrashing hand. Striking blindly, Sarah's entire world shrank to the ringing impact of her fist upon the side of his head. Survival—not only for herself, but for her baby—was at stake. Nathaniel's slight stagger from the blow splintering through his head allowed Sarah the edge she needed. In an awkward attempt to wrest herself free, her elbow found the vulnerable spot.

Grabbing his groin with a moan of pain, Nathaniel would have lost her had not his free hand thrust instinctively outward, snatching the tail of her jacket as Sarah ran. Thwarted by the constricted collar imbedding itself into her throat, Sarah clawed at her neck, fighting to breathe.

"If you ever . . . do that again . . ." he heaved his words through the slowly subsiding pain, dragging Sarah to a standstill, yanking her about to face him. "I'll . . . by heaven I'll . . ."

"Kill me?" coughed a bitter challenge. "Kill the mother and the helpless young will die, of course. Isn't that the strategy of the mighty warrior?"

"My, my." He bowed and gestured toward the road. "Not only have I had the good fortune to find a true Southern gentlewoman, but a philosopher as well. Do you think, madam, that we could *possibly* return to camp now? Even with your magnificence in hand-to-hand combat, I truly doubt that you would make much of a showing with these brigands roaming about the countryside."

The hushed voices of two men beyond interrupted them. Young Davidson lowered two tattered blankets stuffed and tied with a rope, politely inclining his head at the new addition to the company before proceeding with his task. Reacher was not as hospitable, however, and his scorn was obvious.

"Will the . . . lady be riding, Cap'n?" Disliking him instantly and intensely, Sarah swallowed a strong compulsion to run from the man. Small, closely set eyes blinked at her with unconcealed dislike, and a gnarled hand reached to stroke a beard more than a little matted with tobacco juice. The surly infantryman would cut her throat in a second.

"Uh . . . I suppose she'll double with me," said

Nathaniel, obviously concerned with other matters. "The logical move would be to make her home our base until we can recoup ourselves," he added.

"Yessir." Reacher did not appear to be overly enthusiastic about his commander's decision, yet he made no open indication of his disapproval.

"Davidson!" barked Nathaniel. "Where's my saddle?" He indicated the bare back of his mount.

"Under Matthew, sir," Davidson wavered, peering out cautiously from under light brows at the man a full head taller than he.

Searching the faint moonlight, Sarah's eyes found the great red-haired giant they were discussing. The huge man slumped on his large horse, resting, his head on his broad chest. It was obvious that the man was in considerable pain. A darkened bandage was visible from under the bill of his blackened cap. One of his massive arms also wore a bandage. Sarah only just saw him. She hadn't pieced together anything. She assumed that Matthew had been driving the wagon when the explosion occurred. At least he appeared fit enough to stay mounted.

"Well, where is Matthew's saddle?" questioned the captain wearily.

"Blown to hell, sir." A boyish shrug lifted his shoulders and his half-hearted grin revealed attractively crooked teeth. "It was on the wagon, sir, and you said to get him into the saddle one way or another, so—"

"Never mind, Tim," Nathaniel interrupted wryly. "I know what I said."

As Sarah stepped backward, her foot struck a soft object, causing her to turn. With horror-filled eyes, she stared at the ground. A man's body lay at her feet. A ragged gasp tore from her throat, attracting the captain's attention.

"It's one of the deserters we killed," he explained gruffly, frowning as Sarah stubbornly pulled from his hand to bend over the dead man. Sarah cautiously stooped, turning the lifeless face squarely into the faint light. Drawing a quick breath through clinched teeth, Sarah's wide eyes flew to Nathaniel's surprised gaze. Dropping onto one knee beside her, Nathaniel reached to turn her by the shoulders, staring at her with incredulous curiosity.

"You know this man, madam?" Sarah sensed that he was measuring her reactions very carefully.

"You have killed Lionel Freeman, Captain," stated Sarah. Nathaniel quirked a brow and shrugged. "Jack Freeman's brother."

"Well, explain. Are you going to take all night?"

Fate had favored her. The upper hand was now hers. Now she had much more insight into the Union officer's precarious situation than he could possibly have. Suddenly, a whole plan fit neatly together. Her heart skipped, realizing that her entire future, the rescue of her son and her escape from Rachel, depended on how well she could convince these men that she could be trusted.

Reacher and Davidson drew nearer, and three pairs of eyes studied her with silent suspicion.

Sarah told them everything, omitting no detail. She described precisely what she knew of the large band of deserters, of which the dead man at her feet had been a member. Marta Freeman, the mother of the dead man, lived very near where they now stood. Sarah explained, very carefully, her own purpose for being out on the mountain in the middle of the night. It did all sound rather farfetched, even as she put it into words.

"Whether you believe me or not, Captain, you are in terrible trouble, for these men are at least thirty strong. They have been on this mountain since the second year of the war and rumor has it that they have plundered as far as Mississippi. They don't hesitate to attack anyone—Confederates or Yankees."

She plunged headlong—words tumbling rapidly in her one hope for escape.

"If you will help me get out of Tennessee with my son, I will take you where these men can't possibly find you!"

Silence. Sarah prayed.

Nathaniel stretched his back and placed his hands at his waist. His position was bad, and if this puzzling little vixen were speaking the truth, he might well be in for big trouble. He was feeling a strong compulsion to trust her. A dozen questions annoyed him about this young woman whose fiery brown eyes intrigued him. They were clear, intelligent eyes, not the haunted, shrinking gaze he saw in most Southern women.

Be honest, at least, you Garrett blackguard! It's her bottom, and you well know it! How long had it been since he had seen a pair of legs like that? The devil take it! He couldn't jeopardize his men simply because he hadn't had a woman in. . . .

"It would be my opinion, Captain Garrett," she was offering freely, "that the three who escaped from you have reached their camp by now and have had ample time to begin their return."

"Your opinion, madam, is of questionable worth," he snapped.

"Well, stand here and get killed then. Yankees are expendable."

"This fantastic haven where they could never find us—perhaps we would be walking into a death trap?"

"On the contrary, sir. Charles, my husband, called it The Great Stone Door. It is a cave open on two sides, one of which empties into a type of canyon. This mountain is full of caves." Nathaniel, eyes cast heavenward, pointedly coughed.

"Well, it is, you . . ." she sputtered, incensed by his mockery.

"Of course it is. And would not these deserters, native to the country, know of this place?"

23

Sarah sighed. "Perhaps, but they would not expect you to know of it, Captain."

"I yield on that point, madam."

A harsh, broken sound from the man resting in the saddle just beyond snatched their attention. Sarah had nearly forgotten him, and as they all turned to him a cold panic gripped her belly. She heard what they all heard—the unmistakable sound of moving horses— many horses!

"Reacher," snapped Nathaniel angrily. "Ten minutes?"

"If we're lucky."

Faster than she could comprehend what was happening, the two men moved for the horses. Suddenly, Nathaniel's face loomed threateningly over her, drawn with naked fear for the safety of his men. The deadly strength of the man frightened her, and as his fingers closed about her shoulders and pulled her to him roughly, Sarah could feel the powerful beating of his heart racing against her breast.

"I accept your terms, Sarah Bradley," he rasped harshly. "But be it known that if you are lying to me, by God, I'll break that lovely neck of yours with my own hands. Do we understand each other?"

"Yes," she choked. "I wasn't lying," she half-sobbed, but the words were lost, for he had already turned on his heel to run for his horse.

ea Chapter II

It was a fair exchange—escape for escape. Nathaniel had mounted. He held the stock of his long rifle and the threaded reins in one hand and reached down the other hand to her. Once again she had the sensation that life would never be the same again.

Their breathtaking intimacy on the horse was intensified as Nathaniel slipped his rifle across her legs and pulled her snugly back into the space between his hard thighs. Her slender hips were pressed securely against the hard maleness of him, and as he moved sinewy legs up underneath her own, touching the full length of her, an involuntary tingle shuddered through her body. They were so shockingly close that Sarah felt as if Nathaniel Garrett were her outer skin.

Pleasantly aware of her discomfiture, Nathaniel chuckled softly to himself. Blowing wisps of her hair aside and bending his lips until they touched the shell of her ear, he whispered, his quick breath warm against her chilled face.

"It is your turn to move, Sarah Bradley." Turning to protest the outlandish indignity he was forcing upon her, her tanned cheek brushed softly against his parted lips. But there was no time to argue. Her voice came hoarsely.

"I'll take you up the creek bed. They'll search the road first." Nathaniel inclined his head in assent and turned the horse in the direction she indicated, and the silent caravan wove its way cautiously through the enormous trees, reining sharply every few steps to avoid tangles of undergrowth. Once they paused, but only long enough to unhobble the unconcerned Jackson and secure him with the pack mules.

After many minutes Sarah ventured, "Captain Garrett?"

"Hmmm?" he leaned his head toward her but kept his eyes upon the pack mules.

"The creek turns back to the north just beyond us, Captain," she began, "and there is a deep overhang." Sarah hesitated, and finally the commander turned a frowning stare on her.

"Your men could wait there for us while you and I ride to the cottage. It's hardly two miles, and we could pick them up after we got Peter."

The truth was, Sarah was exhausted by now, and she needed reassurance that he would help her escape with her son.

"How far is the cave from here?"

"Three miles, no more."

Nathaniel shook his head.

"We could be very careful. Cut across the ridge. The sassafras trees are so thick we—"

"Not yet, Sarah. It's too dangerous. If we must ride to the cave and then ride back, we will. But I must get these men to safety first."

"But, Captain," her arguing grew more intense. "The longer we wait the more chance Peter will awaken and Rachel will discover me gone. *Please.*"

"No, Sarah. You will simply have to trust me. I *will* get the child, but not yet."

Her speech thickened. "Please, I'm begging you to go *now. Please*. Can't you see I have told you the truth and intend to help you as I agreed? *Please*. I need to go *now!*" Fingers clawed frantically at the rough sleeve.

Sarah's eyes assumed a brittle stare which Nathaniel recognized even in the darkness. She would soon snap if she didn't regain control of herself. His fingers reached to touch her, but Sarah jerked bitterly backward.

"You lied to me!" she rasped furiously. "You had no intentions of going, you lying Yankee! Oh, God! What a stupid fool I've been! You can't stop me from getting my baby . . . ."

The words ripped from her throat in ragged sobs, and she recklessly sought the reins. Nathaniel's hand shot out, covering her own like an iron glove.

"Sarah, stop it!" he growled.

Nathaniel reassured, his manner tightly controlled and unhurried, "You are exhausted. We all are. I gave you my word that we would get the boy, and we will. I promise you."

Nathaniel was frightened, for if Sarah lost her nerve at this stage, disaster could overtake them. Knowing little else to do, the dark captain followed his natural instincts, folding his arms about her a bit awkwardly and drawing her trembling body securely against his own. For the next moment the three mounted men watched in no little awe as their fierce commander calmed the frantic woman. Bending his head very low, out of the hearing of his men, he whispered to her. Sarah did not refuse his comfort, and presently Nathaniel was conscious that her shoulders relaxed.

In some minutes Sarah regained a portion of her lost poise. Feeling extremely foolish indeed, she half turned to the men she knew were staring at her in stunned silence. Making an attempt to smile, Sarah spoke to all of them in a low, strained voice, intently watching the water dancing at her feet.

"P-please forgive me," she sniffed. And discovering she had nothing with which to dry her eyes, she wiped them across her sleeve.

"I . . . I swear I didn't mean to do that. It's just that . . ."

"It's all right, Sarah," Nathaniel sighed softly.

The southeastern lip of the bluff lay beneath the hoofs of their horses before Nathaniel bent his lips and whispered, "You have been a very patient lady, Sarah Bradley. I think that we may go back for Peter now."

Not too surprisingly, Sarah's compulsory acceptance of Nathaniel's authority had resulted in a sullen withdrawal into herself for the duration of the trek to the cave. Wisely, Nathaniel had left her to her own thoughts, realizing the complexity of her situation.

Ever since her outburst Sarah had cursed herself, and her vulnerable position in front of Nathaniel on the horse had accomplished very little to soften things.

"We could have been there and back already if you hadn't been so pig-headed. Have you ever noticed, Captain, how a liar always suspects everyone *else* of lying?"

"Well, I suppose I could change my mind and not go at all, if I am such a liar," he drawled. Neither of them spoke again until they were mounted—Sarah had her own horse this time—and on their way once again.

Everything in the house seemed miraculously as she had left it some hours earlier. And, thank the Lord, there was no Rachel up prowling. That seemed hardly possible, and more than a little unnerving. The fire had died, and the house was cold, gruesomely transformed from cottage to crypt since she had last stepped through the door. Swiftly, Sarah sped to the tiny bedroom. In harried seconds, she crammed together the things they would need. For her this consisted only of her single dress and a change of pants and shirt. Peter's clothing consumed more precious space in the tattered tapestry bag, but in minutes it was all done.

Suddenly, on a whim, she whisked up the bag and sped lightly across the living room rug, dropping to her knees before the bookcase beside the hearth. Charles's books, all her treasured volumes of Bach, Mozart, Clementi—how ever could she leave them behind? She didn't need to read the titles; she knew them intimately, by placement, by touch. Finally, two small leather-bound volumes of poetry and two manuscripts were all she placed in the little bag.

Later on, Sarah never believed that she had awakened Rachel. She must surely have been awake all the time. Whirling abruptly to find Rachel standing just behind her, Sarah started. Neither spoke for seconds. They stood—squared for battle.

"And what are you about at this time of the morning, my dear Sarah?" Rachel broke the silence, and Sarah could almost see the workings of her mind as Rachel strove to fit this new puzzle together.

"Nothing. Go back to bed." Sarah didn't think she could survive another row. Not tonight.

Rachel shuffled to the window, pulling back the curtain and squinting into the darkness. If she saw Nathaniel she gave no sign. A gnarled hand reached to set the rocking chair in motion. It creaked, rocking twice before it came to rest.

Sarah held her breath.

"In a pig's eyes, as the saying goes, you deceitful little bitch. You've been gone for hours. Do you think I don't know? Have you been out whorin' with some of this Tennessee scum, now? Won't that sound pretty before a judge? Such a good mother you . . ."

Rachel's little eyes caught the bag now, and she screeched.

"You were tryin' to leave here! Where could you go? You will never get away with it!"

"Old woman, I've finished with the name calling, and the degradation, and the cruelty. You can't keep me—or Peter. You are going to live alone and some day, Rachel, you will die alone. And it's all your own doing. I can't feel any pity for you. I used to, but no more."

Sarah turned her back on the trembling woman and that is where she made the big mistake—turning her back on Rachel Bradley.

The poker slashed its path through the dim light with amazing vigor. Sarah barely saw it move, but sensed its stroke. Her quickness saved her, and the force of the poker caught her viciously across the upper part of her back, instead of on her head. The blow sent Sarah crashing through the delicate panes of the window near the door, thousands of glassy splinters showering as she crumpled to the floor. With the last breath she had, Sarah screamed.

The hinges barely held the door, so savagely did he burst through the opening like an avenging god. Rachel's shock at seeing the big Yankee, legs astride and rifle aimed, was complete. Nathaniel's lips curled back dangerously, his gun gaping at Rachel like a cannon. Before he could even stoop to touch Sarah, lying beside his boots, Rachel's eyes rolled back into her head, and she fainted before the hearth.

Sarah felt all Nathaniel's fury as he lifted her gently and carried her to the bedroom. She wanted to thank him and say a thousand other things, but she could only strangle, clutching at her chest in a frantic effort to breathe. He stepped through the bedroom door and laid her carefully upon the bed.

Sarah's cry had roused the sleeping Peter and, as his little blond head bobbed up from the pillow, a rosy mouth opened wide to give a lusty yell at the terrifying figure bending over him. Nathaniel scooped him up, quilt and all, and deposited him neatly beside his mother. Tossing his hat aside carelessly and dropping down near them, he panted, pointing a lean finger at the wide-eyed toddler who fearfully clutched his mother's jacket.

"And you must be the famous Peter who has caused me so much trouble," he growled in mock ferocity.

Peter's mouth curled down at the corners, and Sarah reached out a reassuring hand to touch the tousled head.

"Be quiet . . . Nathaniel," Sarah managed. "You'll . . . scare him to death."

"Nonsense. You Bradleys are made of pure steel." Nathaniel grasped her hand as it rested upon Peter's shining head and frowned at the thin line of red at her wrist.

"It's nothing. Strange. The glass really didn't . . . hurt me that much. Only the poker." But Sarah didn't object when he rose to tear the flimsy curtain from the small bedroom window and tore a strip with which to wrap her wrist. As he absorbed himself in bandaging the small wound, Sarah studied him anew. She could see the tiny muscle flexing in his jaw as he worked.

"Nathaniel?"

"Yes, Sarah," he responded, finished at last and lifting his head to smile at her.

"You can help us get away, can't you?" Once again she needed reassuring words.

"Don't worry, Mrs. Bradley. Saving damsels in distress has always been my favorite hobby." He grinned broadly, and Sarah weakly returned the smile.

"All right now, Peter, my lad," Nathaniel's tone was deep, warm. "Introductions are over. I do hope you can manage to remain dry for some of our little journey."

Chapter III

THE STONE FLOOR of the cave was cold, torturing her bruised back. Surely her aching body had wrapped itself in the flimsy blanket only minutes ago? Peter pulled himself up beside her head and poked at her nose with an inquiring finger. With scalding eyes she surveyed her surroundings in the dimly lit cave— dusty ledges and myriads of crannies.

She sat up with a start, wincing with pain. At least the place was dry. Too dry, for dust was everywhere, and thick clouds of it shifted and reshifted with each movement.

Peter needed changing, and Sarah tried to ignore the fierce shattering in her head while tending him. Except for an occasional movement from a sleeping man, nothing disturbed the stillness of early morning. Thank goodness that Reacher had remained up on the bluff for the night, the horrid man! It had proved too dangerous to walk the horses down the narrow path in the darkness, after all, yet the commander had seemed satisfied with her choice of hideaways. She had been so weary that she could have slept on the bare ground, but Nathaniel had brought her a blanket and securely covered Peter and her before taking his place with his men at the narrow mouth of the cave.

Spring was in the mountain air, and the early sunlight had already begun to warm the craggy face of the bluff as Sarah and Peter made their way down a narrow path fashioned by deer who came frequently for water. The narrow trail inched its way along the side of the bluff to skirt a natural pool, trapped by ragged rock. An unexpected grassy knoll spread just past the pool. The small patch of grass had always fascinated Sarah. It seemed so out of place. The spring bubbled its way out the side of the bluff, caring not at all to whom it delivered its constant supply of fresh water—animal or human.

"Well, Peter," Sarah announced, "it feels so good being away from your grandmother's voice that I think we can even bear the cold water. I know you're hungry but first things first."

Peter's steady stream of chatter was, as usual, mostly unintelligible. After the first quick gasp Peter took his scrubbing like a man, dodging what he could and interspersing the rest with excited *mama's* and *look's* and *see's*. Presently he sat clean and rosy-cheeked upon the dried grass, as Sarah spread his clean diaper to dry in the sun.

Pulling grassy tufts from the earth proved to be a rather interesting pastime for Peter's busy fingers. After making certain that no one was stirring, Sarah stepped as far behind the jutting escarpment as possible. Quickly she peeled off her dirty clothing and scrubbed with cold water until her skin glowed pink. On came the clean pants and shirt she had brought. She did wish the fragile old fabric didn't betray her bosom so distinctly. She sucked in her breath and stood very straight, staring down at the firmly tipped peaks. Then slumped her shoulders. It didn't help.

Combing her hair took a bit of doing, due to the trials of the night before, but at last the tangles surrendered and Sarah finished with a heavy, shiny braid down her back. Much refreshed, she glanced about the narrow projection.

Her body flushed cold, then terribly hot.

"How long have you been sitting there?" she lashed

at him. Nathaniel sat in the path, resting his folded arms across his knees.

He grinned boyishly. "Long enough," and ran long fingers through tousled black hair, eyes shining with a burning that couldn't be mistaken, even from where she stood.

Nathaniel had roused after only two hours' sleep, anxious to rid himself of his prickly stubble and battle grime. A cold bath would work wonders, he knew. But the arousal he had felt from the scene spread before him sent a fire plunging through his veins more quickly than any bath could have done.

She was beautiful, as he had known from the beginning she would be. There was a slender, leggy, coltishness about her, and there were traces of a summer's tan most women would not have dared. The curves of her breasts were pink-tipped, tapering into a narrow waist he could easily have encircled with his hands. Only the nasty purple bruise across her shoulders marred a perfect back. Her hips were narrow.

"You, sir, are the most despicable creature I have ever had the misfortune to know!"

"Shhh, you'll wake everyone." A warning finger crossed curving lips as he scooped up the saddlebags and unfolded himself. Ambling jauntily down the path, a rakish, loose-jointed stride, Nathaniel grinned good-naturedly as if his voyeurism were of no consequence whatever.

His lazy smile still curved as he stood towering, the end of a very errant thumb reaching out to *almost* touch the tempting peak of her breast, but he seemed to think better of it and kept his hand poised in mid-air. His meditative stance and poised hand, coupled with the knowledgeable direction of his gaze, acted more violently upon Sarah than if he had actually touched her.

At last he moved aside, and Sarah started, involuntarily clutching both hands to her bosom. Nathaniel retreated with mock caution.

"Truce?" Nathaniel knew exactly what his eyes were doing to Sarah. He tossed the leather bags absently on the brown grass. "Come, pretty Sarah Bradley, and sit with me while I shave. The men will be up in a bit, and you're better off with me."

"Well, I find *that* hard to believe!" she retorted. She lifted Peter to cover the revealing shirt, and withdrew as far as possible. "We're starving," she changed the subject. "Did I hear you say you had food? I haven't eaten since noon yesterday. But that's no matter—Peter must have something."

Nathaniel wet his face and fished a small tin, a straight razor and a sizeable piece of soap from his bag.

"There's some hardtack in my saddlebags," his voice came muffled from behind his hand as the razor moved deftly along the line of his jaw.

After an envious sigh at Nathaniel's soapy luxury, Sarah found the hard wafers. "With sympathies, my darling," she said glumly to Peter, biting at a square with little enthusiasm.

Nathaniel had removed his shirt, revealing tanned shoulders, lean but well muscled, and a light smattering of curly black hair running down the expanse of his chest. Sarah, pretending to amuse Peter, stole glimpses of the virile Yankee. No paunchiness . . . a scar—not a neat, clean sliver, but a thin jagged line which began just above his lower ribs and travelled downward until it disappeared beneath the waist of his trousers. His legs tapered leanly. All in all, a very attractive man. Sarah felt flushed as she realized she was staring at a half-naked man. The added color in her cheeks didn't escape Nathaniel's shrewd eye, and he wasn't nice enough to let it pass.

"If you could pull your greedy eyes off me for just a moment, my dear, I could use your assistance," he drawled. He laughed softly, rising and grasping a pan of water. He poured it over his head, catching his breath a little as it ran coldly down his chest. Brushing the streams of water out of his eyes with the tips of his fingers, Nathaniel proceeded to work a lather into his black locks.

"Sarah!" he sputtered momentarily. "Do you mind? I'm getting soap in my eyes. Blast, that stings!" Flinging lather off his fingers he turned, squinting one eye as Sarah sauntered lazily to his side.

"Is the conquering titan overcome by a bit of soap, sir? No stamina, perhaps?" Such an uncommonly long amount of time she was taking, indolently catching another pan of cold water and slowly drizzling it over his head as he bent, long legs astride and soapy hands braced on his knees. The scene struck Peter as enormously funny, and he gurgled and crowed.

"Damn," groaned Nathaniel. "Taunted by an infant. Is that as fast as you can move, woman?"

"Oh no, Captain. I can move much faster than that!" And so saying she tossed the entire contents up into his face, fighting back the laughter as he blinked streaming eyes and spat out the soap.

Sarah had been seventeen when the war had begun and had seen few opportunities to be carefree, to laugh, or to tease. Her playing with Nathaniel was new, and she had no inkling of her allure.

"Well, I suggest you move as quickly as you can then, miss!" The swift arm that swept Sarah from the ground caught her short. Nathaniel didn't ask for the kiss—he took it, forcing her twisting face still and crushing her lips hard with his own. A bruising, burning mouth forced her lips apart, and his tongue thrust hard against her teeth, forcing her mouth open. Sarah fought against the search. He tasted pleasantly of soap. The water from his dripping face trickled over hers.

"Peter," she whimpered, half drugged from sensations so foreign to her, hands that seemed everywhere at once, upon her waist, touching her breasts and coaxing the buttons of her shirt.

"It won't hurt him," he argued against her lips, forcing the back of her head still with one hand and pulling the shirt free of her breeches with the other.

"Hold me," his breath was hot against the coolness of her throat, catching as her fingertips hesitated, unwillingly skimming the broad expanse of smooth back, palms pressing, drawing her on tiptoe.

Sarah didn't want to return the kiss. Even those lips that kept pulling her up into some blurring spiral couldn't make her forget herself. A confused memory couldn't recall what love had felt like before. Like this? Never like this! She should feel shame, but still Sarah couldn't stop the small gasp as Nathaniel pulled open her shirt. Creamy bare flesh was crushed into the fine curls upon his chest. Her cry was lost in his kiss. What was happening? His mouth kept robbing her of resistance, and Sarah's bones seemed to melt against his huge, strong, warm body.

Peter had never seen a man touch his mother. In fact, Peter had not seen many men at all. He crawled across the grass and hefted himself up on Nathaniel's leg. Clutching the snug edge of Nathaniel's black boot, he balanced himself, latching onto a fistful of Yankee-blue trousers.

Nathaniel struggled to shut his mind to the little hand. The starved need he felt for Sarah made him ache. He cupped his hand under the curve of her hips, pinning her tighter as she wriggled in his arms. Nathaniel moved against her, drawing her to the hard desire he wanted her to feel, and his raging fire spread, seeping from him until finally she stilled, molding to his need. Now nothing existed except a man and a woman coming together.

No longer able to ignore the babe clutching his leg, Nathaniel's mouth gentled its assault until presently he was playing with her, teasing, caressing with his tongue, and smiling against her lips. Only when she wonderingly opened her eyes to look at him did he relinquish those lips.

Sarah's head dropped, resting on his arm until she could see him clearly. He did not release her—the full length of her limbs was still melded to his hard man's body. Reality rushed at her quickly. She was in the arms of a strange man.

"Peter, my man," Nathaniel remarked firmly, "I think we should have a long talk very soon." He grinned. "You know I shan't be able to ride for a week, don't you?"

"Perhaps if it were permanent, the South would win the war," she said dryly.

Nathaniel laughed, pulling her shirt together. The pretense of brushing the throbbing peaks of her breasts by accident fooled neither of them.

"Sir!" hissed Sarah. He had bent to place Peter back on the grass and was retrieving his bread for him.

"Yes, love?" he replied lightly, buttoning on a clean but wrinkled shirt and reaching over to button a place on her shirt that she had missed.

"That's what I mean!" Sarah stamped an exasperated foot. "I'm a woman," she began.

"Oh, I'm fully aware of that," he interrupted.

"Will you listen to me?"

"Before you enter upon what I predict will be quite a lengthy speech, do you mind if I sit beside your son?" The tall frame folded and propped itself on an elbow.

Sarah's defiance was diminished somewhat, for she felt silly lecturing someone who didn't seem the slightest concerned.

"Sir," she began again.

"If you call me 'sir' once more, I vow you will live to regret it," he admonished wryly, inspecting his fingernails.

"And if you interrupt me once more, Captain, I vow

38

one of those blue eyes will be blackened!" she cried. "You are the most irritating person I have ever known."

Nathaniel shrugged.

"I wish to speak with you about. . . ." How should she put it? "I wish to speak with you about the manner in which you . . . touch my person." Sarah's eyes narrowed forbiddingly.

Nathaniel laughed and wiped Peter's drooling with the tip of his shirttail.

"How dare you laugh, you . . . you. . . . I will not tolerate these outrageous liberties, Captain Garrett. It is true that I need you. And you did give me your word that you would help me, but I am beginning to think you intend demanding a far higher price for your services than I am willing to pay."

Nathaniel drawled. "And what liberties might you be talkin' about, Sarah?"

"You know full well what I mean by liberties. I have known you one day, and already you have . . . assaulted me," she finished weakly.

Nathaniel was grinning. "Well, I would hardly call it assault, darling, judging by your response. What you are trying to say is that you are offended because we were not properly introduced at some elegant ball or a formal tea before I slipped you out into the garden to steal a kiss." A dark brow quirked. "The South is slightly behind the times, Sarah."

Sarah crossed her arms. Then she uncrossed them. "A gentleman would not presume so much in so short a time, Captain."

"That's hardly a satisfactory answer, Sarah. We have lived more in one night than many do in half a lifetime."

"You have a most distorted sense of values! If you think I am afraid to do this on my own, you are mistaken. I don't need you *that* much, Captain Garrett!"

Nathaniel brushed away the irate finger pointed at

39

his nose. "And how far do you think you'd get, Sarah mine? Do you have any idea what it's like off this mountain? Many of the roads are not safe for an armed man alone, much less a woman and child. Freed slaves are wandering around by the thousands, many of them hungry and angry. There are dangerous bands of deserters. And you, a Southern woman going North? I would give you perhaps one day before you were both dead in a ditch somewhere, or sitting in jail if you were very lucky. And that, my darling, is the truth of it."

Sarah paled, knowing he was right. Nathaniel picked himself up, scooped a handful of clear water, and drank.

"Well, it seems I must always be at the mercy of someone or something. So be it. But you, Captain, must honor your word as a decent man and keep your hands off me!" She backed away, always uneasy when this man was moving about.

"Ah, you cut me to the quick," he groaned. " 'Tis a fact, though, that I have already set my word to the first request. But the second?" He shrugged. "I never made any rash promises. Nor would I be so foolish as to do so now. I'm afraid you'll just have to take your chances in that respect."

"I can deal with you," Sarah hissed, not at all sure she could. But it never hurt to seem positive. "I have been outwitting men like you for years, you . . . you abominable Yankee!"

"Oh, you really know how to hurt a man, my love."

"And don't call me that."

"Yes, Davidson, what is it?" he smiled.

Sarah whirled, and Nathaniel suffered a bit of difficulty deciding who was more embarrassed, his young aide or the trembling woman before him.

"I beg pardon, sir. I didn't realize . . . I mean I didn't know it was a private conversation." Tim

Davidson's blush reached clear to the roots of his blond hair.

"It's all right, Tim," smiled the commander. "Mrs. Bradley is not angry, in spite of the evidence to the contrary. She was simply explaining to me some of her thoughts on propriety."

"If you'll excuse me, Captain, I think I shall return to the camp. With your permission, that is," Sarah managed.

"Well, I don't permit. Wait a minute, and I'll go with you. Is everyone awake, Davidson? I think we may as well spend a few hours here. We need the rest. Build a small fire—keep the smoke down—and have Reacher make some coffee, if any is left. I'll have a look at Matthew and his horse."

"Coffee," Sarah echoed silently. How many days since she had had even a cup of real tea?

Sweeping up the fretful Peter, who was not receiving much satisfaction from the hardtack no matter how diligently he persisted, Nathaniel began the steep climb back up to the cave. Sarah started to protest, then gave it up, glumly folding the blanket and diaper and offering Nathaniel's saddlebags to Davidson.

"How did a gentleman such as yourself ever manage to survive the likes of Captain Garrett, Mr. Davidson?"

Nathaniel was well up the path, chatting happily to Peter. With a light toss he perched him on his broad shoulders, and Sarah viewed with satisfaction Nathaniel's "Eee-ouch!" as Peter grabbed a large handful of his black hair.

"Peter has never ridden like that before," she murmured. "I hope he pulls it out by the roots."

Davidson laughed. "Oh, he's not too tough when you get to know him, ma'am. I have served several officers, and he's the best man I've just about ever known. Not that he doesn't raise the dickens sometimes. But you'll get used to him."

"Heaven forbid."

Tim Davidson was not a great deal taller than Sarah, and in some respects he reminded her of Charles. The same gentle air radiated about him. Too, his features were fair as Charles' had been. Davidson took off his cap and stuffed it into his hip pocket.

"Where is your home, Mr. Davidson?"

"New York, ma'am. But not near the city. I live in a tiny little place at the bottom of the state that you never heard of." His smile was charming.

"You're a long way from home, Mr. Davidson."

"Oh, I've been all over. When the Captain nearly got killed and was brought to the hospital at Chattanooga, he convalesced quite a while. Reacher and I were assigned to him then, and this past winter we've been at sixes and sevens trying to keep the railroad between Nashville and Chattanooga in one piece. The scurvy Rebs tear it up almost before we can get it repaired."

"Is the Captain from New York, too?" She could have bitten her tongue. What did she care where the beast was from? An attack of curiosity about that long scar he carried down his side annoyed her.

"Oh, no. He's from Maryland. His father's a senator. A lot of the congressmen live in Maryland 'cause it's so close to Washington."

But Sarah wasn't listening. A senator for a father? How could such an impressive background produce that rascal? Some of the man's arrogance was beginning to make sense to her now. He had probably never been denied anything in his whole life. What disdain he must feel every time he looked at her and remembered the way she lived—the widow of a simple country tutor.

Before Sarah could question Tim further, men's voices reached her ears, bringing home the reality of her plight. The war itself had never scared her as much as this moment did. She was taking Peter, running away from Rachel, and she had no idea where they would go. Nathaniel would help her for awhile, but in the end she was alone. She wished desperately for Charles. She must not give in to panic.

"Are you all right, ma'am?" In her sudden devastation Sarah had lost her balance, stumbling against the young man.

"I . . . suppose it's having not eaten in so long," she lied, apologetic. Anxiously she raised her eyes and saw Nathaniel on one knee with Peter balancing on a finger of each hand between Nathaniel's legs, deep in concentration. With a paternal caution Sarah would not have imagined in him, he released the child to walk the few feet to his mother. A frown creased Nathaniel's brow as he took in the forced smile she gave her son.

"Second thoughts, Sarah?"

She stooped for Peter, eyes glancing sharply upward. "Does it matter?"

"Don't be silly. Of course it matters. You could still go back, you know. Perhaps you and she could make some arrangement."

Sarah shook her head. "No. Rachel doesn't make arrangements." Nathaniel's interest was intense as he watched her eyes harden. How was it that he felt so good everytime he watched this girl stiffen up and take on the world?

"You will see me dead first, Captain Garrett, before I will let Rachel have Peter." The hint of a smile tweaked the corner of his handsome mouth as Nathaniel busied himself with tucking in his shirt. He had never doubted her for a moment.

They remained in the cave two days. Nathaniel's plans to leave for Chattanooga the same afternoon were aborted, for a violent spring storm drenched the bluff, swelling the creek below in only a matter of hours. The horses remained on top, turning their tails into the rains. The men took turns guarding the animals. Most of the time was spent in periods of rest. Much of Sarah's time was spent alone at the far opening of the great fissure, Charles's Great Stone Door, sitting on the blanket, absently entertaining her son. Sarah saw no more of Nathaniel than she did of any of the other men and, much to her relief, he made no more attempts to touch or taunt her.

Matthew McCarey turned out to be a very decent sort, the son of an Irishman who had come to America during the famine. Peter struck up a fast friendship with the gentle bear of a man, sensing that he had an ally in Matthew. He sat quietly on his lap for long periods of time as Matthew rested from his wounds. Peter plucked at his buttons or practiced his new walking trick going around and around the great figure.

Sarah awoke very late on the morning of the second day. Hearing her name spoken quietly and raising herself in quick alarm, she relaxed to find young Davidson kneeling beside her in the dim light, leaning back on his heels with two tin cups of steaming coffee in his hands.

"Oh, dear," she yawned, glancing at the promise of bright sunlight outside and quickly sitting up. "It must be quite late." Blinking heavy sleep from her eyes, Sarah gratefully reached for the coffee.

"A bit late," he smiled. Peter bobbed his head up, making sleepy expressions on his round face. "Just a minute," Tim said, hastily disappearing, only to return in a few seconds with a cold biscuit left over from the day before. Peter removed it from his hand before Davidson had a chance to offer it, and Sarah giggled into her coffee tin.

"Breakfast will be ready soon, Mr. Bradley," he consoled Peter. They chatted, Sarah propped against the wall with the blanket draped across her knees,

44

Davidson smiling cross-legged at her feet, and Peter dribbling biscuit crumbs.

"You don't sound much like a Southerner, Mrs. Bradley."

"Well, I'm not from Tennessee, Tim, which may make a difference. May I call you Tim? You see, my husband and I came to Tennessee only just before the war began. And too, I had some of my education further north. I lived with my uncle for many years." She sipped. "You must have been awfully young when you joined the service."

"Well, I lied about my age," he grinned. "I'm nearly twenty, though. I'll bet you're not much older yourself."

Sarah laughed, her beautiful teeth flashing. "Naughty, naughty to ask a woman's age, Mr. Davidson. But actually I'm twenty-one. A very old lady by your standards, I'd guess."

"Not old enough, I'm thinking," growled a deep voice beside her. Sarah could feel his furious scowl even before she raised warm brown eyes to his steely ones.

"Won't you please be seated, Captain? You are precisely what I needed to begin my day."

"Tim, I think Reacher could use your services about right now." Young Tim looked as if he had been caught with his hand in the cookie jar. He hastily rose, straightening his blue jacket and nodding to his commander.

"Very good, sir. I was just—"

"Dismissed, Tim," Nathaniel sighed heavily.

"Yessir." Davidson performed a hasty exit. Nathaniel stood for some minutes with his legs apart, arms akimbo. He had shaved already, and by some means had managed to coax his uniform into presentability.

"Madam," Nathaniel's voice was strained. "I would consider it a great personal favor if you would cease to fraternize with my men. It will cause nothing but trouble. I can ill afford trouble right now."

Sarah blinked in disbelief.

She raged, "Just who do you think you are? You have the manners of a. . . ."

Nathaniel's dark head bent over hers until his blazing blue eyes were just above her face.

"Manners have nothing to do with it." He snarled. "Don't you have a brain in that beautiful head of yours? Do you realize how rarely these men ever see a woman, much less get close enough to touch one? And here you are running around with that tempting little fanny setting every man's teeth on edge. Why, I'd trust Matthew with my life but, damn it, woman— even he can stand only so much. Now stay out of their way and leave them alone."

Not to be excluded from the excitement, Peter tugged at Nathaniel's trouser leg. "Tee," he repeated. "Tee." At last Nathaniel bent to sweep the boy into his arms.

"What's he saying?" he inquired dismally.

Peter hooked a finger at each side of his mouth and stretched it into a ridiculous grimace. "Tee!" he repeated impatiently, puzzled that this man did not understand plain English.

"He's showing you his new teeth, stupid!" Sarah snapped.

"Oh, I beg your pardon. Yes, they're charming."

Sarah snatched the wide-eyed child from his arms and proceeded to march into breakfast. "Never mind the old grizzly bear, darling," Nathaniel overheard her. "Your great-grandmother was not much better." The defiant saunter of her tantalizing hips was not lost on the brooding commander as he followed.

The biscuits and gravy with hard, dried beef was not tasty fare, and most of the consumers gladly washed it down with the scalding coffee. At least *that* was good, for Matthew had brewed it with the soft

mountain water. The water was said to be so bene-
ficial that summer people used to come from Nashville for it. Sarah found her thoughts slipping into the
past to a time when Charles had tutored the wealthy
daughters of Nashville's society matrons as they sum-
mered at the grand hotel. Life had been so uncom-
plicated in those days, and Sarah was unaware that
her brown eyes had assumed a lovely, dreamy quality
as she sat, feeding Peter from a tin plate. A nostalgic
smile graced her lips. She unconsciously created a
charming picture, and Nathaniel glanced uncomfortably at his young aide to see him sitting immobilized,
as if in a trance, absorbed in her. Matthew coughed
lightly, and Nathaniel flicked his gaze to the older
man to find him smothering a grin at the scene.

Nathaniel finally broke the silence.

"Would you get the horses ready? Reacher, pack
up here. Matthew, let's change those bandages once
more. And Mrs. Bradley," he paused uneasily, "just
. . . do something. Anything." The men began to stir.

"I want this camp to be ready to move in an hour,"
he ordered as Sarah snatched up Peter and swept out
of his way.

Peter's blond locks nestled against the broad expanse of Matthew's chest for a good portion of the
journey to Chattanooga, and Sarah was grateful that
the weather cooperated. The terrain was difficult,
threading in and around, but the journey went well.
At long last Lookout Mountain towered before them,
hovering protectively over Chattanooga. They were
all thankful to see the end of their trip.

Occasional groups of blue-uniformed men dotted
the countryside as they neared the town. Some were
bringing wood from the forests, some fashioned cross-
ties for the railroad. Most of the travelling bluecoats
were on foot.

Buildings were visible now, and tree-lined streets.

The town appeared half empty, yet there was always some activity. A number of the homes had been vacated, but several were still occupied by their owners, and Sarah saw a few Negroes moving about. Grassland sprawled with bivouacked men and piles of covered supplies which changed every few days. The railroad terminal bustled—blue uniforms everywhere, wounded disembarking, and sacks of food being loaded onto wagons. A glance aside revealed a group of men gathered around an ancient pump to water their animals, two mules of which were harnessed to a conveyance carrying a mud-splattered cannon. The sight of it brought the whole living nightmare back into Sarah's head—visions of Charles lying dead, of weapons smoking, and the cries of wounded men.

The building before them served now as headquarters for the Union forces. Men were everywhere. The wide expanse of roadway through the center of town still bore the battle scars of earthworks and trenches.

Surprisingly, Nathaniel's men seemed pleased to see the town again. Reacher dismounted swiftly to wipe a dusty sleeve across an equally dusty face, and Davidson slipped to the ground to receive Nathaniel's orders. Chattanooga would be their home for now. Before she could gain her bearings Sarah found herself deposited on the ground and Peter placed into her arms. Matthew led his horse farther down the battle-scarred thoroughfare. Very quickly, Sarah and Nathaniel were standing alone before the steep incline of steps beside the hitching rail. Nathaniel slapped at some of the travel grime on his uniform with his hat as Sarah blinked at her strange surroundings.

"What am I supposed to do?" she touched his sleeve timidly, bewildered, nervous, and painfully aware of her begrimed appearance.

"Don't do anything right now. Just follow me and stay put where I tell you while I make my report to

Colonel Yarborough. After that we will find you a place to stay for the night."

"But Reacher took my things. I can't go in looking like this."

Nathaniel's long steps took the climb easily, and Sarah pulled against his lead. He chided mildly, "Female vanity." But seeing genuine distress, the teasing gentled. "You're all right. Come along and don't worry about it."

Sarah followed him up the steps, loath to admit that what she was feeling for him was respect. She had not known Nathaniel Garrett long enough to see him in his element. The man beside her now revealed an easy confidence. The men who stopped him with a comment or a casual greeting treated him as a respected officer. Nathaniel's calm assurance was evident in his relaxed stance, the secure movement of his shoulders, and the dignity of his walk. It was easy to be dignified if one was winning, but somehow Sarah knew that Nathaniel would be much the same if he were on the losing side. Just what would it take, she wondered, to bring this man to his knees?

Envy made Sarah more painfully aware of her own unseemly appearance, and she burned with humiliation. Every man who passed them must surely have turned to gawk at the ridiculous mountain woman and her brat. She found herself standing beside a wooden bench against the outside wall of an office, the door of which was standing ajar. A timorous glance inside showed an orderly desk and a seated officer. He must be Colonel Yarborough, she decided.

"I'll be back out in a little while. You wait here," Nathaniel directed. How could the man be so callous? If he would simply touch her hand and say, "I know how you must feel, Sarah," it would mean so much.

"I don't want to stay out here by myself," Sarah whispered hoarsely.

"Well, you have to, Sarah. You wanted to play the

game—this is it. I will be back after I make my report. If he wants to speak with you I will come out and get you." And with that, he was gone.

At last the door opened. "Come in, Mrs. Bradley." Sarah hastily adjusted her clothing and stepped through the doorway. She was so unnerved that all she could see was a blue uniform behind the desk. The uniform stood courteously and walked over to her, offering her its hand. She raised her eyes to the face. It was a very nice face. It wore eyeglasses. It smiled.

"This is Colonel Yarborough, Sarah," Nathaniel's voice steadied her. "He is a very good friend of mine, and he wants to help you if he can. Just tell him what he wants to know, and then we can get you settled." Nathaniel's fingers touched her elbow firmly.

"Thank you." Sarah's voice sounded tiny and very high, and she didn't know why she thanked them.

As soon as she was seated, questions issued from the Colonel: where was she from; who had her husband been; where had he been killed. And then she gave the entire account of why she wanted to leave Tennessee. Presently her voice lost some of its quiver, but Peter began to fret. Nathaniel took the boy, and Sarah did not miss his frown at the wet diaper. He said nothing, however, and walked to the window with the child.

"Nathaniel," concluded the Colonel at long last, "I am assured that it would be satisfactory to take her over the state lines. And I could arrange for the time you would need to help her in exchange for the service she has rendered the military. The red tape it will involve is unbelievable but the confirmation has to come from Carpenter and since he has done this before, I don't see why it couldn't be confirmed in a few weeks."

Sarah's jaw dropped. "I must wait *weeks?*" she gasped.

Colonel Yarborough raised a hand. "What I am telling you is that if you wish to cross the state lines under auspices of the United States Army the recommendation must go through the proper channels. Perhaps you do not realize how great the problem of spies has become, Mrs. Bradley. For a time we accepted a certain amount of espionage as natural. But the number arrested each month now is astounding."

Sarah burst out frantically, "Then I will go on my own! I can't linger, not with that fiend trying to take my son."

"Sarah, please," cautioned Nathaniel.

Colonel Yarborough removed his glasses and wiped them clean with his handkerchief. "The chances of your making it even out of the state by yourself . . . well, it is foolish even to consider it." Sarah slumped miserably, assured he was being honest.

Silence thickened, and suddenly both Nathaniel and the Colonel started to speak at the same time. Politely Nathaniel inclined his head.

"I was about to ask, Nat, if you had ever heard Belsing recount that tale he is so fond of, the one about General Grant's infantryman who got the bucket of water tossed at him by that woman, while marching through the streets of Nashville."

"Should I have?"

"Well," shrugged the Colonel, "there's not much more to tell . . . except that he married her and took her to his farm in Vermont."

Silence.

"I don't get what you're driving at, unless . . ." Nathaniel stopped, sighed heavily, and abruptly moved to place Peter in Sarah's lap. Sarah blinked, aware that she must surely have missed something, but unable to figure out what it was.

"Are you suggesting that—er—I could arrange for a—"

"No, Nat, not at all. There is a matter of ethics,

and for me to breach them by advising you to . . .
uh . . ."

Nathaniel's brows puckered deeply, the mobile
mouth pursing.

"Aaaah, no. What you find unethical I find unsatis-
factory. Even if all concerned were willing, there's
still . . ."

Finally Sarah could stand it no longer. "For pity's
sake," she demanded, "will someone in this room finish
a sentence?"

Nathaniel cleared his voice uneasily and ventured,
"Don't you see what he's saying, Sarah? I mean he
hasn't *said anything*, actually. . . ."

"Stop it!" And this time Sarah raised her voice.
"Either say it or stop talking!"

If Nathaniel was expecting help from Colonel Yarborough, he was tilling fallow soil, for the Colonel
simply laced his fingers placidly and refused to compromise his ethics more than he already had. The
captain lowered his voice and, with a difficulty
extraordinary for his usually glib tongue, began to explain.

"Probably the best way to put this, Sarah, is that . . .
uh, what I'm saying is . . . Oh, *hell! If* we wish to be
married, and *if* I wish to take you North as my wife,
Michael, uh, Colonel Yarborough would do what he
could to help. Is that right, Colonel?"

"I would have no reason to object to a marriage of
two mature adults, Nathaniel, no." The most charming shade of crimson flamed Sarah's cheeks, and her
head shook slowly from side to side in disbelief.

"I think both of you are insane. I could live with
Rachel and her lawyers as well as I could . . . play
such an imposter. I can't believe you're serious."

"No, dammit. I'm not serious! It's a terrible idea,
and I regret he . . . I . . . ever thought of it!" Nathaniel's anger bunched the muscle tightly in his jaw, and
he snapped to a curt military bow of dismissal. "Good

day to you, Colonel. Thank you so much for your time. After you, Mrs. Bradley." The hand upon Sarah's forearm shoved her out the door.

"Sorry I couldn't have been of more help, Nat," the Colonel called.

Quickly Nathaniel propelled Sarah out the door and down the front steps, turning only once to shush her sputtering protests with a furious glare. "I don't wish to hear another word. We can talk after I get you settled."

"But—"

"Matthew?" he called out.

The red head nodded. "Old Mrs. Simpson said she could stay with her as long as she needed to, and there is a girl to help with the laddie. You'll have to see to 'er food, though. She'll be comfortable enough." Matthew's voice was as smooth as it was deep, and Sarah was soothed by the charm of his quaint Irish brogue and gentle manner.

"Good enough. Up with you, Mrs. Bradley. This little beggar is soaking wet." Nathaniel forced a grin, lifting the sniffling Peter to Matthew who had already swung his great hulk into the saddle. "With my compliments," he wryly touched the brim of his hat to the older man.

Sarah didn't have the heart to utter a single word during their short ride to the two-story frame house at the outskirts of town. A wary smile to the pleasant little Mrs. Simpson was all she managed. Peter went willingly into her capable arms as if he had done it every day of his life, and the cheery hostess hugged him to an ample bosom, hypnotizing the boy with a constant stream of happy chatter.

With little formality they were ushered into a room which revealed the effects of the war in several ways. But the winged chair which accepted Sarah's exhausted limbs cuddled her with the most heavenly comfort she had experienced in a long time.

"Mrs. Simpson, I fear Peter is drenched. We have been riding hard for some hours. Did the sergeant give you my bag?" Mrs. Simpson's cameo brooch, the only adornment gracing her dark dress, bobbed as she nodded, immediately catching Peter's rapt attention. Busy little fingers worked in earnest to remove it.

"Yes, dearie. Now don't you worry about a thing. I know you must be exhausted, and I'm so excited at having people in the house again. We'll get along famously, won't we, Peter? Can he eat potatoes?" Sarah nodded, heaping silent blessings upon the gracious woman.

"Wonderful. Rosy!" she called, and a brown-skinned girl peeped with dark eyes around the door. "Heat some potatoes and fetch the bag here. We have a guest. Now just you come along with me, my darlin' little man. We'll have you comfortable in the time it takes to say 'Jack Robinson.' Hurry along, Rosy."

Her cheerful voice faded, and Sarah turned to view a somewhat easier-tempered Nathaniel leaning a hip casually against the front window frame, something akin to astonishment written upon his face.

"Whew!" he whistled softly. "Something tells me we may never see him again."

"Right now I think it's wonderful," Sarah murmured, leaning her head back against the worn velvet, pressing her temples against the dreadful throbbing. Only Matthew saw the mellowing of Nathaniel's eyes. He was, perhaps, the only one who would have read correctly what lay exposed for those brief seconds. Even Nathaniel didn't know of the warmth he was projecting toward the small woman in the chair. Near the door, his large arms crossed, Matthew watched his friend.

Sarah popped upright suddenly, eyes piercing sharply into Nathaniel. "Whatever expense has been incurred on my behalf, Captain Garrett, I shall keep a strict accounting of. It will all be paid back, every single penny. I meant to speak with you about this before now," she announced crisply. "I make my own way. I never want it said that I was a burden." She paused, her voice decreasing to a wistful whisper. "Though I suppose I already am. Always obstacles, obstacles. I don't understand. Why can't Peter and I live like anyone else? From the day the war began . . ."

Mrs. Simpson returned, interrupting, with a tray bearing a squat china teapot and three delicately patterned cups—fragile, as scarce a thing now as graciousness. It was just as well that she came in now, for an aching compassion knotted in the pit of Nathaniel's stomach would have driven him to hold Sarah, to comfort and reassure her. That, he knew, she would never accept. Not now, anyway.

"My faithful old Sam refused to leave me when the others did," she explained. "He does some odd chores for a few of the officers in town, and they repay him with some of the luxuries we cannot get. This tea is weak, for we use the leaves many times over, but you will still find it refreshing, I think."

"Mrs. Simpson, you are priceless," Nathaniel smiled at the little woman as she gingerly wiped her hands on her apron, glancing about to reassure herself that everything was as hospitable as she could make it.

"A fact I often reminded my dear husband of, sir, but I don't recall that *he* was ever convinced." She chuckled to herself, delighting in a memory long past. Her brisk footsteps had hardly disappeared down the corridor again when Matthew spoke.

"What suggestions did the Colonel have, Nat?"

"Well," drawled Nathaniel carefully, "it seems that Miss Sarah and I will have to be married if she intends to leave here much before summer."

Sarah's cup clattered noisily in its saucer, and she made a startled grab for it before springing to her feet. Brown eyes widened and her jaw dropped mutely.

"Shut your mouth, Sarah."

"Shut your own, Captain! I thought I made it *quite* clear in Colonel Yarborough's office. I'm *not* entering into any sinful arrangements. No lies! No deceptions!"

She was doing it to him again. Fists on hips, legs so bewitchingly outlined, breasts straining against the pathetic inadequacy of that old shirt. And those sparking eyes! How could he reason coldly when such a delicacy was within a fingertip's reach?

"I won't discuss it further," she choked.

"I think the term is a 'marriage of convenience,' little one, and you would not be the first to avail yourself of such a recourse." He sounded so nonchalant about the matter.

Sarah seated herself to pour tea, and Nathaniel watched as her hands betrayed her—she had to hold the chattering cup with both to keep from spilling it into her lap. Light steps moved him to the small table, and he poured for Matthew and himself.

"As you wish," he agreed. "I will pay Mrs. Simpson for two days' lodging and escort you back to the foot of the ridge, from which point you may return the rest of the way yourself."

Sarah knew it was hopeless to deceive herself any longer that she and Peter could go North on their own. That much she had learned. An unbidden tear splashed into her cup. Her touseled head dropped. She whispered, "Do you think it would help if I went to this man Carpenter and talked with him myself?"

"No."

"Matthew?" implored Sarah of the gentle giant.

"Ah, Miss," his smooth voice tried to comfort, "you are in a difficult situation, and I cannot advise you."

Matthew spoke again later. "One point to think on, it comes to me—the old woman's chances'd be smaller if your name was Garrett for a time."

Sarah sat still. Nathaniel stepped to the window, intently studying the trees.

"I suppose there are things we should discuss, Captain," she whispered finally.

Quietly, Nathaniel stepped from the window to settle a leg upon the arm of her chair. His voice was more gentle than Sarah had ever heard it.

"Well, Sarah, each state is different regarding annulments. But, if the marriage can be proved to have been attained upon false pretenses or invalid circumstances the courts *will* grant them. I don't really think you'd find it too difficult to convince a judge of the facts. Embarrassing, perhaps, but not impossible. It is, of course, a serious step. But it has been done before, and the more I think about it, the more I think it's a good plan."

"You seem to know a lot about annulments. And you sound more calm about the whole thing than you did in the Colonel's office."

Nathaniel laughed. "Now, Sarah, what man in his right mind would pass up a chance to marry such a beautiful woman . . . and so sweet-tempered and docile to boot?"

"You're obscene," she retorted weakly, and he bent to flick away a stray tear.

"But in this instance an obscene husband is better than none, unless you'd rather marry Matthew here," he gestured toward the big man.

Matthew started, and Sarah thought wryly that it was the quickest movement she had ever seen him make.

"I need some time," she said.

"Of course, dear heart. It's quite indecent to accept a proposal and be married in the same day, anyway." Nathaniel continued to speak lightly, but he was wrestling with the compulsion to scoop up this vulnerable slip of a girl and cradle her in his arms like an infant. For her bravery amidst trying circumstances he ad-

mired her. No, more than that, he truly respected her.
And *that* was something he had rarely felt. For anyone.

"After you have rested a few hours, put on your
dress, and if we can persuade the marvelous Mrs.
Simpson to tend Peter we will have some dinner at
what laughably serves as an officers' mess. Then we'll
decide."

Sarah searched the lean face above her, the strangeness of the man a constant amazement. He displayed
dominance with the boldness of a pirate, yet sympathy
lurked somewhere just behind his mockery. Was exhaustion the cause of her nagging need to trust Nathaniel Garrett, to rely on his judgment?

"I will expect you sometime around dusk then, Captain," she finished, taking care that her need was well
hidden from him.

The men took their leave. Touched with the thought
that human frailty was never meant to survive in this
world, Sarah silently observed the two Yankee figures
striding down the long path to the gate. Their heads
were bent as they talked, and Sarah decided it was
just as well she couldn't hear the words that passed
between the two.

"I've lived a considerable time, Nat," Matthew observed in his quiet manner, "and I don't recall ever
knowing a woman quite like that spunky little thing."

Quick blue eyes darted to the frank grey ones of
his old, old friend. "Spit out what's on your mind."

"Ah, you know I have no great love for Beth," began Matthew.

"I knew this was coming."

"Hold on, lad. It's only for your parents and her
father that I say a word. She's been the only woman
you've looked at twice since Charlotte died, an' you
can't blame 'em for hoping like they do."

Both men swung into their saddles, considering the
future in the light of the past.

"I don't blame anyone, Matt, not them, not even Beth. I don't intend to hurt Beth—I never have. But I'll be blown to hell before I can find it in myself to leave Sarah at the mercy of that old witch."

"Is that all it is, Nathaniel?" Matthew's voice was kind.

"I want her, and if I get the chance, I know I'll take her. But I don't intend to ever *need* a woman again. And that includes Beth Simms."

"I wouldn't put it past Beth to cause quite a nasty mess if she ever finds out just how far you've gone to help Sarah."

The horses began moving toward the town.

"Beth will never know anything. I don't know sometimes how that thing ever got started." Nathaniel grinned. "To tell you the truth, Matthew, I never thought I'd have much to worry about, because I never thought I'd live through the war."

A thick hand pulled Matthew's hat low on his brow. "There were times, laddie," he murmured, "when I didn't think so myself."

✎ *Chapter IV*

THE BEDROOM Sarah had been ushered into wasn't much different from the one which had been hers at Uncle Gene's. Though frayed, it was immaculately clean, the dark mahogany furnishings glowing richly from many years of loving care.

Early spring evenings grew quite chilly in southeast Tennessee, and Sarah hugged the thin coverlet about her naked body. She inclined her ear, listening for sounds of Peter, but stillness pervaded her end of the house. Sarah lay down on her stomach, gazing idly through the sheer curtain to the dusty road beyond. A passing wagon moved through the reddening rays of the sun as it bore its cumbersome burden of firewood toward the town. Two dusty figures dangled their legs off the back, leaning on the water barrel between them.

Putting herself into some semblance of order for her evening with Nathaniel was no small task, and she peeped into a porcelain pitcher on a small table beside the bed. It was empty. A tiny sliver of soap caught her attention instantly however, and she smiled.

Quickly slipping back into her travel-stained pants and shirt, Sarah stepped into the narrow corridor and followed faint voices until she found the large kitchen. Nearly as big as her entire cottage on the mountain, the kitchen consisted of a dining area at one end and a roomy living area sprawled before a fireplace on the other. Two aging samplers, neatly stitched, graced the face of bricks. A kettle of water steamed serenely on its hook over the fire. Sarah imagined that this kitchen had been a bustling place before the war. A contented Peter sat playing with an assortment of items, and Mrs. Simpson glanced up from her knitting.

"Here she is. Come in, come in, Mrs. Bradley." Plump cheeks reflected the flames. Sarah began to recognize the woman's charming mannerism of nodding agreeably along with her words. "Peter has been the most fascinating company for me all afternoon." The old fabric of her dark bombazine skirts spoke with a soft, weary rustling as she arose from her rocker to draw a tapestry-covered footstool nearer the fireplace.

"Please, just Sarah, Mrs. Simpson. And thank you." Sitting quietly at the feet of the older woman, savoring the soothing narrative of inconsequential things, a relaxing glow spread the entire length of Sarah's body. Rosy bobbed a curly head into the room, and Mrs. Simpson beckoned to the shy little Negress.

"Rosy, I think Sarah needs some water in her room, if you would please." The affection in the old woman's eyes, the inflection of gentleness in her tone prompted Sarah to sadness. If only Rachel had been so kind. How they could have comforted each other! Blind and foolish—that was Rachel. She and Peter were everything the old woman needed in her later years, but selfishness had blinded her to what lay just under her nose. What a terrible waste.

Sarah furiously blinked back the tears. "I find you to be a very nice lady, Mrs. Simpson. I'm grateful to you for your kindness. In all truth I had forgotten what it was like."

Sarah sat politely, knowing the older woman was measuring her, unaware that her iron will was obvious to anyone who cared to look closely. A soft hand closed over Sarah's calloused one.

"No need to explain, Sarah. The good sergeant

spoke to me briefly about you. I understand somethin' of your difficulty. I wouldn't worry too much about the old woman. Your captain seems to be clever enough to handle most anythin'."

Sarah opened her mouth, ready to object to the "your captain." But Mrs. Simpson had already arisen and begun to busy herself with Peter.

"Now if you have plans for the evenin', my dear, you'd best be seein' about them. We do have a few candles, and there's one in your room. At least we don't have to sleep in the cellar anymore, now that General Sherman has moved on." She lifted Peter, who was perfectly content to rest on her ample hip. "Don't you fret about the baby. I'm happy to have him. Since the war I've had very little companionship. I was too old to leave here, and I had nowhere to go, anyway. So Rosy and Sam and I stayed. Not that the Union soldiers have mistreated me, but I must admit I enjoy another woman's voice. Which reminds me—there is a lady in town I want you to meet. Oh my! Listen to me run on. And I know you're eager to get dressed."

Sarah laughed, planting a kiss atop the blond head of her son. Her spirits considerably lifted by Mrs. Simpson's infectious cheer, she left the room to confront the task of preparing herself with no materials except herself. Well, there was one print dress and the boots.

Horrible things, she grumbled, pausing to glare at the scarred leather boots. They would have to do, for she had no slippers. Perhaps no one would even see them. At least she had a nice figure and good teeth. She would see what a good half hour of improvisation could do.

Not bad, she decided, turning to view the draping of the dress over her hips. Not bad. The bodice was just right, and the fine wisps of hair teasing down from her coiffure with such studied carelessness were a nice touch.

"Look at what you're doing!" Sarah caught herself and scolded. She was deliberately doing everything she could to make Nathaniel think she was beautiful. Humph! Pride was her trouble. To be honest, if she had had the clothes she would have rubbed it in until he rued every rude thing he had ever said to her!

Sarah sniffed her wrists, pleased that the fragrance from the soap still clung to her. With one last satisfied glance at herself she left the room. She walked slowly, taking care the offending boots would not glare so defiantly from under the full skirt.

Mrs. Simpson enthusiastically approved the change. "Oh, yes. I understand that little spark in the Captain's eyes when he looks at you, my dear."

"Spark?" You mean his temper, she wished to say.

"Only the kind that an inveterate old matchmaker would see, Sarah," Mrs. Simpson chuckled. "Ah, that must be your young man now. Just wait here a moment."

"He's not my young man," protested Sarah weakly to the closing door. Mrs. Simpson's happy welcome rang cheerily, followed by Nathaniel's resonant response. Sarah's stomach began to fill with butterflies. For pity's sake, she was long past that sort of thing. Schoolgirl silliness! She reminded herself that Nathaniel Garrett had not changed in the last few hours—he was still the same horrible man who constantly insulted her with innuendos and condescending smirks. His ego demanded a minion, and *that* she would never be. The butterflies receded a little.

"I hope you don't mind coming back into the kitchen, sir," Mrs. Simpson apologized. "It's really where we live now."

Peter's sober eyes lifted as Nathaniel followed Mrs. Simpson into the room. Pushing himself up onto his new legs in a wobbly fashion, Peter cautiously made

his way to the familiar black boots. The child's eagerness to see him evidently pleased the tall, dark man,
for he swept him into the air with an easy toss,
causing the boy to squeal with delight. Mrs. Simpson
beamed approvingly. Sarah pursed her mouth in disdain. So like a crafty Yankee to ingratiate himself
with a child in order to impress Mrs. Simpson.

If Nathaniel noticed the metamorphosis in Sarah's
appearance he did little more than raise his brows.
She gritted her teeth in annoyance. Well, so it had
been wasted time and a foolish error that she would
not repeat. At least it was a private misjudgment,
and of no lasting concern. And, anyway, she had
done it only for Peter's sake.

"Are you ready to go, madam?" his deep voice interrupted her thoughts.

"Since when have my wishes been of any importance to you . . . *sir?*" Alarm sent Mrs. Simpson's alert
eyebrows flying, and the ill-concealed undercurrent
of animosity drew an uncomfortable cough from her.
Dear, dear—this would never do.

Taking Sarah's arm, the matron escorted them both
to the kitchen door. "Now you two children enjoy
a lovely supper," she patted Sarah's hand, "and don't
you worry about Peter for a second. He will be sound
asleep when you return. Rosy and I will see to that. I
will put out a candle in the living room before you
return in case you should . . . ahem, need to talk."
She beamed optimistically upon them as Nathaniel
held the door for Sarah.

"There's no need to pretend to be a gentleman,
Captain. Everyone sees straight through you," Sarah
murmured sweetly, sweeping haughtily past and
jumping sharply as he allowed his hand to move
across her buttocks in a daring caress.

"There are times I wish I were a man!" she
stormed, visualizing him knocked cold by her fist.

"But I wouldn't do that to a man, Sarah . . . even if he were as pretty as you."

Viciously Sarah snatched the handle of the front door and stepped out into the dusk before he could assist her. This promised to be a memorable evening, he sighed to himself. Lord, but she was beautiful! Her dark hair caught the last rays of the sun to glow a rusty copper, contrasting with her complexion. He drew her fragrance into his lungs, wishing dreadfully to bend his lips lower, to taste the creamy nape of her neck and—

"What's the matter?" Abruptly Nathaniel raised his head. Sarah had stopped suddenly on the steps just as he was following, almost sending him crashing down on top of her. He took her shoulders to steady himself, the feel of her against his chest shooting fire through his veins.

"It's the wretched boots!" Sarah wailed softly, hiking up the edge of her skirts and sticking out a foot. Nathaniel choked back laughter as he glimpsed the small, scuffed culprit from over her shoulder. This time he did place the tiniest peck onto the nape of her neck.

"Not to fret, Sarah mine," he consoled. "Tomorrow I promise we will purchase a pair of slippers if there is a pair to be found in this entire town." He caught the suspicious eye turned upon him and raised a reassuring finger. "To be carefully applied to your list of expenses, of course."

They walked the several blocks through what had once been the main thoroughfare of the town. It was still the busiest section, but a number of shops were boarded up or left standing empty. Men milled about by the dozens, crossing over the wide battle-scarred expanse between the parallel rows of buildings. A number cast envious glances Nathaniel's way. Sarah smiled to herself. Now she wasn't a mountain woman. She knew that look.

Women, haggard and ill-clad, took clothes down from drooping lines and scolded dirty children. Camp followers like these followed troops from county to county and state to state.

"This makes me sick." Nathaniel's distaste of the occupation was obvious.

"Sherman was not in his prime when he left here." Sarah watched two young boys, filthy and barefooted, peep furtively around the end of a building, as if afraid that some villain would snatch their kitchen scraps. "The only thing Rachel really ever feared," she mused.

"Hm?"

"William Tecumseh Sherman. He was the only thing that really frightened Rachel. I suppose that was why she refused to go back to Charleston. She often remarked that the mountain was the safest place to be in the whole country. It wasn't for me, as things turned out." Sarah smiled, her jest somewhat timid. She felt Nathaniel's hand slip into the folds of her swinging skirt and touch her thigh as she walked. It was firmly removed with a frown. Probably even Nathaniel didn't fully understand the protective urge which placed it there.

"The Yankees came to the cottage several times," Sarah recalled quietly. "They took what few tools Charles had, and they only paid a fraction of their worth. Rachel wouldn't allow me to go outside, or they wouldn't have taken them quite so easily."

"In that instance, Rachel did you a service." He smiled bitterly. "Your beauty is rare indeed and would not have escaped their notice."

"It escaped yours."

Nathaniel grinned. "I thought as much." He chuckled. "You're miffed at me because I didn't tell you how nice you look."

"No I'm not!"

"Yes you are, and let's not discuss it further. You'll

just keep on lying, and then I'll be responsible for corrupting you, turning you into a liar."

Seeing an occasional Yankee on the mountain had been different somehow. Even the briskness of military order at Yankee headquarters had been different. This was not the same. Men swarmed over sprawling verandas, smoking, whittling, rereading tattered letters, but mostly huddling in small groups, fingering suspenders and just listening—listening to grim predictions, to descriptions of a wife, a sweetheart, a child. Homesick, lonely men, commanded to do too many things not in their nature to do, had been taken from the land and their own futures. Sarah understood these men. She shared a war-induced kinship with them. They didn't dream any more. Neither did she.

She supposed, eating her dinner in silence as Nathaniel drew maps on the table, that dreaming had attracted her to Charles. Charles could always dream. When had she lost the ability? Perhaps it had begun to slip away when she finally accepted that her father had really left her and would never come back. A cold realism had become part of her thinking. Now as she peered into strange faces, the same quality met her. War had taken young dreamers and crushed them into what she herself felt crushed into.

Did Nathaniel Garrett see life through some magic vision, that he could so frequently laugh? Why was he different? He wasn't insensitive. For long minutes Sarah pondered the man who carried in his hands so much of her future and Peter's. He turned to smile at her, quirking a curious brow at her pensive face. Sarah wondered if maybe Nathaniel could laugh because his life was not a burden, nor the holding on to it. He might die for his country. But she had Peter, and for him she couldn't die.

Sarah smiled wryly and Nathaniel paused. "What is it?"

She shrugged. "It wouldn't interest you."

"Tell me."

"You accused me of being a philosopher. Perhaps I am," she stared ahead, speaking softly. "You have everything to live for . . . and yet nothing, I suspect. I have nothing to live for and everything—Peter."

"Is that all you want to stay alive for, Sarah?"

"Yes."

"There has to be more, love. One can't survive just for another's sake."

Nathaniel cajoled her a bit, walking home slowly, savoring each step, baiting her until she relented and lost her temper. In a way Sarah was grateful for the rapscallion's ability to do this. It was a talent—this mockery. But before she could analyze it the time had come. The subject which had been uppermost in their minds throughout the evening must be discussed. Nathaniel lightly placed his arm about her waist, only to have it promptly shaken off.

"Sarah," he chided gently, "you must learn to accept a few husbandly attentions for the sake of appearances, if nothing else."

Sarah turned. "That's a nice way of telling me you couldn't find any other way, isn't it?" He reached for her, wishing she didn't hate it quite so much. His long fingers moved absently, back and forth upon the smoothness of her bodice, feeling the outline of her ribs. Strangely enough, she didn't resist, not even when he drew her very close and wrapped his arms completely about her. Small hands rested, unmoving, against his waist.

"I considered wiring my father, Sarah, and asking him to just come for you. But a politician's life hangs by a tenuous thread most of the time, and I am afraid talk might do irreparable damage. The Lincoln administration is having a difficult time, and my father has many enemies. Any scandal, even an annulment, could be devastating. I just couldn't ask him."

"I understand, Captain. Say no more." She moved away, shaking her head dolefully.

"Nathaniel."

"I beg your par—"

"My name is Nathaniel. You have called me by my name twice. You were in considerable pain from Rachel's poker. Do you have to be in pain to call me by my name, Sarah?" His voice was so husky that Sarah looked up sharply. What lay in those blue eyes? Genuine honesty, for once?

Cautiously Nathaniel took a step closer.

"Well, I—"

"It is very old-fashioned for a wife to call her husband by his surname, or even 'Captain,' don't you think so, Mrs. Sarah Garrett?"

"Stop it!"

"I'm sorry, darling. I didn't mean to tease," he brushed a stray curl from her forehead with oddly trembling fingers.

"And quit calling me all those names of endearment," she moaned.

"I'm truly sorry, love . . . Oh, hell! Now you've got me behaving like a tongue-tied schoolboy."

He stuffed his hands into his pockets, pulling aside his dress jacket as he took a few stormy strides away from her. Sarah stood quietly blotting at her eyes and observing the smooth lines of his back. She was suddenly caught in a compulsion to touch him, and she impulsively slipped beside him to place her arm through his in a placating manner. It seemed the only weapon she possessed was the playing of this immoral charade.

"Are you quite sure this annulment can be accomplished, Captain? I mean, are you absolutely, positively, beyond-any-shadow-of-a-doubt sure? I don't wish to put my foot into any more traps than I already have. I think we're both insane, I really do, to even consider this. And once we satisfy this Carpenter person and complete the trip, it *must* remain an absolute secret. Agreed?"

"Nathaniel," he reminded, "and the secret part is no problem, if you don't mind a few raised eyebrows. And if you want an annulment, I'm sure you can have one."

"What do you mean 'if' I want an annulment. Of course I'll want an annulment. Are you mad?" Sarah squinted cautious eyes up at Nathaniel, causing him to stop in his tracks and grin down at her.

"Well," he shrugged sheepishly. "You may enjoy being Mrs. Garrett so much that you might just . . . well, you know."

"No, I don't know, and quit teasing me." She began walking again. "You can't be poor," remarked Sarah tactlessly. "Well, I mean, with your father being a senator. I wouldn't even consider this if it were going to bankrupt you. I hope you understand that . . . Nathaniel."

"No, you frugal little witch, I am not poor. In fact, money is one of the last of my problems, at the moment."

"What other problems, pray tell? A wife should know these things."

"Now who's teasing?"

Nathaniel reached out an arm for her, but she stepped from his reach, her skirts swaying provocatively.

"Er—Sarah," Nathaniel began, and something in his tone made Sarah measure him closely. "I've been wondering all evening how to approach this, and I still don't know quite how to do it."

"Well, saying it straight out might help."

"There is a woman whom my family has had me married to several times," he continued rapidly, as if he were anxious to have it said. "By that I mean that it has been practically understood by both our families that we would marry if I came through this war alive." He sighed heavily and leaned against a tree, brushing his forefinger against the tip of his narrow nose as Sarah had so often watched him do.

"Do you . . . love this woman?"

Nathaniel drew a long whistle through his teeth.

"Blast it all, woman! You don't hesitate to go for the jugular, do you?" He took a few paces from Sarah.

"That hardly answers the question, Captain," Sarah replied glibly. So there *was* a woman in Nathaniel's life. The fierce commander was practically engaged. This put her in a more favorable position, for he would be just as anxious for an annulment as she was. And this sweetheart might well prove to be an effective weapon to control Nathaniel's behavior.

"I'm very fond of her, if that's what you mean. I've known her for a long time. But I can't actually say I'm madly in love with her. No . . . I guess I couldn't say that."

This little vixen was getting under his skin again. Right now she was so maddeningly desirable that he didn't want to think about Beth Simms or anything else. He only wanted to hold her and kiss her to her toes and caress her and strip her naked, bury himself deep within her, and just drown! No! She must want *him*, whatever it took! And there lay the dilemma.

"I accept your suggestion of this . . . temporary solution, Captain," she said suddenly.

"Nathaniel," he corrected dreamily, grinning down at her.

"All right! Nathaniel, I accept because I have to. You have as much to lose by this as I do. In some respects," she added softly, "you have *more* to lose than I. There's Peter complicating things . . . and your parents and your betrothed."

"She is *not* my betrothed," he said, extending a cautious finger and slowly tracing the gentle line of her jaw.

"Almost. Anyway, tell me what to do next." So here she was, calmly planning to be married to a Yankee officer whom she had only known for a few days. She could do it without a single qualm about Charles's memory. Had the war done this to her? Maybe God would forgive her for taking a sacred oath in vain to save her child.

"You don't have to do anything. You fulfilled your end of the agreement by helping me and my men, and I will see you out of this as I promised. I do have one request to make of you. Tomorrow, do some shopping. I want you to have the things you need for yourself and Peter. We are going to a much cooler climate, for one thing. You will agree?"

Sarah hesitated, and he grinned. "On account, naturally," he qualified himself. "On second thought, you are so stingy I had better come with you to see you do it properly. I have my own idea of how a wife and son should be cared for."

"All right, Nathaniel." Sarah relented and laughed softly, honestly, and openly for the first time since he had known her. And then, suddenly, he drew Sarah brusquely up the path to Mrs. Simpson's front door. She could not fathom his sudden change of mood.

"Please go in. I will see you sometime tomorrow morning," he ordered roughly, the muscles across his shoulders trembling with the urgent hunger to hold her in his arms.

"The sharpness of your tongue is your most valuable asset, madam." Nathaniel whispered against her cheek, "For without it, you sink to the level of a mere woman—the most desirable woman I have ever known."

He disappeared so quickly into the shadows surrounding the porch that she leaned against the hard jamb of the door, wondering whether he had complimented or insulted her.

A firm knock just outside her window awakened her from slumber. Footsteps softly echoed through the corridor, and she snatched the fragile sheet about her naked body. Good heavens, the sun had been up for hours! And Peter was nowhere to be seen. How could she have slept so soundly?

"Come in, suh," the soft black dialect of Sam invited. "I don' b'lieve Miz Sarah's up jes' yet, suh." Before Nathaniel could reply Sarah opened her door just a crack.

"Yes, I'm up. I'll be dressed and in the kitchen in just a moment."

"Ah, little lazy bones, have you succumbed to a life of leisure so soon?" There was no trace in his voice of the curtness of the night before. Only a small part of Sarah was visible to his approving inspection, but just knowing that only a sheet lay between him and that sweet, sweet flesh was a torment. Those burning eyes, however, did not deceive Sarah. She knew it would be the same for any woman standing as she was.

"Does your greed know no bounds, you evil man?" she reprimanded, making a move to close the door. A quick knee prevented her.

"I only suffer the agonies of any ardent bridegroom, Sarah mine," Nathaniel grinned, drawing a knuckle softly across her pouting lower lip.

"I suggest you remove yourself before Mrs. Simpson begins to wonder what has happened to her guest. I will be in as soon as I can dress," Sarah called through the closing door.

She did not pause in her toilette to analyze her haste. A strange excitement pricked at her bones. But then, she was eager to see Peter. Pinching her cheeks and biting her lips, giving herself one last critical view in the mirror, it did not occur to Sarah that she was taking unusual pains for Peter.

"Ah, there's our sleepyhead." Mrs. Simpson was placing slices of hard brown toast, tea, and a small jar of honey on the table. Peter scooted across the floor on all fours with an excited cry of "Mama!" and Sarah hugged him tightly, planting noisy kisses all over his sweet face. Nathaniel was leaning back in Mrs. Simpson's rocker, extended legs propped on the wide hearth. He gave only a cursory glance toward her as he concentrated on tamping tobacco into his pipe. Sarah chose to ignore his rudeness, giving Peter her full attention. Peter was eager to try talking, and now he released all his pent-up chatter, very gravely, and even she only halfway understood it. But she agreed and nodded as if each word were an eloquent jewel, and a lazy smile curled Nathaniel's lips as he watched them.

"I suppose you're on official furlough," Sarah casually murmured without looking at him, meticulously spreading a bit of honey on her second piece of toast.

"Beginning today for two whole weeks. Don't you think you should inform our hostess of our wedding, love?" The careless statement seemed to shatter the entire room. Sarah jumped. The least he could have done was to give her some warning, the beast! Her toast caught in her throat and she nearly strangled, glaring at Nathaniel.

Mrs. Simpson could but watch in astonished amazement as the handsome man was by the side of his intended in an instant, taking her in his arms solicitously and patting her on the back to ease her gasps. The bride-to-be covered her mouth with both hands and coughed until her face was scarlet and tears streamed down her cheeks. Fetching a glass of water, Mrs. Simpson handed it to the unruffled groom.

"Here, my darling," he crooned, holding her shoulders *quite* firmly with one arm and replacing the glass of water on the table. He went through the pretense of patting her back with his supporting arm as he warded off a dangerous hand that threatened to pinch a piece of flesh from his ribs.

"Sarah, I've warned you before not to talk with your mouth full," he admonished in a husbandly tone. Sarah brushed by him reproachfully to take a long sip from the glass.

"It's the excitement, I think," she sputtered, smiling wanly at Mrs. Simpson, and threatening to kill Nathaniel with her eyes.

"We were not quite certain when I could get time off to have a proper wedding, Mrs. Simpson," he explained. "We shall have to be consoled with a whirlwind affair, I fear, much like our courtship. But I suppose this is not uncommon during wartime," Nathaniel concluded, smoothing Sarah's locks.

"Oh, my dears," cooed Mrs. Simpson, elation all through her round face. "You can't possibly know how thrilled this makes me. You know, I lost two sons in the war. I am not proud to admit that at times I have felt very bitter toward this country. I have believed that I would not live to see the day of healing, when hands could reach over a dividing line that was never meant to be there at all. To see you two young people take such a step consoles me." The sweet face tried very hard not to reveal painful memories. "Perhaps," she whispered, blotting at her eyes with the corner of her apron, "perhaps it was not all for naught that they died, Captain Garrett."

She sniffed loudly. "Sarah, dear, I would be so proud if you would allow me to give you this wedding here in my own home. I know it would not be elaborate, but the preparations would be made by those who have grown fond of you in a very short time. I would like to take the place of your mother, for just a few hours, if that pleases you."

Taking Sarah's shocked silence to be an affirmation, the gracious little woman placed an excited kiss upon Sarah's pale cheek. "I must get word to my friend Irene. We don't have much time, do we, dear? Ah, yes, and there is the reverend to notify. I will get a note off right away, as soon as you give me the specifics, Captain Garrett. Oh, this promises to be *the event* of the spring. We will plan a splendid wedding supper. And, of course, you may spend your honeymoon right here, if you like. Irene will be beside herself with excitement."

As the hostess took her hurried but happy leave Sarah mouthed a silent "damn you" to Nathaniel's satisfied countenance. Then she flew across the room, prepared to claw his eyes out.

"You knew she would do that, you wretch! And how could I tell her otherwise? You are contemptible! I hate the sight of you!"

"No you don't. One can't hate the groom." Nathaniel placed a quick kiss on the tip of her adorable, outraged nose and dodged a palm aimed viciously at his jaw.

"I would have agreed to a civil ceremony, but she's sending for a minister," she groaned. "That will be a sacrilege. I will damn my soul, Nathaniel. I can't go through with it."

"Yes you can. One can always do what has to be done."

"That's easy for you to say. *You* have no honor," she wailed, and Nathaniel reached out a comforting arm and drew her unresistingly into his arms. At that particular moment Mrs. Simpson chose to return. Finding the couple in tender embrace, she beamed upon them.

"I knew from the outset this was a match made in heaven."

A few moments was all it had taken—the bridges were effectively burned. Her only choice was to see the thing through somehow, as she knew she must. Squaring her slender shoulders as she had so many times the last four years, Sarah bravely took the bit. Casting one last glare of contempt on her prospective bridegroom, she withdrew from his gentle embrace.

"I am so grateful to you, Mrs. Simpson, for your kind offer." Placing a sweet kiss upon the round cheek, Sarah sighed. "We must put our heads together. Time, I fear, is scarce. My dear Nathaniel rescued me with only the shirt upon my back, quite truly. I am ill prepared for a wedding."

"We must see Irene immediately. She has a daughter only slightly older than you who has been in England with her husband during the war. Irene forbade her to even come to visit until it is over. She can help us with some of Tess's things."

"It seems to me, sweetheart, that you are in very good hands," Nathaniel interrupted. "If you will excuse me, ladies, I have several matters that need immediate attention."

And without so much as a by-your-leave he drew Sarah into his arms and bent his head to place an intimate kiss on her mouth. Her cheeks flamed scarlet as she withdrew.

"I will see you to the door, Nathaniel dear," she purred.

Once out of earshot of the household, Sarah's wrath fell on Nathaniel Garrett like a maelstrom of hailstones. But Nathaniel only struck one of his casual postures and let her rage spend itself as his eyes roamed indulgently over her heaving bosom.

As Sarah's fury began to subside, she became aware of his indecent consideration, and she gave him her back angrily.

"If you wish to dampen my desire for you, that did not accomplish it, Sarah mine," he laughed softly.

"You promised me!"

"Ah, Sarah love," he protested, "you have a very

bad habit of hearing only what you wish to hear. I promised only to take you out of the South and to keep our marriage a secret until the annulment. Nothing else."

Sarah whirled to face him. "One more promise is necessary then, sir."

"I will hear your proposal."

Sarah moistened her lips, phrasing her demand as tactfully as possible. "You must agree . . . you must promise . . . not to make demands of . . . marital privileges on me once we are married."

"Would you mind explaining that in detail, my pet?"

"Well," she hesitated, "I suppose we will be forced into very . . . close quarters. You must not think that you can . . . damn it, Nathaniel! You knew all along what I meant."

"Yes," he laughed. "Will it bring comfort to your little heart if I promise that I will not bed you against your will?"

Sarah thought a moment, her brow puckering. "I do not find it over-comforting, no. But I suppose it's the most you will concede."

"The absolute maximum, madam," he agreed wickedly. "You—"

"Well, I don't understand what you've got to lose by refusing. This is not a real marriage, for pity's sake!"

"Sarah, Sarah, Sarah. I've made no attempts to hide the fact that I want you. Not to kiss you, but to make love to you."

"Well, that's a fine attitude in a predicament as delicate as this one!"

"No one's forcing you."

"That is the most flagrant understatement— You *could* just get a couple of horses and just *take* me out of here, you know!"

Nathaniel's frown darkened. "I don't relish a dishonorable discharge, if that makes any difference to *you.* And I don't ever want it thrown in my face that I didn't pursue every means at my disposal. You know damn well that if there were another way I would have taken it!"

"Oh, God help us!" groaned Sarah.

"God didn't create this war, Sarah. Greedy, stubborn men did. We'll just have to help each other. Now be ready for me this afternoon. There is a matter of some slippers, I believe." Cramming on his hat, he left with an oddly pleased look on his face.

The remainder of the morning slipped through Sarah's busy fingers as if it were so much water, and the afternoon was half spent before she saw Nathaniel again. Sarah had some qualms about taking another woman's clothing, no matter how dire the need, but she was assured by the taciturn Irene that Tess had no need for the things and had probably forgotten their existence. So, with Rosy tending Peter on the floor beside them in the sewing room, Sarah, Irene, and Mrs. Simpson set about making alterations.

The wedding gown was a soft beige silk with a high lace collar and long sleeves edged in matching lace. Tiny pearl buttons ran down the entire length of the gown, ending with a shorter scalloped overskirt and a lace underskirt extending to the floor. Tess was a bit taller than Sarah, requiring that the hems be shortened. Much to Sarah's interest, it was agreed that she should be laced.

Lacing had once been an everyday routine with Sarah, when she lived with her uncle and aunt. But, after she and Charles had moved to the mountain she had discarded the fashion. Of course, the war would have ended it anyway, for Sarah rarely had a dress. After selecting a batiste shift, a proper petticoat, and hoops, Sarah submitted to being laced. But when she presented her back to Mrs. Simpson for the adjusting of the stays, the plump lady gasped, "Irene," she choked. "I wish you'd look at this!" The two women stared at the large bruise spreading the entire width of Sarah's small back. Presenting her back to the oval, free-standing mirror, Sarah pulled her hair aside and craned her neck in an attempt to see the extent of her injury.

"It is rather nasty, isn't it?" observed Sarah, wincing as Mrs. Simpson gently probed the edges.

"I just can't believe an old woman could do such a thing," marveled Irene. "Forgive me, Sarah. Frannie told me about your problem."

"Well," snapped Mrs. Simpson. "Sarah's just lucky it wasn't her head. I shudder to think of the possibilities."

Slithering into the wedding gown, Sarah stood patiently as they buttoned the dozens of tiny buttons down the front of the gown. All eyes, including Peter's, gaped at her with something akin to awe. She looked elegant, alluring, with a dash of the pixie thrown in. Her already trim waist was demurely small, and the laces only emphasized the fullness of her bosom, filling the dress in exactly the right amount.

"I can't believe it," she murmured to herself.

The entire afternoon was a miraculous fantasy. When Silas Hartman had climbed the stone steps to his brother's house many years past, a broken, stooping man, he had left a tiny girlchild whose mother died at her birth. Silas never saw Sarah again. Gene Hartman had loved Sarah, cherishing her as his own until the day he died. Something of this had been guilt for having loved Sarah's mother and doing nothing about it until, from utter loneliness, Caroline had married Silas, his brother.

Though Sybinna Hartman had never complained about rearing an unrequested child, had never struck Sarah, had never dealt harshly with her, she had never loved her, either. In all her life Sarah had never known the love of a woman. And not until she nursed her own son had she realized she had been cheated. She had lived with a great lack in her life. If pressed, she might even admit to being frightened of older women.

Frannie Simpson was the first woman to show any love to Sarah. Her affection for the older woman was a fresh, exciting thing. The beautifully flushed brunette who laughed at her own reflection in the oval mirror was almost a stranger to Sarah. She was beautiful. She had two new women friends. Her son played happily upon the floor by her feet. And a wealthy Yankee captain was going to help her, even if the method was not of their choosing. Did Sarah see a spark of hope for the future? Yes! After all, there was a glimmer of hope.

Sometime well past mid-afternoon the three women took an accounting of what they had. Six gowns— three of which still had hems to be altered, a button or two to repair—two petticoats, two shifts, one of which Sarah was wearing, and the lacing. All that remained unaccounted for was a nightgown, stockings and a hat.

"I doubt that you can find stockings in Chattanooga, Sarah. And if you do they will be terribly expensive," warned Mrs. Simpson. Sarah didn't care. She would go bare-legged. There was nothing like a new gown to lift the spirits, and she had six!

"Now if your young man sets the wedding for tomorrow afternoon, my dear, we can have all the alterations done in time."

Sarah sobered, surveying her great gift and the planned marriage which had instigated it all. The hour was bittersweet, and her words a bit trembly.

"I wish to thank you both, but I don't even know how. You've done a wonderful thing. Rachel could have taken that child, you know. If Nathaniel Garrett hadn't helped me leave that house three nights ago, and if we were not leaving this town and this state . . . well, I . . ." Mrs. Simpson moved to slip a plump arm about the tiny waist.

"Don't dwell on it, Sarah dear. These are strange times we live in, and you have a new life before you now, a life that Rachel can't touch. Comfort yourself that you have a fine man who loves you and will be a good father to your son, and don't let the circumstances spoil your wedding day."

Sarah could hardly look at her. If you only knew what a fraud I am you wouldn't be saying these comforting words to me, she thought miserably. To have to lie to these wonderful new friends!

Sharp rapping at the front of the house interrupted them. "That's the Captain," assured Sarah. "I'll answer the door."

Before she could stop herself she glanced in the mirror one last time. She had almost fallen into the same trap—wishing to show off for the captain. Nathaniel's lady was without a doubt a gentlewoman, and Sarah's fierce pride wasn't content with coming up short. Perhaps the captain would not be so quick to mock her since she had shed her backwoods attire? Perhaps he would show a little respect, now that she looked more like a lady. Quickly Sarah smoothed back a few stray wisps of hair from her forehead and ran her fingertips along her arched brows. The knock at the front door became insistent.

"Patience is not one of your virtues, Nathaniel," she murmured, swinging open the heavy door. For one split second Sarah stood, stunned. Then, with a small cry, she grasped the brass doorknob hard, throwing all her weight back against it.

"No!"

"I've come for Peter, you devious girl," Rachel sneered as she jerked the door open with amazing agility. Expensive leather gloves, a flowing velvet cape, wiry grey sprigs effectively covered with a tasteful hat—Rachel looked like the influential dowager she was. Two well-dressed men stood behind her, one with his arms folded. The other carried a brown leather case and a cane. Sarah trembled. Control, Sarah, control!

"How did you manage to find me so quickly, Mrs. Bradley?"

"Oh, that proved no trouble at all in a town of this size, my dear," purred the vengeful old woman. "Well, Sarah, are you going to ask us in or shall we discuss our legal affairs before all the neighbors?"

"Forgive me," murmured Sarah, gesturing for them to follow and stepping to the entrance of the living room. Wasn't this hilarious? No "damnable little slut," no "wretched bitch." Rachel was terribly polite when it suited her.

Politely Sarah inclined her head to the man with the brown case who nervously moistened his lips, obviously a bit surprised to find an attractive young woman instead of a raving maniac. "Please be seated, gentlemen. I will fetch the mistress of the house."

She backed out the door, careful to keep her head erect and not to bump into anything. Then her feet literally flew to the back room where they had all spent such a happy afternoon. Throwing open the door so sharply that the two women started, Sarah stood shaking before them, eyes huge with terror.

"It's Rachel!" she choked, leaning against the wall and gesturing wildly to the living room. "And two men. Probably her lawyers!"

"Oh, good lord!" gasped Irene, but Mrs. Simpson was already moving with surprising fleetness.

"Rosy, tell Sam to fetch the Captain—wherever he is. Irene, take this boy and go home!" Hastily she glanced about the room, taking a deep breath and pausing to smooth her collar and the bodice of her dress. "Now, Sarah child, calm yourself. Let's see to our guests."

Drinking in the older woman's strength, Sarah sighed. At least this time she wasn't alone in her battle with Rachel.

"I have been scrapping with Rachel Bradley for a long time, Mrs. Simpson. I shan't fall apart now." Forcing herself to smile, Sarah left the room. She had learned well that the more one feared, the quicker was the stand and the harder the fight.

The power of the legal strength behind Rachel Bradley permeated the room like strong incense. The dark-suited man without the case stood behind Rachel's chair, resting one smooth, manicured hand upon it. His dark eyes frightened Sarah. The other man appeared less offensive and more likely to be reasonable so Sarah directed her words primarily to him.

"Mrs. Simpson, this is my late husband's grandmother, Rachel Bradley. The names of the two gentlemen I do not know." The seated man had risen as the two women entered, and he now presented his hand to Mrs. Simpson.

"Gerald Aveley. An' this is Mistuh John Pollard. We ah from South Carolina, as you may already know, an' we have a legal mattuh of custody with Miz Bradley."

"Pray tend to your business, sir. But remember, you are a guest in my home, and I will not tolerate any abuse of Sarah."

"Of course, Mrs. Simpson. It is suhtainly not our intention to misuse anyone. We have come in good faith that th' child's mothuh will listen to reason an' not necessitate any unpleasant court actions. It is suhtainly to th' advantage of all con—"

"There will be no negotiations, gentlemen," interrupted Sarah, coming straight to the point. "I am the child's natural mother, and I have no intention of relinquishing my rights."

Sarah paced a few steps before stopping to stand before Rachel. Their eyes locked in the familiar battle of wills. "Forgive me. I do not care to listen to legal niceties. State your case quickly and leave."

"You're a little fool, Sarah." Rachel curled her pinched little mouth into a smile. "I'm even prepared to pay you more money than you have ever dreamed of. You don't have any use for that child. If you don't listen to common sense I'll only have you before a judge, or even the provisional governor if I have to. You will lose. Be smart. Give me what I want and I'll leave you alone."

"You forget that I was married to Charles, Mrs. Bradley, and I am not entirely ignorant of the law. You can't bluff me into surrendering Peter."

"She can adequately prove that you have no means of support for th' child, Miz Bradley," interjected Mr. Aveley. Sarah whirled upon him like a trapped animal, hair swirling.

"And *you,* sir, are bought and paid for! How much is she paying you to misrepresent the facts?" Gerald Aveley flushed, compressing his lips together tightly. His companion spoke.

"Mrs. Bradley, the simple fact is that you may as well give us the child immediately, for if you don't we shall be on your steps tomorrow mornin' with the provost marshal. The papers are complete and only need to be filed. That, Mrs. Bradley, is a mere formality, quickly accomplished. We came here today hopin' to spare you."

"I don't suppose her husband would have any say in the matter, gentlemen?" drawled a voice behind them. Sarah lowered thick lashes to her cheeks as relief washed through her. Wiping her wet palms lightly against her full skirts she turned to cast a grateful glance toward the uniformed figure leaning against the doorway. His booted ankles were casually crossed, and his thumb hooked carelessly beside the holstered pistol at his waist.

Astonished eyes darted in his direction, and a small sound escaped Mrs. Simpson. Gerald Aveley rose, the muscle in his jaw twitching as he surveyed the captain. He did not dismiss this unexpected adversary lightly. The two men waged a silent battle of wills until Rachel's brittle laugh filled the room. Pulling her small body forward onto her elbows, she narrowed gleaming eyes at Nathaniel.

"Now I recognize you, you Yankee brigand. And spare us your lyin'. She's not worth it, sir. You do yourself a disservice to ally yourself with her." She gestured to the serpent-like Mr. Pollard.

"I assume that you have documents proving your alleged marriage?"

"I will show you my papers when you show me yours, sir." Nathaniel smiled easily and straightened himself to carelessly toss his hat upon a chair. Sarah smiled. She had seen that posture before and well knew the danger it hid.

The cobra bent its head to Rachel's ear and murmured something, and Gerald Aveley shifted his weight uncomfortably. At last Rachel stood and looked at Nathaniel, moving a few steps until she stood before him. Raising a twisted finger before his bemused face she rasped, "You are bluffin'. Tomorrow we will investigate this alleged marriage and come with th' provost marshal. And not only will we leave here with my great-grandson, but this little charade will cost you your commission—Captain, is it? Always leave white trash alone. It will only drag you down."

At that, Mrs. Simpson made a move toward Rachel, but Nathaniel placed a staying hand upon her arm as she stepped forward. He bowed to Rachel and slowly straightened himself to cast a deadly look at Mr. Pollard.

"Welcome to the arena, gentlemen," Nathaniel spoke carefully. "I must warn you that I cut my teeth on little antics such as this, and I play your game extremely well." Mr. Aveley's composure suffered slightly, but he made no reply. Finally he gestured to his companion to escort Rachel from the room and without further comment took his own leave.

As Rachel and her legal artillery made an awkward departure, Nathaniel availed himself of the few minutes to feast his eyes upon his trembling bride-to-be. The black boots traced a slow circle about her, his quick eyes missing no detail. Her girlish exuberance of less than an hour past was shattered beyond repair, and she did not mind when his arm encircled her from behind.

"Well, ladies," he said, "I suggest you fetch the reverend quickly unless you desire to enter the battle without a weapon."

ⅇ⅄ *Chapter V*

WITH A LAST, silent apology to Charles' memory Sarah dressed herself. She had indulged herself in the luxury of a tub bath, complete with a small piece of scented soap, and then dried herself slowly. As she sat arranging her hair, she decided to apply for a position as a governess, or advertise her qualifications as a music teacher just as soon as they arrived in Maryland. She would do ironing if she had to. Then she could begin to pay back her debt to the strange man she was about to wed. She would do what she had to do, for Peter's sake.

A light tap sounded on the door. "Look what we made for you, Sarah," Mrs. Simpson popped her head inside, offering a beautiful spring nosegay composed of early sprigs of delicate forsythia surrounded by sprays of bridal wreath. Such an attack of conscience battered Sarah's poise that the older woman mistook it for prewedding jitters and patted Sarah as she dried her tears.

"It's nearly time, my dear girl. Let's get you laced and dressed, for the groom has just arrived. He is so handsome, Sarah, you would not believe it. I know that you two will have the most beautiful children ever born." And, strange to say, Mrs. Simpson had to comfort another stream of tears.

The minutes ticked away, and another light knock announced that the waiting was ended. Mrs. Simpson opened the door to Matthew's huge form, and Sarah could hardly raise her eyes to him. She was very fond of Matthew, caring a great deal about his opinion of her, and as Mrs. Simpson gave her one last kiss and slipped out to her guests, Sarah reached out a hand to touch his sleeve.

"Please don't hate me, Matthew," she pleaded.

"I understand, lass, perhaps more than you know," his smooth voice soothed. "One thing I would tell you, Sarah. Nathaniel's a fine man, for I've known 'im since 'e was a tad. Just give 'im a chance."

"But we don't love each other, Matthew," she whispered raggedly. "I can't be honest with anyone but you and Nathaniel. You know what we're doing. It's wrong."

The Irishman smiled. "What could be so wrong in two people givin' of themselves to save an innocent boy?" Matthew smoothed his moustache and beard. "Now take the arm of a crusty Yankee sergeant, and I'll take you to your husband."

"Crusty, my foot. You're a pussycat, Matthew McCarey."

"Shhh! It's a secret."

Sarah survived the wedding ceremony. Nathaniel was, as Mrs. Simpson had reported, quite the most handsome man she had ever seen, towering well above everyone except his sergeant. As the simple ceremony began, even the reverend seemed to be sympathetic with the undue haste of it. The groom was obviously overcome with ardor for his bride, for he was quiet and a little pale. And the bride was so awestricken that she was rendered speechless. The reverend was afraid she would not be able to repeat her vows, but she finally did manage to say the words. As Captain Nathaniel Cameron Garrett's steady hand slipped a narrow gold band on the trembling finger of Sarah Catherine Bradley, the reverend pronounced the happy couple man and wife.

Nathaniel's kiss was gentle and properly executed.

"May I kiss the bride, sir?" Tim Davidson's crooked grin flashed at his commander. Sarah smiled as Nathaniel glowered. "With a great deal of restraint, if you please." Obediently Davidson placed a very polite kiss on her flushed cheek. He shook Nathaniel's hand very warmly.

Mrs. Simpson stepped to place a thin-stemmed glass into the hands of the bride and groom. "I couldn't believe it when Sergeant McCarey handed me a bottle of wine for the occasion, Captain." Under her breath she inquired, "I wonder where he got it."

Nathaniel bent his dark head nearer her ear and chuckled. "If I were you, Mrs. Simpson, I wouldn't ask."

"Oh, dear," she laughed.

"I must congratulate you on your choice, Captain," said the reverend. "The bride is charming, and it's obvious how she feels about you. Why, I believe her eyes have scarcely left you for a moment."

"She adores me," said Nathaniel solemnly, his gaze flicking over Sarah.

"To the bride and groom," proposed Matthew, and Nathaniel lifted his glass, turning his new wife in his arms and very gently tightening his fingers about her waist. Sarah's glass trembled dreadfully, and for a moment Nathaniel feared she would give the whole thing away.

"To us, Sarah," he murmured, his eyes steadying her. She lifted the crystal to her lips. Her profanation was complete.

The guests traipsed to the back of the house to be seated for Mrs. Simpson's intimate little wedding supper. The matron had wanted to open up the dining room in the Southern tradition, but Sarah had put her foot down. She was sacrificing what they could ill afford. So the ladies had made do, amidst sighs and memories of times past.

Sarah and Nathaniel found themselves alone in the living room, and Sarah sensed Mrs. Simpson's hand in this contrived moment of privacy.

"May I say your beauty is exceeded only by your ability to play your role?" Nathaniel maneuvered himself so that he towered between Sarah and the door.

"I was wondering how long your restraint would last. I must admit I thought it would last a *bit* longer."

"It will go with me only as far as the bedroom door, madam," warned Nathaniel softly, bending to touch his lips to the tempting lobe of her ear. He gently bit her ear and smiled at Sarah's quick gasp. "You aren't really going to refuse me, are you? After all this?"

"Nathaniel! Listen to me, here and now!"

"I'm listening, sweetheart," he murmured, moving his lips upward, following the curve of her eyebrow. He smelled so pleasant, and the nearness of his strength did strange things to Sarah's legs.

"Nathaniel, I promised myself, less than an hour ago, that I would be as pleasant as possible to you for what you are doing for Peter and me. You didn't have to do it, I realize, and this is costing you money as well as a lot of inconvenience. As soon as I can I will free you from our entanglement. Until then, all I can do is apologize for ever getting you into this mess." Oh, dear. He was still looking at her as if he might eat her alive.

"You apologize for the wrong things." His fingers traced the delicate bones in her back until they found themselves entangled in a long brown lock. "You should beg my pardon for the hours that I couldn't sleep for thinking about the sweetness of your mouth and that soft, naked body underneath—"

"Stop doing this! You promised me!"

"Sarah, sweet, this one fault I would remind you of."

"Don't say it!" she snapped, feeling his silent laughter. "Please, may we go in now?"

Pensively Nathaniel sighed, lifting the palm of her small hand to his lips and gently kissing the rows of callouses there. "Ah, you are a hard woman, Sarah Catherine Garrett. It may take me years to mellow you. Come now, love, the guests will think you lured me into the bedchamber."

Nathaniel amused everyone at the table with his seemingly endless supply of husbandly niceties. He leaned on his elbow and traced circles on her sleeve while the reverend told one of his favorite stories. And besides impudently stealing the bits of spiced peaches from her dish, he insisted on trading her his glass of wine two times after Irene had filled it.

"Are you trying to get me drunk?" she whispered behind her hand.

"Yes," he answered pleasantly.

At last Nathaniel could stand no more. Quirking a brow to the perceptive hostess, Nathaniel vowed her a friend for life for tactfully drawing the evening to a close. Somehow Sarah found herself maneuvered beside the door to bid the guests adieu as her husband slipped up snugly behind her to wrap one arm around her waist and reached about her with the other to shake hands with the men as they left. She could feel him crushed against her skirts, every move he made rubbing against her.

The dreaded sound came at last—the ominous knell as the lock bolt slid into place. Her impulse was to throw open the heavy door and scream for Mrs. Simpson, but amazingly enough Sarah found herself quietly sitting at the small dressing table taking the pins from her hair. Her fingers lined the pins into a neat row as she waited, painfully aware of his every move.

From the reflection in the mirror, Sarah watched him catch the leg of the red velvet chair with the toe of his boot and effortlessly turn to face her before he eased lithe limbs down into it. Inattentively she put a brush through her hair, covertly watching him reach into his pocket for his pipe and tobacco. She brushed mechanically stroke after stroke, watching those fingers tamp the tobacco.

Nathaniel's feet just reached the mahogany frame at the foot of the large bed, and Sarah's eyes followed the black boots as they crossed at the ankles and came to rest on the carved footboard. The pipe lit, its pleasing aroma already filling the room, blue eyes suddenly lifted to lock tenaciously upon Sarah's pale reflection. She jumped, her eyes widely staring into his. They both sat, unmoving.

"Pray continue," his deep voice broke the silence. He smiled and settled low on his backbone. "I enjoy watching you, Sarah." Sarah began to draw the brush through her hair again, wishing frantically that he would make a snide remark, lose his temper, or do almost anything except just sit there. Presently she dropped her head onto her arms with a moan.

"Oh, God, this is impossible. I don't know what I'm going to do, but I can't go through with this."

"Ah, what are you thinking, love? Are you afraid I will ravish you after all, leave you a battered heap upon the bed? Do you think I'm a rapist?"

Sympathetically Nathaniel studied the forlorn little figure. Perhaps her fears were not without cause, for his control was hard come by.

"This has been a long, hard day for both of us, Sarah, and we had best come to grips with it if we want any peace." But when he stirred to lay his pipe aside, Sarah jumped up and whirled on him.

"Don't be nice, Nathaniel. It doesn't become you! You said you wouldn't force me, but that's what you are trying to do just as surely—"

"Ah, so we have begun the game at last, my love." Nathaniel swung his legs aside and pulled off one black boot to drop it beside his chair. "Now we will wrestle over words. I do enjoy playing this game with you, Sarah, for you always lose." He grinned at her glare and pulled off his other boot.

"You said you would not bed me against my will."

"Oh, I don't deny that. I am working on the problem of bedding you *with* your consent," he murmured as he began undressing.

The sight of his browned chest with its long scar caught her breath, the light curling of black drifting downward until it disappeared beneath his belt. Nathaniel was not sleek, but sinewy and hard. He smiled.

Slowly she retreated until she felt the wall hard behind her back. Groping for the right words, she gasped the first thing she could think of: "Don't you think this is unbecoming behavior for a betrothed man?"

He was suddenly before her, a strong arm bracing itself on the wall on either side of her. Once she attempted to duck down and escape from under them, but he only shifted them down to keep her pinned.

"Two things, Sarah," he warned softly, no longer smiling. Sarah nodded mutely.

"Don't ever taunt me with her again," his voice was as sharp as a razor. "And don't compare me to Charles."

"I wasn't comparing you to Charles!"

"Then don't." He smiled that chilling smile again. "When I make love to you, Sarah, and you can deny it all you want to, but you know I will . . . when I make love to you, you won't think of Charles. Or any other man. It will be as if you had never known a man before."

His finger began to move down the line of tiny buttons, beginning at her throat, pausing as it rambled over her breasts, then down her abdomen. He continued.

"I will tell you the truth now, and then you will know. I have no intention of forcing you. You will desire me—you probably do already and you're too stubborn to admit it. We have both known it since the first time I kissed you. Well, I don't care how long it takes. I will wait until you desire me as much as I want you right now."

Sarah shook her head, watching his lashes lower and his lips reach for hers.

"You won't be nursing memories of a man that's gone when it happens, Sarah," he whispered.

She struggled. "I told you I wasn't thinking of Charles."

"Then yield to me. Let me love you."

"Nathaniel, *please!*"

With a heavy sigh Nathaniel relented, and Sarah took advantage of this to place some room between them. Dropping into the chair she covered her face with her hands.

"This is madness, Nathaniel. Please, let me go sleep somewhere else."

"No!" He added more gently, "I'm a very patient man, Mrs. Garrett, and I never break a promise."

He tossed back the bedcovers, and Sarah didn't move as he undressed and got into bed. Presently she thought he slept, and the candle sputtered, leaving only a curl of silver smoke.

Sarah undressed. With the wedding gown a wilted cloud upon the floor, she searched for comfort in the chair. This was her wedding night, she reflected grimly, and she was huddled in her shift, sleeping in a chair.

"Sarah?"

She started. Sarah could see him well enough, propped against the headboard, studying her. He seemed oddly vulnerable, like a small boy—wistful, easily hurt, needful of reassurance.

"What is it?"

A full minute passed. "I want to hold you."

Nathaniel's words were simple and honestly spoken. She had no doubts about his honor. He would respect her wishes. Arising from her chair, Sarah slipped into bed beside him.

Nathaniel gently straightened and opened his arms to take her. For many long moments he sat, listening to her breathe as her head leaned against his chest. Absently his fingers laced in and out of her hair, tracing around the delicate shell of her ear.

"Nathaniel?" she murmured, almost lulled to sleep.

"Hmm?"

"What will happen to Peter and me when we leave here?"

"I'll take you home, Sarah. It's all I know to do. I really do want to see you settled happily, in spite of how it seems."

There was no pretense between them. And Nathaniel talked, telling her things of little importance. Nice, comfortable things. Presently she felt his fingers under her chin, turning her face up to his. He moved down beside her, and Sarah shrank as he touched her.

"Kiss me, Sarah."

Nathaniel's mouth pleaded with hers. And Sarah didn't know how to say no, for the night had been insane. But she had to say no, for this was wrong. She should not be here.

She felt her lips parting beneath his, and her cry shattered the stillness. Sarah's weeping was not coy. It was a body-wracking grief at herself, Nathaniel was sure.

As one will force a small child who refuses the medicine to make him well, Nathaniel reached out pulled her into his strong arms. "It's all right, Sarah. Things between us will work out, and in good time you will love again. In good time."

"I loved Charles. I really did," she wept. "He took me to that strange mountain place. All those horrible nights of fear—the fear was the worst." Sarah covered her face with her hands, and Nathaniel tried to pry the wet fingers away so he could understand her. She shook her head, distraught. "I begged him not to go, but he wouldn't listen. God forgive me. I hated Charles for leaving me. I hated him for a long time. There was no food—no money. He came back just that once. And later on I got so sick with Peter. I slept in the closet. The cannons . . . I could hear the cannons in the valley, and I was afraid *all* the time. I nearly starved. I can't believe in anything. Not again."

"You will Sarah," he said. In good time you will.

Poor little soldier, Nathaniel wondered in amazement. And he waited until she fell asleep before he let himself do the same.

"Cap'n, suh," a light tap sounded on the door. "Cap'n, suh."

"Coming, Sam, coming," yawned Nathaniel, throwing back the sheet to reach for his uniform trousers. Sarah drowsily watched the muscles ripple through his legs and hips to the lighter skin below his waist.

The snap of the lock shouted its message—the marriage was done. She had spent an entire night with her husband. She was free of Rachel.

Hushed voices murmured outside the door, and presently Nathaniel stepped back into the bedroom, calling over his shoulder. "If Sergeant McCarey arrives before I get dressed, have him wait for me in the kitchen. Thanks, Sam."

Sarah raised on an elbow to stare at Nathaniel. His eyes dropped down to hers. A strange expression etched his handsome features.

"What is it?" she demanded.

"It's over," Nathaniel muttered, sitting down on the

edge of the bed beside her and leaning his elbows on his knees. "The war. It's over. Lee surrendered Richmond yesterday."

Over! Somehow, she had never pictured the ending of the war. She knew only the beginning and the hardship. And what about the marriage? Had she done it for nothing? But no—there was still Rachel.

"Nathaniel?" she queried softly, reaching out a hesitant hand. Tears sparkled in his eyes, and suddenly it struck her—the wealth of compassion in this teasing man. "What does this mean? To us, I mean."

"Well, nothing, actually," he replied. "This will delay us considerably so that I may finish up a lot of paper work. And my discharge, I suppose. But I will need to get home to help my father, now, as soon as possible. President Lincoln will undoubtedly call a special session of Congress." His eyes carried a distant look.

"If you think the war was hard, wait until you see what this country will be like now, Sarah. There are pardons, amnesties, economics, to say nothing of the black people. And half the South is in ruins."

Nathaniel stepped to the dresser to give his black hair a few strokes with Sarah's brush, bending his knees to bring his tall body down within sight of the mirror.

"I really wouldn't *have* to go with you now, would I?" Sarah mused, half to herself. "I mean, the army doesn't have any say now—"

In two strides Nathaniel was by her side, pulling her out of bed.

"Stop it!" she snapped, jerking her shoulders from his rough grasp. But he took them again, this time more firmly.

"Oh, no you don't!" he rumbled. "You are my wife, and where I go, *you* go! If you are entertaining any ideas of leaving on your own, forget them!" His face darkened.

"Well, I actually wasn't!" she spat, drawing herself up to match his anger, inch for inch. "But I am now. And I am *not* your wife, not in the way you say. And I may go anywhere I so choose without asking permission from you, Captain Garrett!"

"Just you try it and see what you get for your troubles, miss!" With blue eyes flaming Nathaniel loomed over Sarah. "There's no place where I won't find you. And when I do I will tan the daylights out of that stubborn hide of yours. Now, get dressed before I anticipate myself and give you a good thrashing here and now!"

"You are a misuser of women, Nathaniel Garrett, and it would please me very much if I never had to look at your wicked face again!" she burst out.

For the performance Sarah gave Mrs. Simpson and Matthew at the breakfast table, Nathaniel felt she deserved applause. A just-right smile, a subdued happiness, and Sarah was the picture of a happy bride.

Mid-morning found all but Matthew still at the breakfast table sipping a third cup of tea. Irene returned with Peter dressed and fed, and the new family prepared for an outing together.

"I'm rather looking forward to showing off my new bride," Nathaniel grinned. Hearing something, he strode quickly to the window, casting aside the drape with an impatient movement. He swore.

"What on earth—" Sarah stood just behind his shoulder, and it occurred to her as she stared, that she already depended on him to protect her. Assisting Rachel from a splendidly polished and appointed coach was John Pollard, her attorney.

"Nathaniel!" Nathaniel's steady fingers closed upon the anxious ones clutching his sleeve.

"It would appear the reverend didn't beat them to the clerk's office."

"I don't think I can stand another of these terrible scenes. I thought we were finished with all that!" Sarah complained.

"Well, *you* are finished, love. I'll talk to them. There's no need for you to even be here." Nathaniel bent his head to rub noses with Peter. "Just to be on the safe side, slip to the back of the house and tell Mrs. Harrison they're here and ask if she won't please tend Peter for just a little longer. And ask her not to be seen leaving with him."

Nathaniel moved to leave, Sarah following closely. Chubby arms clasped her neck tightly, and Nathaniel ruffled Peter's hair.

"I'm scared, Nathaniel," she confessed, all pretense gone. "Are you sure she can't . . . do something?"

"Positive. Trust me." He stopped to place a warm, reassuring kiss on her lips. "Run, now."

Not really expecting Sarah to return, Nathaniel was surprised to see her slip into the room hardly two minutes later. Rachel was accustomed to dominating a room, her two legal representatives positioning themselves much the same as before. Today Rachel's face was aglow with triumph.

Nathaniel placed himself before Rachel, standing silently poised. The silence became unbearable. Just as she drew a breath to speak, Nathaniel interrupted, giving her a rather stiff bow and gesturing with a flick of his wrist.

"Ah, Mrs. Bradley, age has its own kind of courage. Isn't that fortunate?"

"Don't small-talk me, Captain Garrett. I have come here to take your hide an' you know it. An' I will hear you ask for my mercy before I'm done with you."

That, apparently, was the cue for Gerald Aveley to present Nathaniel with a folded sheaf of papers. Taking a few minutes—much more than he needed—scanning, turning pages, perusing points of interest until Rachel began to fidget, Nathaniel finally lifted his head with a serene smile.

"I think not."

"Damn!" whispered Mr. Aveley. "Ah told Miz Bradley Ah'd hold mah tempuh with you, Garrett, but Ah declayuh—"

Reaching inside his jacket, Nathaniel withdrew the certificate of marriage and placidly presented it to the wary man. Gerald Aveley read the document, frowned, and passed it to John Pollard.

"This certificate carries yesterday's date, Captain. You aren't serious, surely."

"Quite."

"Give that to me!" snapped Rachel, squinting to decipher its content before she lifted sharp eyes to study the captain. Nathaniel smiled. Of all the men this old woman had met, he probably was the first who wasn't in awe of her. And she knew it.

"If I had three like you I could control the world," she observed to him wryly. "This is fraudulent, of course. But I can cause you enough discomfort, sir, that you will give me what I want. That will be interesting for me."

"You think so?" replied Nathaniel, taking the document from her gnarled hands.

"I never make empty threats," Rachel snorted. "Do you think we've been idle since yesterday, sir? We have spoken with your commandin' officer. We'll just see what a few months of needlin' can do."

Nathaniel didn't like being threatened. "Save yourself, madam. Even if you should make a semblance of a case against Sarah you wouldn't get support of that child, nor could you prove her incapable of support."

"Humph!"

"Where did you live during the past year, Mrs. Bradley?" snapped Nathaniel, weary now of the two jackals leering at him.

Rachel's eyes narrowed. "I've been residin' with Sarah, in the Cumberland you know that. What's your point?"

"And who's been supporting *you* for the year's residence with Mrs. Sarah Bradley?"

"I . . . I've supported myself, sir, and you're quite out of line askin' such a question." Nathaniel shook his head.

"I don't think so, Mrs. Bradley, for we both know you haven't spent one penny for your own support, that can be proven through your own financial records, by subpoena. Let me ask you, Mr. Pollard, don't you think such a point would be of as much interest to a judge as the validity of a whirlwind marriage? Sarah's support of Mrs. Bradley is a matter of record, whereas your allegation regarding our motives for marriage are only conjecture, and quite impossible to prove."

Nathaniel smiled into his collar. "The truth is, gentlemen, it was either a quick marriage or live in passionate sin. Now, what would you have done?"

"Insolent Yankee!" spat Rachel, gnarled hands clinched, and Nathaniel knew she wished she could slap his face. He shrugged.

"Hardly seems worth the trouble, does it? Now I really must ask you to excuse us. Darling, would you like to take a stroll? We're on our honeymoon, you see, and she doesn't like to be left alone."

"You liar!" shrieked Rachel. "I don't care what it takes, I'll have you dragged—"

The next minute and a half were not pleasant, and Sarah simply turned her head, having seen Rachel's tantrums often before. Finally Gerald Aveley calmed the old woman enough that she could leave. Gloves and bag were gathered, the briefcase snapped shut, and Rachel rose, shuffling to stand before Nathaniel.

"You make one false move, young man, and I'll know it. I hope you believe that. I have a few years left in me, and I am warnin' you that I shall amuse myself awaitin' your downfall. You even sneeze crooked, and I'll have you subpoenaed. Oh no, my Yankee friend, this little game isn't ended yet. You wait and see!"

"Mrs. Bradley, this isn't helping matters any," cautioned John Pollard, his uneasiness showing for the first time. Taking the old woman's arm and guiding her firmly, John gave Nathaniel a brief bow.

"Captain Garrett, I trust we shall meet under more pleasant circumstances." Nathaniel inclined his head silently. For the second time in two days, Rachel and her lawyers departed the Simpson house. Would there be another meeting?

Chapter VI

THE WORST THING about trains was the filth, and the second worst thing about trains was the weariness. Sarah's knitting needles ceased their soft chatter, and she allowed her head to drop wearily against the hard seat as the smoke-belching machine gradually heaved its way through the rolling lands of Virginia. Drowsily her thoughts slipped back upon her past weeks as Mrs. Sarah Catherine Garrett.

Abraham Lincoln had not had time to call that special session of Congress; he never would. Sarah didn't think she would ever forget the sound of Nathaniel's run through the house, doors slamming loudly behind him. She had looked up in shock to see the pale man, his eyes so full of pain, lips tightly compressed. Finally he had said the words and Sarah had gone without hesitation to the arms that reached for her.

But grief had faded, and workdays had grown tiring. Sarah's days had assumed a pattern, revolving around Nathaniel and their talks late at night. Her mind was quick. She hungrily absorbed knowledge of Washington and inflation, industrialization and social reform.

As she had rubbed his aching shoulders, Nathaniel had talked and had been amazed at her eagerness to learn. He had talked and talked and talked.

As she looked back, she realized that something had imbedded itself deeply within her mind. Sarah Catherine Garrett had slowly begun to see herself as a person and not just a war casualty. More than once during the past weeks the thought had come to her that she would miss Nathaniel when they went their separate ways. Wasn't that one of life's ironies?

The leavetaking had, of course, been emotional and wrenching for everyone. Mrs. Simpson didn't know what she would do, now that she wouldn't have Sarah and Peter to fuss over. And Rosy! How she would miss the little girl!

Though only ten, Rosy was as solemn as an adult. Born into slavery, she had worked hard all her life. Now, she would be part of a wealthy household, and the Garretts would treat her kindly. Rosy would learn to read and write! Though she was miserable about leaving Mrs. Simpson, Rosy looked forward to a good life. Even at ten, she knew how lucky she was. She hugged Peter tightly as the carriage clattered away from Mrs. Simpson's waving form. She dared not let go of her charge, so she didn't wave back.

Closing her eyes, Sarah allowed the steady sway of the railcar to lull her almost to sleep. A rare sense of optimism flooded through her. The tall man sitting beside her arose to stretch his long legs in the crowded car, and Sarah's eyes fluttered open. He was restless. Though most passengers generally dozed during the warmth of the spring afternoon, Nathaniel prepared himself a pipe and turned to stare at Sarah with sober eyes.

"Where are your thoughts, Sarah mine? You're awfully quiet this afternoon." His manner was wistful.

"Oh . . . about Virginia, I suppose," she said, picking up her knitting once more and taking swift stitches. Nathaniel stood a moment watching the nimble fingers as they controlled the clicking needles. He took a secret interest in Sarah's hands, and a faint smile tugged at the corner of his lips as he noted their recovery from past hardships. Her nails were neatly tended, and the gold band graced a slender hand that had readily absorbed the moisture from a mysterious vial found on her dressing table. Nathaniel had remained staunchly closemouthed concerning its appearance, to say nothing of the cost of such a commodity in Chattanooga's scarce market. Sarah had finally given up asking him about it.

"What about Virginia?" Nathaniel prodded, and Sarah's brow puckered.

Allowing her gaze to sweep outward once again, shyly returning the waves of white sharecroppers leaning on their hoes in a nearby patch, Sarah surveyed the burned land. She sighed. Thoughtful eyes grew misty, and Nathaniel had to bend low to catch the words.

> "So deem'st thou—so each mortal deems
> Of that which is from that which seems:
>> But other harvest here
> Than that which peasant's scythe demands,
> Was gathered in by sterner hands,
>> With bayonet, blade, and spear."

"Ah, my love has read Scott," he murmured after several minutes of quiet. "It makes me wonder about all the rest of Sarah Garrett that I have yet to see."

Over the monotonous clatter of wheels, Nathaniel studied his wife. The weeks had been tedious. Instead of becoming her husband, he had made an investment —he had become her friend.

Now, because Sarah accepted him as her friend, everything changed when he took her hand. She thought it was the way he followed the bones of her wrist with a fingertip.

In mere seconds the sounds, the light, and the distance between them were different. She faced him honestly, her eyes wide. Feelings she had thought were discarded suddenly reappeared.

"No," she said, stunned that she had not seen it before. It was all plainly written there—in his eyes and in his touch that said I have not changed, I mean to have you.

Dusk found the over-filled cars creaking to a stop in a small town in northern Virginia, youngsters romping beside the noisy iron dragon and squealing when it puffed its steam in great hissing snorts. Nathaniel decided they should get out and spend the night in a hotel, for which Sarah was grateful. Her bones ached miserably, and even if a bath turned out to be an unattainable luxury, a bed would improve everyone's disposition.

After arranging for the trunk to be delivered at the town's only hotel, Nathaniel scooped up the fretting Peter and they dragged themselves across the poorly lighted thoroughfare and up the steps of the unimpressive Main Way Hotel. The candlelit lobby was almost as deserted as the street, but there were the inevitable blue coats. Several people were taking advantage of the dining room. The place looked terrible, and Sarah prayed that their bedrooms would be clean. The balding proprietor stared at Rosy, causing Sarah a moment of uneasiness, but the moment passed without any quibbling over their black nursemaid. He escorted them to their rooms.

"Would it be possible to have a small tub of hot water sent up? We need a tray of food prepared as well, and I would like to speak with your cook, sir," requested Nathaniel, evidently satisfying himself that the room was clean. A small room adjoining boasted two cots and a window, and the larger bedroom was adequately appointed.

"If yawl kin pay, Cap'n, yawl kin get mos' anythin', suh." The round face smiled to reveal startlingly large, white teeth.

Nathaniel returned the knowing grin with a wily one of his own and, after bidding Sarah to make them comfortable, he departed with the proprietor. The trunk arrived as he was leaving, and Sarah busied herself. Hardly any time had passed when Nathaniel returned with a napkin-covered tray bearing cooked cereal and boiled eggs, bread, butter, and fresh milk. Sarah rearranged the furniture to create a makeshift table and chairs, and Rosy attended the feeding of Peter and herself. Sarah was still not used to having a servant for Peter, but Nathaniel had insisted. Rosy was still a child herself.

"I thought perhaps you might enjoy eating downstairs, Sarah. The stew is delicious. I tasted it myself. He's right. You can get anything if you have the money. So tonight it's cheese and bread with stew, and a bottle of wine." Nathaniel grinned at Peter, sitting with his mouth open, patiently waiting for Rosy to put something into it. "Ready yourself for a night out. I suppose I will torture myself with the plumbing."

Sarah had already poured herself a bowl of water and had eagerly scrubbed the travel grime from her face. Removing the pins from her hair she frowned as Nathaniel watched it tumble free about her shoulders. He yawned lazily and sat on the foot of the bed. Lacing his fingers behind his head he dropped back to scrutinize her movements. She ruffled her hair then stopped.

"Don't stop, Sarah. I've watched you do that often enough." At her glare he moistened his lips. "You're disenchanted with me, I believe."

"You're darn right I'm disenchanted, Nathaniel!" At Peter's wide-eyed look she clamped her mouth shut.

"Just consider that your education has been considerably broadened." He paused to add softly. "Probably in a few ways you haven't even discovered yet."

"What?"

"Nothing."

"I really hate to leave the children in a strange room. Can't we just have something to eat up here?" She stooped to give Peter's hands and face a vigorous scrubbing as he wriggled.

"Mercy, Sarah, don't take the hide off," cautioned Nathaniel, pitying the toddler as he stalwartly blinked away the discomfort of his mother's attentions. "And yes, you need to be away from Peter for an hour or so. They are both exhausted and will sleep like logs, won't you, little man?" he growled playfully as he plopped the boy upon his chest.

A knock interrupted Sarah's protest, and as she oversaw the preparations for her bath behind the screen, Nathaniel absented himself for his own bath. Removing her dusty clothing, Sarah bathed with as much comfort as a footbath allowed. Streams of soapy runnels ran down her legs and dripped off her elbows. She patted herself dry with a towel that smelled of fresh outdoors and wrapped the long linen about herself. Tucking the loose end between her breasts she sat down before the mirror to brush her hair dry. Ah, she felt almost human again! Before her hair was dry, Nathaniel's key clicked in the lock.

Their eyes met in the mirror as he turned from relocking the door, and he grinned at her, freshly shaven, his own hair still damp and curling about his face. His shirt was unbuttoned, and he tossed his jacket on the bed, still studying her face. He was so unnervingly handsome. Why did he persist in wanting her? She refused him at every turn.

"Perhaps you could go amuse yourself in the lobby until I finish," she attempted.

"Wear it down tonight," he commanded with casual authority, gesturing at her hair.

"Will you go somewhere and leave me to my

own dressing? You're so possessive. You remind me of a . . ."

"A husband? Who can't quite get his wife to come to bed?"

"More like a vulture, waiting to pick the bones of its victim clean. That's all you've thought about lately, isn't it? Getting me into bed?" Sarah slammed down her brush.

"That's not true," the words were serious. "I have thought to myself, now here is a smart woman who has insight, an ability to learn quickly, and who doesn't have a penny's worth of knowledge about herself. Maybe if I just give her time, she'll learn."

Sarah glanced up as his voice sounded by her ear. He was smiling at her, calmly resting his arms across the upper rim of the screen.

"There is no escaping you!" she cried, holding the back of her dress together and turning from the screen in a flurry of yellow silk. "You are everywhere! When I go to bed, you are there. When I get up, you are there. When I dress, you are there. Every time I turn, to eat or tend the baby or even to think—you are there!"

"That, I fear, is the way of husbands."

"I suppose your family is expecting you," she searched for a change of topic.

Nathaniel stepped to take a clothesbrush from the tray and proceeded to give the jacket of his uniform a thorough brushing as Sarah observed with pretended disinterest. This husband of hers was a careful man.

"They also know that I am bringing you, and why." Sarah's eyes flew wide and a small whimper escaped her.

Nathaniel laughed. "Sarah," he chided gently, "don't you believe anything I tell you? I kept your secret. I only explained in the wire that you had done

me a great service, and that I planned to see you settled. That's all."

"It's your secret, too, you know," touching his sabre
in the trunk.

"Yes," he sighed. "It's my secret, too. I swear to
heaven, Sarah, I don't know who's the bigger fool—
you or me."

The dining room was small, but so was the crowd,
sparsely scattered throughout. Nathaniel selected a
table next to four men who apparently were enjoying
the same dinner they had decided on. Sarah lifted
the yards of yellow silk skirt as Nathaniel held her
chair. Hardly had she murmured her thanks than she
wanted to box his ears for brazenly drawing his
thumbnail up her backbone.

"You never stop, do you?" She shook her head,
then smiled as he adopted a little-boy look of innocence. "I'll try to be . . . good," he sighed.

Her laughter was soft, and she began wondering
what it would be like not to see him every day.

"You've never told me much about your family,
Sarah," coaxed Nathaniel as the stew arrived. Sarah
smiled, buttering bread and thanking whatever lucky
stars she had that he had chosen to wear his "friend"
hat downstairs instead of being a wolf.

"It would require one paragraph, I'm afraid. Father left me with his brother when I was three—that
you know. He didn't leave me anything of his or my
mother's. Uncle Gene and Aunt Sybinna had no
children and we lived in South Carolina most of the
time. There were two years or so in Richmond. I met
and married Charles when I was just barely seventeen."

"Did you go to school?" Nathaniel had often marveled at Sarah's abilities. She was quite able with a
needle, well-read, quick of mind.

111

"Uncle Gene was a professor, and he just enjoyed spending time with me, teaching me things.

"I will teach you things as well, Sarah mine." There was a knowing gleam in his lively blue eyes. Sarah sniffed.

"Take care, Nathaniel Garrett, that the teacher does not become the student," she warned, lifting her glass in a subtle challenge.

They returned to their meal, both of them caught in the silent communion people develop when living together.

"Are you discharged now?" she asked at last.

"Officially, yes." Nathaniel smiled, lowering his gaze to roam leisurely over the tiny yellow pleats above her breasts.

"Well," she coughed lightly. "I just wondered. I mean, you are still in uniform."

"Want me to travel naked, my dear?" He lowered his voice. "Some beautiful damsel might say to herself, 'Ah, what a fine specimen!' and steal me away. Then what would *you* do, Sarah mine? Hmmm?"

"I would reply that she had made a fine choice and was welcome to you. You are sinful and entirely impossible!"

Voices rose annoyingly at the adjoining table, and Sarah cast a glance aside. They were behaving badly, almost deliberately making a nuisance of themselves. She raised puzzled eyes to Nathaniel. He shrugged.

"Have you ever been drunk?"

"I should say not, sir! Why, I have had less than a dozen glasses of wine in my entire life. The very idea!"

"Would you like to get drunk?" he teased. Bracing an elbow on the table Sarah shook a chastizing spoon at him, half a smile playing about her mouth. The voices rose again, quite loudly this time, drawing the attention of practically everyone in the room.

"Ruddy rotten turncoat! Tennessee man. Damned

if a Tennessee man don' plan t'grind our faces in th' dirt. Gonna make that Southern boy bow an' scrape an' say 'Yessir, King Andy,' and 'No sir, King Andy.'"

The man appeared well-educated, even though drunk, and Nathaniel shifted uneasily, sweeping an eye their way.

"Ain't that right, Yank? Ain't that what yawl wanted all along? New Year's Day, they say—niggers on th' rampage! Wahoo! That hothead in Washington tryin' to stir up th' coloreds and kill us all off. And whoever don' git killed will play slave to th' Yankee King. Wahoo!"

Noisily, his three companions agreed, slamming fists on the table, jarring glassware. Nathaniel glanced about to see if the drunken speaker could possibly be addressing someone besides himself. He appeared to be the only "Yank" in the room. He gave a brief nod to the man and lifted concerned eyes to Sarah.

"Are you ready to go?" he urged quietly, not wishing to get involved in the drunken scene. Another of the four arose, advancing a couple of faltering steps as Sarah began to push her chair from the table. At first she thought he was attempting to be gallant. He bent over her, his breath reeking. A wave of her hand kept Nathaniel in his seat.

"This here Yank b'long to you, ma'am?" Sarah turned to him with a look of disgust. "Can't stay up in their own country, can they? Have t'come down and run over somebody else's," putting a hand beside his mouth in a loud announcement to the entire room. "Can't go t'sleep in our beds without fear of gittin' cut up by a buncha gol-durned niggers. Yanks always fillin' 'em full o' murderous talk, stirrin' 'em to rape our women and burn our barns and steal everythin' their troops didn't already take."

The clamorous man jerked his expensive rust-colored vest into place. "What we oughta do is teach a few of 'em a lesson. Cut a few of 'em up. Give 'em th' message, loud an' clear. Show them damn politicians that we won't stand for 'em treatin' us worse'n coloreds. Why, a man won't even be able t'vote 'lessen he's nigra or white trash!"

Nathaniel stood slowly and reached for Sarah's hand. Drawing her around the table, he pulled her hand through his arm and began to draw them around the speaker. The drunk threw himself at them. Pushing Sarah from him with a strong shove, Nathaniel raised an arm to ward the irate fellow off.

He smiled, a small amount of drawl slipping into his tone. "I think you've had a little too much to drink. Why not let it go tonight? We'll talk about it in the morning."

As his quiet voice droned on, quick eyes sized up his potential opponents, Sarah's nearness to them, the distance between her and the doorway.

"Who would you be, Yankee?" sneered another voice to his right.

"I don't think that matters, do you?" Nathaniel answered with feigned disinterest, maneuvering himself more to the center of the room.

"If you will excuse me, gentlemen, I must see the lady to her room." He pretended to step toward Sarah, and what he anticipated happened. One of the men, whom his companions called Giles, motioned to the other three standing men with the flick of a slender hand. Giles was nearly as tall as Nathaniel, somewhat more slender, and his neatly trimmed beard and moustache accented good-looking features. He was young. And very drunk. As Nathaniel watched his eyes, he suspected he saw true madness there.

"Why don't you three just detain this damn Yankee for a few minutes while I say some things to him?"

Giles leaned back against the edge of the checkered tablecloth, and the other three lunged at Nathaniel.

Nathaniel waved away the advancing proprietor, not wishing to involve another.

Nathaniel caught one neatly below the ear, sending him sprawling into a neighboring table. As the candle tipped, the anxious proprietor swept it up, hoping his hotel would not be wrecked.

Sarah covered her open mouth with shaking hands. A sick dread formed in her stomach as the other two went for Nathaniel at once, one of them managing to land a blow to his abdomen. Nathaniel bent, then braced himself for a real battle. As he straightened, steeling himself, he could almost feel the three become sober.

As one aggressor grabbed for a blue-clad arm, Nathaniel caught the man sharply in the chest. Two made good their intentions, one latching onto Nathaniel's arm and twisting it behind his back, and the other grabbing a foot.

"Hold him!" shouted Giles, and they did. Giles hit Nathaniel with a bottle from the table, not breaking the heavy bottle but laying open the flesh above his eye. Nathaniel's free leg connected with Giles's groin, and Giles doubled to the floor, groaning. Blood drizzled down into Nathaniel's eyes, half blinding him, and he savagely kicked against the man hugging his leg with both arms, unable to free himself. Holding a chair by its legs, a man came at him, and Nathaniel had time just to shield his eyes before it slammed against his chest with a thud.

Giles began calling to his friends. "We'll show 'em with this one. We'll show 'em what will happen every time one of those freedmen gets himself a white man!"

The blade flicked from Giles's boot, and Sarah screamed. Nimbly Giles stepped before the blinking Nathaniel, the glittering steel cutting the air as he slashed it back and forth before his face. No one in the room was moving. They were all going to sit there and watch.

She took two steps toward the center of the room, saw Giles turn in her direction, and stopped. "Are you all just going to sit there?" she cried.

The room was silent except for the ragged breathing of the assailants.

Giles made a sound and Sarah moved toward him.

"Get back, Sarah!" Nathaniel choked, coughing hard from the blow to his chest. Sarah obeyed him, slowly backing from the men and drawing toward the coat rack. In her daze she wondered if she could make it to the front door. Yankee blues, of all she had seen today, where was one now?

"I think I'll just give you a little something to remember the South by. Get his other arm, Trent!" Sarah heard Giles laugh as she inched her way past. "I won't kill you, Yankee. I'll just carve on you a little. Come, pretty baby," the man cooed to the steel.

"Hellfire, can't three of you hold one Yankee?" barked an angry Giles, and before Nathaniel could regain his balance, the blade flashed. A long streak of blood stained Nathaniel's trouser leg.

Sarah whirled, slamming herself to the wall. The coats fell about her and Sarah cried, flailing herself free of them.

One of the men holding Nathaniel whined, "Hey, wait a minute, Giles. I don' think yawl oughta—"

"Shut up, Bobby! This has to be done! Now, dammit, hold him still!"

Trent threw about two hundred pounds against Nathaniel, managing to grasp the free arm, and the slashed leg almost gave way beneath the burden.

"This time I'll open up your belly, Yank, and just see what kind of blood you bleed. Maybe it's blue." Giles straightened his impeccable jacket.

Sarah turned, praying to get to the street. As she moved, her fingers closed over the barrel of a rifle that someone had leaned in the corner. Drawing it out from under the heap of coats, Sarah didn't even worry that it might not be loaded. At least it was something. She felt as if she were gliding, not walking, toward Giles. She moved so he could see her, positioning Nathaniel and his assailants to her right. Nathaniel's face revealed pain and a primitive hatred more terrible than she had ever seen.

"Stop now!" Her voice sounded pathetically small, but it rang clearly enough. Giles froze in mid-stroke.

Fear was on Giles's face for a few seconds. Sarah read it clearly in his strange eyes. But then he began to smirk.

"Hold him, I said! This little piece isn't going to shoot." Giles began to chuckle. What had she done wrong? The hammer! Quickly, she reached, almost dropping the heavy weapon, but she managed to pull back hard on the hammer. She straightened and leveled the rifle.

"Ah, madam," Giles threw at her. "You don't think I would kill him, do you? I'm just going to mark him up—put a little something on this pretty face."

"Turn him loose!" demanded Sarah.

Giles smiled. His teeth gleamed white below the dark moustache.

"Now you just stay put, boys. This little miss is bluffing. I'll just give her man a nick like this—" His hand reached toward Nathaniel, and Sarah saw the candlelight glance off the blade. Only then did she pull the trigger. Sarah didn't even aim, and she never remembered pulling the trigger. She saw only the surprise on Giles's face. The explosion was deafening in the closed room, and the kick from the rifle sent her spinning back against the table behind her. The rifle slipped from her hands.

A large red stain on Giles's vest was in her view for only a second, but his strangling cry would haunt Sarah for years.

She wasn't aware of much after that. There was a vague memory of the slender man who lifted her from the floor before he disappeared, and of the proprietor peering over the dead man. Nathaniel began to slump to the floor.

You're late, she thought, as the military police arrived. Far too late.

After thirty minutes of stitching, Nathaniel was ashen. He had refused chloroform, as it made him very ill, and vomiting might injure his ribs further—or even send a broken end through a lung. The ribs were taped with a warning to avoid anything strenuous for a few days, and as the doctor took Nathaniel's pulse he nodded his head with satisfaction.

"You're as strong as an ox. You'll be sore as hell for a few days. Keep him quiet, Mrs. Garrett. I'm leaving you something for pain if he should need it. With all that brandy he may rest fairly comfortably without it. Those stitches will have to be removed after about a week. No traveling for two days, and that's an order, Captain."

Sarah saw the doctor to the door. Grasping his skilled hand in both her small ones, Sarah's eyes blurred. She wanted to throw both her arms about his neck in a gratitude she didn't quite fathom, knowing only that it was huge.

"Th-Thank you so very much, doctor. I will come by or send payment in the morning."

"We'll just let the army take care of this one, Mrs. Garrett. Goodnight." Soberly he tipped his hat to her, and Sarah watched him walk tiredly down the hallway, his feet dragging slightly. She locked the door. Nathaniel opened one red eye.

"I think you're drunk," she teased. "Do you want a fresh shirt or do you want to keep that one?"

"Are you my new serving wench?" he grinned, lifting a finger to probe at the bandage over his eye. Sarah brushed his hand away.

"Leave that alone. And yes, I suppose I have the dubious honor for the next couple of days, sir." Putting her hands on her hips, Sarah smiled. "I demand perfect obedience from anyone I fetch and carry for."

He didn't answer, and Sarah's smile faded. She couldn't think of anything to say, and the room was so still she could hear her own heart. Sarah couldn't look anywhere but into the depths of those blue eyes.

"Oh, Sarah, Sarah." Nathaniel's eyes brimmed, spilling their hunger. She knew she would kiss him, and she knew that Nathaniel was waiting for her to come to him. Her lips parted as her lashes fluttered closed. With a great deal of care, Sarah covered his chest with her own.

It was an oblivion where nothing mattered except the endless mingling of their breaths and their ventursome searching. Sarah held his head to her lips, fearing the moment it would end. She stilled herself, even as he molded to her, awed by his trembling.

Placing both her hands upon his warm face, Sarah compelled herself to interrupt the flow of their desire.

"Uh-huh," Nathaniel shook his head, protesting the losing of what he had searched so long to find.

She was responsible for this, she chided herself. What a time she had picked!

"Would—would you like a pipe while I get ready for bed, Nathaniel?"

"As a matter of fact, yes," he said, trying to catch her eye. "But first I must get dressed for a journey to the end of the hall." Nathaniel swung his legs over the bed. Sarah fetched him a pair of breeches and a pair of clean socks.

"Is it hurting much?" She bent to help him dress. The touch of lean, hard muscles jarred her once again.

"It hurts a bit, my pet," he murmured to her back,

119

"but not that much." Sarah turned, grimacing as he grinned and tested his leg. Sitting once more to draw on his socks, he probed his ribs. "They're not so bad since they're taped," he said to her absently, standing and finishing the buttoning of his pants. By the time Nathaniel returned, Sarah had changed the sheets and put the room to rights. Even his pipe had been placed on the small bedside table.

"You've been busy," he nodded, glancing at his watch. It was after midnight.

"Get off that leg. You know what the doctor said."

"What does a doctor know?"

"How to sew that leg back up again if you pull those stitches loose, Captain Garrett. Back into bed."

Nathaniel turned to stretch the leg upon the bed with care, sighing with relief as his dark head found the pillow. Closing his eyes, he listened to the sounds of Sarah undressing. He could picture exactly what she was doing, how she would look as she wriggled about trying to reach the hooks down her back, how she would bend to step out of her skirt. If the little tormenter thought the last weeks had been easy—damn! His only reward for holding a rein on his passion had been her gradual easing of manner.

The question of desire had always been with him—on the mountain, in Chattanooga. But love?

Looking squarely at death cleared one's head, and Nathaniel knew how it was with him. Perhaps he had known it from the beginning. Sarah was a part of him now, and he could no more free himself of her than he could sever the leg that had spilled his blood.

What was it he had told Matthew? That he never intended to need a woman again?

Sarah lifted the covers, slipping in beside him carefully, partly because of his leg, and partly because she was afraid to touch him at all. Keeping well to her side of the bed, she turned just so that she could see his face.

"Nathaniel?"

"Yes, Sarah mine," he murmured.

"Oh. Have you . . . made love to many women?" She closed her eyes tightly. Oh, why couldn't she have left well enough alone?

"Dozens and dozens," he finally answered.

"Be serious."

"I am. Loving dozens of women is serious business."

Nathaniel pressed a wisp of her hair to his lips, a strangely earnest gesture amid the teasing of the moment.

"The kiss. I wished it would last forever. You did too, Sarah. Tell me."

"No," she lied. "I mean, I . . . yes."

He kissed her eyes, as if by doing so he could make them see the truth. "Let me love you, Sarah. It's been so long, sweetheart. I've wanted you so long."

Softly moaning, she turned her head from side to side. He lay still as she battled with herself. Her tiny sounds of despair were lost and bitter in the hatred of her own weakness.

"Tell me, Sarah. Say the words. Please say the words."

"All right, all right," she choked, and the tears spilled. She wanted to tell him she was fragile. She wanted to say she was ashamed. But she only lifted her trembling hands to her face.

"I want you, but I don't love you!" Nathaniel lowered his hurting chest and braced on his elbows. Half lifting her, he drew her arms about his neck. Sarah clung to him. "I don't love you." She knew already that she would belong to him tonight. "I don't love you."

"For now, Sarah," Nathaniel's lips found her cheek and tasted the salty tears, "that is enough." The touch of his fingers was beautiful and knowing. And Sarah resisted, even in her yielding, trapping them tightly between her knees.

"Don't," he murmured, and she kissed the bones of his shoulders, seeing their shape even with her eyes closed. "I can't fight you tonight."

And in the end, Sarah helped him. She felt she should have known, all her life, that she would give in to him.

His mouth, when he found her lips, was not gentle. Sarah gave as he gave—hungry, eager, demanding. Small hands smoothed the muscled back and the sinews that flexed in his hips, and the knee that slipped between hers to part her legs was not unwelcome.

He had been right: it *was* a new thing, as if for the first time. He took her with care. He made love as he lived—impetuously and yet earnestly, whispering tiny words of love in her ear and upon her open mouth. Together they let the world go its own way, their urgency growing into one need.

And when they tumbled back, together, Nathaniel rolled to his back with a soft moan and drew Sarah to his chest. He kissed her again and again.

A lazy finger brushed back and forth against the curve of her breast. As her mind cleared, the realization of what she herself had helped him do dawned upon her with fear and wonder. Nathaniel felt it. He raised his head.

"Sarah, love," he murmured, shifting his wounded leg. "Now is the time we must talk. I know you're sleepy, but for a few minutes we must talk."

"What is it?" Sarah's voice was small.

"Please don't be sorry," he leaned to kiss her lips softly. "It was right. You know it was. How do you feel?"

"I . . . don't know," sighed Sarah. She knew she wasn't angry. "But Nathaniel?"

"Yes, Sarah."

"It must never happen again," she whispered.

"If that is what you want, love," he lied easily, kissing her neck. Certainly, he knew how *he* felt.

"Nathaniel?"

"Yes, Sarah."

"Does your leg hurt?" Sarah turned her head about.

"Yes."

"Do you want something for the pain?"

"I will take a swallow of brandy." Sarah rummaged about in the dark, found the brandy, and managed to pour a sizeable amount into a glass. She was back to the bedside before she realized that she had not put her gown back on. Nathaniel was grinning at her.

"Oh . . . here! Take this!" she choked, thrusting the glass at him and searching for the gown. She slipped into it and tied the ribbon.

"After that, Sarah mine, I hardly need the brandy. Now be quiet and let a dying man get some sleep." He smiled into the darkness.

Sarah lay down and moved her back gently against his chest. She spoke without turning around "Quit smiling."

Nathaniel laughed and gave her fanny a pat before he settled down with the throb in his leg.

Chapter VII

SARAH AWOKE with the unromatic worry of being pregnant. The greyness of dawn opened Nathaniel's eyes also, and he roused himself to find Sarah, wrapped in the bedspread, pacing.

A full five minutes elapsed before Sarah realized he was awake and was openly staring at her attack of nerves.

She started, then snapped peevishly. "How do you feel?"

"Not bad, considering I may have to pay the hotel for a new rug to replace the one you're wearing out."

With wifely concern, despite her own ill temper, Sarah moved to touch his forehead. It was cool and smooth. Nathaniel caught her wrist as she turned and propped himself against the headboard.

"You're a small package of good cheer, Sarah Garrett."

"Oh, don't be trite, Nathaniel. I'm in no mood for it."

"You were in a splendid mood last night," he grinned devilishly.

"You're such a typical man. You don't have to worry the morning after. Did it ever occur to you that this mistake could render me pregnant with your child?"

Nathaniel proceeded to nibble her fingertips one by one, and Sarah jerked her hand free. She remembered too much—how new his passion had made her feel.

Even remembering made her feel guilty and sharpened the edge of her panic.

Once again she slipped into her private world of fears, wanting to bargain with God, to promise Him she would never do another bad thing if He would just let her escape being pregnant.

"What?" Sarah asked. Nathaniel had spoken.

"I *said,* if you're pregnant, we'll just grin and bear it, sweetheart. And redo the nursery."

She didn't need that!

"A shotgun marriage? Don't you think I have any pride, Nathaniel? Oh, no."

Testing his leg with a wince, Nathaniel arose to the chill of the morning and pulled on his pants. Sarah was so nervous she brushed at her hair and threw the brush aside impatiently.

Nathaniel shook his head at her. "You can't escape the binding power of the marriage vows as easily as that, love."

As if they were duelists, Sarah measured him, straightening herself for impending battle. Nathaniel controlled himself, but he was angry.

"This marriage began as a lie," and her eyes dared him to deny it.

"Perhaps it did," he shrugged. "Now it's a fact."

"You play me for a fool, Nathaniel. Last night didn't change anything, except . . . well, it didn't change anything. My plans are the same. I will proceed with the annulment. One emotional moment of bad judgment . . . well, there has to be love between two—"

Nathaniel whirled, an irate finger pointing at her face.

"You play yourself for the fool, Sarah! We're married. The sooner you accept that as a fact, the easier it will be for the both of us."

Sarah's jaw dropped, and she stood blinking. She

struggled to think. The annulment—he had said it would be a simple matter to reverse.

"Then you lied to me. You told me, Nathaniel, that—"

"I *know* what I told you, sweet innocent. The truth is," he explained to her as if she were a child, "it would now take a divorce. And I'll be damned if I'll say I'm sorry."

Sarah paled, feeling she had been struck. A full minute thudded past.

"Di-*vorce!*"

"The marriage has been consummated. Once a marriage has been consummated, Sarah, there exists the possibility of pregnancy. The only way to set it aside would be a divorce." His manner changed and he smiled.

"I will never give you a divorce, little one, and you have no grounds to sue me. It would appear, Sarah Garrett, that you have a loving husband, whether you want one or not. And don't set that jaw at me. I can hear your rebellious mind from here. Besides," he added, "I don't think even you could have pretended the desire you felt last night."

"Desire has nothing to do with it. Nothing at all." Sarah's voice was quiet now. And intense with determination.

"I shall retain a lawyer," she promised, "and we will see whether this marriage can be annulled or not."

"I'm as qualified as any lawyer you can retain, and I say it cannot."

For long moments they stared at each other. Sarah's inexperience frightening her, making her feel as if she were lost in a strange city.

"Yes," she whispered, her eyes growing distant. "It all does sound very legal—quite legal."

"I assure you that it is."

Slowly, fragmented pieces of her memory shifted in her mind. They turned, sliding into place like a puzzle.

126

His confident manner with Rachel and her two attorneys, the skilled explanation of annulments and their process. The law *would* do this and the law *wouldn't* do that. Of course he knew the law. *He was the law!* And he had known last night what would happen to their plans. He had not had the decency to warn her. She had been tricked.

Sarah's eyes burned brilliantly. "If I ever hated anything more than I do you at this instant, I don't know what it is."

Nathaniel reached out a hand, and Sarah ignored his desire to explain.

"It was pride. Your pride couldn't stand it because I could resist you. Well, I yield the victory to you in that, Nathaniel. I may pay a long time for that, but I have pride, too. I lied my way into this, and I can lie my way out. I will deny *everything!*

"And if I should be pregnant with your child," she sobbed, "I would say it was a bastard child before I would admit it was yours! All those weeks in Chattanooga, I trusted you."

Nathaniel loomed above her. What would she care if he loved her? He didn't want to love her. Not to lose her. He couldn't live through that again.

"You beautiful little bitch!" he rasped, his fingers biting her shoulders.

She stamped her foot emphatically. "I won't go any farther with you! We'll stay here. In Virginia."

"No, madam. You will not stay here. And no child of mine will ever be called a bastard while there is life in my body. If you wish to play the adultress and deny an honest marriage, so be it!"

He was hurting badly.

If Sarah had even appeared to relent, Nathaniel would have stayed his fury. But her stance, and the way she lifted her chin, inflamed him. Nathaniel went too far, knowing it as he did it.

"I won't let it happen again!"

She didn't understand his hoarse words. His angry lips bent to ravage her mouth, kissing her brutally. He meant to force her, his mouth more wounding than a blow to her face. She tasted blood. His fingers bruised her body, and they bruised her spirit as well.

In her mind Sarah fought him; she hated him. Not because she was ashamed of wanting him, but because he had deceived her. He had let her believe a lie. Twice.

Her breasts were crushed against him painfully, and Nathaniel's fingers closed about her skull. His tongue raped her, driving her against his knees in whimpering defeat.

She refused to cry. And she vowed she would never, never forgive him for this.

Abruptly he released her.

"Oh, *God!*" he groaned miserably. "Oh, God, what am I doing?"

Spinning to face her, the horrible regret drawing his face, Nathaniel moved toward her, then stopped. She stood before him like a battered child, and he despised himself.

Sarah knew already he was sorry, but she wanted to hurt him in return, so she pulled her mind beyond his reach.

For once Nathaniel could not find the right words. After long, painful minutes, he lifted his hand in a helpless gesture, his shoulders dropped wearily, and he turned to leave the room.

When he returned later, the tempest of their wrath had cooled. He wanted to go home, he said. Wisely she didn't argue but determined that she would help him, though she knew he suffered dreadfully with his wound and his remorse.

Sarah's heart yearned for Nathaniel to say he was sorry; she needed to hear the words. But he never said them. Yet, when he caught her by surprise, laying a large hand against her cheek, she felt she would break from the gentleness of it.

"I care for you," his voice shook.

And she thanked him with her eyes. She knew he cared.

The remainder of the journey to Nathaniel's home was more comfortable than the first part had been. Though not luxurious, the carriage was well made and reasonably warm. It was necessary to remove Sarah's brown cloak from the trunk only as the ferry prepared to take them across the Potomac River. Now, as they stood on the deck, the wind whipping at her cloak until she thought she would be turned wrong side out like a great umbrella, she took Peter from Rosy. Nathaniel's limp was worse, and after they were all settled for the last lap of the journey, Sarah put the children on one seat with an order to sleep! Then, in spite of Nathaniel's glower, Sarah made him turn to his side and place the aching leg across her lap.

"You aren't a Spartan, or even close."

"Humph!" was the only reply she got.

The further North they had come, the more prosperous the country appeared. War, Sarah decided, had been good for the North. She wondered if these people had any idea of what it was really like. She wouldn't feel sorry about leaving the South, though. Nor about leaving Rachel!

Dusk was settling. The countryside still bore some traces of winter and a mist rolled in to shroud the bare trees. In the distance Sarah observed several scattered estates, their brick chimneys reaching above the clusters of trees that approached from the hills and surrounding farmland.

A growing excitement began to tell on Nathaniel, for he kept twisting about to stare at passing scenery. Finally he pulled his leg about, straightening his uniform.

"How long is it since you've been home, Nathaniel?" Sarah ventured over the noise of the coach. He contemplated a moment.

"About two years, now. Did I ever tell you about my brother, Clarke?" Sarah shook her head. "Clarke was a mean little dickens." Nathaniel laughed for the first time that day. "Believe it or not, I was the good one when we were little. If there was mischief underfoot, you could be sure he started it. You see that hill there? Well, there's quite a nice lake to the left of it. Runs back, oh, forty acres. Clarke had this idea, see, that we'd be Vikings. He had a book with pictures of those big boats and all, and we worked for a week building a raft. Quite a piece of workmanship, if I do say so. Didn't even resemble a Viking ship, but that was immaterial. The thing was, Clarke got up in the attic and picked himself out a very handsome sail. We put up a mast and rigged up this sail."

Nathaniel laughed again, and Sarah smiled, engrossed. "Just so happens that what Clarke selected was a very large piece of Irish linen that belonged to Mother's mother. Did Mother ever get sore about that!"

"What happened?"

"As I remember, we cut wood for about a month." He smiled dreamily. "Clarke was so proud of that raft. I don't think much else registered. He could never stay out of trouble for more than a week at a time, anyway."

Nathaniel turned, a grave anxiety lining his face. "I think I ought to tell my family the truth about our marriage. I know we agreed to—"

"You promised me!" she cried, quickly pressing her fingers across her lips. "You said," she whispered, "you *said* you wired them I was coming for a brief time until I could get settled. Everything was arranged you said."

I wasn't playing for keeps then, Nathaniel thought. "I'm thinking of you, Sarah. It would look much better all the way around for you to come as my wife than for me to just . . . bring you with me."

"I'm not your wife!"

"Don't start that again.

Sarah rubbed her forehead. "This whole thing is quite insane. I mean . . . I have a son. I intend to make a home for him. I intend to see what sort of sense we can make out of all this . . . legal involvement, just as soon as I have a little money. Now, if you don't keep your word to me, I shall leave your house tonight. I promise I'll run. I care about how things look, too. And I'm not a . . . a *gold-digger,* or whatever they call women who trap men. I'm not a tramp. I . . . I'm just a person, and *all this is moving much too fast!* I can't think anymore, can't you see that?" Sarah was near tears now.

"Sarah—"

"You talk about the way things *look?* Your family doesn't know me from . . . anybody. Nathaniel, don't you realize I'm what people call 'poor white'? My daddy was a lumberjack. He never owned any property or had a name of any worth. I don't even know if he's still alive. I'm nobody from nowhere, and you already have an understanding with a woman."

Nathaniel clamped his jaw. "You've managed quite a high opinion of yourself, haven't you? Sarah, honey, can't you trust me—just for once?"

"I *did* trust you. That's my difficulty."

"Do you want a divorce, Sarah?"

"What?"

"You heard. I asked you if you wanted a divorce. Or—I can go before a judge and lie for an annulment if you want me to."

"I . . ."

"Divorce or annulment, Sarah, if Rachel hears of it, she'll be on you before you can blink."

"Not if I'm employed. Don't talk like that! She couldn't . . . Oh, I don't know anything anymore.

Everything I do is wrong! I'm so confused I can't think straight anymore. Please don't yell at me!"

Nathaniel had wanted for weeks to blurt out the truth of his feelings to Sarah. This marriage could work if she could see past the things it didn't have to the things it *did* have. He had pride. And feelings. Their one night of love had been no flirtation and no accident.

Sarah just wished he would put his arms around her and hold her. She hated it when Nathaniel was angry with her. She cared a great deal for this man. Why couldn't she just tell him that? She almost wished he were a poor farmer—most anything but the wealthy son of a wealthy senator. Oh, she didn't think his family would ever say anything to her face, but how she dreaded taking Peter and herself into this! She didn't want to see looks of cold distance.

Peter was rousing, and Rosy rubbed at her eyes and slumped over again.

"Up here, Peter, we're almost home." Brushing aside a strong compulsion to hug his wife, Nathaniel hoisted the sleepy baby on his good knee, Sarah gratefully took the few minutes to arrange herself for their destination.

Hoofbeats clattering across stone sent Sarah's heart right up into her throat, for the coach had slowed and turned. They were nearly there. She couldn't see too much, for darkness was upon them now, but the rolling driveway necessitated a much slower pace. Shadows loomed on either side of them as they made their way down the tree-lined road. Peter squirmed in Nathaniel's arms, and as Sarah reached for the child the blond head surprisingly drew from her to nestle back against Nathaniel's broad chest. The distinct word, "Papa," widened Sarah's eyes. Her jaw dropped in amazement, and she turned on Nathaniel.

"How could you? Using an innocent baby! How long have you been working on that?"

"Not long. He learns quickly," chuckled Nathaniel, "and don't lose your temper in front of the children."

As Sarah was gathering her forces, Nathaniel gave Peter's nose a tiny tweak. "I suggest you sheathe your claws, little kitten, for we are home!"

The huge doors of the mansion had swung open. Awestruck, Sarah gazed up at all the windows. The lines were simple and elegant, wide marble steps with heavy black railings ascending to the entrance of the brick house. Through the increasing darkness, Sarah received an impression of great size, only faintly viewing the archways and walks to each side. She had not been prepared for such magnificence!

The marvelous smells of cooking food and freshly plowed earth assailed her, and Sarah took the proffered hand of a young man standing beside the steps of the coach. Shyly, Rosy took her proper stance just behind Sarah. Nathaniel placed a barely awake Peter into her arms, and Sarah hugged him. The night was quite chilly.

A tall, slender woman dressed in an exquisite black gown, her hair slightly greying but still lovely, lifted her billowing skirts as she flew down the marble steps toward Nathaniel. Nathaniel began to run to her, but Sarah caught his quick gasp of pain. Knowing this was his mother, Sarah turned discreetly, trying not to intrude. Opening his arms to his mother, Nathaniel held her close, his head bent downward. For a few moments, the servants waited quietly on the steps and the drive as the woman wept, burying her face in his neck and lifting her head at last to hold his handsome face between her hands.

"Nathaniel," she whispered. "I have prayed for this day for such a long, long time."

Soon several of the servants ventured forward, clasping his hand or grasping a shoulder with fondness. Mrs. Garrett stood back proudly as greetings were exchanged.

"How did you beat me home, David?" queried Nathaniel of a young man wearing a sling and dressed in smart stable livery.

"Ran all the way, sir, ran all the way," the man laughed, pumping Nathaniel's hand with vigor.

Sarah began to wonder if his grin would split his face. She was proud of him. He fit. He belonged here. She smiled with him and for him, while weeping somewhere down inside herself for the home she would never have.

Nathaniel smiled and turned to his mother, placing an arm about her waist. He wanted to say "Mother, this is my wife, Sarah. She has brought me more happiness in a few short weeks than I ever knew existed." He wanted at least to say "Mother, I love Sarah very much, and I want to build a life for us like the one you and Father have." But he could say neither of those things.

Mrs. Garrett touched the bandage above Nathaniel's eye, but her son smiled, "It's all right, Mother."

They turned to Sarah. Feeling embarrassed, out of place, Sarah inclined her head toward Mrs. Garrett.

"Mother," Nathaniel smiled, "this is . . . Mrs. Sarah Bradley." He swallowed uncomfortably. Now it was his turn to share a bit of the awkwardness she had endured over the past weeks. "I'll speak to you at length about her later. But for now, it's enough to say that if it were not for her I would probably not be standing here."

Sarah didn't know quite whether she had expected Mrs. Garrett to scream at her that she was white trash or what. She was taken aback when Mrs. Garrett placed both hands on her arms.

"Mrs. Bradley, whatever the circumstances, I am very grateful to you. Please be welcome in our home, and feel free to ask us for any assistance we can give you. Come along now, the night air becomes chilly here. Nathaniel, this child needs a coat."

Nathaniel chuckled indulgently. "She has one, Mother. We have had wraps in the carriage. Come on, Sarah. Follow Mother, for Mother waits for no man." He took Peter from her and assisted her up the steps. Rosy following timidly, Nathaniel refused to favor his leg, which Sarah took quiet note of—that and the little arm that curled about his neck as Peter promptly went back to sleep.

Once inside, the driver having been paid and sent on his way, Mrs. Garrett took her leave to arrange for Sarah's room. Though Nathaniel reassured Sarah, telling her not to be overwhelmed, she was. Slightly dazed, she allowed the children to be taken to their rooms.

"Is Father in Washington? I started once to go directly there." A great chandelier shed its brilliant light into even the wings spreading above them on the second story. Nathaniel reached as high as he could to flick at a drooping chain of cut glass, setting up a cheery tinkling.

"I would never have forgiven you if he had gotten to see you first! Yes, he and Senator Herschell drove in early this morning, but he said he'd be back for a late supper. Clarke and Tabby are coming. And Beth and her father. Tabby is to have that baby any day now. The assassination still has us all so upset that we hardly know what we're doing. Nathaniel, I have put Sarah in Clarke's room because of the extra chamber for the baby and his nurse. Now I insist you have a bath and take a rest, for you know that once this house fills up you won't have a minute's peace." Mrs. Garrett gave her tall son one more kiss. "Introduce Peggy to Sarah, dear. I know she must not have heard the carriage, or she would have beaten us all down the steps."

Sarah had little time to take in the splendor of her surroundings—the large elaborate dining area to her left or the tastefully appointed drawing room just beyond, for Nathaniel steered her toward the stairs. Once his mother had disappeared toward the rear of the house, Sarah perceived that he limped noticeably, and as they ascended the carpeted stair he stopped several times to favor his aching leg. The wide staircase opened onto a very broad, carpeted hallway, several doorways opening off it, and Sarah was escorted to the last one on her right. Reaching about her to open the door, Nathaniel stood back, letting her precede him.

"You will be comfortable here, my love," he murmured as Sarah moved past him into the cheery room. The interior was abundantly supplied with candles which had all been lit, and a lovely oil lamp sat on the reading table near the bed. It was a large man's room, but furnished with such exquisite taste that Sarah loved it immediately. She smiled in wondrous appreciation and walked to the well-stocked bookcase to survey the titles. Drawing one out, turning the pages wistfully, Sarah felt much as if she were renewing old acquaintances—Shakespeare, Dickens and Dumas, all the Greek works, and more besides. The seconds slipped past, and for a moment Sarah forgot herself. She gave a start when he spoke.

"I thought you'd be pleased. Come in and see your bedroom. Nothing in here bites," he grinned, unbuttoning his jacket, slipping into the old, easy familiarity. Warm eyes smiled down at her, and that tugging began all over again—that irresistible something that had brought her so far. And when slender fingers reached to smooth back her hair, Sarah jerked back.

"Please, someone might see you," she protested lamely.

"Peggy's the only one who would come in this room, and Peggy would never tell on you. Even if you were naughty," he teased.

He walked past a very tall, wide expanse of windows, to a door. Opening it quietly, peering inside, he motioned to her. Sarah poked a curious head around the door facing to find Peter dressed in his nightclothes, snuggled up in a round little knot under the blanket. Rosy was in a small bed nearby. It was a long way back to Tennessee, a long time since she had stood in the mountain cottage and stared at Peter asleep on his cot. A long way back.

"Sarah," Nathaniel drew her away and closed the door, "I know you are not used to having people all about or asking anyone to help you. But this is a large household, and my father has paid these people long and well for their services. They will be happy to assist you. If you want Peggy to have a gown pressed for you, as I expect you will, just give a tug on this cord." He indicated a gold-braided affair hanging by the carved mantelpiece.

"Wait here," he smiled curiously, clasping a hand on each side of her shoulders. In a moment a door in the wall beside the fireplace opened, and Sarah gasped with surprise.

"This way," he curled a long finger, taking her by the hand and drawing her into a spacious closeted area and further past into a room equipped with a linen closet and bathtub and various other necessities. "Since we were both boys we shared the bath. This adjoins my room across the hall and opens to the stairway outside."

There was no indication from the hallway of the existence of this small passageway. The door opened to his chambers, and Sarah entered rooms much like the ones she occupied except for the difference in furnishing tastes, Nathaniel's a bit more conservative, the colors more subdued.

"Of course, there's a key," Nathaniel grinned wickedly, answering her next question before she could ask it. Teasingly he touched her nose with it before slipping it into the pocket of his pants. "Shall I ring Peggy for your bath?"

"Oh, yes!" This was a luxury she had no intentions

of passing up. And she decided she might as well select a gown for pressing, sure that servants were something she would never get used to.

Reentering her rooms to summon Peggy, Nathaniel carefully lowered himself into a chair as Sarah opened the trunk. Thank heaven Nathaniel had made her shop! There was a light tap on the door, a deep "Come in, Peggy," and the Garrett firstborn unfolded himself to greet the robust, middle-aged woman whose round face glistened with tears as she spread her strong arms wide.

"Mister Nat!" she cried, throwing her arms about him so heartily that Sarah feared for the ribs. "I heard you'd come sneakin' in this house. Land sakes! Is it ever good to see you! I can't tell how many times I wondered if I'd ever lay these old eyes on that face again!"

Nathaniel's hug was lusty, giving her a turn about the floor and setting her white cap awry until she scolded and demanded that he stop. . .

"Sarah," he laughed, reaching to straighten Peggy's cap, "if it hadn't been for this woman I would never have survived childhood. Besides keeping Clarke and me from killing each other on several occasions, she even saved me from a couple of well-deserved tannings from my father." Slipping a fond arm about the ample waist, the tall man placed a resounding kiss on the ruddy cheek.

"Peggy," he continued, sobering a bit, "this is Sarah . . . this is Sarah. Um . . . yes. You may think a few things strange . . . ." The gleam of caution in Sarah's sharp brown gaze was caught quickly. "Whatever Sarah needs, see that she gets it, if you please. I trust your discretion, Peggy. There is a rather unique problem here. . . ."

"Nathaniel!"

She began on her own.

"Peggy, what this man is trying so ineptly to say is

that we have just been through a war together. We have experienced some rather bizarre circumstances, and our relationship is a rather difficult thing to explain to someone who was not there with us to experience it as well."

Nathaniel's shrug was definitely on the sheepish side, whether on purpose or by accident there was little telling. But his body was hurting badly and he leaned heavily on the back of the chair, agony covering his face.

"Mister Nat?"

"Peggy, see that hot water is brought to Nathaniel's room. We will need salve, cotton, several wide strips of linen, and any antiseptic you have. Please don't alarm Mrs. Garrett. And," she added, viewing the lines of exhaustion drawing his face, "perhaps a little brandy, also."

Sarah smiled at the servant, and it seemed that a message spoke to her from Peggy's warm hazel eyes —an understanding, a respect, and perhaps compassion for the things Peggy did not yet comprehend.

"Would you like for me to have this gown readied for you, Miz Sarah?" she offered as she departed, indicating the burgundy muslin Sarah had draped over the trunk.

"Oh, yes. Thank you, Peggy, that will be fine." How easily she had done it—acquiesced to a service that before she had known Nathaniel she might well have been performing herself for someone else.

"And you, sir," pointing an irate finger straight at her husband's handsome nose, "left a lot to be desired. At the rate you're going, the entire household will know our secret before morning."

"Oh hell, Sarah. I find it very difficult to lie to Peggy," he objected.

"Pretend she's Mrs. Simpson, and perhaps it will inspire you. Now go to your room and get out of these clothes. When Peggy returns I will come to dress your leg."

Nathaniel assumed his most wounded air and grudgingly permitted her to shut the door.

Presently, the needed supplies in hand, Sarah slipped across the hall, following Peggy. Without a glance at either her husband or Peggy, she drew a low stool to his feet and carefully lifted the wounded leg to rest upon it. Nathaniel sighed, leaning back and feeling the first absolute contentment since daybreak.

Sinking to the floor in a cloud of skirts, Sarah pulled aside his robe to bare his leg. There was no hesitation, no self-consciousness at being between his legs and unpinning his bandage. Nathaniel smiled at Peggy's amazed stare, and Sarah would have been astounded at what passed between the man she had yet to accept as her husband and the older woman who had practically raised him. Nathaniel couldn't have told the story to Peggy much better, if he had spoken their whole account to her out loud.

No angry red streaks spread anywhere on his leg as Nathaniel leaned to peer at his wound. "It's fine," he muttered, and Peggy bent over Sarah's head.

"Mister Nat, that's quite nasty doin's you're wearin'. How old a wound is it?"

"Was it just last night, Sarah?" he asked in disbelief.

"Last night!" Peggy was bristling. "How——? The war's over."

"Not in some places, Peg. It's a long story, and I'll tell it later. Just say nothing to Mother. Let her think it's . . . anything. I don't want to get involved in any explanations tonight."

Sarah had straightened and was leaning very near him to peel off the small bandage over his eye. He could almost touch those pink lips with his own. He grimaced at her as the antiseptic burned into the open cut.

"Don't be such a baby, my fine war lord," chided

Sarah softly. Touching the cut with an extra dose she murmured, "This is for me," and touching it again, "this is for Peter." He knew exactly what she meant. "I would suggest that you don't cover that, Nathaniel, but if you want to and Peggy has some kind of adhesive, we can replace the bandage."

"Find it, Peggy," Nathaniel requested meekly. "Fewer questions. Sarah, will you finish? You're hurting me more than Giles did. Peggy, have one of the boys bring up a bath for Sarah and some water for me. Tell Mother if you run across her that we are settling in for a short rest, and I want to be called the minute Clarke gets here."

Peggy nodded, talking to herself as she left. It was a mystery to her how he always managed to be where trouble was. And the war was *over*.

Once she was back in her rooms and had collapsed into a gold, velvet-covered chair, Sarah closed her eyes.

What a nightmare the past twenty-four hours had been! Sarah did not feel as if she had taken a man's life one day ago. The strangeness of this room with Nathaniel's mother just below her, new people—everything was happening so fast. How could she have let desire overwhelm her like that?

Taking a candle from the mantle, Sarah touched it to the orange flames dancing in the fireplace and walked naked into the small dark chamber with her light. It was a nice feeling—the freedom to walk through a room stark naked. She took a deep breath. Posh! She was becoming as worldly as Nathaniel.

Quietly she opened the door to the linen closet and inspected the items for the bath. She found the soap and a washcloth and towel. Stepping into the warm water brought instant bliss, and she sighed as the soothing warmth melted the weariness away from the center of her bones. Her teeth held the corner of the washcloth as she repinned some of her hair. The crackling of the bedroom fire was so subtle in its whispering, the closeness of the chamber so cozy. She wished she had hours to bask in this marvelous solitude.

The hinges on the door from Nathaniel's room whispered their objection when he entered. The catch slipped into place beneath his fingers, and he paused for a moment to listen to the faraway sounds of life below them. Nathaniel smiled at Sarah's small expression of surprise, satisfied in his assurance of a few uninterrupted moments with his alluring wife.

His wife. Yet not his wife. How could this be? All his life things had been there for the taking . . . except the one thing he really wanted. And that? What *did* he want most at this very moment? To be the most important thing in the entire universe to someone, he supposed. Selfish, wasn't it? How much more noble it would be to say he wanted to give of himself for the good of mankind. But he wasn't noble. He wanted to be needed, loved, given the chance to pour out all the tender things he knew were locked away deep inside him. Until he had this, he was half a man.

"You look very handsome," Sarah admitted honestly. "And, I wish you wouldn't . . . don't sit down. You must leave."

"No." The stool scraped softly as he drew it beside the tub and leaned his hips on the edge.

She could see he was in no teasing frame of mind, and when his hand reached to lift a fallen lock of hair, she jumped.

Carefully Nathaniel replaced the tress, taking up her towel, holding it open for her. Just for a second he had seen that warmth in her eyes.

Sarah hesitated, then rose dripping to accept his assistance from the tub. Rivulets of water streamed in the candlelight, glistening in tiny rivers as they traveled to drip off the peaks of her bosom, off her elbows, and down her slender legs.

She sighed, "If I could lift that key from you, you might find it a bit more difficult to intrude on a lady's bath." Her hands reached for the towel and he snatched it back.

"A key would never stop me, Sarah," Nathaniel grinned, and he turned her around so he could dry her. Lingeringly he took his pleasure. Sarah started to speak a dozen times but, somehow, the words just wouldn't come. She stood speechless, barely breathing as the palm of his hand curved about her hip. With tantalizing slowness he reached about her waist and drew her back against him, kissing the nape of her neck. Her heart raced. His lips moved to her ear.

Sarah had never stood before a man so long and so naked before, not even Charles. Nathaniel's fingers caught in the soft down of curls below her belly. She gasped and tried to stop him, but he only cupped her breast in the palm of his hand, teasing the little tip until it sprang taut in his fingers. Sarah felt herself slumping back against his shoulder, her hair on his face and her head lolling toward him.

"No more," she moaned in his ear, her voice sounding foreign. Nathaniel turned her, her hair catching on his buttons as his hand found her breast. He was kissing her, saying something against her mouth. But she couldn't hear and didn't care.

Dismayed, Sarah jerked herself from his arms. Nathaniel stared at his hands shaking upon his knees. He would know she was lying if she said it had been a mistake.

"I really just came to kiss you. And not like that, either—to tell you I'm sorry for what happened this morning."

He folded her in a large, soft towel. As usual, his honesty disarmed her, though she wanted to cherish a list of his mistakes.

"I wanted to make you sorry," she confessed.

"We said some pretty hard things, didn't we, love?"

"I suppose so." She swallowed hard. "I, uh . . . what I said before, about your baby. I would never say it was a bastard child. I don't know why I said that."

Nathaniel didn't move for a time. "I know that." Sarah glanced upward, and he smiled. "Because I know you."

They laced their fingers together, as if to say it was all right now, and Sarah walked him to the door.

Sarah found it necessary to pull the braided cord for Peggy after all, for now the dining room loomed before her like some forbidding black forest. Standing in her shift, feeling a strong urge to confide, Sarah waited as Peggy's deft fingers laced her, fluffing her skirts and adjusting the flounce of lace at her elbows.

"Peggy," she began, and the moment Peggy turned those kind eyes on her, Sarah knew she could talk. Peggy was her kind of woman, hardworking, used to taking over when necessary. Peggy was Uncle Gene in woman's form—solid, accepting.

"Yes, Miz Sarah," replied the servant, gesturing toward Sarah's brown locks with raised brows. Sarah glanced at her reflection in the huge heavy, ornate mirror. Natural beauty could go only so far. Why not? She sat meekly and watched Peggy empty her pockets of comb, brush, pins, some small jars and a sparkling length of something or other that Sarah didn't recognize. Peggy had come prepared.

"As you have probably guessed, Peggy, I am a simple woman who had a simple upbringing. Nothing like this," and Sarah waved her hand about. "It's unnerving for me to go down and mingle in this society. I don't have the proper clothing, for one thing."

"This is nice, Miz Sarah. You've got a pretty face, and a bit of doing with your hair will turn you into a real beauty. And I wouldn't worry about downstairs.

The Garretts look more deeply into people than their clothes."

"I wish you'd tell me about Nathaniel, Peggy. About his life as a young man. I really don't know him too well, and he doesn't talk about himself very much."

Peggy's smile was so understanding that Sarah would have blushed, had she been anyone else. "Well, Miz Sarah, Mister Nat is a complicated piece of machinery sometimes, and I think I know him about as well as any. Maybe better than his mother in some ways. His happiness couldn't be more important t'me if he was my own. I started tendin' that child when he was about the age of your little son. Oh, I think a lot of Clarke, don't get me wrong, but my Mister Nat is special."

Sarah smiled and nodded at Peggy. "Not that Mister Nat has been easy to live with always. He was a scrapper in his teens, an' more than once he's bit off more than he could chew. His daddy made him finish law school, and Mister Nat practiced law for a while. But I always believed he'd rather be here in the country, workin' on this land. 'Course I never said much.

"He got hisself involved with a pretty young thing, but she died of typhoid, and I don't guess he's been serious about anyone since, lessen it be Beth Simms. You'll meet her tonight. She's a pretty good girl, I guess. I don't really know her like I knew Miss Charlotte."

Sarah understood some things now—Nathaniel's mockery, and his contradictory stubbornness.

"Peggy, my life is rather a mess just now." She sighed. "The one thing I don't want to be is a burden. To anyone. I plan to make my own way, and perhaps you might help me. I don't mind working, I always have. There must be some family who could use my services. Nathaniel won't help me there. He . . . feels obligated and all that." How was she going to live with all these half-truths she was spreading about?

Sarah dropped her chin to rest in the palm of her hand. Peggy beamed at her handiwork. The reflection that stared back at Sarah was unaffectedly simple— refreshing, natural, and Peggy had managed to twist her heavy locks into a becoming fashion, allowing a trace of golden glimmer to peep out here and there. The smooth forehead was accentuated and the slender neck was bared to curve gently into her modest decolletage. Only a small pale roundness teased above the neckline.

"Just a touch?" and Peggy withdrew a small container of rouge from the bountiful pocket. Sarah laughed.

"Just a touch." She was ready.

"You look lovely, Miz Sarah."

She couldn't put off leaving for another second.

"Don't be nervous. You're sitting by Senator Herschell," Peggy smiled. Sarah opened the door. "Miz Sarah?"

"Yes, Peggy."

"Miz Sarah, I may as well be honest with you. I've been so long in this house that I sometimes put my foot right in my mouth, and I'm probably doin' it again. But I want you to know right from the start that I like what I see in my Mister Nat. When he left to go fight in this war, neither his mother nor myself thought that we'd ever see him alive again. That man didn't care if he died. I don't know what's made the change, but I figure you had something to do with it, and I'm obliged to you for that. Whatever you want, no matter what, all you have to do is tell Peggy. If I can do it, I will."

Sarah touched her thick, tireless arm. "Thank you, Peggy. I won't forget."

⳼ *Chapter VIII*

SARAH KNEW THE disease from which she suffered was the universal fear of the unknown. Knowing it didn't make her entrance into the Garrett family any easier. Her slipper pressed into the rich carpet of the stair, and her hand rested apprehensively against the smooth balustrade. Smells of polish, wax, and hot coffee blended with the marvelous aroma of food, and it all spoke good taste and breeding.

A bustling stir sounded over the quiet murmur from the drawing room. The front door swept open, admitting three dark-suited men, one of whom was unmistakably the father of Nathaniel Garrett. The height was Nathaniel's, though the older Garrett was slightly heavier, and the raven-black hair was beginning to silver. The deep resonance of his voice carried the same authority, and Sarah saw where Nathaniel got his brilliant blue eyes.

The appraising gaze caught Sarah's hesitation as he followed his guests through the entry, and for a moment he paused, a gloved hand resting on the ornate hardware of the door. He nodded up to her, a generous smile spreading across his face, and Sarah knew that very little would escape the man.

Beside him, a shorter, slightly stocky man, dressed in a dark tweed suit and vest, traced the direction of his companion's eye, and Sarah stared back into friendly black eyes, as black as the immaculately trimmed beard and moustache he sported. The slender, blond man standing back apace, attractive to the point of being striking, was watching her descent also. She held her skirts very carefully. A stumbling debut into Washington's society wasn't quite what she desired.

"You must be Mrs. Bradley," Senator Garrett stepped to the landing with a small bow of welcome and drew her arm intimately over his own. Like father like son, she mused. "I am Nathaniel's father, and I welcome you to our home, Sarah Bradley. May I present a friend of very long standing, Senator George Herschell? George lives quite near here, and our families have practically grown up together." Blue eyes twinkled. "Except that nearly eighteen years ago they had themselves a set of twins. We never did quite match that, Eleanor and I."

"Thank you, Senator Garrett," replied Sarah demurely. Her instinctive poise in company began to evidence itself, in spite of all her apprehension. For a few seconds, memories of Uncle Gene and his myriads of guests, educators and scholars, coming and going at all hours, flooded her thoughts. Though she would have denied it, Sarah flourished in this setting, for she had conversed with thinking men as far back as she could remember.

"And I am most pleased to meet you, Senator Herschell. I must admit, Senator Garrett, that though you hail from the North you speak with the gallantry of our famed southern gentlemen. I had thought their manner unsurpassed until now." Sarah's tiny curtsey earned her a rich laugh. She liked Senator Garrett at first sight, and she was sure he returned her feeling.

"This young man is a new associate of Senator Herschell's, Mr. Adrien Ronsard. He has just returned from the South himself, on a research project for the government."

Sarah inclined her head at the languid study Ronsard made of her. "I'm afraid the South isn't very pretty just now, Mr. Ronsard, or should I say, *Monsieur* Ronsard? Have we met before?" she smiled, toying with the sensation that she knew the man.

"Please, just call me Adrien, Mrs. Bradley, and I assure you that I would recall it if we had met, for such a meeting would not be easy to forget." Perfect teeth flashed in a dazzling smile.

Sarah bowed politely and the senator took her hand, escorting her to the drawing room where the other guests mingled. "And you, Mrs. Bradley," he murmured, "seem to have been born with a politician's blood running through your veins. May I be so bold as to say that I look forward to many delightful hours of your company?"

Inclining his head to the room of people before him, the senator courteously handed her over to his companion as he excused himself to find his wife. Sarah searched the room for Nathaniel.

The room was very large, and closed double doors closed off even another area. The entire room was probably opened only for special occasions, like a large ballroom. Crystal chandeliers sparkled with lit candles and drooping scallops of cut glass. A patterned floor gleamed with fresh wax, and the rich fabrics of the furnishings blended artistically with several selections of greenery and fresh flowers.

Sarah saw him then, wearing that same careless affability of his father but with more animal ruggedness. The blond woman at his side was stunning. The room revolved about this man, just returned from the war, as he signaled a greeting to friends across the room with the quirk of a brow or motioned to them with a gesture. The pair blended into the gracious setting as if it had been fashioned only to compliment their beauty. They moved with grace—privilege amid smiling faces.

Sarah winced. A shattering weakness struck her knees, and she stumbled on the feet of Senator

Herschell. Rosy lips of the taffeta-clad woman reached to whisper in Nathaniel's ear as his dark head bent, and Sarah flushed hot, then cold, forcing a faint smile of apology at the senator. Slender fingers closed about her shoulder, and Sarah was grateful when Adrien Ronsard saved her from making a spectacle of herself.

"Since Mrs. Bradley and I are both strangers in the room, Senator, perhaps you would allow me the honor of entertaining her while you greet your friends?" he offered tactfully. If he guessed the reason for her discomfort he never showed it.

"May I get you some champagne, Mrs. Bradley?"

"What? Oh yes, thank you, Mr. Ronsard. I think I would like some. Very much. Yes."

"Mrs. Bradley?"

"Oh, Senator Herschell, please. I beg of you to forgive me. It's been a very tiring day, all in all, and I'm afraid I quite lost myself for a moment." She was a master at hiding pain.

"Mrs. Bradley, I have a feeling that I put you on edge. That is not my intention at all. I wonder if I might have a word in private with you. In the senator's study, perhaps. I may not have a chance to speak with you again this evening." George Herschell inclined his head to Adrien. "I think he will manage to find you again," and a white smile flashed through the black beard.

"Why yes, I suppose so, Senator Herschell, but I can't imagine why—"

"This way then, please."

Sarah allowed herself to be drawn to a room down a short hallway. She was mesmerized by the image of Nathaniel smiling down at one of the most beautiful women she had ever seen.

There was leather-covered furniture, the faint aroma of tobacco, a large desk surrounded by tall bookshelves, a photograph of two boys and one of Mrs.

Garrett. Abraham Lincoln's portrait hung from one wall. Senator Herschell motioned for her to sit, and she did.

"Mrs. Bradley, I know this must seem rather outlandish. I know I would think so if I were you." His voice was very pleasant. Senator Herschell was eloquent and disarming, and Sarah finally managed to gather her wits enough to give him her attention.

"Samuel told me two days ago of your existence, Mrs. Bradley. He told me what he knew about you, which wasn't much, only that Nathaniel spoke very highly of you and that you were coming to relocate. Something about a custody suit regarding your son, I believe?"

"Yes, Peter," she nodded.

"I think perhaps, Mrs. Bradley, that you could be the answer to a very large problem my wife and I are facing just now."

"I?"

"As you know, President Johnson has not called a special session of Congress, and many of my associates, including Samuel, are quite concerned. I am needed in Washington, and I very much need my wife with me." The senator paused, and Sarah nodded. "Mr. Ronsard, my new secretary, has worked for me for only a few weeks, and I'm afraid he can't give me the assistance I need. We have the twins that Samuel spoke of. My wife and I hoped we would not have to take them into the city this summer. So it occurred to Samuel and me that perhaps you might, well, since you have not had time to settle yourself anyway, at least I thought I would meet you, and kind of look you over, so to speak. Forgive me," he laughed softly, and Sarah surprised herself by responding so readily to the man.

"Well, I hope I passed, whatever it was," she laughed, and the senator sighed a small sigh of relief, nodding and smoothing at his beard.

"I pride myself on being an astute judge of character, Mrs. Bradley. I see in that face much that impresses me. A certain strength, and perhaps a bit of pain, too, I think."

"A bit, sir," and Sarah slowly nodded at the senator. "If I could be so bold, sir, I think I see a bit of pain on that face, as well." Sarah gestured to him lightly.

Senator Herschell looked away and then raised his hand to rub his moustache. His hand trembled.

"Senator?"

"The twins, Patty and Vance. We have older children, of course, but they are married with families of their own. Patty's a bit of a rounder, but you'd get along famously with her. Vance . . . was always the problem. From birth. Something with Margaret's blood, the doctor said. He, ah . . . well, none of us thought he would live. But he did," and Sarah watched the habitual smile turn his mouth up at the corners, but the eyes gazing into space weren't smiling. Not at all.

"Vance is quite the young artist. A fine violinist, they tell me. I'm afraid everything sounds good to me, but he did study. It's his lungs, I think. Well, I'm sure. They . . . are slowly collapsing. Oh, Vance knows he's not in good health. There was no way we could ever keep him from knowing that. For a number of years we hoped they had made a mistake about the lungs."

Sarah couldn't see too much behind that black beard, and perhaps that was why he wore it. And Senator Herschell was too proud to pretend he wasn't crying. Why tears started sliding down her own cheeks Sarah didn't really know. Perhaps some of them were for herself. The room was absolutely still.

Presently he cleared his throat and reached into his hip pocket for a handkerchief. When he could talk again he continued, but he didn't look at her any more.

"We have to be gone for several weeks. Two

months, maybe. Margaret doesn't want to take Vance out of the country. And I really think she needs a break. It cuts her up something terrible to watch him. She's trying very hard, but eighteen years is a long time to live with something like this."

"You need someone to be a companion to the twins while you're gone." How trusting he seemed.

He sighed a long, weary sigh. Sarah wished she could go to this great, wonderful man and hold him as one would hold a weeping child. But she laced her fingers together firmly instead.

"Of course, Margaret would want to speak with you at length, but I told her I was going to meet you. And if you were even half the person Nathaniel told his father you were, I was going to speak with you about it."

"There are three of us, sir," she offered.

"Oh, yes. Yes, I know that."

He was waiting for her to say something. Since she really didn't know what to say, Sarah examined her fingernails intently and finally began to talk—more like thinking out loud, actually. Senator Herschell listened without interrupting, even when she paused.

"I'm so touched that you thought of me. I mean, not knowing me at all and well, looking me over, as you say. I wouldn't wish to make a hasty judgment about this. And I really do need a place to live. And work. It's not that. In fact, it would really be perfect for me. I have considerable experience in arts and languages.

"I don't know, Senator, really. I don't know if I could handle a situation like this or not. You're right, I have lived through some painful times myself, and even now I find myself quite . . . unsettled, you might say. I really need some time to think this over, Senator. My inclination is to decline. I've never dealt with a problem of this nature before."

Sarah looked at him, then, and she knew that he would not blame her if she refused.

"Of course. If you feel you can't, we can take them with us. Vance hates it in Washington, and it's hot there at times. Perhaps I could send Adrien for you in the morning and then you could meet Margaret and the twins. Hm?" He rose and extended her a hand which Sarah took and waited for him to open the door.

"Who else knows of this, Senator Herschell?"

"Only Samuel and Eleanor and his mother, whom I don't suppose you've met yet, have you?"

"No, sir."

"I'll understand, Mrs. Bradley, if you feel you can't."

"I know you will, Senator. And please, call me Sarah. And, sir," she held out her hand on impulse, sensing a strong, comforting courage that she wished she had, "you have given me one of the greatest compliments I ever received."

Adrien Ronsard found her the minute she and Senator Herschell returned to the drawing room. Unexplainably the first person she saw was Nathaniel's father, from a considerable distance, and those blue eyes smiled at her. He knew they had talked. Now Sarah began to wonder just what Nathaniel had said about her in those telegrams.

"I thought I had lost you, Sarah," Adrien smiled that dazzling smile, and Sarah forced herself to return it, promising herself that she was able to conduct herself well, despite that off-the-shoulder dress Nathaniel's fiancée was wearing. Very effectively, the woman managed to turn herself so that Nathaniel could view more than half her bosom. He seemed to suffer some malady over bosoms anyway, so Sarah supposed he was delighted.

"Would you like some champagne now, perhaps?" murmured Adrien.

"Yes, I suppose I might as well, Mr. Ronsard. And this time I'll try not to run away."

"Mrs. Bradley?" the deep voice called her name, tightly guarded, very controlled. Nathaniel moved forward with the betrothed upon his arm as Adrien returned with a glass. He adroitly placed it into her hands without spilling a drop.

Nathaniel's dark head bowed casually as Adrien drew himself well into her skirts, and the vivacious blond gave an aristocratic bow to Sarah, allowing her bright green eyes to take in the details of her coiffure and gown. Sarah returned her scrutiny with a look which she prayed was casual. Soon, Nathaniel would find himself in a dilemma over the introductions. Sarah wondered whether he would defer to his wife or his betrothed. It wasn't difficult to see that the same question plagued him, for the slightest frown crossed his features.

"Mrs. Bradley," Nathaniel made his choice without faltering, "may I present Miss Beth Simms, a close friend of our family for many years."

If Beth Simms was offended she was too well-bred to show it. "Beth, Mrs. Sarah Bradley." Waiting for him to make some attempt at conversation, Sarah tried not to purse her mouth at him. Nathaniel only breathed deeply and drew an unreadable shield over his eyes.

"Never mind his rudeness, Mrs. Bradley," Beth's voice was refined, like fine silk, and Sarah did not fail to note the possessive timbre. "These stuffy Northerners are a snobbish lot. I've heard everyone is so friendly in the South. Oh, my! Well, the war's over now anyway, isn't it? So don't be discouraged if you have to hit them between the eyes to get their attention. It's a little difficult, moving into a new place. Of course, my family, and Nathaniel's too, have lived in this county for, oh, I'd say nearly a hundred years, so I've never had to start all over, making new friends and all. Where did you say your family lives, Mrs. Bradley?"

"I didn't say."

"Oh. Nathaniel, you neglected to tell me that your associate was so pretty."

Beth smiled beautifully. She was tall. Sarah had always wished to be tall. Tall women were almost always graceful, no matter how they moved or what they wore.

Beth's honeyed words continued, and Sarah felt an underlying message. She wasn't certain, however, until Nathaniel introduced himself to Adrien, and the routine amenities began. His attention averted for a few seconds, Beth's cool green eyes locked in a majestic challenge with Sarah's calm brown ones. The look was direct and confident—unerring in its message. Sarah was not to touch Nathaniel. And before Sarah could think, she returned the look with one of her own. The two women now understood each other. There was no mistake.

"Beth," Nathaniel began to drawl, and Sarah nearly smiled, "I would like Mrs. Bradley to meet Grandmother, if you and Mr. Ronsard would excuse us for a moment."

"Certainly, darling," cooed Beth, and she lifted a soft hand to cup about his jaw in a possessive caress. A smile flitted across his lips, and with a curt nod to Adrien, he moved off. The hand that extended to draw Sarah across the room was not gentle.

"Where have you been?" he growled under his breath as soon as they were a safe distance from Beth and Adrien.

"What concern is it of yours? You kept yourself well occupied!" Sarah smiled through gritted teeth. Nathaniel's fingers tightened around her arm, warning her to behave, and Sarah paused to set her untouched glass of champagne upon a table before she spilled it.

"It didn't take you long to find an attractive escort,

my sweet wife." Nathaniel whispered from the corner of his mouth, and his eyes intimately touched her lips.

"I only just met the man."

"I don't think *he* knows that."

"Don't use that tone with me. Gawking down her dress so far you could see her legs!"

Nathaniel's grandmother sat in her special chair like a throne. Her eyes were alert, though Sarah had doubts about her health. Behind her sat a prim, black-haired girl, perhaps Sarah's age. Sarah guessed her to be the nurse.

Affectionately Nathaniel bent to place a kiss on her wrinkled cheek. "Grandmother?" he grinned, leaning so low that Sarah could barely hear him. "Can you keep a secret?" He winked slyly, and his grandmother winked back, a little slower but well enough.

"Have I ever told one of your secrets, Nathaniel Cameron?" Fragile, almost transparent hands reached to touch his lips with her fingertips.

"Well, then, I have a very special person I want you to meet. This is Sarah Catherine. Grandmother has always demanded two names, Sarah. She says a person is naked with only one."

"Well, what is the secret, young man? Don't keep me in suspense." Her eyes were blue, but age had bleached them to so soft a hue that they seemed clear, like her hands. Nathaniel folded his long frame until he was level with her face.

"Sarah Catherine is the prettiest woman I have ever seen."

"That doesn't appear to be a well-kept secret, my man. Have you told Beth?"

"Now, Grandmother, you know Beth couldn't keep a secret if her life depended on it," retorted Nathaniel playfully, tweaking her nose.

"Beth what?" inquired the silky voice, its speaker gliding smoothly up to rest her hands on Nathaniel's shoulders. "You shouldn't tease, darling, and you

157

shouldn't talk about people behind their back. It's not nice," she purred, as if they were the only people in the room.

"Whoever said he was nice?" clipped Sarah before she knew it. She could have strangled herself. Grandmother Garrett chuckled into her handkerchief, and Nathaniel became fascinated by his shoes.

Nathaniel wisely began to draw Beth toward the dining room. But a tall, fair man entered the room with a very pregnant young redhead on his arm. Sarah looked up, as did everyone else, to see the rousing reunion of the two brothers. Clarke Garrett was nearly as tall as his brother, with much of his mother's coloring. Brown hair framed his fair face, and clear, greyish-brown eyes swept across Sarah as she retreated to lean across the back of Grandmother Garrett's chair. Sarah relaxed, comfortable with the old woman.

"Clarke Terrance is a physician, Sarah Catherine," commented the older woman. "It's a good thing, too, bringing that girl out into the chilly night like this. She'll be lucky if she can get home before that great-grandchild comes. This will be our first, you know."

"You like babies, Grandmother Garrett?" Was there a pain keener than this hunger for what this family had? By law she had a right to stand by Nathaniel's side, and from the corner of her eye Sarah watched yellow skirts brush the lean leg of her husband. *The* leg, that *she* had killed a man for. *She* had knelt between those legs to dress his wound. *Her* naked limbs had pressed against his.

But was she capable of claiming her place in a family like this? No, she doubted that such a family would open their arms to the child of a simple tutor. She had lived as an outsider for too many years to subject her son to a lifetime of it.

"I've heard you have a young son. I am anxious to meet him. You must bring him down tomorrow morning so I can see him."

Sarah avoided her eyes.

"Draw closer to me, Sarah Catherine," commanded Grandmother Garrett, and Sarah glanced about, reaching to pull a small stool from the wall. She sat at the woman's feet, hands clasped about her knees.

The cheerful buzz about the room continued, and Sarah watched, disheartened as Beth took the place rightfully hers. Much to her surprise, the old grandmother reached a wrinkled hand to her, and Sarah's head lifted to peer deeply into the eyes that held a vast storehouse of wisdom. She felt naked as she took the proffered hand.

"Try not to be lonely, Sarah Catherine. Life is too short to be that lonely," the woman spoke quietly, drawing Sarah's hand into her lap, smoothing the lace about Sarah's sleeve and leaning her silvery head to Sarah's brown one until they almost touched.

A long, thoughtful moment passed, and Sarah forgot the others in the room for a lovely space of time. Somehow the old woman knew her hunger—it didn't matter how. Her eyes filled with hot, stinging tears, and she forced herself to smile through them. And Grandmother Garrett understood that, too.

"You are a very wise woman, do you know that, Grandmother?" whispered Sarah.

"I think they are going into dinner. Would you mind giving me a hand into the dining room? I grieve for Mr. Lincoln, and for all our other dead, but it is a very happy occasion to have this boy home alive."

Below Sarah the ring of a chime struck one shimmering beat, and she sat in the light of a single candle. Her mind refused the sweet balm of sleep. At the request of his mother, Nathaniel had escorted Beth and her senile father home. His hurried comment over her shoulder had been unapologetic.

"If you're up when I get back, I'll come in to say goodnight."

Well, she was up, and Nathaniel should have been back long before. What was there about darkness, late at night, that made the truth so hard?

Miserably Sarah tried to recall the blond, gentle man walking through the forests of Tennessee, hands stuffed into his pockets and a pipe clenched in his teeth. She almost managed to focus on the vision, but all she could see clearly was Nathaniel's face. Nathaniel, not Charles. The tears slid their way into her lap until the soothing black curtain of slumber mercifully took her.

Sarah started. It was nearly dawn. Her muscles ached from remaining cramped in the chair all night. She was cold, and quickly built a fire, scraping her hands as she laid a split log across the kindling. She peeped into the water kettle. Good, it was full, and soon she could wash the heavy grogginess and wretched memories from her face.

Sarah opened the draperies. The heavy fog only added to the dreariness of an already cloudy morning. It would surely rain. The stables below her were quiet in their security against the forthcoming storm. Sarah began to enjoy the cozy warmth of her rooms as she surveyed the dark clouds moving in. Sounds of boiling water bubbled cheerily. Soon she would ring Peggy for some tea and toast. She would dress, and think on more pleasant things.

The lone rider slipped into view and Sarah watched transfixed as Nathaniel reined up before the large swinging door to the stable. In horrified silence Sarah's jaw dropped as a long leg swung around the saddle, the dismounting accomplished in no small discomfort. She hoped it killed him, for she was sure he had had a tryst with Beth Simms. Gone was her hard-won cheer.

"Fool, fool! What a damn little fool I've been!"

Sarah wished to strike the window and send the splinters hurtling down on him, to hurt him the way she hurt. No. Anger felt better. It was easier to hate than to hurt. Beth Simms was welcome to him.

She turned to give the braided cord a vicious jerk. Sarah made the bed, sorted her garments, and straightened the room. Savagely she scrubbed herself and paced. She didn't want memories, blends of jealousy and hunger, hopes for the future. *She just wanted away.*

"Come in, Peggy," Sarah tried to speak normally and spread a forced smile across her face, taking a slow, deep breath to calm her voice. Peggy stepped into the room and closed the door over-carefully, placing a tray on the foot of the bed. Sarah stood woodenly as the servant smoothed her white apron and glanced warily about the room.

" 'Tis a good thing I brought the coffee with me, by the looks of you this mornin'," she observed succinctly. "Or would you rather have tea, ma'am?"

"Coffee is fine, Peggy, and I know I look terrible. I have had a horrible night. Do you think you can pull me together?"

"Ah, yes, Miz Sarah. Should I ask the trouble, or do you wish me to satisfy myself with assumptions?"

"The assumptions could not go too far amiss, Peggy. What time does Mrs. Garrett rise?" Just managing to keep the spout in the vicinity of the trembling cup, Sarah poured herself coffee from the fat little pot and turned her back to Peggy for the final adjustment of her dress. As Peggy cinched the trim waist and hooked the basque of Sarah's grey suit, giving the white collar and cuffs a smoothing, she responded with subdued enthusiasm.

"She'll be up early. She always is. Do you want to see her?"

"Yes, Peggy," and Sarah's decision was made without thinking—as the very words fell from her lips.

"Senator Herschell is sending a coach for me this morning, and I have an appointment with his wife. If things go well, I will be staying there for a few weeks to oversee the twins so they may remain in the country. I only wanted to inform Mrs. Garrett of my plans."

The coffee was clearing Sarah's head.

"Does Mister Nat know of your plans, Miz Sarah? Can't this be delayed a mite?"

"No. They're leaving today, and the twins will have to go too unless I agree to stay. And it doesn't matter, Peggy."

Sarah's deliberate answer snapped so brusquely that Peggy pressed her lips together and said no more. She brushed and arranged Sarah's hair into a shiny mass of twists on the back of her head. The smoothness back from her face made the tired eyes seem wider, more childlike, and her paleness took on something of an ethereal quality.

"Now you look like a typical professional lady. I assume that's how you intend to go, ma'am?"

Sarah stiffened. Peggy was going to be difficult, and she knew the woman didn't approve of her making plans independently of Nathaniel. Well, let her disapprove. Peggy didn't have to watch the miserable cad come creeping in at dawn.

"I look as I need to look, Peggy. I would appreciate it very much if you would take all of Captain Garrett's items from the trunk and place them in *his* room. I may be sending for my things today," Sarah requested curtly, wishing she could rid her thoughts of Nathaniel as easily as she could dispense with his clothes.

"Mister Nat would want to know, Miz Sarah," reproved the older woman cautiously, and Sarah read the disturbance about her mouth.

"I don't give a damn what Mister Nat would like!" Before she could stop them the bitter words burst forth. Peggy accepted the wound for her beloved Nathaniel without a comment. If possible, Sarah was even more miserable.

"Oh, Peggy, forgive me. Nathaniel has placed me in a terrible position. You know there is more to the situation than appears on the surface. I can see it in your face. You have known since I first set foot in this house. Well, I *must* get out of this house. I can't tolerate this arrangement!"

Abruptly Sarah turned, staring down at the stables without seeing. Scuttling clouds grumbled with thunder.

"As you wish, Miz Sarah. Would you like me to bring breakfast to the room for the three of you?" Sarah didn't turn to answer.

"Yes, please, Peggy. And tell Mrs. Garrett that I wish to speak with her as soon as possible." Peggy sighed loudly, and only when Sarah heard the door shut softly did she turn.

Mrs. Garrett was attired in a crisp silk gown of pale green with a large white collar. Her slender hands were soft, graceful, and a mass of silvering hair streamed down her back. She sat at coffee, in her splendid home, aristocratic—everything Sarah would never be.

"Come in, Mrs. Bradley. Peggy informs me that you wish a word this morning. I always arise quite early —a habit for many, many years. It's the only way I can keep ahead of Samuel!"

Sarah returned her smile and murmured, "Please call me Sarah. I felt it proper to inform you of an opportunity open to me, Mrs. Garrett, one which Senator Garrett and Senator Herschell have been considering for several days, apparently. The Herschell family leaves for Washington today, and after I speak with Mrs. Herschell this morning, it is possible they might leave the twins at home under my charge."

Mrs. Garrett smiled and motioned for Sarah to sit beside her on the powder blue settee. Thanking her for the cup of coffee placed in her hands, Sarah settled back. Mrs. Garrett didn't make her as nervous as Peggy did, for, of course, she had no inkling that anything existed between her and Nathaniel.

"Samuel told me he and George had been talking about it. I understand your hesitation. The situation with Vance is quite delicate."

Sarah nodded, wondering if she should even be talking with this woman, she seemed so perceptive.

"Nathaniel is very fond of you, I can tell, and though I haven't had a single minute to speak with him alone, I sense a settling in Nathaniel." Her eyes slipped into a distant gaze. "You see, Nathaniel is so different from Clarke, much more reckless. Well, I am sure you already know what it's like to worry over the life of your son."

Finally Sarah answered, "I have had both, Mrs. Garrett. I have lost and I have feared to lose. One is almost as cruel as the other."

"Yes, of course, Sarah," Mrs. Garrett agreed sympathetically and continued to study the strong young woman neatly attired in her modest gown. Eleanor Garrett could sense a defiant courage in the posture of Sarah's head, and she could begin to see what Nathaniel admired in Sarah. She was quite lovely, no doubt of that, and the quiet independence perhaps hid a more impulsive, fiery temperament than she allowed on the surface. This woman was complex, but then, so was her son.

"Well, I think I may speak for Margaret. She will be grateful for someone like you to be with the twins. Probably this last year with Vance has been the most difficult. He hasn't done well at all, and though they restrict his activities, there has been a marked decline. I really don't see how Margaret bears up. I hope she will go on to Washington with George and be away from Vance for a few weeks."

Because of Mrs. Garrett's kindness, Sarah felt older

than twenty-one, and she smiled her gratitude. Eleanor Garrett treated Sarah as an equal, a woman of worth, and Sarah arose to extend her hand. Holding it in her own soft one for a moment, Eleanor nodded.

"Do I hear a carriage now, Sarah? Perhaps not, let's look." Together they watched the fine coach being pulled up the drive by a pair of stunning blacks. "Ah, yes," murmured Eleanor, I suppose you will take your son with you for your meeting, Sarah."

"Yes."

Adrien Ronsard's boots sounded on the steps. A costly coat was unbuttoned on his tall frame, and Sarah was reminded that she should perhaps go back upstairs for her own.

"Mr. Ronsard, if you don't mind waiting, I think I had better bring a wrap with me. Rosy, take care that Peter doesn't touch anything 'til I return." Sarah smiled at the timid little black girl. Rosy stood with Peter's blanket draped across her arm, standing with as much dignity as a thirty-year-old matron.

"Come in, Mr. Ronsard. Would you like a cup of coffee? You are out early this morning." Mrs. Garret was drawing Adrien into the room, and Sarah lifted her skirts to run up the stairs. Drawing out the lovely brown cloak—Nathaniel's gift—Sarah straightened, brushing the soft nap, then turned to view Nathaniel leaning in her doorway.

"Where are you going?" he questioned roughly, sharp eyes sweeping her attire, a deep groove cutting between his brows.

"Out!" snapped Sarah loftily, turning contemptuously to slip past him into the hallway. She might have guessed that she would not escape so easily. Stern hands reached to whirl her about as she attempted to pass.

"Out where?" Pinning her shoulders against the doorway, he forced her head up.

"It's none of your business, Captain Garrett. Remove your hands from me this instant!"

Blast him! Let him suffer a little and wonder where *she* was! It would do him good, the philanderer!

"Stand aside," Sarah clinched her teeth warningly, "you will soon be free to go back to your lover. You don't frighten me anymore. I have my grounds for suit if it must come to that, Nathaniel. And don't pretend innocence. I saw you when you came in this morning. Did you enjoy it? I see the wound didn't give you too much inconvenience. Well, take her! I'm as anxious to be free of you as you are of me. Now stand aside! I have a living to make, and I, for one, cannot afford the luxury of *dallying!*"

Nathaniel grew deathly pale, flinging his hands from Sarah in a frustrated gesture to lower his face until it nearly touched her own. "You try my patience to the limit, you little witch! Go, then! By heaven, you'll tell me where before you leave this house. Is *he* here for you? You belong to me, and unless you wish to see every bone in his body broken, you'd best remember it!"

"Oh, you men make me sick! You can be unfaithful to a wife by right of law and breach a promise to a fiancée. And now you have the nerve to reproach me for taking an honorable position?"

"What position? You're not leaving this house to take any damned position! And for the last time, I have *never* proposed marriage to Beth Simms!"

"I'm leaving this house, Nathaniel, and I shall take the position—with the Herschells, if it's any of your business. It seems clear to me that you have made your choice. And some way, I will have this marriage annulled."

Past thinking, Sarah just let the words come, anything she thought would hurt. She steeled herself, for she knew he would match her, pain for pain.

"Believe what you like, you are still mine. You're

more of a fool than you are behaving at present if you think I'll let you toy with that."

Nathaniel strode to his door and yanked it open viciously. Spilling tears of bitter victory, Sarah flew down the stairs. Mrs. Garrett and Adrien were involved in a conversation of politics that could go on for hours. Impatiently, she lifted Peter and walked about the drawing room with him, chattering to him under her breath, her nerves stretched nearly to the snapping point as Adrien carefully expressed his disagreement with Thaddeus Stevens.

"No one has the best interest of the freedmen at heart when they preach total and immediate emancipation. Do you agree, Mrs. Garrett?"

"Even with the Thirteenth Amendment, Mr. Ronsard, I seriously doubt the black man will experience total and immediate emancipation. Hello, Mother," Nathaniel's voice drawled as his dark head bent to place a kiss on his mother's cheek. Mocking eyes raised to issue Sarah a sharp warning. "I am surprised to see you about so early, Mr. Ronsard. I hope nothing is amiss?"

"Certainly not, Captain Garrett. On the contrary. Everyone is in quite a frenzy to finish packing, as the Senator must be in Washington by tonight. The Senator asked if I would not bring Mrs. Bradley to spend the day, on the chance that the twins might remain under her care for a time. That is, if all works to everyone's satisfaction."

"I see," muttered Nathaniel.

"Nathaniel, you returned rather late, didn't you?" Eleanor's casual inquiry as she sipped her coffee drew a hearty laugh from her son. Sarah's heart skipped a beat.

"You never change, Mother. Yes," he agreed lightly. "Old man Simms and I sat by the fire, and he plied me with brandy to stay and listen to his tales of days at sea with *Circe.*"

Nathaniel's steady hand poured a cup of coffee, and as he balanced the cup in its saucer he began to roam about the room leisurely. Adrien watched him, and Sarah knew Nathaniel well enough to know the tall man was aware of the scrutiny. Mrs. Garrett's back was to them, and Nathaniel moved his eyes over Sarah, appraising her with such lingering boldness that Adrien could not help but see it. Sarah stiffened, but she could do nothing lest she attract the attention of Mrs. Garrett.

"An old wound was plaguing me a bit," he offered casually, resulting in a concerned countenance from his mother which he lazily brushed aside. "Oh, it's nothing, Mother, don't concern yourself. As I was saying, it was bothering me a tad, and the both of us being quite full of brandy, we dozed off to sleep before the fire. The next thing I knew, it was daybreak. The old scoundrel had gone on to bed and deserted me. I expect he will receive a sound scolding from Beth this morning. Spare me that! If there is one thing I don't need, it is the tongue of an irate female." Sarah whirled indignantly and strode to stand beside Adrien.

"If you would forgive my rudeness, Mr. Ronsard, don't you think it is about time we proceeded on to the Herschell's? Mrs. Garrett, thank you once again for your hospitality, and yours too, of course, Captain."

Sarah gave them her most dazzling smile.

"By all means, Mrs. Bradley," drawled Nathaniel. "I will come over later today and finish up that legal matter we discussed earlier, so that you may rest your mind on that score."

Nathaniel stepped to her side and ruffled Peter's blond locks. Sarah held her breath, terrified that the child would utter that word again. Before anyone could do or say anything she swept to the door.

"How very kind. I shall look forward to your visit. Mr. Ronsard?" Glancing at Rosy, Sarah exited the room with a regal lift of her chin. However, he followed her to the door, Adrien in his wake.

"Take care, my love," he warned under his breath. With that, she and Adrien departed.

The rains finally came during the brief ride to the Herschell estate. Torrents turned the ruts of the road to soft mush, and the carriage groaned and leaned, jerking crazily. Sarah could catch glimpses of the brick home from where the driver stopped the carriage to inspect the rear wheels.

The driver banged on the carriage door with a heavy fist, and Adrien swung it open, allowing a great gust to force them farther into the recesses of the coach. Winds were bending the trees low to the ground by now, ripping small branches to send through the air.

"I best go fer 'nother team!" he roared above the tempest. "Back any more an' she'll tip over th' embankment!" Sarah braved the wet gusts to lean around Adrien's knees and look. The wheels balanced precariously over a rocked culvert. Adrien yelled his agreement over the winds and strained to pull the door shut. Disheartened, sinking even lower into an already sizeable discouragement, Sarah slumped back against the seat.

"Do you suppose it will take very long?" she raised her voice to inquire dismally, rearranging Peter's blankets and settling him back snugly into the corner. "Don't be frightened, Rosy," she encouraged as cheerfully as she could. "This will probably be over in a very few minutes." She hoped she was right.

Adrien said smoothly, "He should be back in a half hour or so, Sarah," and his grey eyes smiled with the rest of his face. This was really the first chance Sarah had had to take a good close look at Adrien Ronsard. Once again, a nagging familiarity about the man pricked at her, but she dismissed it.

"You have been assisting Senator Herschell for

some weeks, I understand, Mr. Ronsard," Sarah raised her voice to be heard against the pelting of the rain.

"Enough to suit my purposes here, my dear. Why?" Adrien glanced at the children who were as quiet as could be, a little frightened of the storm. A slender, trousered leg moved against Sarah's skirts with an alarming boldness, and her gaze darted to him. But he wore his usual placid expression. The rascal had done that purposely, and Sarah was in no mood for flirtations. He certainly was cool—about the storm, about her. Ah, the confidence of the French!

A fierce bolt of lightning struck nearby, and thunder burst, terrible and deafening. Peter cried out, and Rosy grabbed him, clutching. Before Sarah could move to them, Adrien had slipped across into the seat beside her. He drew her into his arms. Though he did not appear to be a strong man, he was, undeniably, and Sarah found it futile to pull away.

"Sir!" she cried, her voice lost in the violent peals of thunder that echoed, rolling heavily, one after the other. The carriage jerked, the horses threatening to bolt. Now Sarah was truly afraid. If the horses threw themselves against the harness, there would be no predicting what would happen to them.

"Don't panic, Sarah, you'll be safe as long as you're with me," cautioned Adrien, smiling curiously and placing a possessive hand inside her cloak, just under her heaving breasts.

"Get away from me! How dare you!" The explosive crash of lightning shook the vehicle again, and the horses lurched against the coach.

"I'll scream!" Sarah cried desperately as Adrien ignored the terrified children and covered her protests abruptly with his mouth. His lips were ice cold. Sarah shuddered, struggling. His mouth seemed not to desire her but to threaten her in some strange manner.

Sarah tore herself from him at last in a frenzy near hysterics.

Scrambling wildly for the baby, Sarah felt Peter's tiny arms grasp her neck so tightly she nearly choked. "Rosy!" gasped Sarah above the boisterous melee. "Put your shawl over your head *and come!*"

Adrien wasn't quite quick enough to stop her as Sarah raised a slippered foot and kicked hard against the handle of the door, causing it to snap back against the side of the carriage with a loud crash. He lunged. Tormenting needles of rain invaded the carriage, and Sarah's cloak slipped free in his hands. Before Adrien could reach for her the second time, she had leapt from the door, barely keeping her footing in the mud torrent. The mud sucked around her ankles.

"Are you crazy?" Adrien yelled above the wind as Rosy followed Sarah out the door, gasping. The rain drenched them to the skin in seconds, and Sarah began to run as best she could for the gigantic protection of a huge oak some distance away.

Frightened sounds from the horses rent the air, and their thrashing hooves pawed madly. Jerking about to see how near Adrien was to her, Sarah gasped as the wheels of the carriage slid down the embankment, dragging the screaming animals along. It did not turn on its side, but slid to a halt, sitting at a crazy angle, and imprisoning the horses half on, half off the slippery drive.

Sarah stood for a few seconds, her clothes heavy with freezing rain, weighing her down and burying her feet deeper in the slush. She disbelieved the vision of a large horse and rider, appearing from nowhere.

"Nathaniel!" Her cry pierced the storm and the familiar blue-clad figure dismounted to stride toward her through the thick muck. Sarah attempted to run toward him but nearly lost her footing as her skirts were caught in the mud. Swiftly Nathaniel's eye grasped the situation. How much of the truth he guessed, Sarah had not the faintest idea, understanding by the unflattering oath only that he was displeased with Ronsard. She fell into his arms and huddled Peter and herself against his comforting chest, shivering and crying as Rosy clung to her skirts. Nathaniel hugged her close, bending over her to shield her with his back.

"The tree!" she cried. She pointed toward the oak.

"Not in lightning!" he shouted back. "Where's your coat?"

Sarah shrugged helplessly, remembering it was in the carriage. He peeled off his jacket to place it over her head. "Come on," he motioned to Rosy, who clutched her little knees in fright. Taking Sarah's hand, Nathaniel half dragged her, half carried her to the horse. By some means Sarah found herself mounted and Peter placed sniffling into her arms under the jacket. He tossed Rosy up behind them.

"Keep a tight rein and go to the house," he called at her, drawing the animal away from the other horses.

Adrien stood back, his shoulders braced against the stinging rain, and Sarah caught a glimpse of his eyes. Was it a warning or a request? She did not care. All she wanted was to get out of there. Up ahead the returning team of horses and several men were making their way toward them, heads bowed against the downpour. Nathaniel slapped the rump of his mount to urge him on. He walked a few feet with the horse to see him past the returning team, his large hand resting firmly on Sarah's thigh. Sarah, never so glad to see someone, reached for his hand and held it tightly. Her teeth were chattering uncontrollably.

"Thank you," Sarah mouthed silently as Nathaniel urged the horse away. He chuckled and shook his head at her sorry state, making a kissing motion with his mouth. Sarah wanted to smile at him, his black hair plastered to his head as he stood blinking the water out of his eyes, but she only turned to duck her

172

head farther under his jacket and let the beast carry them to the house.

The household was waiting for them as the large horse made his way to the front steps. They were assisted down by two young men of the stables, and then quickly they were up the steps and bundled into the warm entrance.

"Mrs. Bradley," welcomed a smiling, plump woman dressed in blue. "Don't try to talk now. I'm Margaret Herschell. Patty, bring that folding screen and assist Mrs. Bradley out of these muddy things."

Before Sarah could orient herself to the strange surroundings, she found herself ushered into a make-shift chamber of the folding screen and stripped of the freezing garments. Margaret Herschell slipped into the little fortress and unfolded a blanket warmed at the fire, enfolding Sarah's naked, shivering body in the luscious warmth. Barefoot, her dripping hair hanging in straggly strips down her back, Sarah wished she could hide, but Margaret seemed unconcerned as she led her into the large living room. A great fire blazed, and Sarah curled herself in the readied chair. Margaret wrapped her bare feet in the edge of the blanket, mud and all, and one of the servant girls bound her wet hair in a towel.

"The girls are taking care of the children, Mrs. Bradley. Your son is probably in a warm bath by now. How dreadful for you to arrive under these outlandish circumstances. I'm very sorry. Drink this. It will warm you."

In grateful silence Sarah sipped, the woman giving orders to care for the soaked men at the kitchen entrance. Lounging her head back into the chair, Sarah closed her eyes. What an introduction! She couldn't contain a quick laugh.

"Would you believe I took great care in dressing, Mrs. Herschell?" giggled Sarah, adjusting the towel on her head. Both women chuckled, and a bustling from somewhere behind her told Sarah that Nathaniel and Adrien had arrived.

Margaret bent to pat Sarah's hand reassuringly. "As soon as the children are bathed and settled in the nursery, we'll fix a bath. I'll have Patty tend them until you are comfortable."

Something drew Sarah's eyes to the woman's face. The lips smiled, but no guard shielded those eyes— what pain, what suffering lay in those eyes! Footsteps were nearing, and quickly Sarah reached her hand, without pretense, without hesitation, and Margaret grasped it tightly.

"We'll talk," she whispered, not even as woman to woman, but as one who was losing to one who had lost.

Sarah was of two minds as she watched Nathaniel pass by the wing of her chair—immense gratitude and flagging wrath. His tall frame was fitted into a borrowed pair of cotton pants, not quite long enough, and a plaid flannel shirt. His hair had been combed. The people were gathering before the fire, and Nathaniel dropped to the rug to sit cross-legged before his wife, presenting his broad back to the warmth of the fire. Lifting amused eyes to Sarah, he surveyed her with an unsettling gaze.

"It's been quite some time since you received a scrubbing in my house, Nat Garrett," laughed Senator Herschell as he entered, bearing a tray of spicy toddy. "I think Adrien got about the worst of it. Not used to this good Maryland mud yet. Well, I suspect he'll be down presently."

"What did your new secretary do during the war, George?" Nathaniel moved away from the fire and braced himself in a rather possessive fashion against the leg of Sarah's chair.

"Served in New Orleans, Nat," explained the senator between sips. "One of the Confederates that switched early on in the war. I examined his war record—looked quite good. He came highly recommended by Everett Kenton. You remember him—newspaperman. So far Adrien has performed with exceptional ability. He gets a bee in his bonnet over the Radicals, but," the senator laughed, "I guess he's got company there!"

Nathaniel nodded, smiling. "New Orleans," he repeated, sipping his toddy.

"My husband and I spoke about you at length last evening when he came home, Mrs. Bradley," said Margaret, changing the subject abruptly, smoothing a simple dark brown coiffure.

Margaret was quite attractive, not a beauty like Nathaniel's mother, but the two Herschells were the image of a socially poised and attractive couple. Their secret grief had imbued in them an air of tolerance and depth of character. Nathaniel seemed not the slightest ruffled at the talk of Sarah's taking a post.

"Tell us something about yourself," urged Margaret, as she arose to fetch an ashtray for her husband's cigar.

"Oh dear. Well," Sarah began, noting the hint of humor in the blue gaze of her husband, "most of my teaching has been done in music." Nathaniel straightened to peer at her, quirking a brow at this new piece of knowledge. "I did a smattering of study in mathematics at the university at Richmond when we lived there. Of course, I do have some knowledge of languages, as my late husband was a French teacher. I am afraid, however, that my German is dreadful. And my understanding of political theory leaves something to be desired."

"Perhaps you would play for us before we leave. We have a piano. Not one of the new larger ones, but Patty has done a bit of study on it. However, we have never been able to convince Vance of the necessity of the piano. He knows how to find A to tune that fiddle of his, and that's about it."

"From what I've heard of him, Senator, he just

might take exception at your calling a violin a fiddle. And are you asking me to enter your employ, sir?" She sensed their genuine approval of her, the silent urging deep in Margaret's eyes, and even felt a little excitement. Perhaps this *was* the answer for her—a place to rest, to teach, to think and do some study for herself.

"There was never any question in our minds, from the other day when Sam fished out that telegram from his pocket and said, 'George, I think I've just solved all your problems'. Though you may wish to withhold your decision until you've met our Patty!" the white slash in the black beard appeared again, and Sarah returned the smile with one of her own.

"I doubt that she could frighten me off, Senator. Actually, I'm very pleased, and I . . . I hope I can be the help you need." Suddenly she said, "About the money," lest Nathaniel might begin talking. But the senator anticipated.

"Nathaniel said that's what you'd say! He will tell you about the financial arrangements. I discussed this with him in the kitchen, if you will forgive me, as he said he was handling your affairs—at your insistence —until you were settled. I'm sure you'll be quite satisfied."

Sarah clamped her jaw! As usual, there was no escaping him! Handling her affairs! Meddling was more like it. But it would serve no purpose to pursue the matter now. It was uncanny how he out-maneuvered her at every turn. But his day would come.

During the next hour, the rain stopped, and the sun shone feebly. Sarah had her bath and was offered one of Patty's gowns. It fit fairly well, and after shampooing her hair and brushing it dry, Sarah felt almost normal again.

For a few brief moments she and Margaret were alone, and Sarah had to admire the courage of the woman. Explaining Vance's symptoms, severe weakness upon exertion or mental stress, difficulty in breathing during bad weather, and explaining how to watch his color for signs of trauma, Margaret gave her his medication. Vance despised coddling, and his inability to be like other boys his age only drove him deeper into his music.

Patty, she said, was patient overall but tended to throw it in Vance's face if he brought her a great deal of inconvenience. The doctors offered no hope, not even advising a change of climate. And so they had lived with it, knowing deep in their hearts that it was only a matter of time until Vance himself would know. Margaret didn't cry when she talked of it, and the fact that she didn't even made it sadder, somehow.

"Mrs. Herschell," began Sarah delicately, not quite knowing how to form her question. "I think I understand everything you've told me. I'm sure there is no chance of it happening, or you wouldn't leave Vance, and I certainly wouldn't agree to stay, but . . . if an emergency should arise . . ."

"I don't think it will, Sarah. Vance usually does quite well during the summers. We let him ride—he knows to be careful, and he and Rick Mayer, that's one of the neighboring boys, practically live together. Rick has always had an instinct about Vance. He has watched over Vance since they were quite small, though he doesn't suspect a thing, I am sure."

Margaret left Sarah to finish her dressing, and the meeting of the twins was accomplished before lunch. Patty Herschell was quite taken with Peter, somewhat to the annoyance of Rosy, Sarah suspected. The little black nurse's bottom lip protruded considerably.

"Are you to be our governess?" questioned the attractive and vivacious Patty as Sarah completed dressing in her room.

"Well, I suppose that's what I'm to be, Patty. Do you think I am fierce enough to control that brother of yours?"

177

"Vance is a brat! You and I will have a marvelous time, but we should lock him in the barn with the work oxen. Have you seen your suite yet? You'll love it. It's on the ground floor and has its own little courtyard." The girl's eyes twinkled merrily, and Sarah suspected that she could be quite a little minx if she were so inclined.

"Wait a minute, Peter!" she cried. "I'll be right back. I have just the thing for you."

Sarah rose and surveyed herself. Well, she supposed she was presentable. Patty had hardly been gone for a moment when she reappeared with a small ball of yellow-orange fur in her hands.

"See, Peter, it's a kitten. Can you say 'kitten'?" Peter crowed with delight, promptly crawling under the bed after the wary cat. Assured she would never be missed, Sarah departed to find her way back into the living room. "Kitty . . . kitty" echoed softly behind her.

The senator and his wife were not present, but Adrien had reappeared. Sarah paused long enough in the doorway to sense the hostility bristle between the two men. As usual, politics was the order of conversation.

". . . would have to disagree, Captain Garrett. From what I've seen of the Southern cross section, Northern supremacy is accepted throughout. I've heard it. In fact, I've seen it for myself, sir."

"I would not argue that point, Mr. Ronsard, but slavery has always been only the emotional thorn. The real debate has only been interrupted, not solved."

"And that is?"

"The constitutional rights of the states. Don't you agree?"

"I would not disagree."

"And, Mr. Ronsard, since there are factions within

the North who hold strong positions regarding how the South will be allowed to rejoin the national body, it is my opinion that the South does *not* accept Northern supremacy. To the contrary, I contend that the South is disturbed, and rightly so, concerning the half million new Negro votes."

Adrien shrugged, sipped his drink and turned at the rustle of Sarah's skirts. With the slightest mockery the blond man raised his glass to Nathaniel. "To the survival of the Negro, Captain. May he see it."

Nathaniel frowned but turned his eyes to Sarah and unfolded himself to step toward her. Fingering the tiny lace at her throat Sarah's eyes caught Adrien's over Nathaniel's shoulder.

She should tell Nathaniel what Adrien had done. After all, it had been no light kiss but a strong and demanding one. And besides telling Nathaniel, she really ought to tell George Herschell.

But Sarah had played too many scenes in the many dramas. She was beholden to the Garretts and to the Herschells for helping her find a place to live. Neither of them needed the sort of trouble this would create. Adrien had been outrageous, but she would hold her tongue.

Sarah realized with a start that Nathaniel was talking to her. She forced a smile.

"They tell me that it's taxing the entire staff to restore your garments, madam," he chuckled. He moved closer. "You make me appear to have robbed the cradle in that garb, sweetheart," he murmured under his breath. Adrien discreetly moved himself across the room to study the bookshelves.

"What in the devil were you doing out of the carriage, Sarah?" Nathaniel's gaze flicked suspiciously to the silent Adrien who casually lifted his head from his book and innocently sipped his drink.

But they were interrupted as a short, round man

stepped into the room to announce that lunch was ready. The meal was served informally, and Sarah felt more at home than she had in the formal Garrett household.

When their clothing was brought in shortly after lunch, Sarah could hardly believe the small miracle someone had wrought. In a matter of minutes she and Nathaniel were restored almost to their original appearance. Peter was bedded down for a much-needed nap. And then Vance arrived with apologies for missing lunch.

Vance resembled his father, though taller, and if Sarah had not been told that the two teenagers were twins she would never have guessed. They did not look at all alike except for the black hair. Sarah hoped she wasn't staring, but he was such a *beautiful* boy, with fine, sensitive features. Patty was pretty, but Vance really should have been a girl. Except that he was a little too frail and his eyes were set deeply, giving him a pensive look, Sarah would not have known he was ill. No wonder his parents kept hoping.

Nathaniel shook Vance's hand, and Vance placed his free hand on the larger one, restraining Nathaniel from clapping him on the back. It was a subtle action, and Nathaniel never noticed.

"Well, Vance, you have quite outdone yourself. I should think all the hearts around here have taken quite a start already," the tall man observed as he made a slow circle about the lad, much to the amusement of his father.

"Don't swell his head, Nathaniel," scolded his twin, coming to place an arm through Nathaniel's. "It's several sizes too large already, and he will be quite unbearable in Mother's absence as it is."

"Aren't we going?" interrupted Vance, lifting a black brow to his father.

"This is our new governess, Vance, and mind your

manners. I have already warned her of every nasty habit you have, so watch yourself!" snapped the teasing girl, bouncing her black curls.

"Hello, Vance." Sarah studied the young man before her as he smilingly returned her scrutiny. "I'm Sarah Bradley."

Vance bowed and reached for Sarah's hand and kissed it. A frown darkened Nathaniel's brow as Sarah curtsied slightly, smiling and extricating herself with such charm that the youngster withdrew to admire her from a safe distance. Nathaniel despaired. Good lord! All he needed was another Timothy Davidson to complicate an already delicate situation!

Later, Sarah was cajoled into playing the piano. After an excellent performance admired by everyone, especially Nathaniel, she returned to her seat and said, "Vance, I am eager to hear you play. Would you oblige me?"

The young man looked shyly away from her and said, "Oh, I haven't been working on anything much lately."

"It doesn't matter," protested Sarah, reaching out a hand. "I'll accompany you. Let's select something easy."

Margaret's eyes filled, but no one saw it except George. Conversation buzzed quietly as the two heads bent over a small stack of music. Sarah didn't know her young charge well, and she mentally crossed her fingers that she was not doing the wrong thing. They selected a Haydn sonata, and Sarah watched Vance approach his instrument. She learned more about him in those moments than he would have dreamed possible. The care he took as he lifted the instrument from its velvet nest, placing it in the crook of his arm, and the care he took in tightening the bow—these things revealed his nature.

The fluid wrist, and slender-tipped fingers flying up

and down the scale told her the boy was an artist. It didn't take a genius to see that. Brown eyes darted to Nathaniel's blue ones to see if he saw it too. Nathaniel knew little of music, yet his instincts were uncannily sensitive. Their eyes concurred as Vance bent low over his violin, knee slightly flexed as he tuned with bold strokes.

Who would have thought that a single half hour could change so many things? For Margaret, her poor heart so torn by love and grief, a certain objectivity seeded in her mind. As her son worked with this young woman she saw an individual strength she had been too close to see before.

Nathaniel's pride in Sarah strengthened. And he knew that sweet sadness that touches all who love. It made him want to tell them all, "Don't love her too much. This is *my* Sarah. She is easy to love, but for my sake, don't love her too much."

For a young man Vance played brilliantly, stumbling a bit at intricacies near the end of the movement. Sarah lost him and glanced up to hear "at the triplets again, please." Again, breaking at the same passage, Vance swept the bow upward, letting it fly off the string.

Now it was just the two of them and the music, and Nathaniel sat absorbed, watching his surprising wife at work. Only Patty saw the hungry path of those blue eyes as they watched Sarah rise and go to the boy, touching him here, prodding him at his shoulder.

"You're buried in the chin rest, Vance, and that tenses the hand."

"Do you play?" demanded Vance, irked at himself, edginess creeping into his voice.

"Not a fraction of what you do, Vance, but I know some physics." Sarah slipped an index finger between the neck of the violin and that slender hand. "I'm glad my neck isn't in there," she cajoled. "Now begin at the triplets—don't think of the fingers. Shoulder loose and lift your head."

Vance executed the passage magnificently, finishing with a flourish to laugh at the ceiling in utter delight. Nathaniel was so proud for Sarah and Vance that he couldn't speak. He applauded hard, along with the rest of them. Vance coughed, several times, turning his back, and Sarah stepped quickly to take the instrument, loosening the bow and putting it away. Nothing was said.

Finally, the Herschell departure was made, the guests left, and the remaining household settled down. Nathaniel took his leave, too, but not before seeing Sarah alone.

"Don't you think that it would be proper to leave that door open?" she asked.

"And wreck my image as a rogue? Never. And I won't stay long, just to say goodbye." Sarah whirled.

"Goodbye?"

"I go to Washington tomorrow. Will you miss me?"

"I . . . *Must* you go now?"

Nathaniel grinned. "I thought you would rejoice since you won't have to look at this beastly face of mine for a while. Mother and Father are leaving in the morning, and I have a bit of snooping to do. There's a small war brewing in Congress, and some of the newspapers are printing lurid stories, firing up the radical faction and agitating the South. Some people would like to know where they're getting all this borderline truth they're printing."

"It sounds dangerous. Maybe someone won't like you poking your nose in."

"Everything is dangerous, sweetheart. Living with you is the most dangerous thing *I've* ever done. For one thing, I've been celibate so long I'm probably ruined for life." Sarah swung a haughty palm at him, and Nathaniel caught the weapon, holding it tightly.

"How you can laugh, I can't comprehend. What if Rachel should send some of her bloodhounds up here to Maryland to snoop around?"

"Rachel won't come snooping around. Not this soon. Oh—you'll have to buy your hand back," he teased. Sarah flushed. "I can have you undressed in less than two minutes."

"That's all you think about." Sarah found herself memorizing the way his hair curled on his neck, how long his fingers were, the tiny crinkles at the edge of his eyes. She didn't want him to leave. Face it, Sarah.

"Well, what else *can* I think about, with Vance watching you like a hungry puppy, and that French wretch. I'd like to smear that smile of his—"

"And I suppose Beth is nothing? Fawning over you like she owned you, *wearing* you like some jewel around her neck!"

Nathaniel laughed. "You're jealous, little one."

"I am not!"

"Yes, you are!" Swiftly the play was gone. Cold reality claimed the room. Releasing her, Nathaniel told Sarah how to reach Clarke and where to send a telegram to find him or his parents. Soberly Sarah listened. She would have time, he said, to think. And when he returned, decisions could not be put off any longer.

Sarah knew he wanted her to make a gesture. And what kept her from it? Was she too proud to say the words first—I care about what happens to you. Nathaniel. Why couldn't she just say it?

At last Nathaniel sighed and walked to the door.

"Nathaniel?" Sarah's voice was so small, torn between pride and shame.

Nathaniel turned and stumbled toward her. He was holding her so quickly. Sarah raised her lips to his, and Nathaniel took them, fiercely, ravenously. His fingers found the pins in her hair and dropped them on the floor. Sarah's fingers fumbled at the buttons on his shirt, and with a moan of impatience Nathaniel jerked it free of his pants. Soft hands smoothed his waist, and Nathaniel scooped her up and fell with her to the bed.

"Oh god, I'm hurting for you, Sarah!" he groaned in her ear.

"Not here!" she gasped. "You can't think of it! Not here!" Agile fingers undid the buttons of her tiny basque and pulled loose the ribbons of her chemise, freeing the soft flesh to his caress.

"Nathaniel?" Her fingers closed in his hair, pulling hard until the pain in his head forced him to look up.

"Dammit, don't do that!"

"Stop!"

"No!"

Sarah sobbed a tiny sound, knowing why she must force him to stop when she didn't even want to. "Please, you can't do this here. These people trust me. Please help me. *I* want it too. Please." Nathaniel stilled, his breath coming in hard gasps. Finally he swore and pulled himself up. Running his fingers through his hair, he struggled to clear his head. Forcing a grin, he lowered his eyes to the moist ones blinking up at him.

"Why do you *ever* fight me when it's so good, Sarah? You taste so good and feel so good to me."

"You understand why."

Nathaniel heaved a sigh. "When I return you will find yourself quite at my mercy, madam."

"Really? Do I stand in line to become acquainted with your manly prowess?"

"I'll work you in, don't worry," he retorted. "I didn't force you, you know. See how painless it was to say you wanted me?"

"Are you satisfied?"

"Aside from the fact that you've nearly ruined my masculinity, I guess so. Very satisfied. No! I'm not satisfied. Are you crazy? I'll never be satisfied until you're my wife for real." And he kissed her one last time, thoroughly, before he left.

Sarah sighed. She would miss him. Oh, she would miss that man!

ळ Chapter IX

THE SUMMER OF 1865 moved more slowly for
Sarah and the twins than it did for the rest of the
country. Though newspapers were picked up regularly
in town, along with the faithful weekly letter from
Margaret Herschell, Sarah rarely read the papers. Nathaniel wrote only once, enclosing a brief letter from
John Pollard in behalf of Rachel. Rachel, it seemed,
had set aside a trust for Peter, his when he turned
twenty-one on the condition that he alone would be
the beneficiary. It made Sarah so angry she hardly
glanced at it before cramming it in the trunk and slamming the lid. But it was nice to have Nathaniel's note.

Don't worry, Sarah. We'll send her a broomstick
for Christmas. Kiss Peter for me.
Nathaniel

He didn't have a single personal word for her. At
first Sarah was offended, then she was lonely. Memories about Nathaniel had such a habit of rearranging
themselves.

Sometimes she was angry and it lasted for days. She
grew sentimental and tried to recall each touch, each
kiss, each word. But they were memories, and she
couldn't bring back the feelings.

So she took out the note and held it for awhile.
Then she pressed her lips to the paper where he had
written her name.

The hours spent working with Vance were sheer

joy, their passionate discussions of interpretation, of style and technique, were as wonderful as the talks she'd had with Uncle Gene. Not too many days elapsed before she knew that Vance was suffering a terrible crush on her. She wondered if perhaps she were in over her head. After all, there was not that much difference in their ages, and Vance was a temperamental young man.

In her own way Patty also excelled in the arts, and she began to flourish under the good tutelage. Sarah earned the respect of the twins quickly, and they accepted her authority.

As the sunny days of June lengthened, a letter from the Herschells created a small stir in the household. Vance was the bearer of good tidings, waving the letter teasingly above the head of his frantic twin.

"And what am I bid to hear the contents of this document?"

"You'll have your eyes clawed out for your troubles if you don't hand over that letter!" shrieked Patty. Sarah dropped her books and rushed from the drawing room.

"Vance, stop it this instant!" she commanded.

"As you wish, Mrs. Bradley," replied the handsome boy, bowing. "It is my pleasure to announce a grand ball, my dear ladies. It seems the Garretts are resuming their custom of giving a bash on the Fourth of July."

Patty snatched the letter. Vance stepped before Sarah, lifting her hand to his lips.

"May I have the pleasure of this waltz, madam?" and before Sarah could protest, she felt herself crushed against him as he grinned down at her. With a whirl Vance spun her out into the spacious living room, twirling her in a magnificent pattern across the waxed floor. He was a splendid dancer, even without music, and in spite of the objections just on the tip of her tongue, Sarah laughed in a breathless flurry of billowing skirts.

Then it happened—one arm holding tightly about her waist, knees bending until Sarah was afraid he would fall to the floor. Vance buried his mouth in his sleeve. Sarah held him while hard dry spasms racked his lungs. Patty came quickly.

"Mother's told you and told you!" her voice was strained. She's afraid too, Sarah thought. "Don't fight it! I'll get your medicine!"

Finally it began to subside, and Vance fished about for his handkerchief.

"I won't go . . . to bed. And no medicine. It makes me sleepy." Those dark eyes were teary and bloodshot, and he looked once at Sarah and moaned. "Don't . . . look at me."

"Don't be foolish, Vance. Of course I'll look at you," Sarah kept her arm about his waist and drew him toward the landing. "And you will rest in bed, at least for a little while. Come along now. I'll sit with you for awhile, if you wish."

Though he tried to argue, his breath so short that Sarah found herself trying to breathe for him, Vance finally yielded.

Sarah removed his boots, and Patty helped him get the medicine down. His feet and hands were freezing. How did Margaret stand it? It was all she could do to keep from bursting into tears.

"Patty, you run along and eat your lunch. Set aside a tray for me. I'll sit here for a few minutes, and perhaps Vance can doze off."

Whatever the medication was, it was potent. Soon Vance's body process slowed, his breathing became more stable, and his eyes drooped. He smiled at her.

"Makes me drunk," he drawled, and Sarah reached to take his hand, perching herself on the edge of his bed. Rubbing the slender, artistic hand, Sarah cursed the injustice of it all.

"You remind me of Chopin," Sarah teased softly, watching those red lips curve in a sleepy smile.

"Because I'm dying?"

She gasped, then smiled quickly, maybe too quickly. He couldn't know! He couldn't!

"Vance! What a terrible thing to say. Of course you're not dying, you silly boy!" Dear God, don't let her go to pieces.

Those dark, half-lidded eyes just kept looking at her steadily.

"Figured you different, Sarah," his speech became slurred, and Sarah reached to smooth back the tousled black locks. "Thought you were . . . straight with me." Vance shook his head very slowly. "Don't tell Mother." The eyelids closed.

"Shhh, Vance. It's the medicine talking. You'll be all right. Go to sleep."

Sarah started to withdraw her hand, but he tightened his fingers, and she knew he wasn't yet asleep. So she began talking softly, saying just anything that came to mind. He breathed so slowly!

"You know, Vance, I was looking at one of the compositions you began. You have something very special there. It's not ready to publish yet, of course, but some of your harmonies—they are quite different from anything I've ever heard. Quite lovely. You know, a man's performance may be wonderful, but a man's work—that part of him that he gets down on paper—well, that reaches far beyond."

Sarah paused. She thought he was asleep at last, but his fingers moved in her hand, and she continued, blinking hard so the wretched tears wouldn't come.

"You must finish it, Vance. Don't let anything keep you from it. If I had half your gift I would be so thankful. But I don't. I can help you, though, and maybe that will count."

Now he was so deathly pale, and Sarah moved her hand from his fingers. She had to get out of this room.

Oh, how could this be? One who had so much to give? How *could* this be? The first door she touched opened, and she couldn't hold them back any more. The tears came, and she sank to the floor, holding her breast because it ached so. She didn't make a sound. Nathaniel, please come home. I need you!

During the next days Sarah fell into the same trap which had claimed Margaret so many times over the years. Vance appeared to thrive. In fact, he looked better than he had in weeks, and there were times when Sarah wondered if she had exaggerated it all. But Vance soon began working on his composition, without a word about the long hours he spent at the piano, slaving over it, without any consultation with her about points of theory. And then Sarah knew. Vance did know he was dying. And he never spoke of it. He was protecting his mother.

It was for his sake, Sarah supposed, that she fought herself, forcing gaiety over the upcoming ball. Patty had her own excited plans, and literally dragged Sarah into town with her for a shopping spree. Suffering a terrible attack of conscience at spending some of the funds Nathaniel had arranged for her, Sarah gave in to the infectious spirit. Vance accompanied them, teasing and baiting his twin to exasperation, and watching Sarah with mellowing eyes.

The large brown parcel seemed so innocent sitting on the seat of the carriage, and in all truth it contained only some yards of pink silk, pink satin, and yards and yards of pink scalloped lace. The extravagance of it took her breath. A smaller package contained the daintiest pair of white slippers she had ever seen. Their neat, raised heels and delicate straps across the tops, crisscrossing in the fine meshwork, would set off her new gown to perfection. As the wheels squeaked home the twins and she ceased their chatter to become lost in their thoughts.

The governess would attend the ball. Not only

that, she would surprise Nathaniel and be breathtaking. Perhaps she would even outshine Miss Beth Simms. Silly! She was too old for such fantasies. Still it would ease some of the lonely hours that Nathaniel's absence had created and dull the edge of her grief over Vance.

On an afternoon during the fourth week Patty burst into Sarah's room.

"Mrs. Bradley, it's Nathaniel! Perhaps he's bringing some news from Mother and Daddy. Quickly, let's go see."

Dropping what she was doing, Sarah hastily pushed the dress form with its half-completed gown into the wardrobe and shut the door securely. She and Patty flew to one of the windows in the spacious living room. Sarah's hand trembled in anticipation as she drew the sheer drapery aside.

Nathaniel sat his mount easily, allowing the animal to take a leisured walk up the drive. He was dressed in a brown buckskin shirt and pants, and scuffed work boots. He was bareheaded.

"Ah, Mrs. Bradley, you should set your cap for that man," sighed Patty wistfully, adjusting her crisp pink-and-white checked gown. "Isn't he the most divine thing you've ever seen? I suppose there's not a prayer of a chance for me, but I would have him in a minute. Say!" The mischievous girl whirled upon Sarah, a gleam sparking in her dark eyes. "That's an idea, you know? You're much better suited to him than that awful Beth Simms. I can't stand that show-off. And I think he likes you already. I could tell by the way he looked at you when you played the Chopin piece."

"Patty! I would leave Nathaniel Garrett alone if I were you. He eats little girls alive. Where's Vance, by the way?"

"He's out riding with Rick. He said to tell you he would be especially careful and be in before dark."

Patty resumed her idolization of the man outside as

he swung lithely from his mount, suddenly coming to life in time to dash madly for the front door and snatch it open before Nathaniel had a chance to knock.

"Come in, come in," she cooed coquettishly, slipping her arms around his neck to bestow a resounding smack upon his cheek. Nathaniel closed his surprised arms about the laughing girl and twirled her about, his hungry eyes peering over Patty's head to devour Sarah.

"My! I wish I got that reception everywhere I went," he chuckled, placing Patty lightly from him upon the floor. "And how are you doing, Mrs. Bradley?" His eyes spoke volumes, and Sarah prayed that hers were discreet. She smoothed her forehead.

"Fine, thank you, Mr. Garrett. Or do you still desire Captain Garrett? I'm never quite sure just what to call you," and Sarah's voice feebly dwindled down to a very nervous swallow.

"Nathaniel will do nicely," he grinned, as usual seeming to thrive upon her discomfiture and allowing the uninhibited Patty to drag him to the sofa.

"You will stay for supper, won't you? Please say yes. I have been working on this little Bach piece, and you will be simply overwhelmed by it. You must stay. I'll go tell the cook." Placing her hands on her hips impressively, Patty impatiently awaited his response as if it were only a formality to her imperial wishes. Nathaniel nodded. "Ah-ha! It was the Bach that did it, I'll be bound. Be back in a minute. Oh—and don't you think Mrs. Bradley is looking especially pretty today?" And she swept from the room with her usual flair.

"I really must do something about that girl's manners," vowed Sarah.

" 'Tis wasted effort, love. And, yes, I *do* think Mrs. Bradley is looking especially pretty today," leaning to place a reckless peck on her rosy lips.

"Nathaniel Garrett! Are you trying to get us both in

trouble? Control your lust. How was Washington? What did you do? And how is your father?"

With practiced ease Nathaniel explained the congressional war between the radicals and Andrew Johnson. "President Johnson gives Southern pardons very freely, Sarah, and he even gives them to the landed gentry, though they claim he has a vendetta, which he undoubtedly does. It just doesn't set well to go on bended knees to get pardoned. The radicals would destroy them if they could. There's error on both sides."

"You could have read a newspaper and told me that. Now why don't you tell me why you *really* went to Washington?"

"You don't trust me. *You* think I went to crawl between some lady's thighs? My, but you're a jealous little wench!" Nathaniel sobered. "I'm sorry, sweet. I worry about you and can't believe you'd worry about me." His voice lowered to a whisper. "And if you weren't my wife I wouldn't tell you smut."

"Smut?"

"Political smut. The kind that ruins careers. Half truths in anonymous letters, newspapers. One man even received a letter tied to a brick thrown in his window. We call it the Faceless Scourge."

"We?"

"We—Johnson Cooke and myself, my law practice. For three weeks we cross referenced every voting record for the past six months. The next week we tabulated results."

"And?"

"One common denominator is all we could see. Everyone, every man who has been a smear target has made no public record of how he plans to vote on Trumbull's bill to extend the judicial powers of the Freedmen's Bureau. Already the South sees it as a partisan weapon, and I fear they are not entirely wrong, Sarah."

Sarah turned on the sofa, unconsciously placing her hand on his knee. "Your father, Nathaniel, is he one of these targets?" Nathaniel paused, taking the small hand in his large browner one. The depth of her eyes, the sound of her voice—as always, he wanted to hold her.

"Not really, Sarah," he said. "Only through his secretary, and they don't have anything to use against him unless it's just lies."

"Do you think anyone could possibly . . . find out about us?"

"How?"

"There are ways, surely," and Sarah watched him smooth her wrist, her fingers, and the palm. The callouses were barely visible now.

"I doubt it. Someone started a rumor that Thad Stevens promised the land of all Confederates owning more than two hundred acres would be confiscated and given to the Negroes in January. I don't think that will set too well with Rachel. What do you think?"

"No, it won't. Shhh. Here comes Patty. Give me my hand." In the teasing boldness of a husband he trapped it between his legs. Only with considerable effort could she remove it.

"I want to see Peter. Would you like to go for a ride before dinner?" Nathaniel ventured with a pleased smile.

"I don't have a riding habit. Besides . . . I can't ride sidesaddle."

"Can't ride sidesaddle," Nathaniel choked. *"Every* woman can ride sidesaddle. You're not serious, Sarah? You are serious! Patty, did you know this woman cannot ride sidesaddle and can barely maintain her seat astride a horse?" he accused soberly.

"That's not true and you know it," Sarah protested adamantly. "It's only that Uncle Gene never kept a horse, and the only times I rode were astride. Then down there in Tennessee, I didn't even have a saddle most of the time." She knew exactly what was going through that head—the ride where she had sat crammed between his legs half the night.

"I have culottes. Papa got me some. Oh, let's do go riding! Mrs. Bradley, I'll let you wear the culottes, and I will wear some of Vance's pants. To heck with that habit! May I run tell someone to saddle some horses? Please say yes." Sarah agreed.

"All right, but not for too long. And the first one that laughs at me gets . . . well, I'll think of something," she giggled.

Patty bounded toward the back of the house, and Nathaniel arose, drawing Sarah to her feet. "Where's Peter? I want to take a look at him, nap or not," and Sarah measured the matter-of-fact eyes. No, she was not mistaken—the bond between this man and her son was real. Nathaniel loved him.

The sway of Sarah's hips absorbed Nathaniel's full attention as he followed her through the schoolroom into the Herschell nursery. How long and tedious the days in Washington had become, chasing dead-end rumors and knowing at the end of the day she would not be there to rub his shoulders and talk. Oh, Sarah, habits are so quickly formed and so hard to break. Did you miss me? What would you do if I told you how much I love you?

Nathaniel bent over the sleeping boy, smiling at the slight changes of expression upon his face as he dreamed and reaching a finger to carefully brush a wisp of blond hair out of his eyes.

"He's beautiful. Very much like his mother," he murmured, moving to slip an arm about her waist, breathing her name and drawing her closer and closer.

"Shhh! You'll wake him. And he's liable to pop up and yell you-know-what!" Sarah whispered, detaching herself to brush past Nathaniel into the schoolroom.

"I refuse to apologize for that, my spouse, and I

don't intend to argue. I am Peter's father—he is mine, as are you, and I will see to his needs as I see to yours."

"I see to both our needs. And I don't know whether or not this has occurred to you, Nathaniel, but your parents just might have an opinion about another man's son calling you 'Papa,' regardless of how much they love you. You forget, I only met them once, and they don't even know me."

Nathaniel's eyes widened in mock innocence, and he steepled his fingertips together maddeningly.

"Don't strike that arrogant pose with me, Nathaniel Garrett. I'm trying to tell you something. Your parents have rights. Has it not dawned on you just once that someone beside you has a few rights in this world? You are so used to getting your own way all the time—"

"No, no," holding up a finger, "I don't get my way all the time. I must differ with you on that point." And then he touched his finger to the end of her petulant nose, right in the middle of her tirade. He was so big! She wished he would hug her until her bones cracked.

"Have you seen Beth since you returned?"

"And why do you ask about her every time your control slips a notch, little witch?" Slowly he moved toward her, and Sarah inched away from his deliberate stalking, the quiet sound of that tread reminding her of all the days she had not heard it. She was so vulnerable just now. It seemed that his presence filled the entire room.

"Do you have any idea how bad the nights were in Washington? I kept seeing you in my bed, naked and willing. Like you were. Once."

A large hand reached to take her face in its palm.

"Oh!" she breathed, her mouth a tiny circle as she watched his thick lashes flutter down to the chiseled cheekbones.

"Shhh."

"Patty will be back in a min—" Sarah had no desire to resist, and he smelled faintly of tobacco and leather. The hardness of his chest made her giddy, and as Nathaniel slanted his mouth to taste her deeply, Sarah's eyes closed, her caution fleeing. His cheeks were still slightly chilled, but his mouth was hot on hers. Sarah held him tightly, allowing him to bend her far back over his arm as her skirts spread as a wide fan behind her. They clung to one another until a gentle cough behind them caused Sarah's eyes to widen in horror.

Nathaniel released her slowly. Sarah was so paralyzed she couldn't move. Raising his blue eyes to Patty's mischievous ones, he spoke.

"Well, Patty, I hope there is not too harsh a penalty for getting caught kissing the governess," he chuckled.

Patty giggled. "Oh, it depends on who does the catching, I'd say. Now me, I'm as closemouthed as a mummy. Your secret is safe with me." She handed the culottes to Sarah. "Don't be embarrassed, Mrs. Bradley. I told you he liked you, didn't I? I'm never wrong about these things."

"Patty," choked Sarah. "You are too old for your years."

"Are you two going to have one of those secret romances like I read about in those French novels my sister has? If so, I—"

"Patty," growled Nathaniel as he moved toward the girl. "Are they preparing the horses? And did you tell them not to use sidesaddles?" He loomed over the youngster as sternly as the devil himself, legs astride and arms akimbo.

"Oh. Yes, sir," Patty feigned a ridiculous expression of fear and Sarah groaned.

"Will the two of you please leave this room before I suffer a nervous breakdown?" she wailed. "And don't believe a word the beggar tells you. I will talk to you about this wretched business myself. Understood?" She turned to point a warning finger.

"Sarah," Nathaniel placed a hand over his heart.

"Get out!" Sarah gasped. "Both of you, out!" They retreated in a flurry of Patty's giggles and Nathaniel's feigned grimness, which was broken only by a sly wink as he turned to shut the door. Sarah mouthed a silent obscenity at him as he left. Then she leaned back against the wall. Her heart was still in her throat.

Sarah wondered, as she dressed in the soft grey culottes and the old pullover sweater that carried such memories, about the chances of a man like Nathaniel Garrett truly falling in love with her. Well, she had broken down and asked him a number of things, and had even admitted a few, but that was one question she could never ask him.

Sarah tugged on the little scuffed boots. As she moved, she stumbled, grabbing out to balance herself. Bracing herself for a few moments, she caught her breath. This was the second time today she had experienced this vertigo. Slowly she straightened, eyes straining far out into space as she groped for a chair. How long had it been—her mind raced back over the last weeks. They had married the last day of the war —and about a month later she had killed Giles. That night was over six weeks since her last time.

She was pregnant. The one night had been the time for her to get with child? He would have to be told. But not just yet. She didn't think she could bear just *telling* him, not without some kind of love between them. He wanted her, and the truth was that she wanted him to desire her. She worried about him, she needed him. Yes. But she would never believe he needed her.

Sarah stood before the mirror and surveyed herself. She didn't look any different. She would wait, for just a little while. And if she couldn't make Nathaniel really care for her, really love her, then she would simply tell him anyway and live with it.

As they were getting ready to leave, Vance and his friend rode home. Leading her mount from between wide, swinging doors, Patty caught sight of them.

"Oh, drat! Do we have to take them with us?" she groaned, unaware of the delightful picture she made in her brother's pants and boots.

"Now, Patty, be nice," coaxed Sarah. "If they want to come, they may. Who is the other boy?"

"Rick. You don't know Rick. *I* have known Rick from day one. He has sworn he would marry me from the time he was five and I was three. He is so stubborn! Oh! He drives me crazy!"

With near uncontrollable mirth, Nathaniel's blue eyes met Sarah's, and he coughed loudly, proceeding to lead the horses from the stables. Vance, near enough to give Nathaniel a small salute, smiled broadly, reining and dismounting carefully to shake hands with the towering Nathaniel.

"Welcome back, sir. Have you word from Father?" Wiping an arm across his face, Vance's eyes met Sarah's, and Nathaniel was not ecstatic to note the strong bond between this boy and his wife.

"Everyone will be coming in for the Fourth. How long they will be staying is not decided. You will hear something soon. Would you and Rick enjoy coming with us or have you had enough of the saddle for one afternoon?"

"Oh, no. I'd love it. What about you, Rick?" The sandy-haired youth, sitting mounted with hands loosely crossed across his saddle, nodded. Suspecting that Patty played heavily in his decision, Sarah giggled. Patty swung a trousered leg across her saddle with a flourish. Sarah sighed. So much for decorum.

"Vance, you mustn't overdo," Sarah warned quietly, and again Nathaniel observed the unspoken messages between them. Sarah smiled. She smiled at Vance a lot.

Rick gave a curt nod of acknowledgment to Sarah and Nathaniel, flashing a smile of white teeth. Tawny brows raised in a challenge to Patty.

"Race you to the lake, Miss Smartbritches," his deep voice goaded.

"Perhaps you won't be so pompous when you get beaten by a girl, braggart!" Defiance blazed as she touched the heels of her shiny boots to her mare, and the horse spurted ahead in a spray of damp earth, causing the other animals to start and Rick to wheel his mount sharply in furious pursuit. Sarah laughed to see the girl ride, her black hair flying in the wind as she streaked across the great expanse of turf.

Sarah walked to the side of the horse and patted him firmly as if pleading with the steed to be patient with her.

"The other side, Sarah," Nathaniel suggested.

"What?"

"The other side. Always mount from the left," he grinned.

"Well, what difference does it make?" she glared, embarrassed that Vance stood watching with equal amusement.

"Just be a good girl and do it."

"Shouldn't there be a thing better to hold to? I've seen pictures of saddles that—"

"Those are western saddles. This is an English saddle, and this is the pommel. And you can hold it. Just put your foot in thusly, and see? That's right." Nathaniel spread a large hand under the curve of her buttocks and gave her a hefty assist upward. "Now, are you ready?"

"I could have done it myself," Sarah snapped, tossing a pointed glare at the offending hand. Nestling securely into the saddle, she carefully observed the easy way Nathaniel mounted and held his reins. Copying him exactly, Sarah congratulated herself and followed as Vance led the way out into the long grassy plain.

Gradually the pace quickened, mounting Sarah's alarm, for she had never ridden strenuously.

"Nathaniel, please!" she cried. "I want to stop!"

"Pull back on the reins," he called. "He'll stop."

Well, she knew he was supposed to, she fumed, but would he? Yet, she did as she was told and sure enough, the animal slowed his rhythm, bouncing her a little too suddenly to a halt. It seemed so simple when he did it, and it was simple, except that Sarah didn't release the pull of the bit in Brandy's mouth. And he resisted the bite by jerking his head about, snatching the reins unexpectedly from her hands. In an attempt to catch the escaping reins, Sarah leaned forward in a quick lunge. The flick of the straps against his legs caused Brandy to prance, placing an ill-timed hoof on the reins, resulting in the bit biting even deeper into his mouth. He jerked, and Sarah felt herself lying on the thick grass just beyond his head. The fall didn't hurt her at all, but Sarah reddened, vowing she would strangle Nathaniel. Due to his fine breeding, Brandy instinctively stood as still as a statue as Nathaniel dismounted in one swift movement, and Sarah found herself swept up in a sinewy embrace almost the second she graced the ground. Buckskin rubbed her cheek, and she raised embarrassed eyes to the humorous blue gaze.

"I'm not hurt," she protested furiously, painfully aware of Vance's curious surprise at Nathaniel's reaction.

"I know that," he smiled. "It was just too good an opportunity to get you in my arms. Sweet, sweet, sweet," he murmured under his breath. Standing her up to brush twigs of grass from her clothing and pick dry leaves from her sweater with over-competent fingers, Nathaniel smiled. "Vance, do you think there's any hope for her?"

"Oh, I'll ride with her every day if you think it will help her." Patty and Rick thundered toward them at a dead run, the twin reining up her horse with enviable skill, Sarah thought, and Rick sliding quickly to the ground.

"Who won?" questioned Sarah. Patty threw herself from her mount in a huff.

"Oh, *he* did, *the show-off!*" Irritably stomping about and smoothing at her pants impatiently, Patty's dark eyes narrowed as Rick gave a short laugh and snorted from his bed in the grass.

"She just can't face the reality of the superior sex, that's all," he informed them. Patty gathered a large handful of dry grasses and stepped above the tawny head to rub them between her hands, peppering his face with the debris. Then she turned her back and walked toward Nathaniel and Sarah. They watched as the tall boy arose to spit chaff from his mouth, flicking the grassy bits from his eyes and hair. In two huge strides he was behind Patty, lifting her from the ground and planting a very robust lick across her backside. Patty screamed and wrestled herself free, and Rick sprinted, missing her vicious swing. He out-distanced the raging girl, much to the immense pleasure of her brother.

"A man after my own heart," Vance approved heartily. "She could use a good hiding."

Brooding, Nathaniel watched Vance and Sarah after supper.

"Before I go, Vance, how about something on the violin? I'm rather anxious to see what you've done in my absence."

With something near pain he ambled after them to the drawing room. They shared a world of music he could never enter. Would he not be able to hold Sarah? He, who had brushed women off his arm all his life? He was ten years older than Sarah, and Vance wasn't that much younger than she was. He frowned as Vance bent over her.

Finding a chair, Nathaniel slumped on his spine.

"Brahms wrote this sonata more as a duet between the two instruments than as a solo for the violin." Vance seemed to forget him as Sarah began the sonata with the clear, moody, bell tones of the piano's low notes.

"Marvelous," growled Nathaniel under his breath.

Brahms was a romanticist, and Vance played him that way. He had scarcely begun when Nathaniel saw it happen.

Vance began easily with rich, flowing passion, watching his music, concentrating upon the give and take between the two instruments. The light in the room was soft, and before Nathaniel realized what was happening to him he began to be caught in the spell of the passionate message. Vance turned from the music, his eyes were somewhere far away from that room. He handled his instrument like a gypsy. Brahms grew sad, tormented, weeping with a grief that seemed to encompass the whole world. The slow tears that slid down the boy's cheeks ran into his mouth unheeded. As if reaching to heaven with a low wail of anguish, the bow flowed, powerfully yet delicately. Sarah's head lifted. She almost lost him, so struck was she by the haunting beauty. Nathaniel guessed that even she had not heard him play like this. Never had he heard anything like this.

Suddenly, Vance stopped, in the middle of a passage. "Please excuse me," he choked, bending to place the violin and bow into Sarah's hands. Not understanding, Nathaniel almost spoke to the boy, but Sarah caught his eye and shook her head. Only after they heard his step on the stair did Sarah let out her breath. She began to put Vance's things away without speaking.

Nathaniel hesitated, very much at a loss. "I . . . I don't know what I did," he began, and Sarah raised her tear-filled eyes to him.

"You didn't do anything, Nathaniel," she whispered. "It had nothing to do with you." What was she trying to tell him, for God's sake? That she loved the boy? Hard fingers ran through Nathaniel's hair, and once he started to speak. Finally he just turned, and with deep strides made his way to the front door.

"Rosy, put Peter to bed," Sarah gave her order quietly. "And Patty, I think perhaps you'd best go on to bed, too." Sarah ran after him, her heart near to bursting. She should never have come to this house. She couldn't take that boy's suffering, and she surely couldn't cope with the pain that had swept across her husband's face.

Nathaniel heard her behind him, and Sarah couldn't quite hear what he said.

"What?"

Spinning on his heel harshly, Nathaniel spat his words. "I said, how long are we going to play this damnable game, Sarah? I can't touch you when I want. I leave you when I don't want. I rarely get to see Peter. And I'm weary of guarding my every word and watching Vance pine away with love for you."

Roughly, he pulled Sarah into his arms. "I sit and watch you from afar, denying all my needs. Madam, I'm stretched about as tightly on this torture rack as I can stand!" Biting fingers jerked her to him, crushing her limp body. Placing a swift, hard kiss on her mouth, he set her free. Sarah groped against the door as he left. Hot, brimming tears filled her eyes, and when she closed them, the tears spilled. Nathaniel's steps quickly faded.

The clock chimed eleven, and then twelve, and still she wandered the halls. Upstairs and down she roamed, checking each room, pausing in Vance's doorway to listen to the labored, shallow breaths. Why did life turn upon itself, taking its finest even before it could blossom fully? She didn't understand.

Wearily Sarah moved about in her darkened chamber until she found her cloak. Pulling the latch and opening her door, she stepped into the small courtyard, the stone cold under her bare feet. The sky drooped, heavy with stars, and she squinted to make them out. But salty tears kept filling her eyes and spilling to her bosom. Oh, Nathaniel, Nathaniel! I must surely love you because I have never been so miserable!

Sarah stumbled, stubbing her foot painfully against the stone bench at the edge of the arbor. She dropped down upon the dew-moistened bench and wept bitterly. Finally, sobbing until she was exhausted, Sarah drew her chilled legs up under herself and huddled into a tiny knot on the hard stone. Fragments of tortured sleep attempted to smother her grief, and she was halfway between sleeping and waking when she heard him whisper her name. With great effort she forced her burning eyes open to find Nathaniel on one knee, his dark head almost touching her own.

"Sarah, love." Nathaniel touched her tear-stained cheek timidly, his voice heavy with compassion. "Sarah, I had to see you."

As a tender vine lifts delicate tendrils to cling to the towering strength of a mighty oak, her slender arms reached to twine about his neck and a small sound of gladness burst from her lips. She happily breathed the familiar scent of him as his arms lifted her. She held tightly as, without a sound, Nathaniel slipped through the still night with his precious burden, silently closing the door with his foot and shutting out the world for a space of time.

"Haven't you slept at all, love?" Nathaniel noted the unmade bed.

Sarah shook her head. "I was too miserable." With great care Nathaniel lowered her to the bed and drew himself up beside her, still holding her. He breathed the delicate fragrance of her hair, the sweetness of her breath, the fresh scent of her skin. He doubted that anything in this life would ever be as sweet to him as those teary eyes blinking up at him.

"What's the matter, Sarah?"

Sarah's arms tightened around him, and her voice trembled. "I didn't want you to go. Why were you so angry? I can't take any more. You've won, Nathaniel. I want to be your wife. I really do, and I don't know where to begin—things are so complicated. I just want you, and I don't want you to leave angry like that again."

He searched her face soberly.

"Don't you believe me?"

Nathaniel reached to smooth her hair. "I think I've waited forever just to hear you say that much, little one."

In the past Nathaniel had cared for her. He had fought Rachel for her. But it had been the repayment of a debt he owed her.

Now there was no debt. He had come because he wanted to. Her life had a center now. She loved him, and her mind closed upon her love like a tight fist. She didn't want to lose it.

After a long silence, he spoke again. "We didn't grow into this marriage, Sarah, like people do. And there is much besides ourselves to consider. But it will be a good marriage. You'll see."

Sarah snuggled in his arms and clutched him tightly. He hadn't said the words, but somehow it didn't matter quite as much. "There are things I fear," she whispered. "I'm afraid for you to be here. I'm afraid for your parents to know we're married. I think of Peter, and I think of Charles and the bitter thoughts I had for him when he left me. I hardly know what to think sometimes. I just know that it hurts to see you go. And perhaps that's just a scar from when Charles left. I don't want to hurt you, Nathaniel, and maybe I'm hurting you right now, just by wanting you. I could be, and I wouldn't even know."

"You can't hurt me. Only if you turn away from me. You're my wife, and I have a right to be here with you, even in this house." Nathaniel grinned.

For the first time Sarah didn't fight him, still a little shy in her desire. She knelt on the bed and lifted her arms as Nathaniel drew the gown over her head, her hair tumbling back down to frame the milky softness of her shoulders and arms. He stood before her, fully clothed, and she felt him tremble as he reached to smooth her arms, pausing to nestle her breasts in the palms of his hands. So gently his arms slipped around her back, and his breath was hot as he lowered his mouth to hers. His lips opened to claim her, and impatiently Sarah returned his kiss with demanding lips. He felt her impatience, but he would not be rushed, and only when she was collapsing against him did Nathaniel relinquish her mouth.

"Wine like this must be savored, sweetheart," he assured her, releasing her to pull off his boots.

He peeled his shirt over his head, and Sarah sat back to watch the play of his shoulders as he tossed it to the floor. A little amazed at her own boldness, she drew herself nearer to wrap her arms about his neck, molding her body to his back. Sarah caught her breath and lowered her fingers to bury in the soft mat on his chest. Nathaniel didn't move, and in the still room the rough edge of his breathing urged her fingers to smooth the muscles in his arms and thread themselves through the hair at the back of his neck.

"How old are you, Nathaniel?" she bent to whisper in his ear, brushing the line of his jaw with warm, open lips.

As she began to move away Nathaniel grabbed her arms, pinning them about him. "Thirty-one," he moaned. "Don't stop," turning in her embrace to search for her mouth. His neck was hot, and Sarah freed her hands to cradle his head, letting him open her mouth again and drink the sweetness of her. She flushed, a blistering hotness spreading through her as those slender fingers buried into her satin buttocks.

"Sweet, sweet Sarah," he whispered. "I love the way you smell, I love the way you taste, the way you look."

It was the nearest Nathaniel had ever come to declaring his love for her, and together with her own new realizations, it proved a powerful stimulus. She hugged his waist. Softly her fingers followed the old scar down into the waist of his pants, and then she hesitated, fingers trembling a bit as she felt for the buttons at his waist. Nathaniel stood stone still as his little wife ventured, testing an infant confidence, seeing just how far she would go to claim him.

Sarah's lips pleaded with Nathaniel to take her as she leaned against his waist, kissing the blistering flesh with tiny little moans, her hands so gentle as she explored the way he was made.

"Oh, Sarah," he breathed, catching handfuls of her hair. They tumbled, Nathaniel drawing her full length on top of him. He took her mouth again, this time not gently, experienced hands finding, caressing, and arousing every secret she had. When at last he slipped between her silky legs, Sarah was too drunk to deny him anything. For a second she felt she couldn't bear the exquisite tightness of it, and Nathaniel stopped, buried within her.

"Sweetheart?" and she arched against him, silently asking. Nathaniel moved slowly, touching deeply, yet giving her the time she needed. Sarah reached, accepted, taking him as close into her as a man can go, even into the recesses of her soul. She would never be the same. He was a part of her body now, and would always be. Their taut guest finished, and Nathaniel bent to bury his face in her hair.

They slept, and Sarah didn't rouse until a small sound from Peter reached through her slumber. Nathaniel was up, pulling on his pants before she could stir.

"What's the matter?" she raised on an elbow to peer through drowsy eyes.

"He's dreaming."

Dropping to the bed again, he grinned. "Sleepy?"

"Mmmm," Sarah burrowed her cheek into the pillow and gazed across the bed at him. Languidly she memorized the curve of his brows, the line of his nose, the small crevice below as it shaped his upper lip.

"Sarah, love," he moved his hand to search for the swell of her bosom, "tomorrow I want you to pack the things you need for yourself and Peter. I'm taking you back to Washington with me. No, no. I will handle everything with my parents. I promise you things will be pleasant."

"Oh, Nathaniel," she sighed, "I can't go back to Washington with—"

"What do you mean, *'you can't'?*" his voice was sharper than she would have liked.

"I have committed myself here, until the Herschells return."

"Well, that's simple enough, love. I'll un-commit you. Margaret and George'll understand. The twins may have to go to Washington with us, but it won't be a disaster for them to spend a few weeks in town with their parents. It won't hurt them nearly as much as it will hurt me to keep denying myself my wife."

Sarah sighed. "You don't understand." How could she explain? She had to keep Vance's secret.

"Vance isn't well, Nathaniel. He needs to be here, and I just can't walk out after I gave my word."

Nathaniel swung his legs to the floor, his broad back to her, and he braced his hands on his knees, pondering. Abruptly he stood.

"You gave your word before a man of God, too, if you remember. You're my wife. I need you with me." He wasn't about to compromise, she could see that. Marital bliss had burst so quickly. Sitting up, snatching the sheet free of its moorings and wrapping it securely under her arms, Sarah groped for a way to stop the impending battle.

"I can't," Sarah muttered lamely, and the silence roiled, Nathaniel just standing there as the glittering in his eyes intensified. With that catlike suddenness he possessed, Nathaniel moved, and Sarah knew him well enough by now to dodge, slipping from the bed in a trailing flurry of white sheet. But he was too swift, whirling her about and biting into her arms until she stood still.

"Are you being unfaithful to me, little wife? Is that it? Can't you pull yourself from the arms of your young lover?" Sarah's look of shock didn't stop him. "And don't deny it. It's obvious when you two are together. How can you *do* this to me after what happened between us tonight? You claim—"

"Oh, shut up, Nathaniel! You're talking like a madman!"

Sarah struggled, wrenching herself from his fingers

only to be caught in his embrace which crushed her hard against him.

"I'm jealous of a boy," he growled. "Does that please you, pretty one?"

"For God's sake!" Sarah cried, tears damming behind her eyes. How could the father of the child in her womb be saying these horrible things? Didn't he care at all?

"You don't deny it, Sarah," his voice grated. Why was he hurting her like this? Why? "You don't deny it," he repeated, and he moved so fast that she was nearly jerked off her feet. "You are mine!" He bent his mouth, but Sarah twisted away.

"You refuse to take my word for this? I *promised* I'd take care of him. I promised his parents." Sarah tried not to say it, but she had to. "Oh, can't you see it, Nathaniel? The boy is dying!"

Sarah clamped both hands over her mouth, grief still drawing her features. Nathaniel blanched so pale that she could see it even in the near-darkness. He froze.

She must have stood there for three or four minutes before Nathaniel spoke.

"Can you forgive me, Sarah?" he whispered. "I had no right to . . ."

With the understanding of new-found love, Sarah reached to smooth back his hair. "There's nothing to forgive. I was supposed to keep this a secret, but I should have told you."

Nathaniel took her in his arms. They talked for a long time, Sarah telling him everything, and Nathaniel agreed to continue with their present arrangement, sad though it made him.

And so they comforted one another as best they could, holding each other quietly until it was time for him to go.

"Do I make you happy, Nathaniel?" How she wished he would say the words that would make her totally happy. But he didn't know what she was longing for, and so he kissed her, gazing deeply into the beloved brown eyes.

"Only until I think I may die," he said.

ℰ𝒳 *Chapter X*

ADRIEN RONSARD was late. Already darkness had necessitated the lighting of one oil lamp and a few candles in the spacious drawing room. The chandelier hung, long unused, and the hardwood floor was pock-marked by horses' hoofs.

Adrien had met several of the twenty or so men before, and in this very house. Dalton Evans, a North Carolina planter with the heavy jowls of a bulldog and a crude tongue as well, could always come up with money. Like John Pollard, from Charleston, given to affectations but with a mind of steel. Tennessee's John Burdette, and Georgia's Seton Haarom with Cleve Schrevers from Mississippi were also present.

Adrien climbed the steps, carrying with him a report, financial and detailed to the penny. These men weren't playing ante-up with matchsticks. They wanted to know how he had been spending their money. Once they saw the report, it would be destroyed. It could put any one of them behind bars.

"You're late, Mr. Ronsard," informed Dalton Evans, the heavy folds of skin quivering as he turned to see Adrien slip into a once-beautiful emerald velvet chair. The long table before Evans had seen better days too, having been repaired so poorly that the mending was almost as bad as the broken legs.

"The road needs a heavier guard, Mr. Evans. And one of my men brought news of Representative Pritchard's daughter. Since I have waited four weeks for this news, I stayed to take it. Thank you," and Adrien accepted a glass of spirits from the slow-moving black man who, very properly, kept his eyes to the floor. Adrien barely touched it, however, for much liquor made him ill.

"Was it of any value, man?" questioned a face he had not seen before. Adrien didn't like new faces.

"William Nansen, Mr. Ronsard. I'll vouch for him," mumbled John Pollard. Adrien inclined his head.

"*I* thought it was, Mr. Nansen. The congressman's daughter went to Spain very much with child and returned three months later, this past week to be exact —no child and un-pregnant."

Dalton laughed, and his jowls shook. "Well done, Ronsard, well done! Gentlemen, I'd ventuh to say, theah's a vote we can count on!"

Dalton Evans owned 1265 acres of burned North Carolina farmland, and his objections to the rumor of it being divided into 40-acre plots put him in the frame of mind to do *anything* necessary to fight the radical faction in Washington. Organized terror was the most effective weapon he had.

The men indulged themselves briefly to heap profanities on the head of Thaddeus Stevens and supporters, and Adrien wished they would get on with it. He could understand why men like John Pollard, backed by thousands of acres of Southern soil, were angry. But as he owned not a square inch himself, Adrien was eager to get to his particular assignment —purchased votes.

"As I see't, Mr. Evans," Seton Haarom, a small, red-faced man interjected, "the fifteen propertied whites I represent kin suhvive with forty acres and a mule. Anythin' 'cept the coluhed vote, if that goes Republican. Why, th' blasted Bureau has such a leash on th' coluheds of Georgia that they'll vote any way they're told, to git that gover'ment handout. An' gentlemen, if th' Trumbull bill passes Congress you might as well blow ev'ry votin' white cleah to hell for all th' good he kin do. All a nigger'll have t'do is make a complaint, an' the whole damn South'll end up behind bahs."

"The president will veto," forecast the deep voice of John Pollard.

"How kin you be shuah?"

"The Trumbull bill is unconstitutional, granting that the Bureau agent may arrest, try, and sentence a white man entirely by himself. Every man is guaranteed redress to a court of higher appeals. Guaranteed by the Constitution. Any thinking man would veto."

The blond head of Adrien Ronsard raised, and the slender man steepled his fingers. "It won't do him any good to veto," he predicted. "The votes I see will overrule any presidential veto. I count only eight votes sitting on the fence, and only if every one voted against th' Trumbull bill would it fail to pass Congress."

"Well, that's your job, Ronsard. We pay you to get the dissenting vote. If it's more money you need, we'll get it, but *stop that bill!* Whatever it takes! Damn politicians. The present Freedmen's Bureau has a year to go yet."

John Burdette chewed on the end of his cigar. "I move we hear what Mr. Ronsard has been doin' with our money before we go any further. If it's goin' to be as close as he says, mebbe we oughta get a little rougher."

"Mr. Burdette, with all due respect, sir, some of those men won't budge easily. A small percentage will not bend to terror at all, no matter what the threat is."

"Any man can be bought, Frenchie. Didn't we almost buy the whole gol-durne country of France for Southern cotton and Maximillian before the end? If you got what they want, they'll buy. And no man wants a public scandal. It's a matter of gettin' enough dirt in one place to grow a pepper, Frenchie. See?"

John Pollard remained silent, and Adrien felt those serpentine eyes on him.

"What names do you consider the most unbuyable, Mr. Ronsard?"

Adrien answered quickly, positively. "Stevens, Fessenden, Mason, Herschell, Black, Garrett, and Rawll."

"Garrett? Maine?"

"Maryland. Samuel Garrett."

The meeting broke up two hours later, none of its participants wishing to linger. Adrien was in a hurry —needing to return to Washington for another meeting before dawn.

"Mr. Ronsard, a word with you, please," John Pollard followed Adrien down the wide steps into the black Virginia night.

"I am somewhat pressed for time, Mr. Pollard," clipped Adrien.

"I always come straight to the point, sir. This Garrett—tell me about him." Adrien narrowed his eyes and tried to read the mask over Pollard's face. He couldn't: Pollard's face was quite devoid of emotion. Adrien fell into step with the smooth stride, allowing his arm to brush Pollard's. This man was strong, ruthless, and Adrien admired strong men. Few were stronger than he.

"Late fifties, well-bred wife, two sons—one a doctor, one a lawyer."

"The sons?"

"Nathaniel, the oldest, and Clarke."

"I *knew* it must be the same! I have had dealings with Nathaniel Garrett. On behalf of a client. What do you know of him?"

John Pollard's eyes rested at length upon the French-American, and Adrien returned the stare, slowly assessing the build, the clothes, the eyes.

"Distinguished Union officer. He's resuming a law practice. He and a man share one near the Capitol. Wealthy, of course. He may be playing with some Tennessee woman."

Pollard laughed. "Sarah Garrett."

"Sarah Bradley? Is that who you mean?"

"Sarah *Bradley?*"

"I think you better tell me everything you know about this Sarah." Adrien told what he knew, and both agreed to keep this new development strictly between them. After all, this might be of monetary value to a man personally, as well as politically.

John Pollard withdrew a slip of paper from the inside pocket of his jacket.

"Here is where I can be located in Charleston, Adrien. Contact me," and the cold eyes measured carefully.

Adrien hesitated and took the proffered paper. The men nodded to one another, then parted without another word.

The calendar read one week before the Garrett ball when the Herschell dining table sat an unexpected guest for the noon meal. Adrien Ronsard appeared out of the blue with news from George and Margaret.

Several families, it seemed, were to be guests at the Herschell estate, as the Garrett mansion could not possibly hope to house all the guests. Adrien had instructions to prepare the kitchens, open the guest rooms for airing, cleaning and a change of linens. Four families were coming, and the twins were ecstatic.

Mid-afternoon, Adrien invited her for a stroll along the stream which bordered the property. What could she do but go along?

"Mrs. Bradley," began Adrien, having the decency to blush, "about that unfortunate occurrence between us in the carriage. Really, I didn't dream it would lead

218

to the dreadful results it did. You must assure me that
you have forgiven me for my outrageous behavior."

Adrien stuffed his hands into the pockets of his blue
linen suit and Sarah drew her shawl a bit closer,
watching his stride, the manner in which he squinted
into the sun. His face was smiling, and his voice was
apparently genuine, but something in his eyes disturbed her. Perhaps she was imagining things.

"Mr. Ronsard."

"Adrien," he smiled. He really was quite handsome
when he smiled. Sarah smiled back.

"All right," she shook her head, "perhaps it's best
that we start all over. I really was quite furious,
though. You know that, don't you?"

"I don't blame you. Thank you for just letting it go.
You could say a lot more." Pausing, Adrien turned,
lifting her hand to his lips in an overly polite manner.
Was it insolence? Sarah questioned her judgment in accepting his apology. Was Adrien playing some clever
game with her? And if he was, then what for?

They strolled quietly. Sarah paused once to snap a
wild flower from a carpet of soft, crushed leaves.
Adrien plied her with questions about her past, some
of which she answered, some of which she avoided.
Drawing Adrien out to speak of himself proved impossible. Why was he so secretive? In answer to one of
his questions, she replied, "I learned of opportunities
to make a living near the capital. That's why I settled
here. And I don't look upon myself as a deserting
Southerner, either, if that's what you're implying."

"Oh, no," his voice slipped into a tightly controlled
impatience. "I was just wondering if your shooting of
that man in Virginia had anything to do with your decision to come here."

Adrien's words fell quietly. Sarah went ice cold from
head to toe. The indefinable look in Adrien's eyes became obvious. Unerringly, she read danger in that face.

As the notion entered Sarah's mind to turn and run,

he read her thoughts. His body readied itself, coiling for the strike.

"Don't try it, my dear," he cautioned softly. "You wouldn't get six feet."

She lifted a cold, trembling hand to her lips to keep from screaming.

"Don't scream or throw a fit, Sarah," Adrien's voice slurred into quiet sarcasm. "Don't do any of those little things women are so fond of doing. And in case you entertain thoughts of escape, I wish you to understand that I could kill you now without even quickening my pulse. I have done it, and with little provocation. You had best heed me."

His smile was not a smile at all, but the drawing aside of his lips. His eyes remained sinister. Sarah jerked her head back, her memory of that night returning.

"You were there, weren't you? It was you who picked me up. I remember now! To my right, in the darkness. You were with a woman. I remember her. But then, you must *know* I did not shoot the man because I wanted to. It was to save Captain Garrett's life. Why are you—"

"Don't question me, Sarah. I will tell you only what is necessary for you to know. I have a message for you. The society with which you are now mingling has much influence. Certain people wish to approach you for your . . . services."

He waited as a cat will wait, poised for the kill. But she was entirely at a loss.

"I'm sorry, Adrien, I don't understand you."

"This is politics. What we need is information. You were not the first consideration, but since you are in such an advantageous position, it was decided to approach you. Our point of leverage will be, of course, that if you decline, your being a murderess will be exploited to its fullest. That would bring no small embarrassment to you, to say nothing of the scandal Senator Garrett would find himself in—his son being involved with a murderess."

"What kind of information would you want me to give you, Mr. Ronsard?"

"You agree to cooperate?" Sarah knew he was testing her.

"I would have to be assured that no harm would come to the Garrett name or family before I would even consider it."

Adrien stirred and began to walk, his steps small, whispering in the leaves.

"Certain people in the South," he began warily, choosing his words with care, pausing every few seconds to study her eyes, her coloring. "Certain people in the South stand to lose a great deal from the Johnson administration. It is necessary to influence certain votes in key areas. Do you understand?"

"Yes," replied Sarah, facing him squarely. She knew she must take her chances with the truth.

"Mr. Ronsard, you know already that I must decline. I could not inform on Senator Garrett."

"That doesn't surprise me, madam," Adrien agreed flatly. "We'll reach the Senator another way. I don't want some hostile woman botching things up. And you, madam, will keep your mouth *shut!* If you cross me, if you report this conversation to anyone, you will pay. I will not warn you a second time. Nothing you do from this moment on will escape me. Nothing. If you do not possess the good sense to leave this place, then you will be watched constantly until our purpose here is accomplished."

Sarah made one attempt to reach Adrien by reason. "Mr. Ronsard, do you really feel this is the best way to approach the problem? The risk you run in even asking me a question like this is of greater importance than anything you could learn from me."

Adrien laughed.

"Oh, Sarah, you are no threat to me." Sarah stepped

back as he moved to tower above her. "Do you have any idea how easy it is to break a woman's neck, Sarah?"

Her skin began to crawl, but she forced herself to look him in the eye. His slender fingers were warm and steady as they fitted themselves securely about her neck near the top of her spine with one hand and tightly underneath the base of her skull with the other hand.

"What you do, Sarah, is to place these fingers here, and apply a little pressure here." Sarah moaned. Had she lived through the war only to die like this? Should she beg him?

"Then, you see, a pressing of the thumbs, a hard snap of the elbow, and it's done. And what would become of your son after they buried you? Why, he might also meet with an unfortunate end." His fingers tightened until she felt her windpipe crushing. Oblivion's black curtain crept from the sides of her vision, and her face grew thick and hot. Peter, *Peter!*

Adrien released her, dropping her to the ground. Sarah held her own hands about her bruised neck, her lungs battling. The tears came streaming down her face. Cruel fingers crushed the top of her skull.

"Women," he breathed, "are the spawn of the devil. I could redeem you, you know. It is within my power to do that if you serve me. I offer you . . . destiny. Destiny! If you want it, and I rarely offer. I offered it to you once before, in the carriage, and you refused me. You see, my mission is above this petty war between mere mortals." He intoned again, "This is your last chance to serve me, Sarah."

Adrien read abhorrence in her eyes.

"Refuse me then." With a bitter laugh he turned her head to his leg, burying her face against the inside of his thigh in an obscene gesture. Sarah fought his hand with both of hers, but he held her face trapped just below his groin. Then he jerked her up, snapping her head backwards and forcing her to stand.

"I could force you, Sarah," he laughed. "You would serve me in ways you have not dreamed of. As the others serve me. But I choose to spare you." Sarah shivered. "Now, let us finish our pleasant walk back to the house. You need a few moments to compose yourself before you resume your position as sweet-tempered governess." Again, the laugh.

Fear for her own life and Peter's took hold again between alternate passions of terror and hatred. Suddenly the Herschell lawn spread before her. *She must just get away!* Objectivity assured her that even if he was insane, he wouldn't kill her here. Reason could defeat madness if only she could control her own hysteria.

"If you've been spending the last moments devising ways to thwart me, madam," Adrien warned softly, a cruel hand grasping her elbow, "spare yourself the trouble. I will brook no bothersome interference by an amateur."

Sarah gasped, pain clouding her eyes, her knees beginning to bend. "I will obey," she moaned weakly, biting her lips to keep from crying out. Abruptly he released her.

He nodded then, indicating that she could go inside.

Rosy was dressing Peter after his nap as Sarah entered her rooms, panting wildly. Glancing up as Sarah entered, Rosy stared with wide, shocked eyes as Sarah closed the door and moved quickly to the mirror. The glass revealed marks about her throat which were becoming purple.

Sarah sank into a chair, motioning to Rosy with one hand and supporting her toddler with the other.

"Rosy," her hoarse voice was somewhat difficult in coming, "how old are you now? Thirteen?"

"Yassum," the little nursemaid continued to stare at Sarah's neck in dumb amazement.

"Rosy, I'm about to ask something of you that requires a very mature young woman."

As Sarah caught her breath and began her explanation, she held the small black hand in her own.

"Rosy, there is trouble in the house. Please, child, I can't explain. All I want you to do is to deliver a message for me, but it must be done in a very special way. Do you think you could do that?" This was an awful lot to ask of a thirteen-year-old child. Sarah straightened her back.

"I want you to get a message to Patty. But you must not take it to her room upstairs. You must wait until you see her downstairs, for Mr. Ronsard will undoubtedly be watching you." Rosy's eyes widened. "Yes, Mr. Ronsard did this to me. You see," she paused, "he isn't well, Rosy. In his mind, he is very sick."

"He's crazy," the black girl stated flatly, and Sarah smiled bitterly.

"Yes, Rosy, he's crazy. And he wouldn't hesitate to hurt a little girl. So you must do as I tell you. All right?"

Rosy smiled broadly at Sarah, nodding her kinky, black head. "Oh, yassum. I know what to do, Miz Sarah." She lifted her head proudly, and Sarah stared. "I knows how to ac' 'roun white men, Miz Sarah. Long time ago Mama done showed me how. She eben showed my sistuh how to ac' lak she crazy, so th' white mens'd leave 'er alone. Dey won' git ya if they thinks ya got th' debil in ya. I's a little bitty gal when Mama showed me how. I kin do it, Miz Sarah."

"Oh, merciful heavens, Rosy!" the angry tears brimmed in Sarah's eyes as she crushed the black girl to her breast. "Now, Rosy, wait until Patty comes down to get a drink of water or something. You'll know when. Just hang around the kitchen and stay out of the way until you see her, no matter how long it takes. Mr. Ronsard probably will not wait around too long watching you if you just help out with little things. Do you understand?" Rosy nodded thoughtfully. "Tell her very casually that she left her music in my room and that I would like for her to come get it as soon as she can."

"I kin do that, Miz Sarah. Is that all?"

"That's all, Rosy. Now I want you to help me change clothes so I can come down for supper as usual. It's very important that Mr. Ronsard does not become upset in *any way,* dear. Now, help me find a dress to cover these marks."

Once she was dressed and Rosy had gone, Sarah waited. And waited. Finally a tap sounded at the door, and a thousand icy pricks stung her from her scalp down to her toes. Sarah called "Yes, come in," but the door opened easily to admit Patty. Sarah watched, unable to speak, experiencing grave misgivings at the wisdom of drawing Patty into this. Patty's astute eyes guessed swiftly that something was amiss. Her manner sobered, and the smiling lips slackened.

Plunging headfirst into her ordeal, Sarah began. "Sit down quickly, Patty. You mustn't remain here long."

"Don't talk for a few minutes, please, Patty. I'll explain as rapidly as I can, and then we must go into the drawing room for your music lesson."

"I was . . . I don't know how to say it . . . accosted by Mr. Ronsard, Patty, this afternoon. He has threatened to kill me. I don't know why. No, don't interrupt. We're going to walk *very calmly* into the drawing room and shut the French doors for a piano lesson. He will be watching us, and under no circumstances must you show any surprise at what I tell you during our so-called piano lesson. No surprise. Do you think you can do that, Patty?"

"Mrs. Bradley," began Patty, "I'm sorry, but what you are saying makes no sense to me." Frantically Sarah stepped forward to hold the stunned girl by the shoulders.

"I'm desperate, Patty!" Sarah choked, fear in her eyes. "You *must* help me! The man is mad. You could be in danger too, child. Look!"

Sarah fumbled at her gown. With shaking hands she clutched open the gown, baring the bruises about her throat. Patty gasped, drawing her hand to her own bare neck. She couldn't make a sound and only stood shaking her head, her mouth agape.

Having at least convinced Patty of the gravity of their plight, Sarah rebuttoned her gown impatiently.

"Mr. Ronsard is insane. Now, do you think we could gather your music and walk *serenely* to the drawing room without arousing any suspicion? The man is as clever as a serpent, and he will detect the slightest error from either of us."

The girl's dark eyes hardened, and an air of composure squared her shoulders.

"I don't understand, Mrs. Bradley," Patty assured her, "but I do trust you. And you are correct. I will be absolutely stunning." The girl gave a deep curtsey, and Sarah could not but smile at the reckless nerve of the young. Patty sobered. "I wonder what Daddy will do when he finds out about this?"

"We will leave that for another time," Sarah admonished gently. "Don't overact, now. He's too clever for that."

The music was gathered, and Sarah made a quick assessment of the two of them. Stepping to the door and opening it firmly, Sarah strode into the hallway and called for Rosy. The nursemaid appeared, receiving a quick pat of approval from her mistress.

"Just talk, Patty, just talk. I will do the rest." Seated in the front room, pretending to read, Adrien observed, as Sarah had known he would. He lifted his head as the two women made their way tranquilly to the drawing room. Sarah met his eyes with a look of bitter hatred, guessing that he would expect it, and his smirk satisfied her. Patty chattered aimlessly, on and on,

Sarah drew the double French doors shut. Not at all surprised, Sarah observed Adrien rise to make his way to the tall bookcase directly in their line of vision. He seated himself some distance from them. Sarah was aware that though he could see their every move, he could not hear what they said.

"Begin with the Mozart Sonata, Patty, and listen very carefully as I talk to you. Play through a few measures rather badly, and then we may talk a few moments without looking out of place."

Obediently, Patty complied. Pulling her chair near the girl, and turning her back to Adrien, Sarah began.

"The first thing you must know, Patty, will be a surprise, so please keep a straight face. You see . . . Nathaniel . . . is my husband. Shhh." Absently Sarah pointed at the page of music before her, playing a few notes herself to give Patty a chance to compose herself.

"I can't believe this, Mrs. Bradley. I mean, kissing the governess, indeed. Grief and hemlock! Well, that explains a lot. Why the secret, pray tell, and does anyone know besides me?"

"You are the only one. Now, prepare for another shock." Sarah breathed deeply. "By some freakish accident that I can't explain now, Patty, I shot a man. He and three other men were drunk and had beaten Nathaniel badly. One might have killed him. I shot that man. There were plenty of witnesses. And Adrien saw it. I found this out today. Now play the passage again and continue on into the next page."

Patty and Sarah followed this procedure until the whole story was out. It was an exhausting hour.

That afternoon, at the Garrett estate, a rented hack crested a lengthening shadow in the tree-lined driveway. A dark-suited man got out. He had red hair and was huge. A tall, slender man rapidly descended the marble steps to grasp the great proffered hand of the red-bearded giant.

"Matthew!" exclaimed Nathaniel heartily, wrapping an arm about the shoulders of his friend. "You made good time. I only just got here myself. I have a bottle of Irish whiskey the likes of which you have never tasted in your life. And I'm most anxious to talk with you about Herschell's young assistant."

"Strange goings-on in Washington these days, Nat. How's your dad?" Wistfully, Matthew's grey eyes swept the waxed floors and polished furniture. It had been a long time. A woman appeared, smoothing a great apron as she came, and Nathaniel peered at his guest.

"Hungry, Matthew?" Nathaniel turned to the servant. "Nothing fancy, Mrs. Fremstad. Just a lot of whatever you have ready." He grinned and escorted Matthew into the drawing room.

"Father's doing fairly well. This business with the threats has everyone pretty disturbed. Now, tell me what you found out." He stepped to a sideboard to pour his friend a drink.

"Only that he was educated in France where he lived with his mother. I looked at his war record from Vicksburg—looked good." Matthew sipped. "I couldn't understand George taking him for an assistant, but it's none of my business."

"Well, I never saw his war record," Nathaniel said, "but George told me Everett Kenton recommended him. You remember when I was in the hospital in Chattanooga after I was wounded?" Matthew nodded. "Everett Kenton was in the next bed. War correspondent—took a shot in the leg. Anyway, I got to know the man pretty well. So later on I looked him up."

A servant entered the room with sliced roast and vegetables, a large hunk of fresh bread, and a good sized slice of peach pie smothered in cream. There was a goblet of apple cider, too. Matthew smiled up at the woman gratefully before she left. Pouring himself a small whiskey, Nathaniel lounged in a chair and watched Matthew eat.

"I asked him about Ronsard, and he told me he was a fine man, that he had seen the man behave remarkably well in several difficult instances. I asked why he had vouched for him to George, and he told me that he figured it was the least we could do for the man—what with his being a Frenchman and giving an arm in the service of the United States Army."

"And?"

"Adrien Ronsard isn't missing an arm."

Seconds passed before the impact struck Matthew, and he slammed his fist on the table.

"What?!"

"So guess who I put at the top of the list in all this? But question one—where's the real Adrien Ronsard?"

"What's the latest on th' smear campaign?"

Nathaniel shrugged. "Mason was discredited in the newspaper, something about investments he made before the war. Father's secretary found another letter in his desk. I'm just hoping nobody finds out about my marriage before I can tell my parents."

"I take it there won't be any annulment?" Nathaniel grinned, shaking his head.

"It took her awhile to be convinced. And things have gone too far for that."

Matthew blushed. "Suits me fine," he grinned through his beard. "Where is . . . Mrs. Garrett?"

"Safe, I think. She's staying with the Herschell twins while George and Margaret are in Washington. She doesn't even know I'm back. As soon as the folks return, I think Sarah will be amenable to my telling them. She insists on easing into it." A warm mist clouded his gaze, and he spoke as if to himself. "She pleases me. More than I ever dreamed possible." He sighed. "Yes, she pleases me."

Matthew seemed to have some difficulty with his throat. "I'm glad for you, Nat."

They were interrupted.

"That's all right, Mrs. Fremstad," Nathaniel spoke more sharply than intended. "It's Miss Simms. I'll take care of it."

He swore under his breath as he stepped out on the marble portal. He should have spoken to Beth long ago, and his own negligence annoyed him.

Beth was attired in a riding habit, expertly seated on a huge grey stallion and escorted by a very young man in his early teens. She had come at a very inconvenient time, but a broad, politician's smile concealed his irritation.

"I didn't expect you, Beth," he reached up to swing her from the great animal. "The stables are to the left," he motioned to the youngster.

"Please forgive me for just riding over, Nathaniel," purred Beth, slipping a familiar arm through his.

"I took a chance that you might be home. Why, I've hardly seen you since you came back. If I didn't know better, darling, I would say you're avoiding me."

Beth's gay laugh rang through the entrance of the grand house, but she stopped in startled surprise when she saw Matthew.

"Oh! I wasn't aware that Mr. McCarey was in Maryland. Why didn't you tell me?" her face pouted prettily, and Matthew flushed at the long look of disdain that raked him. There was no love lost between the two of them. When Beth was only a young girl, Matthew had caught her in an indiscretion in this very house—half clad in one of the upper bedrooms as one of George Herschell's older boys was taking her virginity. She had never forgiven him for telling Trav to button up his pants and go to his mother. Few of their encounters since had been free of anger. Matthew, having never disclosed to Nathaniel the reason for their bickering dislike, allowed him to assume they simply shared a mutual aversion. Matthew excused himself and went to his room.

Rising suddenly to close the distance between herself and the scowling man before her, Beth laughed sweetly, raising pink lips to him with a twinkle in her green eyes. "First I would enjoy a kiss."

Her kiss was passionate. She opened her mouth and searched for his tongue, and he felt her animal arousal as she pressed tightly in his arms and slipped her hand inside his shirt. Presently he lifted his head.

"You haven't lost any of your timidity," he grinned down at her, setting her from him and going to pour himself a swallow of Matthew's Irish whiskey. Tossing it down swiftly he endeavored to make casual conversation.

"What have you done with yourself during the last couple of years, Beth? Sorry I didn't keep in better touch after I got wounded. But, I don't know, days tended to run together after awhile," he apologized.

"Nothing exciting, Nathaniel," Beth sighed. "Mostly I suppose I just took care of Papa and waited for you to come back." Nathaniel doubted that. "I was wondering if you'll be staying for awhile, Nathaniel."

"I'm staying."

"And will I be seeing you, then?" Beth pressed.

"Beth," he began. He knew he had to tell her. He hadn't planned it this way. It would be easier if she were angry, but it would only be cruel to drag this thing out any longer. "Beth, perhaps we should just plan to . . . keep it casual. Kind of . . . like we always used to do. I'll have many responsibilities just now, and . . ."

She touched his chest and, caught off guard, he moved back a step.

"Well, I do beg your pardon," she sniffed. "Have you returned from the wars a little too good for the rest of us, perhaps?" Anger flamed hot in her eyes as Nathaniel's reluctance began to register for what it was.

"Could it be," Beth asked, "that part of those so-called responsibilities include one mousy little governess?"

"Don't push me, Beth," warned Nathaniel. "I don't want to hurt you," he mumbled, and he didn't.

"Hurt me? Oh, Nathaniel! You must think I'm a fool! Did you honestly think I would sit around here waiting, *four years?* I've waited half my life for you. I got tired of waiting long ago."

Nathaniel whirled to face her. How long had their affair been so empty of love?

"No one asked you to wait, Beth."

"Oh, you never asked anything, Nathaniel," tears were flowing at last. "You just took. But you never asked."

"I never took more than you wanted to give, Beth." He wouldn't go to her. This was the way it had always been, and that's why this thing had not ended long ago. A clean break was best, no matter how it hurt. He turned away.

"You! The golden man with everything! It's her, isn't it? I knew it the first time I saw you look at her." Her voice was just behind him, and it softened, hurting. "Can't you even say the words, Nathaniel? Don't you have the decency to at least tell me?"

How had he reached this point? He had never encouraged her. He just hadn't ended it. This *was* his fault.

"Look at me, damn you!" Nathaniel jerked about —angry, guilty, eyes blazing. "I knew you were never in love, Nathaniel. I loved you, though. In the beginning I really did. Does that surprise you, that Beth Simms could love someone besides herself? But no one could love you. Ever since Charlotte died you were the great iron statue with all that armor surrounding you. Do you have any idea how hard I tried to get through that armor?"

"I never intended to hurt you, and you damn well know that, whether you'll admit it or not."

Beth's heels clicked across the long room to the table and she snatched up her things. The strain showed on her terribly, and her words came tightly. "If you will be so kind as to send for my young companion I will take my leave. Isn't it convenient for Mrs. Bradley—the cozy arrangement over there? She and Adrien Ronsard, I mean?" She forced a laugh.

"Ronsard?" Nathaniel quickly strode after her. "You've been by the Herschell's today?"

Beth lowered her eyes and fussed with her hat. "Oh no, I haven't been over there. I . . . picked it up from one of the stable boys." No one knew, nor would they ever know about her assignation with Adrien—not her father, not the servants.

But Nathaniel was far away, caught up in the terror of Sarah's being practically alone with Adrien . . . or whoever the man was. Nathaniel hardly remembered going through the motions of seeing Beth out of the house, but somehow she was gone and he was bounding up the stairs, three at a time. Vaulting to Matthew's room, he pounded on the door with a heavy fist.

"Matthew!" he yelled, and the door jerked open under his raised fist.

"Get your jacket and come with me! It seems Mr. Ronsard is a lone guest at the Herschell house! Come on!"

Sarah had retired to her suite, thankful that Vance was at Rick's for the night. As she lifted shaking fingers to the buttons at her throat her ears caught the sounds of Patty's setter barking, but the animal quieted, and she dismissed it. Taking a last peep at Peter and the amazing little Rosy, Sarah returned to rock wearily in her chair, doubtful she would sleep.

A tap sounded at the door, and Sarah recognized it as Patty's. What on earth was that child doing up?

Sarah stumbled to the door and tugged at the table. It was harder to remove it than it had been to put there.

"Mrs. Bradley, hurry up!"

"Just a minute, Patty," admonished Sarah, finally dragging the table back far enough so that she could open the door. Patty was in her nightgown and robe.

"Nathaniel and Matthew McCarey. Matthew's an old friend—"

"Yes, I know who Matthew is! Here?" Composing themselves, they walked to the living room. The room was tense, highly charged. Nathaniel's gaze flicked anxiously from the doorway back to the good-looking imposter with Matthew. He was so nervous he had half a mind to smoke one of George's cigars. If Sarah didn't come soon, by heaven he would fetch her himself!

Only for the briefest of seconds did Sarah's anxious eyes meet Nathaniel's glittering ones as she stepped from the dark hallway into the light. Nathaniel's breath caught. She was, strangely enough, attired in the gown she had worn when they had both stood so paley before the reverend to take their vows. She looked haggard. Her cheeks seemed transparent. A hollow darkness was about her eyes, and the deep hue of the tendrils that lay in childlike disorder about her face only accentuated the haunting beauty of her features.

Nathaniel trembled, wishing to run to her, to sweep her up in his arms and cradle her and kiss away the fine lines of tension. But he forced himself to stay where he was. Oh Sarah, my precious, what has happened here? Whatever it was stemmed from the blond devil making his way to the side of his wife, he would stake his life on that! But he had to move carefully or he'd learn nothing.

Sarah shook off the warning pressure at her elbow, a wan smile curving her lips. "Matthew!" she

234

breathed aloud, such a warmth of affection filling her voice that Adrien's brows rose.

Sarah's skirts whispered across the floor, bright, un-shed tears sparkling in her dark eyes as she held out both hands toward the giant. Slender arms lifted to circle the big man's neck as Sarah drew herself close, placing her pale cheek against the bristly, red beard. Only Matthew heard the softly whispered words as she hugged the brawny neck.

"I'm in trouble. Help me." She released him. His large hand pressed a promise against her shaking fingers. "How nice to see you again, Captain Garrett."

How lost she was, after Adrien's ambiguous state-ment about her "involvement" with Nathaniel. How-ever, Nathaniel's posture revealed nothing.

"Mr. Ronsard," Sarah called brightly, "this is Mr. Matthew McCarey, a friend of mine from Tennessee. I'm so pleased that you brought him by, Captain Gar-rett. Do you plan to stay for a long visit, Matthew?"

And as if Patty had called his name, Nathaniel's eyes caught hers. There was something for him in Pat-ty's dark eyes. But *what?*

"Since I'm the hostess tonight, Nathaniel," the girl flounced her way up before the brooding figure, as well as one can flounce in a belted robe, "would you mind helping me get some refreshment? I'm afraid the staff retired early. We'll be back in just a minute, Mrs. Bradley." The quick giggle was so typical that no one paid Patty any mind. Nathaniel soon felt himself be-ing led from the room.

Sarah did most of the talking in their absence, wish-ing Matthew would say something. Anything! Adrien was acutely aware of her every word. She plied Mat-thew with inane questions about news of Mrs. Simpson and Irene, and even laughed when he finally pro-ceeded to recount a tale of Timothy Davidson, who, it seemed, could hardly manage to keep himself out of one difficulty after another since Nathaniel had left.

Reacher had returned home. Matthew hinted that he was considering staying with the military and going West in the fall.

Sarah watched tensely as Nathaniel and Patty entered the room, the carefree man bearing a tray with bread, cheese, fruit, glasses and wine. There was a large decanter of whiskey.

"We decided to have a party," he shrugged, flashing a dazzling grin their way. Placing the heavy tray on the rug, he motioned to Patty who scooped up an armful of cushions and scattered them on the rug.

"Nathaniel and Matthew were bored in that big house," confided Patty, very much the gay young hostess. "So I suggested we play cards. Papa says it's unladylike to play cards, but I don't care. Do you play, Mrs. Bradley? No matter," she didn't wait for an answer. "I can play well enough for both of us. And you can watch for the first few hands until you catch on."

"Wait, you!" choked Sarah. "I play very well, if you must know." Something about Nathaniel's mouth sent a strength surging through her. Could it be that he knew? She could not read him, and he refused to meet her eyes. "I have no money," she mused almost cheerfully. "I fear I shall be forced to borrow."

"Mr. Ronsard," drawled Nathaniel as he folded his legs like an Indian and drew Patty down beside him. "Have a seat, sir," he requested idly, giving the impression that Adrien was free to toddle off to bed if that was his choice. He waved Sarah down at Matthew's feet with a smile and reached for three glasses. Pouring a goodly amount into two of them, he raised his brows to Adrien.

"Your pleasure, Mr. Ronsard?" Nathaniel held the decanter poised above the empty glass, awaiting his reply. Matthew muttered a complaint under his breath as he experienced no small difficulty fitting himself into the small space allotted him between Sarah and the fireplace. Now Adrien could do nothing but sink to the rug.

"Whatever you have is fine," he muttered, unbuttoning his vest and slipping a finger around the collar of his shirt.

"Excellent, excellent!" beamed Nathaniel jovially, "Patty, pour you and Sarah a small glass of sherry. Not too much. I don't want to be accused of demoralizing the young," he chattered on happily.

Nathaniel's behavior for the next hour was extraordinary. Sarah would have been fooled had she not known him so well. By the time his ruse became obvious, Adrien Ronsard was so drunk it didn't matter whether he guessed he'd been had.

Adrien's eyes had assumed a glassy redness. Matthew didn't seem at all affected by the amount he had consumed, nor did Nathaniel. As Nathaniel turned a hard stare upon Adrien Ronsard, the ruthless strength manifest itself nakedly, frightening even Sarah in its cold intensity.

Muttering one of his wry quips, sending Patty into gales of laughter, Nathaniel reached over to give Adrien a lusty whack across the shoulders.

"Well, intemperance doesn't loosen everyone's tongue, does it?" he muttered. Matthew's large hand caught Adrien's collar and pulled him back into a sitting position as Nathaniel arose with a disgusted snort.

"Hell, this is taking too long," he complained.

A white-knuckled hand buried into the folds of Adrien's clothing and pulled him roughly to his feet. Adrien mumbled and gestured abstractly with a slender hand.

"You won't remember this in the morning anyway, monsieur," Nathaniel promised sweetly as he moved the man back against the brick facing of the fireplace. Before Sarah realized what his intentions were, Nathaniel's fist tightened until the tanned arm was rigid. "Never, *never* touch a man's wife."

With a quick movement of Nathaniel's shoulder Adrien's head slammed back against the bricks with a crunch. Sarah covered her mouth with both hands, and Nathaniel unceremoniously pulled his unconscious body out from the wall and dropped it upon the rug.

"He'll have a slight headache, I fear," mused the tall man gravely. "Matthew, take the man to his room and make sure he stays there. We'll talk to him in the morning." And then Nathaniel raised his eyes to Sarah.

It had been a long and terrible day, and as Sarah gazed up at the man above her, her chin began to quiver. She could barely whisper his name.

Nathaniel was before her in a second, his arms drawing her to her feet with a moan.

"Patty," he spoke at last, without lifting his head. "Could you brew us a nice pot of tea, perhaps?"

"Right away."

Nathaniel supported Sarah to the bedroom. Her account of the ordeal was told with a calmness she did not feel. Nathaniel's face revealed torn emotions—from pride in her ability to keep her wits to fury at Adrien's touching her.

Sarah wanted him to think her brave. She didn't speak of how terrified and humiliated she had really been. Nor did she want him to see the marks of Adrien's fingers.

With a tone she dared not disobey, he demanded to see them.

Sarah's fingers fumbled with her buttons. And with quite steady fingers Nathaniel bared her beautiful throat. Even in the candlelight, the dark bruises were visible, and the low growl of rage boiling from Nathaniel's chest was chilling. "When I get through with him I guarantee he won't be putting those hands on the throat of another woman. Ever."

"Nathaniel," began Sarah, "please. He only tried to frighten—"

"It's out of your hands now, Sarah," the low words cut her off short as Nathaniel arose from the bed in a deliberate motion.

At last he turned. "I would like to kill him," he said, "but for the sake of everything concerned I'll make a deal."

"What kind of a deal?"

"For information, darling." Nathaniel's shoulders slumped, and Sarah was amazed at the great weariness which came over him.

He held Sarah in the curve of his body like a bruised summer flower. When her breathing steadied, her lips parted in the peace of her slumber, Nathaniel sat down on the bed. His eyes black with anger, he dropped his head in his hands. Far into the morning Nathaniel pondered the fate of Adrien Ronsard.

ᴇᴛ𝒳 Chapter XI

ADRIEN RONSARD AWAKENED in the Herschell stables, and the return to consciousness was an exceedingly painful one. Not accustomed to the excessive amounts of liquor forced into his system the night before, his condition was not improved at all by the bucket of icy water doused over him by a massive, red-headed bear. Adrien found that he was stripped to his waist, but his hands were not bound. Thoughts came slowly, but he knew for a certainty why he was here.

Leaning against a rough partition a few feet from him was the Yankee captain, and as Adrien focused his eyes on the tall figure, the unmasked hatred wrenched a primitive emotion that Adrien rarely felt—fear! This was not the first time he had faced the results of a complicity alone, but somehow his belief in his own prowess had sustained him. Now he was truly afraid.

Nathaniel spoke with controlled terseness. "Get up!"

Adrien arose, struggling to check his surroundings. Two stable hands lurked in the shadows, but Adrien was confident they would not interfere. The certain conflict ahead was to be with the Yankee. He knew that if the circumstances were reversed, Nathaniel Garrett would never walk out alive. Somehow, the woman had betrayed him.

"Say what you have to say!" Adrien snapped, his nostrils flaring. Nathaniel pulled his broad shoulders away from the wall and took a calculated step forward, as Adrien fastened his pants securely.

"I should kill you for what you did, monsieur. Instead I will put you in prison—the case is open and shut—kidnapping, perhaps even murder, impersonating a United States Army Officer, blackmail. The list is endless." Nathaniel sensed Adrien's fear. Adrien wiped his mouth with the back of his hand.

"If what you can tell me is worth anything, I'll negotiate. You know that." Nathaniel bent to draw a small stool nearer to prop a foot upon it. "But for Sarah, I'm going to beat the hell out of you."

"How do I know you would not imprison me anyway, Captain?" Adrien's activities for the past weeks had not borne the fruit that he and his financiers from the South had hoped. How much this Yankee captain was just guessing was something he needed to know.

Nathaniel laughed softly. "You amateurs are all the same. You think everyone behaves in the same unprincipled way you do." He snorted. "I suppose you'll just have to take my word for it."

"Well," Adrien drawled, "some of us amateurs don't have things simply handed to us. Some of us have to do our life's work however we can." Under his breath the words were still audible. "Garrett son-of-a-bitch!"

Nathaniel closed the distance between them. Adrien raised a fist, tightened it until the knuckles were firm, and Nathaniel moved his left arm slightly before him, slowly circling the blond figure with an easy grace, as if each step knew exactly where it would fall. They both seemed to relish the brutality to follow, and Nathaniel's right hand formed a loose fist.

The closeness of the stables was inconvenient, and the other men stayed well back, giving them room. Adrien's swift blow glanced off Nathaniel's shoulder, and the two men moved farther out into the hay-strewn space. Adrien struck again, catching Nathaniel high in his chest, and as the Yankee moved with the blow, he swung up his right fist and buried it heavily in Adrien's ribs.

Adrien grunted and caught Nathaniel only lightly across the cheek. Nathaniel didn't underestimate the strength of his opponent. Though the blond man was lighter, he was agile. Before the man could recover from his blow to the ribs, however, Nathaniel struck first with one quick fist then the other, at his face, one glancing harmlessly, the other cracking with such force across Adrien's eyes that Nathaniel's knuckles were bloodied.

The two men fought like savages. There were no strategies—each only lashed out in bitter fury. Adrien did not back away from Nathaniel's cruel fists. He took the blows and threw as much weight as he could toward Nathaniel's head. Nathaniel's mouth was bleeding now, and Adrien's eye was nearly shut.

Their harsh breaths filled the stable, and Nathaniel stood with shoulders heaving as they glared at each other. Adrien saw his teeth bared, a low snarl grinding from the bleeding mouth as Nathaniel aimed for his jaw. It struck with a brutal crash, spinning Adrien backward. Desperate fingers closed about the nearby stool, and Adrien threw, catching Nathaniel on the scar Giles had created. Nathaniel's shock and pain gave Adrien an edge. A felling blow to Nathaniel's jaw sent his body sprawling, and as Adrien heaved himself across him, Nathaniel rammed up hard with his already bleeding right hand.

The blow caught Adrien full in the face, and his own falling impetus only increased the force of the impact. Adrien's eyes blurred, and he rolled away. Nathaniel straddled his waist in seconds, and he struck hard to his ribs and belly, time and time again, each blow for the seconds his wife had strangled in terror. Writhing in anguish, Adrien struggled.

"The man can't talk if he's senseless, Nat," Matthew

242

warned quietly, and Nathaniel allowed himself to be pulled away.

Stumbling to the water barrel, Nathaniel poured a dipper of water over his head. It cleared his thinking somewhat, and he moved to set the stool upright. Seating himself, Nathaniel waited for Adrien.

With blinding pain Adrien realized he would probably never be the same again, the beating to his abdomen having injured him savagely internally. The murderous hatred in Adrien's one good eye was so bitter that Nathaniel doubted whether Adrien was a man who could be broken. Still, the bastard would talk to him now or sit in prison for years thinking about it.

A half hour elapsed before Adrien could talk coherently. Nathaniel's terms were stated tersely, "I want to know how involved you are in the mischief going on in Washington. It should go without saying that if your answers don't satisfy me you will nurse those bruises behind bars. I want whys and names and places. Also I want to know the whereabouts of the real Adrien Ronsard." Nathaniel turned. "Matthew, I need paper and a pen." Matthew nodded and stepped out to fetch them.

"Sorry to disappoint you, Captain, but as far as I know he's alive. The last I heard, Monsieur Ronsard was being held in a small town in Georgia. Me? I don't give a damn."

"Your name!"

"Ah, Captain, you would have to bury a knife in my gut. And still I wouldn't tell you that."

Nathaniel decided not to press, or he might lose the other information he needed. "I want a place where he may be found." Adrien nodded.

"About the threats," Nathaniel began again.

Adrien, holding his battered ribs, knowing that he might as well give the captain the information he wanted without prolonging his own misery, spoke brokenly, pausing often to cough. "Some of the Southern planters . . . they are afraid of Johnson. Johnson only thinks of the small farmer, and . . . he's going to let the radicals wage a vendetta . . . against the land-holders. All the planters want is to be heard. And they are afraid of the new Freedmen's Bureau bill." He shrugged, then doubled over. His mouth filled with blood. He spat.

"So you've been scalp-hunting. What you have told me, I accept, for I figured out that much myself. Your motives in all this are another matter. I doubt that even your patrons know what makes men like you do the things you do. Take John Wilkes Booth, for instance, and men like that—"

"Don't preach to me!" Adrien started to arise, but Matthew pushed him back down with the toe of his boot. "Booth was a fool!"

Nathaniel grimaced. "For what he believed."

"For what he did, not for what he believed. He was only trying so save the Negro race. They won't last a decade as free men."

"And you intend to take up where he left off?" Nathaniel grinned, having neatly tricked Adrien into revealing what he never intended to—his own motives.

"I will give you names, no more."

"I'm waiting. I should warn you that Andrew Johnson's policy for Reconstruction is not all that much different than Lincoln's would have been. If you have any idea of removing him like Booth did Lincoln . . . The Negro is free, and you can't change that fact, no matter how many men you kill."

"Can we get on with this? You weary me, Garrett."

Adrien told Nathaniel pretty much all there was, except his real identity. His intimation to Sarah about the misuse of women in the past was not mentioned. Nathaniel agreed with Sarah that it was either the man's delusion or a plain lie.

"One more thing before you leave us, Mr. Ronsard." Nathaniel was writing as he talked, occasionally wiping some blood from his throbbing lower lip. "This other source of information you mentioned to Sarah. You said Sarah wasn't the only one who would spy."

"I miscalculated the nerve of that bitch," he admitted softly. The muscle in Nathaniel's jaw bunched dangerously.

"Well, who was your source?" he gritted menacingly.

"Damn you!" Matthew shook a red head at the reckless man. Adrien sighed, his shoulders shaking. "It was suggested that you would be planning to marry sometime after you returned, and I was to make an arrangement with your fiancée." He began to cough again.

"And now you know better," growled Nathaniel. "Well, did you approach Miss Simms?"

"No!" he cried.

"Maybe you didn't, and maybe you did."

"This is not as bad as you're making it sound!" argued Adrien, heedless now of composure. "All these men wanted was some way to protect themselves!"

"I would say the Black Codes are a pretty good start," and Nathaniel continued writing, disdaining to speak further. After some minutes he rose and motioned for Matthew to raise the man into a standing position.

"Sign it," he gritted, "and you three witness it." Cautiously the groomsmen sidled up.

Adrien gave the hastily scrawled document a cursory reading and braced himself against the wall. Placing the papers against the boards he paused to dip the pen into the inkwell Matthew held. Adrien Ronsard signed the document, secretly wondering what his cohorts would do to him when they learned. A list of twelve men from four different states was included in the paper. Missing were two important names—Dalton Evans and John Pollard.

The witnesses signed. Nathaniel directed, "This man will need a coach into Upper Marlboro. Get his horse and saddle ready, and two of you escort him to town." Nathaniel turned to Adrien.

"Matthew will gather your things from your room. If I *ever* see you on this place, or even in this county again, I will be sorely tempted to kill you." Adrien knew this was no bluff. He had been lucky this time because he had had something to trade.

In less than an hour, Adrien was ready to make his way carefully back down the Herschell stairway from his room. Matthew had left the room to take Adrien's bag to the horses and bring them around, and as he vacated the room a bitter smile flicked across the fair man's battered face. Quickly he reached into a case resting on the bed. Searching painfully through a small black box, Adrien finally found the tiny piece of paper.

Opening the scrap of paper, Adrien read the name John Pollard, 3497 Breachway, Charleston, South Carolina. John would know what to do. The mirthless chuckle hurt his ribs, and he coughed. Folding the paper carefully, Adrien slipped it deep into the inside pocket of his suit.

Sarah's assessment of Adrien wasn't too far wrong, Nathaniel mused. The man was a fanatic. Nathaniel's every instinct craved that Adrien spend the rest of his life safely locked away. But that would be an impossibility, even if Sarah charged him with assault, for these names had been obtained under duress.

Hardly had Nathaniel closed the door to the schoolroom when Sarah gasped, "Nathaniel!" Patty's wide-eyed reaction was similar to Sarah's.

"Patty," Sarah requested firmly, not allowing the girl time to start a barrage of questions, "could you be a dear and have some breakfast put on a tray for us? Please make some explanation for Nathaniel's presence here. I don't think he will be presentable at the breakfast table."

"I just can't believe this," she shook her head wearily, stepping to the water pitcher to bathe his wounds. "You're going to be the death of me—to say nothing of yourself! What with the war, Giles, and now this, you'll be lucky to reach thirty-two, Nathaniel Garrett. And I suppose you are going to tell me that Adrien looks worse."

"Much," growled the battered figure. His shirt was torn, his pants bloody and filthy, the corner of his mouth was split and swollen, and a bruise was darkening one cheekbone.

"It accomplished a lot," his hard voice rasped, "and I'm in no mood for any of your sharp tongue, madam." Nathaniel jerked the cloth from her hands to dab the blood off, then winced from his own touch, Sarah smiled. Taking the cloth from him, Sarah bent his head between his sprawled legs to brush the dust from his hair. Running her fingers through his hair, standing between his legs as she was, her thoughts tangled confusingly. Was it love or pride that drove a man to battle for what he considered his?

Raising his head, Nathaniel silently wrapped his arms about her waist, drawing Sarah closer. "Stop fussing and kiss me."

"There's no place to kiss that isn't black and blue or bleeding," Sarah retorted. But she bent to place a small kiss on the smooth arm.

"Thanks a lot," he grumbled. Gently, Sarah rubbed his temples, her fingertips moving to work down the taut muscles of his neck. Her thoughts slipped to the tiny life growing inside her with every passing second, and a pang of guilt slapped at her because Nathaniel had no knowledge of it. Sarah knew from watching the man with Peter that he very much wanted a child of his own.

Suddenly she realized that she was thinking, not of

her own needs, but of *his!* And he had never even told her he loved her.

Unaware that she had stopped massaging his back and was standing perfectly still, staring, Sarah jumped when Nathaniel lifted his head.

"Sarah," he began in a firm voice, "put your things together. The minute George and Margaret return you are coming back with me." Abruptly he released her and rose. Unbuttoning his pants, Nathaniel tucked what was left of the shirt back into them and buttoned them again.

"Just like that?" Her voice carried a warning, but if Nathaniel noted he didn't show it.

"Just like that!" he replied solemnly and with finality. "And what is more," recklessly ignoring the gleam in her brown eyes, "this game has gone far enough. I know I gave you my word that our marriage would be kept from public knowledge until you were ready, but many things have happened since then. One of which was a threat to your life. Now, if you don't want to be there when I tell them, that's fine with me. Do as you please. But enough is enough. I think I've been fair in giving you time to sort things out in your mind. That's what you said you needed to do. Well, sorted or not, you're my wife, and I want you where you're safe."

"Are you finished?" She crossed slender, grey-sleeved arms across her bosom.

"No, I'm not finished, but you are going to burst soon if I don't let you talk. So vent your wrath, my dear. It won't change a thing," and he smiled.

"You are a bully! From the very beginning you've tricked me and deceived me and ordered me about as though I was a serving woman. Well, it's obvious that we are to be forced into disclosing this marriage. I have accepted that." Sarah stormed. "What I haven't accepted and never will accept is the way you take things into your own hands!" Sarah couldn't stop. "Have you considered what we will look like? You—

the husband of one woman and the betrothed of an-other—suddenly moving me into the Garrett house with a child that half the county probably thinks is yours anyway?"

"Beth and I have had . . . an understanding," he said lamely.

"What kind of understanding? When did you see her?" She listened, thinking she heard Peter stirring about. Sure enough, the sleepy-eyed boy made his way into the room.

"Papa," greeted Peter, as though he had been saying the word all his life.

"Oh, lord!" choked Sarah, whirling about and raising her palms to the ceiling in a futile gesture.

"Hurt?" questioned the child, and Nathaniel nearly bent double trying not to laugh at his mother, who turned on them both.

"Sarah?" Nathaniel grinned down at her as he lifted the rumpled boy. "He's dry, and if you want him to remain that way I suggest you run along and tend to his needs. I'll pick you up tomorrow. Arrange for someone to tend Peter. I want to show you something."

Wishing that she could think of something very clever to say to the wretch, Sarah could only grit her teeth as Peter went through his little routine of hand-waving and "Bye-bye."

"Hurt?" he repeated.

"Not as much as I think she'd have me be, I fear," called Nathaniel as he departed.

Sarah waited impatiently for Nathaniel to call. Pacing the hallway, she ran squarely into Vance, knocking her hat askew. Vance didn't remove himself from Sarah's path, but straightened her hat himself. Vance and Sarah had never required much talk, sharing a world of communication by intuition. Since they also shared the secret of his illness, their band was a deep one. Sarah's brown eyes met the beautiful black ones studying her with no self-consciousness at all.

"He's here," the young man said quietly.

"Nathaniel?"

"Who else?"

Sarah blushed. "Thank you. Vance, I . . ."

"You're beautiful. Did you know that?" He smiled.

"I . . . well . . . Thank you, Vance."

"I saw you sleeping in the schoolroom earlier. I almost kissed you." He smiled. "I was too gallant."

"Vance!"

"Quit saying 'Vance.' It's not contagious, Sarah."

Sarah wanted to cup his jaw in her palm. He was so very young. "Don't talk like that."

"I'm sorry."

Once again he was controlled. Control was a fine art with Vance. "You shouldn't keep the captain waiting."

"I've been meaning to speak to you about some of the harmonics you are using in your work. They're somewhat different, to say the least. They remind me of the new music from those daring French composers. Are you sure about them?"

He laughed. "I'm sure. About the harmonics, anyway."

Vance watched them leave, guessing Nathaniel knew how he felt about Sarah. Wasn't he glad Sarah had him? Yes, he was glad. And sad. Oh, he didn't know sometimes, except that Nathaniel wouldn't have been gallant. He would have kissed her.

Nathaniel's lip was almost normal, but he would carry a small scar at the upper edge all his life. Giving him her hand for an assist into the buggy, Sarah lifted her eyes to find those blue ones caressing her.

"You have to tell him, Sarah." Sarah folded her hands in her lap, and Nathaniel covered them with a large one. "It's not fair, sweetheart, for Vance to hear it some other way. It's going to be hard as blazes for him as it is. Look at me. If you don't tell him, I will."

"No! You have never seen him when one of those attacks hits him. You think he's never going to breathe again. I know you're right. I will, I promise I will. It's just that the time has to be right. I . . . I just can't blurt it out, just like that!"

Nathaniel climbed up beside her and clucked to the horse. Sarah changed the subject. "Are you ready to tell me yet where we're going?"

"For one thing, I've never taken a woman where I'm taking you, Sarah." She looked at him narrowly. "I swear," he grinned.

"Well?"

"It's my inheritance. From my grandfather. I inherited my share when I was of age . . . and then I let it lie." Nathaniel shrugged. "For ten years."

"Ten years!"

"Well, I had no interest in it until now. Why should I? I wasn't married. I had no reason to want it." He pointed toward rolling terrain near the Herschell estate. "This land adjoins my parents' at the back. My father was born on this land. It's been in our family for over a hundred years."

"I know. Beth told me," murmured Sarah.

"Witch!"

Brown eyes grew velvety warm as Sarah watched Nathaniel speak of his grandfather and his family history. It seemed so important to him, pride and love of his land.

"Clarke had no intentions of ever living here, so I bought his share," Nathaniel was saying. "Here we are. Things have gone to seed. No one has lived here for many years."

A tree-lined drive only faintly revealed the evidence of travel. It was long, with no sign of a house anywhere as the steep incline reared. Timber covered this section, and the old trees of the drive almost touched at the tops, darkening the carriage in heavy shadows.

Finally, as they reached the crest of the tall climb, Nathaniel stopped the carriage. "I want you to see this from the top of the hill," Sarah climbed out to look down into a small valley. There, below them, spread the old Garrett homesite, backed by a wide stream at the far end of the valley.

"Oh, Nathaniel," she whispered, and Nathaniel caught her hand to his lips. Not immensely large, the stone house gave the impression of being a small castle nestled among invincible trees. It was a storybook picture.

"Your grandfather built this?" murmured Sarah, making a wide gesture to encompass the stream and woods, stables and barn, in addition to a small cemetery and its tiny stone chapel.

"Yes, and I never liked it."

"Never liked it? Are you crazy?"

Nathaniel bent to snap a piece of long-bladed grass. "I . . . I spent a great deal of time with my grandparents when I was a boy, what with Father's campaigning and all. Grandpa's buried down there."

Sarah followed his gaze. "Charlotte, she was a . . . a young woman a long time . . ."

"I know about Charlotte." At his strange expression Sarah smiled. "Peggy."

"Oh. Well, I suppose I had to go through war before I realized that dying is a part of life just like living. And I began to understand what a special thing it is to be committed to a woman and building something during your life, leaving children to begin it all over again when you die. It's only when you've never lived that dying is frightening. And," he paused, "now it seems right somehow that I should come to the place where Grandpa and Grandma lived. Come here with you, Sarah. Do you understand anything of what I'm trying to tell you?"

"Probably more than you know," she whispered.

"This is where we will raise our family, Sarah," and she almost told him then, that he had already begun his future with their child. But she listened, following his pointing finger, turning with his body, enthralled. "Is this what you want, too, Sarah? To raise our family here?"

Sarah only nodded. She loved him so much now, more and more every day.

"There's a lot of work, little one," he laughed ruefully. "I'm afraid when you see the house, you will go into a frenzy. But we'll do the repairs soon. I want everything done to your taste. Can't you just see the lawns, Sarah? Our children running around?"

Sarah slipped both her hands into his.

"Let's drive down to the house. Then there's a special place I want you to see." Sarah laughed. Her splendid husband appeared to be totally happy.

The house was old and did indeed need work. They made their way through the rooms, upstairs and down, picturing how it would look refurbished. The plans for the kitchens were elaborate and costly. There was so much work to be done!

At last they left the stone house and wandered about the once gracious lawns of the estate until Nathaniel began to hurry her along. She caught a glimpse of what lay before them. A small, picturesque grotto was hidden in a bower of trees. A pool sparkled before them, so clear Sarah could distinguish every pebble on the bottom. Wild violets thrust through the moss carpeting of its banks. Nathaniel laughed with delight. Lacing long fingers behind his head, he lay down on the bank.

"Clarke and I used to swim here when we were young. The spring is there," and Sarah followed his gesture to the crystal fountain emptying on a small stairway of grey-blue stones. A small thread of water

spilled into a rivulet, growing into the stream Sarah
had seen from the hilltop.

"Oh, it's lovely! Something that an artist would
paint!" his wife cried. Since he had taken Sarah from
the Tennessee mountains and the war, Sarah had often
seemed far beyond her years, but now her enforced
maturity magically slipped away. The fantasy scene
intoxicated her, and her slippers whispered through the
tender violets, arms outstretched, her laughing face
turned up to the skies.

No sooner had Nathaniel begun to remove his shoes
than a cool spray of water drenched his shirt. Wrenching them off, peeling off his shirt as well, he cocked
a threatening brow.

"You remember the last time you gave me a soaking, don't you?"

"Yes, but I know more now than I did then."

With a rippling girlish cry Sarah scrambled from
his reach, missing a sound ducking by seconds. They
romped with the freedom of beautiful children. Nathaniel tousled and rumpled her hair, kissing her until
she squeaked for mercy.

Sarah cuddled in his arms, laughing and flushed.
She was lovely, and he was sensitive.

"There's something different," he toyed with the
idea. "I don't know. It's . . ."

A great longing welled within Sarah, and it was
very simple. "It's your baby, Nathaniel. We're going
to have a baby."

The ride back to the Herschell's was slow and quiet.
She had experienced a war and the pain of losing a
husband. Their marriage was now fact, and their
child was a fact. That they would live together and
have other children was a certainty. It hardly seemed
important anymore *why* they had married. Things
didn't demand a perfect beginning to turn out beautifully. How very clever of her to discover that! She
smiled.

"What's the matter with you, Sarah?" Nathaniel nudged her, and she came to herself, aware now that he had been watching her.

"I was just a mite pleased with my own brilliance," she quipped.

"Please me with it," he grinned.

"I was just considering how my outlook has changed." Sarah shrugged over the sound of the carriage. "I used to make excuses for my misery because my father deserted me and Charles left me stranded. And now I think I may actually end up being. Do you think I'm becoming overconfident, Nathaniel?"

"No, I do not, Mrs. Garrett. Not at all."

As the carriage turned into the Herschell drive, the setting sun blinded them both for a moment. Nathaniel knew he would look back on this day as one of the best of his entire life. Bright, like the sun.

The same blinding rays didn't evoke thoughts of contentment from Adrien Ronsard, however, as he guided his horse through a series of wooded ravines to keep his assignation with Beth. Damn, he hoped she wasn't tardy. Every muscle and bone in him ached! Blast Garrett to hell!

Anything but tardy, Beth was pacing through the tall grass circling a deserted shack, flicking an impatient quirt against her thigh. Catching sight of Adrien she paused, hands on hips, and her face slowly filled with horrified amazement.

"*Adrien!*" she breathed, stepping quickly beside his stirrup and taking the reins he dropped to her hand. "My god, what happened? Your eye! Can you see at all?"

"Don't question. Help me down."

Shadows cast long, and the hovering woods made the dusk even darker.

"I don't wish to discuss it with you, madam. 'Twas

the Garrett son-of-a-bitch. He *dared* to lift his hand against me—an act soon to pay double, I assure you."

Beth shook her head. "That kind of talk won't get you anywhere, Adrien. People like the Garretts don't get paid back."

Managing to open the rickety door which hung by only one hinge, she motioned for Adrien to enter. "If that were true I would settle a score with Nathaniel myself. Come and sit down and stop dreaming."

Beth's proffered hand was brushed aside as Adrien carefully lowered himself to a rough-planked bench. "There are dreams," he clipped, "and there are visions. Only one who is called is blessed with foresight to tell the difference."

Beth had seen Adrien Ronsard less than a dozen times, and only once before had she met him like this, in secret. He was obsessed with some crazy notion of saving the Negro race from exploitation. She suspected he was a tiny bit mad, for that had been all he'd talked about. When she had objected he struck her— hard across the face, telling her that she was being disciplined for holding a sacred mission in low esteem. And then he had kissed her, explaining that she was special—she would learn.

Indifferent to whether the black race became extinct or not, it was the other that had drawn Beth back to this shack. When Adrien had hit her, even with the pain, Beth had been excited to a passion she had never known. Giving herself to men had never been a matter of serious concern to Beth, and even the brief affair with Nathaniel years ago had been nothing more than pleasant.

Though Adrien had not touched her, other than the blow to her face and the kiss, Beth had desired him ever since. Love had nothing to do with it—Adrien possessed a brutal animal cruelty that ignited molten flames through her body. Beth was driven to Adrien. Compelled to humble herself before him, Beth knelt and slipped her arms about his waist. In a ceremonious manner, Adrien placed both his hands on her head.

"You sense my power, don't you?"

Beth shivered. "I don't know what it is."

Adrien's voice was almost a monotone, as if he had memorized the words long ago. "Men such as myself must choose those who will serve them. One race was not meant to destroy another, but to give to the other and ultimately produce a stronger man. John Booth saw this, but he overstepped the bounds of wisdom by killing the President. There was a better way.

"Men like Garrett and Lincoln put a sword in the hand of the law. Justice is twisted. I must see this does not happen. We are different, and those who serve us are blessed. Do you understand?"

Beth knew she did not, but she was frantic to feel the thrilling sensation she had felt before. "I don't really understand why you think freedom will annihilate the Negro, but I understand when a man feels there is something he must do. And obviously, you feel that way. Every man needs a woman to understand his work, and I will try to—"

Adrien arose swiftly to send Beth sprawling back onto the hard dirt floor with a backhand blow. *"No man needs a woman to understand!"* he raged, and Beth drew herself up to her knees.

"I only meant—"

"It doesn't matter *what* you meant! Women are weak, and *I cannot abide weakness!*"

Holding the side of her face, Beth huddled as far away from Adrien as she could, her golden coil of hair tumbling in a disheveled mass about her shoulders and face. Warily she pulled herself to her knees, and as he made no move to stop her, Beth began to straighten herself. His knee caught her just under her chin to send her against the weathered wall with a crashing blow.

"Stop it!" she screamed, and as Adrien's fingers grabbed a handful of hair, pulling her up with it, pain drew harsh lines down her face.

"Don't command me, my novice!" he snarled, dropping her abruptly before she could balance herself, then standing over her. "How old are you, Beth?"

"I . . ."

"You've known many men intimately, haven't you? Why hasn't one of them married you by now, Beth? You must be nearly thirty, at least."

"That's none of your bloody business!" she rasped.

"Ah, but it is my business," his fingers tightened in her hair again, and Beth reached pleading fingers toward his face.

"You're hurting me," she whimpered.

"But that's why you're here, isn't it, Beth? Because I can hurt you? Hmmm? We both have our special little preferences, and this is yours. And don't start crying on me—you know what you are as well as I do. You're a demimonde, as my people would say. And you had it in your mind that I would degrade myself and join the legions of men who have crawled between those legs. Didn't you? Admit it! *Admit it!*" he gritted.

Finally Beth nodded with a sob.

"It would seem, my dear," he turned his back to her, half muttering to himself, half talking to her, "that we have both suffered a setback. That little Southern gal caught the big man right out from under your nose, didn't she? And now you're grabbing at straws because you don't want to admit you've wound up with nothing. Well, I have the advantage over you, for at least my work here is noble. I have a calling. You're nothing but a tramp."

Moonlight caught his face as he jerked back to her.

"You think I'm mad, but that's because you don't understand my power. You feel it, but you don't understand it. You will obey it, though, and you will do anything I ask. Won't you?"

Beth came to life, twisting her slender body up quickly and flattening herself back, palms flat against the wall.

"No! I will not obey you. And yes I think you're mad! Crazy mad!" She inched along, knowing there was no way she could escape. Adrien loomed before her suddenly, crushing her, his weight against her. Beth's eyes flared wide with the horror of things she didn't understand.

"Ah, yes." Adrien's breath fell on her pale cheeks, and he felt her body melt against him, as he had known it would. "I understand you, Beth. I don't care what you are. And you are alone." He whispered the words tauntingly. "Alone! Alone! And you're afraid of being alone, so badly that you would have even me, and I despise you. All I have to do is touch you, for I have the power to do what none of your men has ever done—satisfy you."

Closing one hand about her beautiful face, pulling it out of shape with cruel fingertips, Adrien pressed until Beth's eyes welled with tears.

"Pain brings cleansing, doesn't it, dear? You see, I know what you need, and if you obey me I will help you. Then you won't be alone. Hm? I can promise you absolution from what you have become, because my mission is above petty men. And it will be done, I promise you that."

He slammed her head back against the wall. "Say you will obey me! Say it!"

She screamed, and his mouth closed over hers, not in a kiss, but to silence her. Tremors, thrilling shudders rippled through her body, and Beth groaned against the eroticism of his mouth. Her eyes were closed, but Adrien's were not, and if she had looked Beth would have seen the naked sadism glittering within their depths.

"It is important that I gain access into the Garrett house without being seen," he withdrew his mouth and mumbled just inches from her face, continuing to trap her against the wall with his body. Slowly she shook her head, lips bruised, breaths coming quickly through her open mouth. Steady hands began to undo the buttons of her dress, Beth shivered.

"You will not do wrong to tell me. By helping me you help yourself," he said. He continued with the buttons.

She moaned, "A stairway . . . outside . . . by the stables. There's no need to enter by the ground floor. Will that . . . do?"

"Perfectly." He smiled, bracing himself for the distasteful task before him. Then he reached for her.

❦ Chapter XII

The morning of the Fourth of July threatened rain, but at last the sun came out in all its brilliance. For Vance Herschell the day would be one of the most difficult he would ever face, for he had agreed to escort Sarah and Peter back to the Garrett estate to live. How long they would stay he did not know. He sensed they would never come back, but he knew he would always hope. He had immersed himself in composing for days, nearly exhausting himself.

Since their outing, Nathaniel had openly "courted" his wife, much to the amusement of Patty and the consternation of Vance, who knew nothing of the secret marriage. The details of the forthcoming announcement had not been worked out. Nathaniel's parents and Beth would be told in private, they had agreed. It was only fair, after all. And Sarah knew she must find a way to tell Vance.

Rosy had had Peter prepared for the move hours earlier. Even with the grooms doing the heavy work, Vance seemed to take forever to have the carriage readied. Special care was required for the pink ballgown, and in the seclusion of the carriage Vance simply sat with it, lifting the wrapping to brush his lips against the satin. *Her* gentle hands had smoothed the soft fabric, and now *his* lips had touched it, reverently. His lungs felt as if they would burst as he smoothed the shimmering folds on his knee.

Rick Mayer was escorting his sister to the dance, and his parents were at this very moment entertaining their own guests down at the lake before departing for the Garrett mansion. Everyone about the entire Herschell household was occupied. Everyone except Vance. His preparation for the ball must be done in private—that deep searching for inner strength to hide his grief. It had made an old man of him, this emptying. Dying was such a solitary thing.

Slowly, Vance made the final, torturous journey back through the schoolroom and into the doorway of the suite where Sarah had lived for over two months. She was gathering her books and papers now, the sunlight catching in her dark locks.

Sarah lifted brown eyes to catch Vance's hungry look.

"Oh! Vance. I didn't know you had finished," she smiled, placing her floppy hat with the bag.

"I wish you didn't have to go," the words flushed his face, black locks falling across that pale forehead.

"We have had some very special moments, you and I, haven't we? You're one of the finest human beings I have ever known. And for certain the most talented one." Sarah closed the bag.

She smiled again, and just to please her, Vance forced the tiniest grin around the edges of his mouth. Her mouth was made for kissing. He wondered if she let Nathaniel kiss it often. The thought of Sarah in Nathaniel's arms, the dark man's lips on hers, made Vance flush hot, then cold. Clearing his throat anxiously, he moved into the room.

"What's the matter, Vance?" she asked. She knew what was the matter.

"Nothing. When you . . ." Vance moved his dark eyes about the room. The house seemed so still. The world was still.

"Oh, hell!" the agonized words tore from him, and he closed the few steps between them in a moment.

The brooding young man took her swiftly into his arms for the comfort he needed, and Sarah didn't resist. He hugged her closely. Then, without any warning, he moved, lips searching, head bent until he found her mouth. This would be the only time he would ever kiss her. "I give her to you, Nathaniel," he screamed in his mind, "but for this one moment she belongs to me! I have the right!"

Quickly the dark head jerked upward, and he thrust her from him with a low wail.

Spinning around hard, Vance began to sprint from the room. But Sarah's fingers closed about his arm, freezing him in his steps.

"Don't run, Vance," she commanded quietly, a calm understanding in her voice that he was powerless to disobey.

The boy's head dropped forward into spread fingers, and Sarah's hand felt his shoulders trembling under her touch.

"Oh, Vance." Sarah drew herself around to stand before the heartbroken lad and pulled him to her breast.

"Shhh, don't weep, Vance. I understand. It is a very rare privilege that I have to be loved by someone as fine as you. Now, don't grieve anymore. Come into the schoolroom with me, and let's talk."

"I can't talk," he mumbled against the wet fingers hiding his face.

"Yes, you can. Don't hide from me, Vance. It's nothing to be ashamed of—loving *or* crying. I respect you beyond what you can know. Now come and sit with me. This may be our last time alone for awhile."

Sarah led him to an orderly table where he had often sat across from her, talking, studying, arguing. He turned, struggling to keep from choking.

"Do you need your medicine? Are you all right?" Sarah seated herself, wishing she could share the burden he carried.

"I'm sorry, Sarah," the strangled words came at

last. "I know you belong to him," he whispered, and their eyes met.

"Vance, listen to me very carefully. This is something I probably should have told you long ago. This entire thing is *my* fault, not yours. No, look at me."

"Vance, Nathaniel and I are married. We were married before we ever came here."

A pained moan tore from Vance's throat as he took a few seconds to let the truth soak into his already shattered thoughts. Sarah started to speak.

"I don't want to know the details," he said through clinched teeth. A searing anger, then bewilderment, then something akin to relief passed across his features. His head bowed low to his knees, and those artist's hands crossed above his head. "I'm such a fool!"

"No. I am proud. We have something between us no one can ever share, not even Nathaniel and I. Do you understand what I'm saying to you?"

Vance threaded his fingers through his hair. "Don't give me any of that damned jibberish about love on a spiritual plane. I want you like a man, not a saint. I love you so much it's killing me!" he whispered brokenly. Then he laughed bitterly. "That's funny, isn't it? *Killing me?*"

Sarah sank to the floor at his knees and grabbed him about the waist. "Don't do this! Please, I can't stand it! Don't be sorry, don't be sorry to love."

Vance clasped her shoulders, comforting her now as she sobbed against his chest. "I *do* love Nathaniel, Vance. And I've never even said the words before."

Vance grasped her face in both his hands. "You listen to me then, Sarah Bradley Garrett. You go to that man. You tell him. Do you hear me?" Bright tears sparkled in his eyes. "Don't let another day pass before you tell him . . ." his voice dwindled. "One has no assurances in this life . . . none at all. Tell him now."

They sat thus for quite some minutes, not speaking. Finally Sarah broke the silence.

"I wish you could study, Vance. In Europe, perhaps. You should be studying with Berlioz. Please think about it. Will you? Your parents would send you if you ask them."

Vance nodded. They both knew they were lying, that he never would. But it helped, so they said the words.

Already the Garrett mansion was filled. The stables were active. Nathaniel had picked the best possible moment for Sarah to slip back into the stream of the household with a minimum of questions.

"Mrs . . . Bradley!" Peggy smiled enthusiastically. "Mr. Nat said you'd be back today. And he also said I was to fetch him the minute you arrived." She bustled through the rooms, adjusting windows and checking arrangements.

"Thank you, Peggy," replied Sarah a little uneasily. Was this now to be her home, until the old homesite could be restored? "It's good to see you again. The big house is in quite a stir." Dropping down in the gold-covered chair, Sarah fanned herself with her hat while Peter pointed cheerily to the busy stables below.

"Horse," he repeated over and over, tugging at Rosy's hand and pointing.

"Yes, yes!" the girl finally cried impatiently, and Peggy laughed.

"I suspect we'll have our hands full, Rosy. I'll bring you two an early supper tonight. What d'you say to frosted cake and sugared grapes? Why, there's enough food to feed a small army, I venture."

Smoothing happily at her apron, the woman gave a smiling nod to Sarah. "I'd better fetch Captain Nat, or he'll have my hide, he will," and she took her leave. Sarah wandered about, browsing through the children's small chamber.

Only a few minutes passed before the familiar step

sounded. Sarah caught her breath as Nathaniel closed the door silently behind him.

"Hello, love." He opened his arms wide to her, and Sarah ran. She belonged here. She held tightly, her cheek pressed against his soft shirt. Her slender arms slipped about his waist, and her smiling lips reached eagerly for his kiss.

"I know you're needed downstairs, Nathaniel. We'll be all right. Do your parents know we're here?"

"Yes, I told them." He raised her long tresses with a finger and stroked her neck. "Aren't you coming down to meet everyone?"

"I need to change clothes and . . ."

"I can help with that," he grinned, slipping a gentle hand to pat her middle where his unborn child lay.

"And you would never get downstairs!" laughed Sarah wisely. Suddenly sobering, she whispered, "Nathaniel? I'm afraid. What if they look at me with disappointment? What if Beth makes a scene? What if someone finds out I killed Giles. Adrien may have said something." Nathaniel shook his head.

"You are so used to trouble, poor Sarah. It's beyond you that someone might see the beauty and the goodness in you. My father is *not* your father. And I promise you that he'll not turn his back on you. Mother might be a little snobbish, I grant you, and ask you who your great-great-grandmother was. But don't pay any attention to that. They really like you. And you're married to me. You're the one I chose."

Slicking back his hair affectedly, Nathaniel fitted an imaginary pince-nez on his slender nose and clicked his heels smartly. He drew himself up, the haughty aristocrat. "Of all the women in the world, dahling, I chose you. Pray tell, who could ask for more?"

Sarah stuck out her tongue at his easy mockery. Sweeping her off her feet, Nathaniel tossed her onto Peter's bed. Falling on her with a ferocious growl, Nathaniel kissed her all over with rough, noisy kisses until Peter laughingly joined the fun.

"I give up, I give up!" squealed Sarah, struggling to free herself. Nathaniel lifted the wriggling toddler off the bed. Spying the dress form, on which Sarah had placed the splendid gown and covered it with a sheet, Nathaniel started toward it.

"Is this the gown you've been working on?" he began.

"No!" she wailed, scrambling off the bed to stand in front of him with arms outstretched. "You can't see it yet. It's a surprise."

Nathaniel sniffed. "Now you do have my curiosity aroused. Are you sure I can't have just one little peek?" he frowned.

"Absolutely not," Sarah remained adamant.

"I have a surprise for you, too, you know," he murmured.

"It's not some terrible thing that *you* think is wonderful and that will embarrass me?" She knew her husband's pranks a little too well.

"No, no. I've had it ready all afternoon, and I'll send Peggy with it after I go down. It's that kind of a surprise." Sarah's brow puckered in delight. "Now, let me help you dress or take a bath . . . or something."

"Fie! You'll teach Peter to be as obscene as you are," Sarah shushed him. She glided to the large window and peered down at the spreading lawns beyond the stables. "I told Vance. He took it hard. It broke my heart. Such a genius."

Nathaniel slipped behind to hold her, then easily pulled her down into the chair with him.

"Hold me," Sarah's voice was muffled. Peter sat at their feet until he drifted off into slumber upon the rug.

"I can't ever remember feeling so . . . at peace with everything. And yet I feel guilty, too, because of Vance, I guess."

Tonight, Nathaniel vowed. Tonight he would take a

deep breath and tell her he loved her. Would he ever hear those words from her lips?

"Honey, Vance doesn't want your pity. I think he's proved he doesn't want anyone's pity."

"I know you're right," she whispered, not that it would make it any easier.

Ambling down the marble steps, shading their eyes in the sunlight, she and Nathaniel raised their heads when Patty called from far across the lawn. Rick strolled indulgently in her wake, perfectly at ease.

"Mrs. Bradley!" Patty cried, her blue skirts and petticoats flying. "There's a woman I want you to meet," she announced between panting and avid gesturing. "She's just come from France, married Jonathan Herricks, whom you don't know, of course, and she is just the cutest thing. Can't speak a dozen words of English, and Jon is having the time of his life trying to interpret. Everyone is in stitches trying to use sign language." Rick finally slipped up behind Patty to place a hand firmly over her mouth.

"A wonder of nature, isn't she?" he observed soberly as Patty trod boldly on the toe of his shoe. He removed the hand.

"Will you stop that, you . . . nasty creature?" Patty turned to give his hair a painful yank before she dodged away from him, walking rapidly away.

"Rick," advised Nathaniel soberly, "she demands a very strong hand. I'm not sure one man can handle it." He shook his dark head gravely.

"With all due respect, sir, I think this is a case of the blind leading the blind." Nathaniel threw back his head in laughter.

"Sarah? Sarah is docile as a kitten! I have trained her well."

Clarke and Tabby and the new baby had not arrived, nor had the small orchestra traveling up from Washington. Several small emergencies had occurred in the settling of the guests in their rooms, as several couples planned to stay for the entire weekend. But, all in all, the Garrett staff was performing admirably. The ballroom was open and in readiness. The outdoor tables were well supplied and well tended. Only the kitchens suffered minor mishaps, for the demands were great. But the Herschells' staff were helping.

Eleanor Garrett inclined her head toward the busy group before them, and Nathaniel's father paused to observe Sarah talking with the French woman.

"I had no idea Sarah spoke French. She's so versatile, Nathaniel," noted his mother, plainly impressed. Samuel raised his brows at his wife.

"One can look at the girl and tell she's no fool, Elly," he remarked. "Don't be a snob, darling."

"I'm not a snob, Samuel Garrett. I'm merely surprised. She's so unassuming that one doesn't pick up all these things at the beginning." Eleanor turned to her quiet firstborn as he stood, hands in his pockets, studying his wife with far more adoration on his face than he realized.

"Margaret told me how pleased she and George were with your friend's management of the twins."

Nathaniel glanced down to find her observing him closely. His parents had never pressed him about his relationship with Sarah, and he was grateful for that. But the time had come. Their marriage must be disclosed. Presently Nathaniel faced his father.

"You may already have guessed," the deep voice offered briefly.

"I thought there was something," his father responded, waiting for his son to continue.

"We have been married since the day the war ended."

Samuel Garrett smiled broadly at his towering son.

"It doesn't surprise me, Nathaniel. I saw the change in you from the very beginning. If it's because of this girl, we owe her a great debt." He chuckled. "Why the secret? Didn't you feel you could tell us?"

Observing the newcomer in the center of their friends, Eleanor absently smoothed her hair.

She smiled. "Grandmother Garrett warned me of something, I must confess." Her eyes turned warmly to Nathaniel's anxious face. "I suppose I'm not terribly surprised either."

Nathaniel peered down at her, an expression of great relief erasing the lines about his mouth. "Are you sure that is all you have to tell us, Nathaniel?" she prompted.

"Now what would you be hinting at, Mother? Hmm?" a deep chuckle rumbled in his chest. "Well, Clarke is not the only one who can make babies, Mother. And don't play the innocent. You may deceive Father, but you can't pull that on me. I will answer everything. But later, if you don't mind." And he left to stand beside Sarah.

"Are you going to object to this marriage, Eleanor?" the elder Garrett murmured over the head of his wife, and only she knew the hidden question behind the one posed. Samuel knew her very well. Was she willing to accept Nathaniel's choice as completely independent of family counsel?

"To look into his eyes and *not* see desperation written there, my darling, I would accept anything. Sarah is genuine. And he loves her. What more could a mother want for her son?" The reply was edged with unshed tears.

"I love you, Elly." It was all he said. It was enough.

The sounds of music were already filtering up to the second floor when Sarah began dressing for the ball. Peter was asleep, and Peggy was just entering.

"Mister Nat said I was to see that you received this immediately upon dressing." Peggy's eyes twinkled as she fished an object from her apron pocket.

The gift was a long, black velvet case with a white bow—obviously tied with a masculine touch. Sarah stood in the center of the floor, clad only in her undergarments, her hair trailing down her back. Her fingers picked at the bow, then tore it off. A tiny creak of hinges revealed a fine gold chain, the loops so delicate that Sarah almost feared to touch them. A single translucent pearl, exquisitely set in a very old pendant, graced the chain.

A slip of crisp, white paper lay folded in the box. Placing the lovely piece on the chair, Sarah opened the paper. The masculine scrawl was neat but bold.

My darling Sarah—

My grandfather gave this to Grandmother when they married.

Now, it is yours. I hope you will consent to my presenting you to our guests as my wife. Mother and Father already know, and I believe they are happy. If you don't want the announcement made, then don't wear the gift. If I see it about your neck, I will know it's all right.

—Nathaniel

Sarah's eyes moistened, and without a word she handed the note to Peggy. Slowly the servant's eyes moved over the paper, and her lack of surprise told Sarah what she had suspected from time to time. In some way the rascal had managed to tell her. With only a slight hesitation, Sarah placed the pearl upon her breast and turned her back for Peggy to fasten the clasp.

"That's a fine girl, Mrs. Garrett," sighed Peggy with hearty approval. She laughed soundlessly. "I've had my private suspicions 'bout you two since the first time I laid eyes on you."

"You know, Peggy, I don't think this was such a well-kept secret, after all." Sarah shook her brown locks. "Ah, I'm glad it's all over. It would never do for you all to think I was an unwed mother."

Peggy's surprise was genuine enough this time, and a sheepish glance fell to her belly. Sarah laughed.

"It's tiny, but it's there, Peggy. Rest assured." Peggy hugged herself, then suddenly became efficient.

"If we don't get you dressed, the dance will begin without you. Now, let's fetch that gown."

Fifteen minutes of intense concentration elapsed before Sarah stood up from the dressing table. The finished Sarah made a remarkably striking picture. The pink ballgown was absolutely regal, and the brown curls piled high successfully completed the transition from governess to princess.

Sarah knew she was stunning, and the flush on her cheeks enhanced the glow that pregnancy had already stimulated. Her neckline was daring, for she could lower her eyes and see her bosom down to the absolute crests. She tugged at it for a moment and wriggled farther down into the gown. Finally she shrugged. She had made it this way deliberately and now she was determined to wear it. The pearl rested in a little nest between her breasts.

"If you want my opinion, I think you're the most beautiful woman at the ball. And I have had a peek already, mind you. Of course, Mister Nat will think so. Don't worry any more that you're not as fine as the rest of 'em. You're about the prettiest thing I've ever seen, and that's not flattery." Peggy finished firmly.

Sarah lifted her rosy lips to the robust cheek of the woman and gave her a warm kiss of thanks. "I'm almost afraid to go down, Peggy," confessed the new member of the Garrett family.

"Nonsense. I'll go with you to the stairs. And I'll peep in from time to time to see about the young 'uns. Don't you worry 'bout a thing but givin' Mister Nat the sight of his life. There's a few faces I'd like to see when he makes the big announcement," the ample bosom quivered as quiet mirth shook her. Sarah assumed she was referring to Beth, but she remained silent.

The hallway was not empty as Sarah stepped from her rooms, a delightful study in pink. Vance was headed toward the stairs from one of the wings, and the look in his eyes told Sarah that she had nothing to fear regarding her appearance. The dark head bent down over hers with such an open mixture of emotion that Sarah impulsively slipped her slender arm through his.

So full was Sarah's heart that she could only look up wordlessly into those pensive eyes. She was happy, and she held her emotions tightly in check, lest he see the faintest glimmer of pity in her eyes.

"Would you mind, Vance," she forced herself to be casual, "just until I get down the stairs? This is quite a giant step for the governess." And Vance forced himself away from her.

"Of course, Mrs. Bradley . . . I mean, Mrs. Garrett," he smiled, controlled, pretending.

Vance battled for an unselfishness greater than he had ever demanded of himself. This was *her* moment. He had his own kind of love with her, and he wouldn't spoil this. He continued that lying smile. Sweet, sweet Sarah—how can I let you go? *How can I let you go?*

What is worse than knowing one is dying? Seeing what life is and knowing it will never be complete for you. One step, two steps—closer now, closer to Nathaniel. For one enraged moment white-hot anger burst on Vance. He saw himself—fingers closing about the balustrade beneath them, ripping it up like some raging Samson to swing it as a mighty weapon, slashing, destroying everything in its path. But beautiful lips smiled back at Sarah as she nervously glanced upward. He had held himself in check.

"Look," Vance gestured gently as they paused halfway down the steps. From this step Sarah had a view of the dance floor far beyond her. Only two people were on the polished floor, slowly revolving to the strains of the music.

Lovingly the dark head of her husband bent above that of the petite Grandmother Garrett. Lightly the tall man held the tiny woman in his arms, and the lacy stole draped about the aging arms trailed smoothly behind the couple. Sarah glimpsed his parents, their full hearts revealed on their faces as the third generation made this loving gesture—the eldest son giving the first dance to the eldest Garrett. The tiny woman having tired, Nathaniel carefully led her from the floor.

No sooner had her entrance been accomplished than Sarah found the searching blue eyes of Nathaniel. She felt him read her message, the flush that marked his tanned face telling her what she needed to know. He slowly made his way to her through the groups of people filling the edges of the ballroom. If anyone spoke to him he didn't hear, for his adoring eyes were filled only with the vision of beauty that stood a little shyly across the long room.

A magical force seemed to descend upon those who observed the striking man. The tasteful white ruffling at his neck only enhanced his tanned virility, and the becoming cut of his black suit revealed his lean strength. Between Sarah and Nathaniel sparked an attraction almost electrical in its intensity, and Sarah's thoughts screamed so loudly in her head she felt sure everyone could hear them.

"This beautiful man is my husband!" they shouted. "Don't you see how wonderful he is?"

An adoration near reverence was written all over Nathaniel's features, and anyone within seeing distance practically held their breath as their fingertips slowly reached, touching at last. No words were spoken. Nathaniel guided her onto the floor among the splashes of color.

Virtually alone on the dance floor, their graceful movements were ordered by the gentle chromatic runs of low flutes and the delicate shading of strings. The captivating turns intensified, and Nathaniel slowly drew his bride into his arms, a half-smile of awe flirting about his lips. The music heightened, adding subtle horns and a depth of woodwinds, and the couple moved inside the sound. The pink froth of color whirled and turned with a magnificent elegance that seemed to float beside the sure steps of Nathaniel's lean grace. On and on they twirled, their eyes only for one another, Nathaniel's smile broadening with the yearning in his blue eyes.

At last the dance was ended. A hush fell over the room as the last chord struck. Before a single sound could be made Nathaniel turned, and the bystanders sensed he was about to speak. The entire room held its breath.

"Ladies and gentlemen," his rich voice carried clearly throughout the room. He slipped an arm around Sarah. "This is my wife, Sarah."

The burst of applause caught them both by surprise, and the couple looked quickly to each other and then back to the crowd. The leader of the chamber group swept the musicians into the next dance, and Nathaniel drew Sarah to a cluster of friends and family.

The next moments found Sarah peeping over the shoulder of Senator Garrett to see Nathaniel being laughingly dragged into a group of older men for congratulations. Sarah's father-in-law spun her expertly across the gleaming surface of the ballroom, and she forgot her husband for a moment under his intent gaze.

"Mrs. Sarah Garrett, I vow I should pull you into the library for an all-night chat," he chuckled, the blue eyes teasing her.

"I'm afraid that I have become quite accustomed to the Garrett velvet sword, sir, and as deflating as it may be to you, you don't frighten me one whit." Sarah felt his eyes upon his mother's pearl about her throat. The tall man laughed and pulled her closer to spin her about the room. Once a man tried to cut in on them, but the smiling politician only shook his head.

"Go to the devil, John, I just got her, and I intend to keep her for a while." Affectionately he turned his attention back to her. "Sarah, we love you already. And we know Nathaniel. I trust his instincts as well as my own. And my own tell me a great deal. Welcome to our family, my beautiful daughter. Now, Clarke is looking at us very wickedly. I fear we may have a family quarrel if I don't relinquish you."

Before the gentle man released her, he took her two hands in his own. In the midst of dozens of whirling couples they stood, Sarah's heart near to bursting. "Sarah, I have known my son for thirty-one years. In that time, as Clarke is my witness, I have known Nathaniel to run roughshod over people. If he dares hurt you, I will personally wring his Garrett neck. And that is a promise, daughter. Here, Clarke, carefully now—you're not to step on her toes."

Sarah knew her heart must be written on her face. A family! A whole new family! It was something she had dreamed of all her life.

"Don't ask me to talk, Clarke, for I swear I can't think of a word to say," she smiled up at him.

"You don't have to say anything when you're in the midst of Garretts, darling. They never give you a chance to get a word in."

"Congratulations on the new daughter," offered Sarah. "I'm sure you already know about the new Garrett offspring Nathaniel and I will be adding to the family this winter?" she continued. "News seems to go by wire in this family. I'm almost afraid to think, for fear my thoughts will be known before I finish."

Clarke laughed, and his grey eyes measured her.

"We're grateful for the one you've already given to us, Sarah," he said sincerely, drawing her closer.

"I . . . ?" Sarah blinked in confusion.

"Peter." Clarke's arms tightened about her, and for a moment no word or look passed between them. Finally Sarah realized what the younger Garrett was saying to her. Why, he's telling me the family accepts my son! Sarah almost burst into tears as her long-endured dread was suddenly disposed of.

Sarah leaned back on his arm with unshed tears sparkling in her eyes. She dared not speak for fear the tears would gush forth. When had she *ever* received such compassionate understanding from anyone beside her husband? This night must surely be a fantasy of fulfilled longings.

"I . . ."

"Don't talk, Sarah. You don't need any words. All of us know without your saying anything. Can you accept that?" A moment later he continued, "Welcome to the questionable haven of the Garrett clan, dear. Tabby and I want you to come and spend a weekend with us very soon."

Sarah nodded wordlessly. Presently she whimpered, "If I cry I shall never forgive myself."

"Well, you may as well laugh. The wife of a future United States senator will get nowhere with tears," he counseled good-naturedly. "I fear you will gain much experience in that respect, Sarah. Talk to Mother. She is a master of the art."

Sarah flashed him a brilliant smile for all his reassurance. Suddenly Nathaniel was there beside them.

"Thank you, Clarke," Sarah tightened her fingers about the hand that held hers. "Thank you for . . . everything." After one more joyful, wordless dance with her husband, Sarah sat with Patty, chatting and laughing.

"Oh, here comes the bitch," Patty murmured as Beth approached.

"Shh, Patty. Don't be ugly." Knowing the game Beth played, Sarah was aware that Beth had positioned herself where her words would be overheard.

"I can't remember the last shotgun wedding we had around these parts," Beth muttered to her companion.

Patty made a rude, spitting noise between her teeth. Sarah reached for Patty's arm and began drawing away, fearing a confrontation.

"A Garrett with horns is a sight I never thought to see. But, I suppose anything is possible. Isn't it interesting that Adrien Ronsard is a blond?"

As Sarah and Patty turned to move away, they were shocked to find Eleaner Garrett standing directly behind them.

"I have known your father for many years, Beth, and what I just overheard is not worthy of him," said Eleanor to the women around her. "Ladies, I would like to introduce my new daughter-in-law. It is rare that a family is favored as much as ours has been today. Mrs. Sarah Garrett and her son are a most gratifying addition to our family. Since Mrs. Garrett's good breeding will not allow her to respond to pettiness, I suggest that Patty and the rest of you escort Sarah to the Senator's suite so you may refresh yourselves."

Eleanor moved her hand in a gesture not meant to be ignored. "You will find everything you need, I believe. Beth, perhaps you and I could share a glass of champagne," and the lift of Eleanor Garrett's brows didn't allow for disagreement. The group moved on. The message was clear, now: Sarah was a member of the Garrett family, and the strongly knit clan would tolerate no disrespect to her or her son.

When Sarah returned from her interlude in the senator's suite, she found her husband searching for her.

"What was that all about?" he demanded hotly, pulling her to the dance floor where no one could overhear.

"Nothing, Nathaniel. Beth is hurt and angry, that's all. You must not have warned her."

Nathaniel sighed heavily. "Damn it, Sarah. I never

thought to tell her about the announcement. Well, I'm sorry, love, but she should have guessed."

"Your mother took care of everything. *My,* did she take care of everything!" Sarah grimaced. "I hope I never get her that angry. I fear that Beth will never be a strong supporter of your wife, my love." Nathaniel hugged her closely and whirled her about, nearly treading on Rick and Patty.

"You don't pull any punches, d'ya?" called the cryptic young man with a flash of a smile for Sarah as they danced by.

Another new face smilingly introduced itself as Robert Something-or-Other, and Sarah matched her steps to his. She could dance all night! She was accepted. She was the best that she could be.

Robert's supporting arm drew Sarah a bit closer than she enjoyed, and she had a feeling that he was enjoying her daring decolletage. He was an excellent dancer, however, skillfully weaving her about the crowded floor, her pink skirts billowing airily, her sandled feet barely keeping pace with his quick steps. Boldly he bent his head to her ear until she could feel his breath, warm against her cheek. She wished he wouldn't do that.

"Be very careful that you make *absolutely* no outward indication of what I'm saying to you, honey." Sarah began to look up but he gripped her tightly. "No sign at all." He tossed his dark head back in a pretend laugh. His eyes were not laughing with his mouth.

"If you ever wish to see your son alive again, do exactly as I tell you."

Robert's arm imprisoned her until their bodies were crushed together. Blindly Sarah stumbled against the man, and he was forced to hold her up. This wasn't really happening! It must be a nightmare.

"Get out of these clothes and be at the stables within ten minutes. If you disobey . . ." he shrugged. "The child's life means nothing to me."

Glazed eyes noted the small scar on his temple, running into his hairline. His center teeth overlapped slightly, and a tiny amount of white flaking from his hair fell upon the shoulders of his suit.

"But—"

"No questions. Obey. Immediately. Look natural. Do not be observed."

The man removed his arms, and Sarah nearly collapsed on the gleaming tile. She never remembered climbing the stairs, but she came to her senses as she reached the top step.

Blindly she groped for the doorhandle and stumbled into Peter's room. Empty. Quiet. There were no signs of a struggle.

Oh, God, help her! It was Adrien! Wildly Sarah tore at the hooks on the back of the gown she had made with such wonderful dreams. She wasn't meant to be happy. Suffering was all life had for her . . . and for her son. Suffering! And everything had been at the tips of her fingers!

Peter! Where are you?!

She managed to pull on the little print dress she had brought with her from Tennessee and some shoes she could ride in. She must go to the back stairway. No one would see her then. What did they want? Would Adrien kill her? If she could only save Peter, that would be the most she could hope for.

She bent her head over the wash basin and retched miserably. Sinking down to her knees, she bent her head in a tormented prayer for the life of her son. *Please, God, please don't let them kill Peter. Please. Only that, and I'll never ask anything of You again.*

✑ *Chapter XIII*

THE STABLES WERE dark. She waited. She heard nothing—not the wary steps as they fell behind her or his breathing when he reached around to slap the chloroform-soaked rag down over her nose and mouth. The bruising jostle of the carriage, the rag tearing at the corners of her mouth marked Sarah's next awareness. Her lower teeth were clamped, cutting into her lip, and she moved with a half-conscious groan, discovering that her hands were tied behind her and her feet were bound securely. As her tongue touched the cloth Sarah gagged—dry, heaving strangles.

The night was dark, and Sarah could hardly distinguish who was in the carriage. The biting tone of Adrien's voice shocked her, though she'd known he was behind this.

"Behave, Sarah, or I will hit you." His rough hands jerked her up, almost into a sitting position, and Sarah's head lolled from side to side.

"Don't hit 'er, Channing. If she's marked up Garrett'll never rest until he kills us for sure," begged a man's voice. Sarah strained to place his voice in her memory, but she was still too drugged.

"Shut up! Get this clear, Artie, I don't intend to fight you the whole time. You wanted to be in on this, so earn your money and do as you're told," snarled Adrien. "And I don't want to tell you again. Don't call me Channing around here—ever."

"Don't get so sore, Cha—— Adrien."

It was at this point that Sarah became conscious of Peter's presence in the carriage. His sniffling prodded her to consciousness. She could just barely see the outline of the tear-stained face across from her.

So bitter was her hatred of Adrien Ronsard that she could have killed him with her hands. In truth, he had been wise in restraining her, for Sarah's terror gave her extra strength. She strained fiercely against the stout twine bonds. A helpless animal sound reverberated in the small enclosure, and she hurled herself against Adrien with unbelievable savagery.

"Damn you, you stupid bitch!" yelled Adrien, another terrified scream from Peter driving him to violence as he sent Sarah sprawling to the floor.

"Shut that brat up!" Savagely, Adrien kicked Sarah and, lifting her, threw her back into the seat. "If you do that one more time, Sarah, I'll put you out again. Now straighten yourself or I might even be tempted to forego ransom and kill you here and now."

Adrien's face, still badly bruised from Nathaniel's beating, loomed over her. "I warned you I would kill you if you told Garrett. Did you think I was just talking?"

He pulled his vest into place and leaned back in the seat. "The one thing I regret is that I won't be there to see the great Garrett's face when he sees all he got from me were a few names and some bruises on my face."

The carriage shuddered to a stop, and her head jerked upward. No more than half an hour had elapsed.

"I hope we don't have to wait," the strange man fretted. Shrill, his tone indicated a very real fear of Adrien. "Garrett probably has the whole countryside out looking for us by now."

Adrien snorted. "You'll never be anything but a two-bit hoodlum, Artie. See if you can hold onto your spleen until we can get this switch made. Damnation, I wish I'd left you back in Washington."

Voices sounded outside, and the door slammed back against the side of the coach.

"They're here!" exclaimed the worried man, making haste to alight. As Adrien stepped across Sarah to the outside, she wrenched herself upright, only to be knocked back down by a cruel hand. Painful thuds of her heart weakened her, and icy fear raced through her body. Not for herself. For Peter.

A dark figure filled the doorway. Unbelievably, John Pollard's serpent-like face leered at the occupants of the carriage. A lantern blinded her eyes, and for several seconds she blinked hard.

"Do you have the money with you? All of it?" Adrien's question came from just outside the door, beside John.

"Rest your mind, my friend," murmured John without turning. "Did you have any trouble with the woman?"

"No!" Adrien laughed softly. "She came easily, just as you said she would."

John took the lantern and swung it high over the babe who squeezed his eyes tightly shut and made soft, fretting sounds. Sarah couldn't help herself; she fought against her bonds.

"Spare us the marvels of motherhood, Mrs. Bradley. I *beg* your pardon—Mrs. Garrett. Rachel Bradley warned you months ago that it would be better for you to agree, but you wouldn't listen. Didn't she tell you she would have this child? But then, I doubt you'll be needing him where you're going. Let us have the boy, Ronsard. We must hasten," urged the deadly cobra, gesturing to Artie to fetch the child. "You'd best not try to reach me until this settles down a bit, Adrien. The old woman will be moving around until we get the mother taken care of."

Sarah cursed against the gag. May God in heaven damn your soul, Rachel!

As the baby was transferred to a strange woman waiting beside the door—an older woman dressed in a dark gown with a shawl drawn about her shoulders—Peter wept and clawed his way toward his trussed mother, but his cries were muffled by the woman. Heavily Sarah fell to the floor of the conveyance and half crawled to the open door, pleading until her bursting throat could hardly utter another sound. She attempted to stand, thrashing against anything that would help her to her feet, the sound of Peter's muffled cries piercing her. Suddenly, the ground thrust itself up at her, and a merciful darkness swept through her. Sarah never saw them leave with her son.

As Nathaniel's pensive frown wandered over his guests, he threaded his way through the crowd.

"Hello, sweetheart," he grinned down at Tabby, scooping up the slender girl in a great bear hug.

"Put me down, you rowdy pirate!" scolded the new mother, crinkling the row of freckles that marched across her upturned nose. "Why don't you pick on someone your own size?"

"Yeah," agreed Clarke, jutting out his chin formidably. "Pick on someone your own size." Nathaniel dropped his brother's wife in mock fright and Clarke lovingly drew the woman into the circle of his arms.

"I beg your pardon," apologized the taller brother with a wink at his father. "Well, I guess I'll pick on my own wife. That is, if I can find her." Once again his anxious eyes raked the room.

"I saw her just a few minutes ago," offered his father, prompting an agreeing nod from Clarke.

"As a matter of fact, Nat, I did see Sarah. I thought she seemed rather pale. Have you looked in her room? Perhaps she began feeling ill. Women in her condition sometimes do, you know," he grinned, enjoying his expertise at fatherhood.

Nathaniel's long strides took him up the stairs two at a time and whispered on the carpeting in the wing, their sound being the only thing to greet his ears as he hurried uneasily down the hall. The slightly open door drew an apprehensive groove between the dark brows. He called her name before he even stepped into the silent room. The heavy stillness was Nathaniel's first warning, and the acrid smell assured him that his wife was indeed ill. Giving a robust yell for Peggy, Nathaniel strode through the empty room. Why did Sarah have to be so darned stoic all the time? Couldn't she for once admit to being a normal expectant mother and let him care for her as he would enjoy doing?

The scene in Peter's room was a further disturbance. The gown was ballooned on the floor, the undergarments lying in a corner. This was so unlike Sarah. The absence of Peter and Rosy was even more frightening. Something was very wrong here, and Peggy voiced as much as she stepped into Sarah's room.

"Good heavens, Mister Nat!" she proceeded at once to dispose of the washbasin. "Where is the girl?" she called over her shoulder from the bath.

Just then, a small but unmistakable thumping sound accosted both of them. Peggy pointed a stout forefinger back toward his room.

Entering his room, Nathaniel heard the thumping once again. A bewildered lunge toward the bathroom opened its door on a small, terrified Rosy. She was bound and gagged and so weak with fright she could hardly hold up her head. Even before he removed the gag and untied her, a sick warning of what she was about to tell them made him tremble.

"Lord have mercy on us. This is all my fault!" wailed Peggy, bitter tears blinding her. "I swear I looked in on those younguns only ten minutes ago.

Peter was nearly asleep, and Rosy was eating from her tray. Merciful saints, what has gone on here?"

"Peggy, fetch Father and Clarke without alarming the house. Hurry now, we have no time to lose!"

The servant hurried down the hall without question and paused abruptly when Nathaniel added, "Peggy?" He hesitated, frowning heavily. "You'd better send . . . Beth . . . up, too." The distraught woman gazed sharply at Nathaniel but rushed to obey.

By the time Nathaniel had calmed Rosy enough that she could talk, the Senator and Clarke were there.

"Sarah has been taken, Father. And Peter," explained a benumbed Nathaniel, spreading his hands in a helpless gesture.

"I damn well know who took her!" Nathaniel assured his baffled father. "Peggy, fetch Matthew and see to Rosy."

Rosy burst into fresh tears, bordering on hysterics, and stood wringing her small hands miserably. "Oh, Lawd, Mr. Nat. Ah didn' do wrong. Hones', Ah didn't do wrong. He jes' hold me hard. Ah couldn' hep it, Mr. Nat," the poor girl sobbed.

"Rosy!" Nathaniel's words were sharper than he wished, for his own anxiety for Sarah was so enormous he feared *he* would break down if he didn't do something quickly. *He should have killed him!*

"Hush, child! That's all right, Mister Nat. I'll take care of her," promised Peggy. "Come along, honey. Of course it wasn't your fault." Peggy's voice faded down the hallway as she went to get Matthew Mc-Carey.

"Are you saying we have a *kidnapping* on our hands, Nathaniel?" asked Clarke in quiet astonishment.

"Rosy told me a man she had never seen before tied her up and took Peter. I suspect Sarah left of her own free will." Nathaniel donned riding clothes, his mouth pinched and drained of color. Matthew's big frame suddenly filled the doorway before another question could be posed, and in a very few words the quiet man accepted the situation without question.

"Ronsard." The single word fell like a rock.

Samuel Garrett and George Herschell had racked their brains about Adrien's list of names, but Samuel had had no way of knowing then the terrible price Nathaniel would pay for the information.

Beth's full skirts rustled in the hallway behind the men, and Senator Garrett turned to her. "Beth?"

Nathaniel pushed past them and, catching Beth roughly by the arm, dragged her back out into the hall. The three men caught only fragments of the angry conversation.

"No!" and Beth shook her head—pale, trembling. Again Nathaniel questioned her, the muscles in his jaw bunching furiously, and once more Beth denied, composure forgotten as she shook her head against the wall, over and over.

Nathaniel jerked from her, then swiftly whirled upon her again, spitting, "You're lying! Admit it, or by heaven I'll beat it out of you right now!"

"Get him away from me!" shrieked Beth, truly afraid and attempting to wrench herself from the crushing hands that bit into her arms. "I don't know anything! I haven't done anything! *I don't know anything!*"

"You damn well do! *Now tell me!*" An outraged arm raised, and the Senator started to lunge.

"Nathaniel!" Clarke dove for Nathaniel's back and grabbed at his arms.

Beth broke then, half flailing at him, half trying to hide her face. "I swear to God, Nathaniel, I didn't dream he would do anything like this!" she cried. "I swear. I just told him about the stairway. I didn't mean it! Oh, please, I never dreamed he would do anything like this!" Tears ran down her face, and Beth turned pleadingly to Nathaniel's father. "You believe me, don't you? I swear, Senator, I never meant for anything to happen to her."

The Senator shuddered and Nathaniel whirled from her. For a second he looked back, pain drawing long lines from nose to mouth.

"Get out of my sight!" he thundered. "I hope you suffer the torments of hell for this!"

Nathaniel lifted a face of naked suffering to his father.

"Go," advised Clarke to Beth.

Yanking on his jacket, Nathaniel removed a rifle, ammunition, and a pistol from his closet and strode to the hallway, followed directly by Matthew, who had also changed clothes. Rick entered the wing and Vance came more slowly. Rick began to speak, and Clarke interrupted him.

"She was dancing with that guest of Scobel's, Nathaniel. You know, I told you she looked very strange?" Clarke interjected hastily. "In fact, she looked like a ghost. I remember smiling at her, and she looked at me so strangely."

"See if you can find the man downstairs, but I'll lay odds that he has left by now and that Jim Scobel knows very little about him," Nathaniel sighed.

"There's trouble, sir?" Rick's deep voice was steady and determined. Vance watched, ashen.

"Not now, boys. Real trouble, and I don't have any time to explain," Nathaniel began to descend the stair, brushing them off in his haste.

"We're coming, sir. We can change and meet you at the road by the time you're there," argued Rick persistently, following the taller man down the stairway and ignoring Nathaniel's reluctance to speak with them.

"You'll be in the way, Rick. Matthew is coming," snapped the troubled man.

"We're coming, sir," insisted the determined young man, revealing a surprisingly mature understanding.

"We'll be at the fork by the time you get there, or soon after. Vance and I will cut through the fields."

Nathaniel was in no way to blame for what happened next, though in the weeks to come he unjustly took much of the responsibility for it. But the fact was, no one could have foreseen it, with the possible exception of Vance. And he only had several seconds' warning.

Somehow Vance knew—as he watched Rick with detached eyes that separated him from the living. Quietly, quickly, Vance was alone in the universe, meeting with the Creator of life. The waiting of so many months and years was done.

He was going to faint. He didn't need to breathe. Not any more. Already black fingers tangled about his feet, and the next step was too far away. Fingers that would never fly the length of polished ebony again clawed into his vest. Sarah? I finished it for you, Sarah. Sarah?

Rick sensed it before he heard. Matthew and Nathaniel were past, and Rick could do no more than cry Vance's name and lunge for the friend he loved so much.

Down Vance tumbled, over and over, blurring limbs that didn't stop moving until Rick managed to clear three steps and grab him.

"Vance!" he cried. "Oh, Vance! No, no!"

How many seconds did it take Clarke to reach the boy? Nathaniel didn't know, for he could only stare, hypnotized as Rick rocked the limp boy in his arms. Then Vance's mother and father were there—and Patty. Clarke was very efficient.

Senator Garrett guided Nathaniel, stunned, his rifle in his hand. Matthew opened the door. Together they managed to get him outside.

"Nathaniel!" his father shook his shoulders hard. "There's nothing you can do for Vance!"

Nathaniel stared. "You know?"

"I've always known. You must not think of Vance. You must go for Sarah. Now!"

Nathaniel and Matthew rode for some minutes before Nathaniel became aware of where he was.

"What do you make of it, Matthew?" Nathaniel's strained question sounded so much unlike him that Matthew was shocked. An unspeakable fear disguised his make-believe calm.

"Nat," the older man advised, pausing to stare at a road covered with wheel tracks.

"Nat," continued Matthew, "I don't see any hope of followin' their tracks. Ronsard wouldn't be foolish enough to leave traces. Shall we go to Washington?"

Nathaniel sighed heavily. "God have mercy on him," he mumbled, and Matthew watched the fingers rub hard against his brow as Nathaniel shoved that particular grief aside.

"Ride into Upper Marlboro and leave word at the telegraph office to give all wires to the constable before delivering them. They must all be checked. Then see Job Puckett and tell him to have one of his boys standing by in case anything comes for us. All wires are to be delivered to my father immediately. Make it very clear. I'll meet you at the town house."

Nathaniel swung off his mount to check the girth, and an owl made a sharp sound, flapping its wings loudly as it sailed out of the treetop. Nathaniel jumped suddenly as if he had been struck, his gun clearing his belt so quickly that Matthew trembled at the bare veneer of control.

"We could wire the marshal in Washington and give it more thought tonight."

"No, I think we should go now. Ronsard knows the capital, and since he was an agent for the South, I think he will head there. The only place I can actually pinpoint him is in Virginia, the night Giles was killed. But we at least know that much."

And casting one last glance toward the lights glowing in the distance, Nathaniel quickly remounted and set his horse toward Washington.

The night was long and nerve-wracking, producing absolutely nothing. After checking with the law officials, the two men met and began a systematic inquiry of every livery stable and gun dealer in the city. Awakening people when they had to, scouring the city until mid-morning of the next day, the exhausted men dragged themselves back up the steps of the two-story brick home near the capital. There they found a hollow-eyed Rick having breakfast. Without even washing, Nathaniel and Matthew seated themselves to begin gulping black coffee.

Rick placed his fork in his plate, fingers trembling. Grey eyes filled as he met Nathaniel's own haunted stare.

"He lived three hours, Captain. He never came to." Nathaniel's jaw tightened. "He breathed through his mouth for awhile, then he just took a few short breaths until he didn't breathe any more."

The three figures ate mechanically.

"Why did you come?" Nathaniel asked at last.

Rick swallowed. "Vance doesn't need me now. I think this is what he would have had me do." He toyed with the meat and gravy. "He cared very much for Mrs. Garrett."

"I know that," Nathaniel tried to clear the hoarseness from his voice. "Thank you." In spite of himself, Nathaniel's dark head dropped down across his arms beside his plate. The couple who tended the house hovered about sympathetically, and the woman placed packs of food on the table—meat, energy-laced sweetbread and cakes, canteens of apple juice. Nathaniel raised burning eyes to ask that the horses be rubbed, watered and fed.

Biting off a large chunk of hard roll, only half chewing it, Nathaniel paused as the knocker thumped on the front door. He swallowed hastily, striding to the front of the house, pulling on his jacket as he went.

"Mr. Garrett?" timidly queried a wizened old man, peering up at the stern figure looming above him.

"Yes!"

"You the fella lookin' to find his wife what was took?"

"Yes, have you heard anything?" Nathaniel demanded impatiently, steering the man into the kitchen and motioning for the woman to pour coffee. "Quickly, man! Anything you know or have heard!" he rasped.

"Gimme time to say it, boy." The old man hunched his shoulders and frowned at being handled so disrespectfully when he was only trying to help.

"Sorry. Go on."

"The marshal said he wanted any information, no matter how small. And I ain't sure this is the gent you's talkin' 'bout. But I clean up th' hotel, see, an' last week these two men was talkin' in the dinin' room. I paid it no never-mind 'til the marshal was askin' 'bout this yella-haired man."

"Go on, go on!" snapped Nathaniel.

"Wal, sir, it's th' man that was with 'im that I overheered talkin' 'bout pickin' him up a horse in Virginia. Seems somethin' wus ailin' his, and he wus makin' plans as to how he knew a man in Trinity Forks who wus goin' to sell him a horse. The yella-haired man give him some money. It was him sayin' how they best take care with what they had until they got th' other money. That's whut I 'member, thinkin' how lucky a gent wus to have money after the war an' all. A man has money now, he could make hisself a bundle. Speculatin', you know. Land buyers goin' crazy. Yep. Well, I don't guess that heps you none, does it? But th' marshal said to come over here and tell ya anyway, so I done it."

Reaching into his wallet, Nathaniel drew out a few bills, and pressed them into the gnarled hand. "It's not a lot, old man, but it gives us a place to look—if you did indeed see the blond man we are looking for. Can you describe him for me? *Anything* you remember, the slightest detail."

After five minutes of laborious questioning, Nathaniel satisfied himself that they were talking about the same man. The chances were very few that he could be traced with such scanty information, but Nathaniel planned as sound a strategy as he could muster. Rick was to visit the Washington newspapers and use the Garrett home as a base of communication. Twice a day, wires would be sent and received from Nathaniel and Matthew to Washington, to the Garrett estate and back. A ransom message could be quickly relayed this way. The older men would travel in a fan southeast and southwest, alerting sheriffs and searching towns, house by house.

Vance was buried two days later in the small cemetery near Nathaniel's property, quite near the grave of his grandfather.

The lack of a ransom note after five days devastated Nathaniel. Only the threat of force by Matthew and his father made him return to the country estate to rest for the weekend. The search was left in the hands of the authorities in every town of any size through Virginia and West Virginia, at the capital, and in Maryland. Every newspaper in the area carried a description of Peter and Sarah and of Adrien Ronsard.

Sarah's eyes finally became accustomed to the dark cellar. During the first few hours of the first day, she cautiously felt her way about the damp walls. Greatly afraid, she moved slowly. Twice every day, Artie opened the heavy oak door at the top of the steps to bring her food. She caught glimpses of her prison when he came. Apples had once been stored here, for several baskets still remained with hard bits of dried fruit still in them. At least there were no rats or snakes. At least not yet.

At first she had entertained hope of escape, but as the days crept past, those hopes had dwindled. Ten days by now, at least, and the weakened woman was suffering grave difficulty in keeping control of her mind. Often she talked aloud, for it seemed to steady her nerves.

Now she carefully climbed her way up the steep steps, banging on the door with a weakly clenched fist. This was the first time today that she had tried to raise someone upstairs. Sarah knew that often she was trapped alone with no one upstairs at all. What if someday they just *never* came back? She would starve, and her baby with her.

She was so weak she could barely make herself heard, having lost a considerable amount of weight on the small amount she was given to eat, and her pregnancy taking most of the nourishment. She did sleep some, though, even with the cold. At night Sarah would brush out the corner, always making certain she was still the only living thing in the cellar; then she would huddle against the L of the wall. After awhile days and nights became mixed, not even untangling when the door was opened.

Now, it was the silence that drove Sarah to bang as hard as she could upon the door above her head.

"Artie!" she called loudly, praying that Adrien was not upstairs. Sometimes Sarah just pressed her ear to listen. Once Adrien had been there when she attempted to plead with Artie through the door. The door had slammed open and he had kicked her back down the steps. She had rocked herself, whispering, "You can't break me, Adrien. You can't break me."

But now Sarah was beginning to fear he might. "Artie!" she cried again, beating harder.

"What d'you want?" came his grumbling voice from the opposite side.

"I . . . I want to ask some questions, Artie. All right?" Sarah pleaded.

"What questions?"

"What day is it? How long have I been here?" Please let the beast answer. "What time is it?"

"It's nearly dark, and you've been there . . . let's see, nine days." Sarah could hear his shoes squeaking above her head.

"Is Mr. Ronsard there?" she coughed.

"No! Now be quiet, or you'll get us both in trouble when he gets back."

"Artie, no! Please don't go away. *Please.* I think I'm sick. Can't you open the door?"

Sarah knelt on the steps, so tired, trying to comb her hair with her fingers.

"Artie? Please open the door. For just a few minutes. I won't try to get out if you will. I just want to talk to you," begged Sarah. Silence. Then, to her surprise, the bar scraped against its wedge, and the remaining rays of daylight burst marvelously into the dark pit, nearly blinding her.

"Now what do you want? You know Adrien'll be furious with us both."

"Artie, I'm sick. No, please believe me. I could promise you more money than Adrien can possibly give you, Artie, if you would just get me to the Garretts. *Don't shut that door!"* Sarah screamed as he moved, and shakily fought to compose herself, speaking extremely quietly, as if by proper behavior she might merit a few more precious moments.

"Artie, I don't know how much longer I can stand it down there. My God, have mercy on another human being. I'm sick. Feel my head if you don't believe me."

Obligingly Artie touched his hand to the pale, pinched face of the woman and sighed. "Well, they ain't nothing I can do except get you some water. And don't ask me any more to let you go. The Lord's sweet truth is I wished I *could* let you go. I didn't do myself no good gettin' mixed up in this. But I'm in it now, and Adrien would almost as soon kill me as you. And that ain't worth no amount of money to me. Now get back down in there before he comes back."

"Please, Artie," Sarah wept as she saw the heavy door close the shaft of light to a mere sliver. "No, please."

The light shrank to an glimmer and then disappeared. *Oh, Nathaniel! I know I will never see you again. I want you to know I LOVE YOU. I wish I had told you. Now you have lost your wife and child.*

Weeping, rocking herself as she clutched her knees to her bosom, Sarah grew so tired she could hardly crawl back down to the chilly floor. Tomorrow, she promised, tomorrow she would feel better, and she would be stronger. Tomorrow she would fight Adrien.

But tomorrow Sarah's fever would rage out of control. She was demented by desperation. Gradually the effects of the debilitating fever weakened her mind, and after the twelfth day it didn't matter anymore where she was.

"How long has she been sick?" demanded Adrien, bending over the body in the cellar, and Sarah battled fiercely to open her scalding eyes. Painfully she felt her head being roughly lifted and was aware that Adrien was forcing one eye open with his fingers.

"Please, please," reaching thin hands to the voice for help. His grasp felt cool as he pushed her from him, lest in her fevered state she clutch him.

"You should've asked for a ransom when we first took her, Adrien," remonstrated Artie. Artie's worry was a constant source of irritation to Adrien for he had made many mistakes in this kidnapping. And he had no desire to be reminded of them.

"If you don't shut up, I'm going to beat the hell outa you," threatened the fair man, kicking a chair against the wall. What would he do with Sarah? The woman had been delirious for days and had taken no food and very little water.

"With what we got for the boy, her ransom could have seen us both out of the country. We would've been set for life if you'd listened to me," complained the smaller man.

"What did you expect me to do with every damned law officer in the state looking for us, you fool? Everywhere I've been for supplies, that's all anyone can talk about—Garrett, Garrett, Garrett. I can't get near a telegraph office. As soon as the heat dies down I'll contact the Senator. I can't do anything now."

"I'll tell you, Channing, er, Adrien. . . . I'd like my share of the money now. I want to go South. Your life ain't worth a plugged nickel, but no one knows who *I* am. It's only fair. I've holed up here, watching this woman for you, while you've run all over the country. I've done everything you wanted me to, and I think you ought to pay up now." Artie's light brown eyes flitted toward the leather bags that Adrien kept near him at all times. They contained the money John Pollard had given them for Peter.

The blond man's anger flared. "You try it, and I'll kill you on the spot. This girl is dying. You'll get your money when she's disposed of and not before," snarled the slender man. "Since they aren't looking for you I'm going to leave first and see if I can't make it to Canada. Once I get out of Virginia I know I can make it to Canada. Damn, I never saw people so persistent."

Bent over the ghostly pale form of Sarah lying on the floor, Artie grimaced—the curve of her belly was only beginning to swell beneath the faded print dress.

"She's just barely breathin', Adrien," Artie reported gravely, kneeling down and putting his ear to her chest. "Oh lord, I wish I had never let you talk me into this. I never did anything wrong in my life until this. They'll catch me for sure; I know they will," grieved the small man, his unshaven chin trembling.

"I don't give a damn if they hang you, you sniveling coward, but if you tell them where I am I'll kill you myself. Now quit that blubbering and get out of my sight. You make me sick," demanded Adrien, his disgust intense. Artie feared to turn his back on the ruthless man. If he *ever* got out of this trouble alive, the timorous accomplice swore he would never put his foot inside Virginia again.

The sun was beginning to set. Adrien sat on the porch, smoking, despondent, reluctant to ride into the small town nearby. Both men were hungry, for they dared build no cooking fires for fear someone would see smoke.

"Adrien," called Artie, fresh alarm coloring his voice. Cursing the man, Adrien arose, opening the door. "I think she's dead," reported Artie wringing his hands.

"I hope to God she is. I'm tired of this whole thing. Get out of the way and let me see."

In vain Adrien felt for a pulse, both at Sarah's wrist and throat. His ear to the still breast found no breathing. Sarah was dead, and she was about to be buried. Adrien gritted his teeth. Her death had probably cost him ten thousand dollars.

Adrien poured himself a drink, nearly choking as he forced it down. "I want you to take her off somewhere and bury her. I'll give you two thousand for your share of the boy and a thousand for burying her. Then get out of here, out of this state and forget you ever knew me. Do you understand what I'm telling you, you feeble-minded idiot?"

"Are you leaving the buggy with me?" Artie eagerly crammed his belongings into a bag, rapidly checking his handgun.

"Of course. Do you think I expect you to carry her on your back? I'm leaving right now. Be careful. Dispose of the carriage so that no one can trace it back here. And for God's sake, Artie, don't draw attention to yourself!"

"All right, all right. Lay off, will you?" Artie's forthcoming freedom from Adrien increased his boldness. "One thing I'll not miss is that acid tongue of yours."

Adrien counted out Artie's share of the money. Artie snatched it, glancing at the body on the floor. Fetching a quilt from upstairs, he wrapped Sarah in it and dragged her body to the door.

Nathaniel was close to insane. Against the counsel of his father, Nathaniel engaged a dozen workmen to begin work restoring his estate. He recalled every suggestion Sarah had made and covered all the details with his overseer. When he was not exhausting himself in a methodical search of outlying acreages or pursuing hopeless reports, as far as a hundred miles away, Nathaniel stripped down to his pants and boots and worked until he was senseless.

"Son," began his father cautiously, finding Nathaniel seated at his kitchen table late in the afternoon of the third week. The back of Nathaniel's neck was sunburned, for he had been home for three days, driving himself from daybreak until late at night.

The Senator rested his hands on Nathaniel's shoulders, the silvering head leaning to touch the dark one. Together, the two men wept. Tears for Sarah and for one another.

After a time Nathaniel gained enough control of himself to force down some food. He chewed absently, his blue eyes staring vaguely ahead.

"I'm going back in to the telegraph office," he stated between bites. *"Why* don't they ask for a ransom?"

"Nathaniel, let Peggy order you a hot bath. See if you can't get a few hours' rest," advised Samuel Garrett. He could hardly believe what he saw—his son was gaunt, and the dark circles under his eyes made him look even thinner. He hadn't shaved in days, and his movements were slow—broken and defeated.

"Rick or Matthew will bring any word, you know that. It will not help Sarah if you are ill."

The glassy stare focused, piercing through the older man like a stiletto. "You think she's dead, don't you, Father?"

"No, of course not, son. But . . . it's not wise to drive yourself like this. Everyone is doing all that's possible and—"

"Well, it's not enough, damn it to hell!" raged the distraught man, slamming down his cup and jarring the table as he rose. "I'm sorry. I need a drink. I need something. Oh, God! What am I going to do? They can have everything I own. All I want is Sarah."

Nathaniel's words ran together as he stumbled blindly from the room, seeking the solitude of the upper story. His father didn't attempt to console him. He was thankful for the outburst, for Nathaniel had held himself under such tight control that he feared his son would snap if he didn't release some of the terrible pressure he carried.

Nathaniel slept for sixteen hours.

The workmen had gone, and the moon had come. Nathaniel walked the clear spaces of the old house, which was emptied of people. He stared at the paneled walls Sarah had wanted. Fingers smoothed the ancient stones where she had smoothed them.

Hot, burning tears slid down his face.

They had begged him not to work on the house. But not to work would have been like admitting she was dead. Let them think he was crazy. He couldn't stop working. He . . . What had he dreamed? The tears were blinding now, and he stumbled to the mantle, clinging to it with all his might, the deep, racking sobs tearing at his lungs. *Oh, Sarah, Sarah. Please don't be dead. Please don't be dead.*

That was how Matthew found him. The big man coughed quietly. Bleary eyes lifted, and Nathaniel looked up. "I thought you were going to rest for a day," he choked, bracing his elbow on the mantle and dropping his head to his palm.

"Did you rest?" Nathaniel made no reply, and Matthew laced his fingers tightly.

"I never even told her I loved her, Matthew," the lament tore at him, and Matthew wrapped a comforting arm about his friend.

"Ah, lad," the gentle man murmured, "don't do this to yourself. She knew how you felt about her. And she returned the affection long before she knew it."

"Do you think we'll find her, Matthew?"

"Yes."

"But it's been so long," Nathaniel whispered miserably.

"I know," Matthew replied.

"Will you ride back with me to Washington tonight?" Nathaniel pressed the bridge of his nose with his thumb and forefinger. "I sent Rick ahead while I stayed over today."

"You know I will."

Once the ride back to the capital had been accomplished, Matthew coaxed three whiskeys into his exhausted friend, and he and Rick finally saw him undressed and in bed.

Rick pulled the door to Nathaniel's room shut quietly. The lanky youngster frowned up at the older man. "Captain Garrett is in a bad way, sir. I really don't know how to help him. He's a strong man, but I really don't think he can stand much more."

"It's hard on all of us, Rick, but Nat'll make it. A man takes what 'e has to."

"I think I'll take a little walk down to the train

terminal," he mused thoughtfully, tugging at his red beard. "Your company'd be welcome if you'd like to come."

Matthew's grey eyes surveyed the withdrawn lad walking beside him, the trim cut of his clothing making him look even more slender than he really was. He liked Rick—he was quiet and spoke his mind straightforwardly—a quality the big man admired in a man so young.

"Of course, sir. I'd like that."

The mist that settled over the city did little to lift the sagging spirits of the two men as their boots clicked on the cobblestone street. The nearer their steps took them to the train terminal, the more active the streets became, the heavier hung the sulfurous odor of soft coal smoke. Low wails of distant whistles and rumbling of a switch engine at work wafted through the air.

Stepping across several pairs of tracks, Matthew led the way past the green terminal building, past the telegraph room with its almost constant clicking, to Old Dan Franklin's all-night soup kitchen. Old Dan had run his little business as long as Matthew could remember. Upon occasion the stubby man would stroll through the perpetually soot-darkened terminal, vending his packets of shelled nuts, making change from his stained apron of pockets. Matthew smiled deep in the red beard, for it was not a well-kept secret that Old Dan could always be depended on to have a little something tucked away in his cupboard to warm the soul as well as the stomach. More than once over the years Matthew had come to this very place to sit and sip brandied coffee, observing people coming and going in the terminal.

Rick preceded the Irishman up the creaking steps into the small room lit by several coal-oil lamps, taking in the occupants of the room with a quick assessment. Of the four tables, two were occupied. A lone

clergyman sat half dozing over his bowl of beef stew
and a well-handled newspaper. A rather poorly
dressed young couple and a sleeping child sat on a
bench against the wall. The father still wore the trousers of the Yankee uniform. Rick guessed their total
possessions rested in the three bags stacked beside
them. Two men in casual riding clothes sat at the
table next to the vacant one that Matthew lowered his
hulk beneath. The rickety chair complained loudly at
being asked to bear such an unreasonable burden, and
one of the men raised from his conversation to give
the two newcomers a nod of greeting. The clergyman's
newspaper tipped politely, and Matthew returned the
welcome with a mumbled response.

"Matthew McCarey!" called a stout, balding man,
making his labored way from behind the counter as he
wiped pudgy hands on his apron. "Good to see ya,
good to see ya," he greeted, extending a hand as Matthew rose to shake it. "Haven't seen ya in quite a
spell, my friend. Heard about the Garrett troubles,
though. How's it going?"

"Nothing so far, Dan," lowering his voice. "Do you
know Foster Mayer's boy? Rick, this is Dan Franklin.
'E's been here longer than me, and that's sayin' a lot."
Matthew smiled a rare, toothy grin, and Rick laughed,
simply because it was so seldom he saw Matthew
laugh.

"What'll you have, Matthew? Yore usual, or have
yore tastes changed since the war? Don't look to me
like the war shrunk you any," laughed the old man.

Matthew nodded assent, and Rick declined anything.

"I'd like another bowl of stew if you're going back,"
requested the clergyman, pulling a watch from beneath
his cassock and studying it seriously. "What time does
the train to New York come in?"

"Two o'clock, supposedly," shrugged Old Dan with
a skeptical grimace.

Matthew followed the old man back to the counter, leaning an elbow on the wooden counter as he watched Dan lace his coffee heavily.

"How's the Garrett boy doing, Matthew?" questioned the man, putting the cork back into the bottle.

"Not good, Dan. You haven't seen anything of the blond man who's been in the papers, have you? Or even heard anything? It doesn't have to be legitimate. At this point we'll check out anything."

"Matt, I'll tell you the truth. I've watched close at ever'body that has come through here since it happened. I swear I haven't heard or seen anythin'. If you want my ideas, I'd say the girl was dead. That fella would be a fool to pass up the kind of ransom the old senator could pay. If she was alive, you'd a heard somethin' by now. When did the Garrett boy marry this woman, anyway, Matthew? The last I heard he'd set him up a law practice. Then the war come, and I didn't hear no more of them boys, neither one of 'em. Next thing I know'd was this stuff in the papers."

"She's a fine woman, Dan. They were married in Tennessee, the last day of the war."

Matthew placed several coins into the old man's palm and found his chair. Rick knew when not to talk, and together they listened thoughtfully to the bits and pieces of conversation floating disjointedly about them, reassuring in its own fashion that life did manage to go on.

The young couple with the child whispered softly between themselves. The clergyman's chin kept dropping toward his chest as he dozed, and the two other men discussed cattle diseases.

Rick and Matthew sat through the recounting of a scourge of rapid wolves and a hushed response about anthrax, and in the back of his mind Matthew kept searching for a fresh approach to Sarah's kidnapping. Sleepily Rick stared at the sandy-haired man with brilliant blue eyes and slightly nasal voice as the topic of conversation drifted to runaway horses. His companion needed a shave badly, and Rick yawned, rubbing at the stubble across his own chin.

"You take that horse I'm riding, now," the blue-eyed guest was saying. "He's the meanest beast I've ever seen. Tries to fight everything that comes near 'im. If I could take the loss I swear I'd shoot the miserable nag and go on foot."

"I know a guy who'll take him off your hands," volunteered the other man, running fingers through his hair to comb some of the tangles out.

Rick stretched aching muscles and Matthew, weary of looking at everyone as if they were suspect, made a gesture indicating he was ready to go.

"Pray the good Lord the train runs on time tonight," remarked the parson as he folded his paper under his arm. "I've a pressing appointment." Rick smiled politely.

Matthew rose, hitching up his belt, and the pair left, the young man waiting at the bottom of the steps for his large companion. The words "Virginia" and "horse trader" fell on the Irishman's ear, and both had taken at least six steps before Matthew paused, tilting his head. After four weeks of exhaustive search, could such a remark bear fruit? It was highly unlikely. But it was not wholly impossible.

"Hell, we've chased wilder geese," he muttered, and without another comment they retraced their way. Rick followed behind the big man as they reentered the small room. Surprised, several heads lifted to see them return, and the conversation between the two men ceased, discomfited by Matthew's pointed stare.

Old Dan watched the silent figure tower in the center of the room. Every pair of eyes flicked from the seated man to Old Dan, and then back to Matthew.

"May I do something for you?" the shocked man

spoke at last. Self-consciously, he shrugged and made a grimace at his companion.

"It's possible," mumbled Matthew, never once shifting his gaze. The man began to squirm in his seat.

"What's the matter, Matthew?" questioned the worried proprietor.

"Per'aps nothing," replied Matthew gravely. "I would request this man's name and where 'es been for the past four weeks."

The man's temper sparked. "Look, whoever you are," drawing out of his seat, "I don't have to answer any questions. Now, if you'll excuse me, it's time I was leaving."

More from intuition than anything else, Matthew reached out and clapped a hand on his shoulder. "Just a couple of questions, if you please."

"Who *are* you?" demanded the unshaven man, not quite daring to force the hand away.

"Does the name Garrett mean anything to ye?" The words burst with explosive force.

"No!" The man hesitated, then stammered, "Well, I . . . I know there's a search for . . . . some woman, I suppose. Everyone knows that. Good Lord, man, you can't live in this end of the country and not know that."

Matthew had spent a good deal more of his life listening rather than talking, and he was a fairly good judge of human behavior. He trusted his intuition. So, taking a chance, he waited until the man was about to step from the room. The single word resounded through the small enclosure.

"Ronsard!" Before the man could stop himself, his body jerked in reaction, and Matthew knew instantly that he had happened on the one opening wedge they had found in weeks.

The man struggled with a sheepish smile. Rick watched in awe at the quick agility of the huge man.

As the long legs placed him before the man, Matthew lifted him completely from the floor with one hand.

"You may as well tell all, man, before you have it beaten from you, bit by bit."

"Nothing!" whimpered Artie. "I know nothing," squirming against the wall. Matthew dropped him to the floor, and Artie fell weakly to his knees. Artie's dinner companion, having now become the object of Matthew's gaze, drew back as far as he could.

"Please," he choked. "I don't know this man. He told me he had been in Virginia for a while. That's *all* in the world I know, I swear to heaven that's the truth!"

"Over there. Out of the way," Matthew dismissed him carelessly, wheeling about to give Artie his full attention. Artie straightened, inching himself against the wall with arms outspread, sweat glistening on his face.

Without a single word Matthew reached out and found the back of a chair. A quick movement of his arm, and the chair crashed against the wall directly beside the cowering figure, broken splinters clattering to the floor.

"Matthew!" gasped Old Dan. "Have a care!"

Rick started once to murmur a warning to the great man, for he had never seen this type of violence in Matthew. The angry man slowly stalked the creeping figure around the edge of the room, like an aroused animal watching its victim to try an escape. Matthew grasped the table by one leg. Artie gave a cry of horror as he envisioned himself being smashed against the wall.

"Wait!" he screamed as the table rose. Matthew was upon him in an instant.

"Where's Sarah Garrett?"

"Sarah Garrett?"

"Where did Ronsard take her? And the boy?"

"Wait! Stay back!" he choked. "The boy's with the old woman. I don't know where she took him—moving around, they said. The woman Sarah . . . the woman . . ." Artie dropped his head.

"Go on, man!" roared the great Irish figure.

"She . . . she's dead." Matthew made a movement toward the broken man, but Rick interfered, grabbing one great arm in both his hands, holding as hard as he could.

"Dead?" whispered Matthew, the color draining from his face. "Dead?" He turned, removed his hat, wiped his face, his eyes dazed. Glancing at the parson he snapped, "Fetch the marshal." The man left quickly.

Artie began to tell his story, rapidly though brokenly, looking up from time to time to see how near Matthew was. He told of Sarah's being in the cellar for twelve days, and of Adrien's decision not to send a ransom message.

"She took sick, and Adrien wouldn't let me go for a doctor. I did everything I could for her," the man wept. "Oh Lord, the fever. It got worse, and then she just . . . died. Adrien told me to take her out and bury her and then get the hell out of there. He was going on somewhere. I don't know where. Well, anyway, I took her out in the coach, but every time I started to get down and dig a grave for her someone would come by on the road. I was scared as hell, and I . . . I took her out of the coach and laid her down in a ditch. I got out of there as fast as I could. By that time . . ."

Artie was shaking so hard he could hardly continue, but Matthew had heard all he had to.

Presently the clergyman returned with the marshal. "Where did you leave her body?" growled Matthew. "And how long ago?" However, Artie was unable to explain, and Matthew reached toward the broken man.

"About two weeks ago!" he gasped.

"All right!" commanded the marshal. "I'll handle it now. I'll have some men go out and find her. I'll wire the Senator. Now go!"

Matthew forced his way to Artie and stood before him in a daze. "Did . . . did you find a jewel? A pearl? Did you find it on a chain about 'er neck?"

Artie shrugged. "We didn't touch her. I swear on all that's holy. Neither one of us laid a hand on her. I swear."

Matthew would have stayed there forever, asking questions. Anything rather than going back to tell Nathaniel. Anything! What wouldn't he give not to have to look into those eyes with this news? But, after standing there for several moments, he led Rick from the room.

⚸ Chapter XIV

SUNLIGHT PIERCED SARAH'S mind like arrows, stabbing her awake. Green spires viewed through narrowed eyelids bowed and scraped lazily in the wind, flitting in and out of focus. Faraway sounds—a strange voice, mournful in its call, the restless snuffle of a horse, an occasional creak of a passing wagon—all filtered through Sarah's awareness, ebbing and flowing.

Was she crying? No tears moistened her parched face, but sounds of sobbing echoed in her mind as if some poor creature lay weeping at the end of a very long tunnel. Light seared her eyes. Artie would be angry, for she wasn't allowed to see the light. Light was for people Rachel liked. Rachel didn't like her. A thousand vicious needles pricked her, and the cold dew made her shiver. The coveted light dimmed until a warming blackness sucked her up.

Later, the spires were gone. Blinking stars splattered above her, and the blurry memory of a stone-floored courtyard swirled confusing. Wasn't Nathaniel supposed to come for her? She could see the stars, and Peter was crying. Peter was crying! The heaviness of her head wouldn't allow her to go to him. Rachel wouldn't let her hold him anyway. The pain in her belly—was Peter about to be born? The crying—he must be born. And Rachel wouldn't let her see him. Oh, Charles, why did you bring me here so Rachel would take Peter?

If Nathaniel would come and carry her into the

house she would be safe. Didn't he know how cold it was?

You are not Nathaniel. I don't know you. Don't touch my skin—it hurts so. Nathaniel, I died.

The hands are black. The black hands are gentle—not like Daddy's hands. His hands touched my head when he said good-bye. And he never turned around to look at me when he walked away. I waited for him to turn around, but he never did.

I'm crying for Nathaniel. Why am I crying when it hurts my chest so? I wish I could stop crying.

"Missy, is yawl wakin' up? Missy?"

Large black hands changed the damp cloth on her forehead, and the cracked sounds which came from Sarah's throat sounded as though they were in gratitude.

Sarah wished for water, and somehow the stooped black person interpreted that wish, returning soon with a yellowed cup of cool water. Old hands slipped behind her head, raising her as best they could, and Sarah strangled. Gently the hands blotted at her chin and neck. The swollen throat was unable to tolerate water, despite the awful craving.

"Easy, Missy. Don' drank too fas'. Won' stay down iffen yawl drank too fas'."

Sarah followed his voice, and a thin hand lifted to him before it dropped weakly to the old quilt covering her.

"Ah shore is glad to see yawl come 'roun', Missy." The black face glistened, and he stooped, shuffling softly to fetch Sarah a bowl of the broth from a rabbit cleaned only that morning.

Sarah reveled in the strange smells and pulled farther down into the covers. For the first time in many days she was not aching, and her eyes didn't feel as if they were full of sand. What day was it? How long had it been since she was taken from the Garrett's? And where were Adrien and Artie?

Drawing a straight-backed, rickety chair near the small cot, the now familiar hand reached to prop Sarah's head so he could spoon broth into her mouth. Obediently Sarah opened her mouth, swallowing. She tried words, but the grizzled head could barely hear.

"Who are you and . . . how did I get here?" Deep smile lines creased the old face, beads of sweat sparkling his high black forehead.

"Been here 'bout fo' days, I speck, Missy. Yep. Ah done foun' ya layin' by the road, an' Ah thank yawl's daid. I brung yawl up to bury ya. But I watched ya fer a bit, an' then I seed yawl's eyes move jes' a mite. So Ah put ya up on this here bed and waited. Lawd, Lawd, Ah don' know how yawl got on th' road, ma'am. Ah don' know how long yawl laid out in th' open."

The toothless grin touched Sarah, and she knew for a certainty she would be dead, probably eaten by wild animals by now, if this old man hadn't saved her.

"What's your name?" she whispered, carefully moistening her cracked lips with a tongue that seemed too large for her mouth.

"They's allas called me 'Bo,' Missy. So Ah speck that's mah name. Ah don' mean no disrespeck to a fine, white lady, Missy, but yawl want fer Ah fetch th' woman to see 'bout th' babe? Yawl hol' lak it was painin' lotsa times, an' Ah's skeered that it'd come fo' its time."

Sarah shook her head listlessly. Curious eyes studied her, and Sarah strained against her muscles under the cover. So little strength remained in her, she was powerless to move at all. Grimly her hands moved to the swell of her belly. As nearly as she could figure she had been gone about three weeks, or thereabouts. Sarah wrestled with an exhausted brain to figure the months she was pregnant, and then sleep claimed her.

The next two days were much the same. Sarah would rouse for brief spells of wakefulness, during which old Bo would help her outside to relieve herself.

And once he even took the filthy print dress out near the well of the deserted plantation manor and washed it, hanging it over a bush to dry. With a rough rag and cold water Sarah bathed herself as best she could, and once she was attired in the clean dress they both attempted to do something with her hair. It was dirty, but she had no strength to wash it. Awkwardly the black hands removed the tangles with a piece of a comb, and then Bo braided it, explaining between frowning pauses that he had once had a woman of his own and two children. His wife was long since dead. He didn't know where the children were.

"Bo," remarked Sarah pensively during his silence. "Do you think it's August yet?"

"Mite near't, Ah'd reckon," the grey head nodded.

Over four months, she figured. She was over four months pregnant. Her waist was thickening, and the small curve of her abdomen seemed about right for three months. Miraculously, she hadn't lost the baby!

"Are we near Washington, Bo?" Sarah pushed with her palms, dragging herself up onto the pillows to question the old man further.

"Yawl's in V'ginny, Missy. But not too fah frum the Cap'tal, I speck. Is that whur yawl's frum, Missy?" Bo fetched a plate of some solid food for her—cornbread, and some boiled potatoes from his small garden.

"I think if I can get a message to Washington I can find my husband, Bo. They're probably looking for me."

In disjointed segments Sarah related the story to Bo, as well as she could put everything together.

Eager eyes sparked with new life at the prospects of a plan. The pearl! The chain still hung about her neck, and now her thin fingers fumbled with the tiny chain, withdrawing the jewel.

"Bo?" she choked, beginning to cough again and vowing that she positively must not become agitated. "Bo, look. We have money. If we could use this piece of jewelry, perhaps we could buy a horse or something."

Bo cackled. "Missy, d'yawl know whut white mens'd do t'me iffen they saw somp'n lak that?" Again the amused laugh filled the tiny shanty. Sarah's eyes dropped in dismay. It had not occurred to her that Bo had once been a slave, for to her he was a savior. She depended upon him for life.

"Missy," offered the stooping figure, "soon as yawl kin git 'roun' a bit by yawlsef, Ah'll walk to Washin'-ton. Ain't no problem in that. Ah'll git a message to yore people. Ah's jes 'fraid to leab yawl heah by yaw-sef befo' yawl is well."

The third day saw Sarah sitting propped up for a good portion of the day. By the fifth day, however, Sarah's legs could manage to get her about, with frequent stops. Finally Sarah insisted she could manage enough on her own. Carefully Bo wrapped the valuable pearl with its chain, in case he needed it. Casting one last worried look at Sarah, he left.

A hot August sun beat persistently, and the red-bearded man settled a hat low upon an already moistened brow, shielding his face from the brilliant light. Washington was a torment. Finally, though not willingly, Nathaniel had agreed to leave the house for the first time since the news of Sarah's death had arrived. Nathaniel had never returned to his country estate, dismissing the workmen and refusing to speak of it again. In fact, Nathaniel hadn't spoken very much to anyone. There had been no display of grief—no anger—nothing. When Matthew had spilled the tragic news to him, Nathaniel had simply turned his back and walked off. Since then, he had been empty of all emotion.

"Matthew McCarey!" an urgent masculine shout accosted Matthew from a distance, and grey eyes lifted to watch the obese figure of Dan Franklin scuttling along as rapidly as his thick legs would carry him.

"Matthew McCarey, wait up!" Sweat pouring profusely, Old Dan fished about in his pocket for a kerchief to mop at the reddened cheeks before he could speak.

"What is it, man? Don't overdo yerself," cautioned Matthew in a friendly but puzzled manner.

The agitated words fell without preface. "What ya told me th' other time, Matthew! What ya asked the man . . . remember?" Grey brows raised and lowered nervously.

Matthew's nerves suddenly stretched taut.

"Speak up, Dan! Speak up!"

"You remember askin' the man about a necklace? This chain on 'er neck?"

"What have ye heard?"

"It's a bunch of fellas, Matt. They had an old nigger out in front of the place, and I overheard the whole thing. They's roughin' him up pretty bad. Seems he was tryin' to find a likely person to help him with directions to the marshal, but he didn't know nothin' about findin' his way around in the city. Must've followed the rails into town."

"Just say it, Dan! And make it quick!" Sarah's body had never been found, even after an exhaustive search. Persistently, this point had plagued Matthew, for he knew that until she was buried Nathaniel would be in torments of hell, never quite knowing, never quite accepting.

"I dunno, Matt, I dunno. He didn't make good sense when these guys started pushin' him around. He kept sayin' he had to find the marshal, and they wouldn't let him go. Kept makin' sport of him, ya know. And he finally admitted havin' a sick white woman that he was tryin' to find help for. One of the men really jumped him hard when he said that." Dan wiped his face and moistened his lips.

"They's talkin' hangin', Matthew! That pore old man—they threatened to string him up. He didn't know how to handle hisself, and I didn't go out pokin' my nose in. Per'aps I should've. Anyway, he pulls out this necklace, see, and I remembered what you was askin' the other man about."

Interrupting Old Dan's timely account, the door of the town house opened. With the exactness of a stalking cat, Nathaniel moved to stand over the panting man. He had overheard some of the account.

"Where is he? Where's the black man?"

"They all left, Mr. Garrett. They . . . said somethin' 'bout findin' this white woman and givin' her a thrashin' and stringin' up the old man." Old Dan was shivering. Lord, but he was glad this man was not after him! "Those men won't do nothin', sir. They's just angry at the Freedmen and all the trouble with the gover'ment. It's just talk. But I don't know where they went."

"I'm going to have a look at that road into Virginia. It would be near where he put her by the road. I know it!"

Jamming his rifle into his saddle holster, Nathaniel flung himself into the saddle, clamping hard with his knees and jerking the animal about so fiercely the steed reared. Matthew followed, and Old Dan was left standing in the street.

Laboriously the two men weaved their way through the city, Nathaniel's temper growing more raw each time he was delayed by people or horses. Matthew shouted his warning to the straight back ahead of him. "Nat, take care. This may be nothing. Don't set your heart on't, boy. Please."

Matthew's shoulders drooped in defeat, for as Nathaniel twisted in his saddle, hope surged across his face.

"She's alive, Matthew. And don't say a *damn thing!*" Matthew heaved a great sigh. Nathaniel selected the road to Virginia and carefully guided his steed into the tall grasses flanking. With experienced eyes, the two read the signs of recent travel.

"Follow slowly. I'll ride ahead," Nathaniel clipped impatiently, not waiting for a reply as he urged the horse ahead. Soon he was alone, examining terrain for any indication that a sizeable group of horses had passed this way. Leaning low from the saddle, dismounting once, then proceeding again, Nathaniel thought there were tracks—fresh ones. Squinting ahead, he thought he saw a hazy cloud of dust. Probably twelve to fifteen riders would make such a cloud.

Swiftly, taking care not to strain his horse, Nathaniel rode back and signaled to Matthew.

The entire country was disturbed—men were uncertain, angry, and explosive. A mob of men, perhaps out of work and desperate, could easily become enraged at the thought of a black man keeping a young white woman. Care was vitally important.

The afternoon was hot, and their shirts were soaked, clinging to their backs. For well over an hour, and at a steady pace, they followed. Dusk came.

Darkness, when it fell, would be their ally. A simple strategy was easy to plan, for by now their destination was in view. Undoubtedly it was the abandoned plantation grown over with brambles. Slave shanties formed a line just beyond it, and Nathaniel motioned Matthew to draw nearer.

With only the two of them, little remained except to boldly come upon them. Nathaniel and Matthew went back a long way together, and they parted with brief discussion. When the time came, they would know what to do.

"You disgustin' old nigger!" one angry voice shouted, its owner inside a disorderly circle of onlookers. Just barely able to make out the figure of the cowering black man in their midst, Nathaniel pulled back the hammer on his rifle and cautiously placed himself just in the edge of the timber.

Irately the man extended the heel of his hand, catching Bo on the shoulder and sending him sprawling to the parched ground. One of the whites was fashioning a traditional hangman's noose. Though not bound, the black man evidently saw no wisdom in resistance, kneeling mutely.

"Do you want I should bring out the woman?" shouted one of the would-be lynchers, jabbing a thumb toward the shack. "She must not be more'n twenty or so. Trash. If the gov'ment had left the damn slaves like they was, we wouldna had such a mess."

The mumbled agreement rippled, spreading like a spark in a dry field.

"Hangin' ain't bad enough for any black man that takes a white woman. 'Fore you know it, half the kids in the country'll have black blood in 'em," prophesied another.

"Why don't we take him to town and give him to the marshal?" suggested a young voice timidly.

"The law wouldn't do nothin'. Don't you know a nigger can't do no wrong?" a voice sneered.

The leader stepped forward and slipped the noose around Bo's neck. The poor man began to shake, and Nathaniel steeled himself.

Suddenly a woman's form filled the doorway of the nearby shack, a dark shadow, small.

"No!" she screamed, staggering toward them. "The man saved my life! Stop! In the name of God, stop!"

Nathaniel moved and, in the confusion, he quickly closed the gap between himself and the lynching party. A movement dead ahead assured him that Matthew, too, was in position. Fury burst from Nathaniel's throat.

His sharp voice cut through the darkness. "Don't move, damn you!"

Heads jerked about, eyes squinting into the darkness. A man on the perimeter of the circle wheeled his mount, intending to flee, but Matthew's shot sent him hurtling from his saddle.

"I don't mind shooting a few more, if that's your wish," the deadly voice dropped into the stillness. He paused for two seconds, then spoke again.

"I am Nathaniel Garrett, and this woman is my wife who has been searched for for weeks. This old man saved her life and was trying to find me. Why didn't you ask him some questions before accusing him?"

Nathaniel's face was just about as angry as Matthew had ever seen it, and the big man drew his horse nearer, lest Nathaniel's pent-up hatred lash out, uncontrolled.

"Free that man!" Nathaniel snapped, jerking a thumb toward the stunned Bo. And, slowly, they freed him.

The men before him weren't fighters, they were farmers and factory workers. Nathaniel saw fear, sullenness, and contrition on their faces.

His shoulders slumped. It was over, and he wanted to go to his wife.

"What are you doing here, for God's sake? We just ended a war. *Go home!* All of you!"

No one quibbled with him, though a few watched him warily. His saddle leather creaked, and Nathaniel covered the distance between Sarah and himself with long running strides. He bent and swept her up. With tears blinding him, Nathaniel made his way to the cabin.

The great man licked the salt from his mouth and held her tightly to his chest, the quiet, soundless sobs racking deep in his belly as he rocked Sarah back and forth, back and forth.

"I love you, Sarah," he sobbed. "More than anything I have ever known. I've been so afraid, Sarah. I thought I had lost you. I didn't want a life without you. Not *any* life."

"Suh?" the hesitant, gentle lisp drew grateful eyes.

"Nathaniel," smiled Sarah, "this is Bo. There are many things I need to tell you, but in time. This wonderful man brought me in from beside the roadway where I was dying and he has cared for me—brought me back to life. Bo, this is my husband."

"Suh?" ventured the stooped Negro. "Is yawl goin' to tek Missy tonight?"

"I'll send for a carriage, Bo," replied Nathaniel. "Sarah can't travel by horseback as weakened as she is."

"I knows whur one is," said the man. He grinned. "Thur's one in the ba'n, Suh—li'l two-seat rig. Don' know why folkses lef' it. Ah didn' hab no hoss."

"Matthew," called Nathaniel. "Would you go with Bo and check out this rig he has?"

Matthew was just as glad for something to do. He felt awkward, intruding on the reunion.

"Nathaniel," Sarah sighed. "As God is my witness I never thought to see you again." Her eyes closed, and Nathaniel picked her up. She was almost asleep on her feet. "Rachel took Peter." She spoke with eyes still shut. "Adrien sold him for money. John Pollard took him the night of the ball. I know he's all right. Rachel would not hurt him, but—"

"Don't cry, Sarah." The great tears slid down her cheeks. "Your days of crying are finished. I'll find Peter. Just now, our problem is getting you home."

In the darkness of the tiny slave shanty Nathaniel kissed his wife reverently, gratefully. Then he laid her on the little pallet. Sarah was barely able to keep awake until all the preparations were made.

"Bo," she murmured suddenly. "He can't stay here."

"He may not want to go, but I think he'd better," agreed Nathaniel, pulling the covers about her. He approached Bo, who was resting tiredly in the shanty doorway. "Bo," he entreated, kneeling on one knee beside the grey-haired man, "I want you to come with us. I have a place for you, and it would satisfy me if

320

you would let me just begin to repay your kindness. You took a terrible risk for Sarah, keeping her here. You would have your own place to live. I don't want to press something on you, but nothing's left here, Bo. And you would have people who care about you."

It was apparent that Bo had never expected anything in return for his kindness to Sarah. After a long pause, a toothless smile lit his face.

"Ah reckon yawl's right, Mist' Garrett. Ah done tooken a liken' to that Miss mahsef. Ah speck Ah'd bes' tag 'long and see iffen this little 'un gwine be fine. Lak yawl say, ain' nothin' lef at this place—not no mo'."

Soon enough, the three men and their tiny woman were traveling the road back home.

"Nathaniel? How is Vance? Is he all right?"

Why did she have to ask that *now,* before she had begun to get her strength back? What could he say?

Their pace was slow, and the night sounds could occasionally be heard even over the creaking wheels and the hoofs. Hesitating just a few seconds too long, Nathaniel was compelled to look down into those deep, knowing eyes.

"Sarah . . ." he began.

"Nathaniel?"

"Shhh, love. Vance . . . Vance is dead, Sarah. He died the night you were kidnapped. Or the next morning. I wasn't there."

There was a long silence.

"It's all right. It's all right." Sarah buried her face against his chest.

"I think I shed all my tears for Vance before he died, Nathaniel. It saddens me terribly, but somehow I think Vance lived more than all of us."

"He left something for you, love. George brought it to me."

"What was it?"

"A music score. An el—elegy, is that right?"

Sarah smiled. *He had done it! He had finished the score. Oh, Vance, Vance.* Sarah sighed. "A tone poem for the dead. He managed to leave something of himself, Nathaniel. I'm so proud of him. He loved me, you know."

"I felt the bite of that love. More than once. I'm not very nice about things like that."

That's why she loved him. Because he was just a man. And he never pretended anything more.

The Garrett town house was the only one astir on the tree-bordered stretch of cobblestone street, and Nathaniel vowed a yellow rectangle of light must surely be streaming from every window.

"We'll be in presently, Nat," said Matthew, pausing long enough to bend over Sarah. "My hopes for Nat weren't the best while you were away."

"Thank you, Matthew." Sarah reached upward to touch his sleeve. Few words were necessary with Matthew.

Before Nathaniel could open the door it swung wide, revealing the robed Senator Garrett and Eleanor, pinning her hair back from a beaming face. Gently, gently Samuel Garrett drew his frail daughter-in-law to him, the tears coursing down his face. His wife stood beside him, stroking Sarah's arm, the tears streaming down her face just as rapidly.

"Oh, Sarah-girl," the elated father shook his silver head in amazement. "Thank God, thank God!"

Sarah practically fell into the capable hands of his wife as Nathaniel and his father clasped their arms about one another. It was over! As suddenly as it had begun, the nightmare was over.

"Mother," said Nathaniel, "the black man who saved Sarah is here to live with us. Do whatever's necessary to make him welcome. He's an unassuming old man, and I think it will take a woman's touch to make him feel welcome."

"Very well, Nathaniel. I'll be glad to. We owe him so much. But take care with this child. She is *very* weak still. I want Clarke to give her a thorough examination tomorrow."

"Of course, Mother. We Garretts take care of our own."

Sarah couldn't remember feeling so heavenly as Eleanor rubbed creamy lotion on her tired legs and feet.

"I really plan to be up tomorrow," she insisted. "I must be about finding Peter. I'm afraid I can't wait until I'm stronger."

"Nonsense. Samuel and Nathaniel will find him. Already Samuel has set a few wheels in motion to begin a search. This was before . . . anyway, you mustn't worry."

Almost as if she could see it, could hold it in her hands, Sarah felt their concern for her welfare. Her woes were their woes—not an imposition, not a burden. The elegant Eleanor Garrett sat upon the bed and reached out an affectionate hand. Their fingers touched. Each understood the other.

"We both love you, Sarah. I hope you can accept that. I doubt we will ever speak of this again, but I want you to know that I understand what you've never had. A place to belong, the love of a mother. Don't ever be too self-conscious to come to me, Sarah. The life before you will be trying in many respects, for it's my private belief that Nathaniel will follow in the footsteps of his father. It has many built-in hardships for a wife and mother. Once you've lived it, perhaps you will understand my love for what you've given Nathaniel."

The doorway framed a damp-haired man. "Mother," he interrupted, bending low to give his wife a peck upon the lips. Then another, and still another with a murmur of increasing ardor.

"If you please, Nathaniel," scolded Eleanor.

"Huh? Oh yes, Mother."

"Take care of this child. She's very weak, and I won't rest until I see some color back in those cheeks."

As Eleanor left, or perhaps afterward, Sarah could make out only a movement. Or was it even that? Both her arms went around his neck, and as Nathaniel stood holding her, he lost himself in her eyes.

"How many thousands of times have I done this in my mind while you were gone. Tell me. Say again you love me."

Making no sound at all, she formed the words. "I love you."

Nathaniel found her mouth, hungrily opening it with his own. He was almost afraid she wasn't real, that it was all some cruel dream from which he would awaken. Alone.

One kiss became another as he stood there—savage, fierce kisses. Sarah's tongue met his with devouring impatience, and he lowered her with arms that quivered. She didn't understand why he turned away, panting and shaken.

"Is something wrong? *Something is wrong that you're not telling me!*"

Nathaniel pushed her back to the bed. "Hush! Nothing's wrong, love."

Sarah was beautifully flushed, her legs dangling. She seemed bathed in moonlight, and a breeze ruffled the silk about her legs.

"Oh, Sarah," he breathed, kneeling, burying his face in her belly. "Love is such a funny thing, letting blood with the slightest of wounds and accepting pain like the slash of a broadsword. I don't want to hurt you, love. That's all."

"You couldn't hurt me, Nathaniel." Sarah cupped both hands about his face and turned it upward.

"And our baby?"

She smiled. "You're afraid to make love to me, aren't you? I can't believe this—the man who takes and asks questions later. Or something to that effect."

"Don't make me out to be *more* of an animal than I am. But, in all truth, I am, dammit," he grinned, then sobered.

"All the way back I thought of it, promising myself I'd keep my hands off you. Until Clarke looked you over, at least. And now I'm about to burst my breeches I want you so much. You've been *so* sick, Sarah, and I think I hate myself already."

Sarah laughed. "You've been used to ladies, Nathaniel. I worked like a man until the day Peter was born. No, no, my love. I'm not the miscarrying kind."

With his head on her thigh, Nathaniel talked until his words dwindled to nothing. Sarah hardly felt him slip the robe off her shoulders. His mouth moved across her waist, and she couldn't catch herself as she fell backward, her legs still dangling off the bed.

She submitted to his daring play with small gasps of pleasure. Had she no idea at all of the depths he could touch? Moaning softly that she loved him, that she wanted him, Sarah ached.

"Nathaniel," her mind whimpered. "Was I born for this moment? *Nathaniel!*"

Presently he stood, bending low with an arm on either side. "A lifetime," he smiled at her flush, "it's been a lifetime since I took you last. And now it seems like yesterday."

His mouth groped for hers, finding it.

"I will be gentle," he promised. And he would have been but for her upward arch. She was tired, tired of waiting for that splintering caress of manhood. Nathaniel's kisses as he moved within her were warm, then ravenous. Love words grated in her ear. His breath was harsh. Sarah melted to him in a wave that quickly grew. Higher and higher it reached until it dashed itself against the rocks, breaking upward and outward, falling in a thousand diamond drops to move calmly out to sea.

Sarah went to sleep with her head cradled against his shoulder, her hair tangled across his chest.

The papers were full of Artie's imprisonment. Rachel continued to elude them, and the Senator began putting pressure on those Southern landholders who had appeared on Adrien's list. Threatened with exposure and prosecution, they helped in the search for Rachel. But all they managed to uncover was the real Adrien Ronsard, his supporters being most anxious to return him to France.

Channing-Adrien managed to disappear totally after one final grim encounter not far from the Garrett land. Clarke delivered the terrible news at dinner one evening. Beth Simms had been picked up by a passing farmer that day, slashed from one side of her face to the other and half-dead. She was crawling about on the ground, mumbling unintelligibly.

"Is she going to be hospitalized for long?" inquired Eleanor, shocked and horrified.

"Probably," Clarke answered tiredly. "I sewed her up and left orders that she should not be allowed to be alone. One minute she talks rationally and the next she's quite mad. I did the best I could with her face, but she will never be the lovely woman she was. Never. And her father has had a stroke from all this. I'll treat him at home, though. A hospital would be too much of a shock to the poor old man."

In a way Clarke's announcement closed an unpleasant book for Nathaniel. "I really hated that man," he admitted. "Truthfully, I guess I always will. I used to worry that he'd come back. Now I feel cheated that he won't pay for the damage he's done."

Sarah looked up at him with knowing brown eyes. "Everyone pays, darling. Maybe not behind bars. Look at Beth. God knows, she's paid."

Eleanor slipped an arm about her oldest son. "There

was a very wise man who recorded something for us in Holy Writ. 'Vengeance belongs to God.' "

For long moments Nathaniel pondered. He patted her cheek. "And didn't another say the price of a good woman is above rubies? Thank you, Mother."

ᏇᏇ *Chapter XV*

THE FIRST SNOWS were falling when Nathaniel said, "I have nothing against Beethoven." Bending
his knees, he lowered himself before a mirror to brush
his tousled hair. Giving Sarah only half his attention,
he inspected the whiteness of his teeth as she announced her intention of attending the coming concert,
a week from Wednesday. "Second movements by any
composer wear me out. Besides," he grinned, "you
look like a pumpkin."

And Nathaniel bent to give her a loving kiss.

"It's another whole month until the baby yet, and
they're playing the *Eroica Symphony,* Nathaniel. I
promise you'll like it, even the second movement."

Many weeks of rest had resulted in an alertness in
her brown eyes. The hollow cheeks had filled out.
Stepping gingerly before the tall man and obstructing
his view of himself with apparent unconcern, Sarah
studied her swelling middle with interest.

"They are all endlessly slow, tortuous things, and
they try me sorely," Nathaniel continued his critique,
straining to retain a portion of the mirror for himself.
Noticing the gaping back of her dress, Nathaniel proceeded to fasten the increasingly inadequate hooks.

"I'll tell you what, little one, I'll trade you a trip to
the dressmaker's for an evening of Beethoven."

Twisting under his hands, Sarah sternly tweaked a
wisp of hair on his chest. "Ridiculous! You know there
is no sense whatever in having dresses made for me
now. I may as well wait until the baby comes. It's an

328

unnecessary extravagance. *And,* for your information, I intend to hear it even if I have to wheedle Clarke and Tabby into taking me," a tapping foot indicated just how determined she was.

"Headstrong, I declare!" he growled. "I can afford a hundred gowns, and you've put me off ever since we married. Enough is enough, and I'll hear no more about it. Pout if you must, but I shall speak to Madame Cartier tomorrow. If you don't go there, she'll come here. Since she designs and makes my mother's clothes, I venture she'll be able to please even you." He paused, then added. "No dresses, no Beethoven."

"It's not that I can't be pleased, and you well know it, Nathaniel!" Her jaw jutted, and her husband couldn't resist a hug. Sarah leaned back, pretending to become absorbed in his Adam's apple and pressing the tip of a finger against it.

"Stop that!"

Sarah grimaced. "I've never been to a dressmaker's except when you had the cloak made for me in Tennessee. Do you undress . . . down to everything?" she queried, hesitantly.

Suddenly Nathaniel's dark head lifted, his rich laugh filling the room. "Is *that* why you've refused to go?" he choked, placing a large hand on her expanded waist. "My timid little—"

"No! Certainly not!" exclaimed Sarah, flushing. "But no woman enjoys standing stripped before a total stranger when she looks like this! Now will you or will you not take me to hear the *Eroica?*"

"Only if you go in a gown of pale blue silk, madam," Nathaniel's finger waved its warning, "with no hoops, either. I wish it draped so," and with deft hands, his tongue unconsciously clamped between white teeth, Nathaniel arranged Sarah's skirts to resemble the newer style of smooth lines, drawing back a fullness of fabric to stream over slender hips.

"It's a beautiful little round tummy," grinned her husband.

"May we invite Tabby and Clarke to go?" Nathaniel laughed and kissed her nose, enjoying winning.

Nathaniel honestly didn't see how Sarah had recovered so well. Of course, there were terrible days of grieving over Peter, and he suspected her worry about the unborn child was a good deal more than she talked about. To spare him, Nathaniel suspected, Sarah blamed her few depressions on Peter's absence and pretended she wasn't scared to death that her ordeal had deformed the baby.

His father had often remarked how valiant a little warrior she was. "Father," he had said gravely, "you don't know the half. Not the half."

Matthew was sure that Rachel knew they were looking for Peter. Often he had just missed her, and the most he got for his efforts was a description that assured them that Peter was well. Rachel had kept herself South, never once venturing into the cities of the North. Nathaniel and Sarah were endlessly grateful to Matthew for chasing all over the South in an effort to find Peter. Sometimes Nathaniel went, but it was mostly Matthew.

Now, as Sarah stood before the mirror, surveying the shimmering grace of the silk caught just below the curve of her breasts, she knew it would bring a throaty growl of satisfaction from her husband. Even large, she was more fetching in her softly designed and extravagantly expensive blue gown than she had been the evening of the ball. Perhaps it was the certainty that Nathaniel loved her that made the difference, or maybe it was the child within.

"Sarah," called the familiar voice from the hallway, quick steps just outside her door. "Are you ready? We'll be late, and heaven knows I don't want to miss any Beethoven, so please . . ."

Nathaniel's eyes widened at the charming sight of

his wife as she pivoted gracefully before the mirror. "Well, well, well. I'm not sure Washington is ready for this." Coming to stand very close behind her, he murmured in her ear, "I don't suppose you'd consider forgetting the whole thing and just come to bed, would you?"

"No, you wretch," laughed Sarah, loving the way he looked at her.

Before Nathaniel's wits could keep peace with his passions, the kiss exceeded a pleasant gesture, the exciting sensation of Sarah's soft breasts crushed against him resulting in the familiar throb. His arms tightened, and he groaned. "I swear that up to this point I considered raping you only once. But now I find the prospect almost irresistible."

"Nathaniel! You're a long-legged devil! When did you ever . . ." gasped Sarah, surprised. "You tell me when you ever thought of such a thing!"

"You would never guess in a thousand years, and I'm embarrassed to tell you. So forget it," he grinned sheepishly. "Come on, spouse." And he took Sarah's arm, guiding her into the hall.

He behaved very badly indeed during the concert, leaning to whisper the most obscene remarks into the shell of Sarah's ear, causing her to redden often. Clarke could hardly refrain from laughing. What with Tabby's consternation and Clarke's encouragement, the poor Beethoven enthusiast behind them suffered mightily. Nathaniel nibbled at Sarah's fingertips until she snatched her hand free with a withering glower.

"Just you see if I ever go anywhere in public with you again!" she vowed, receiving an impatient "Shhh!" from behind her. Terribly embarrassed, Sarah shifted in her seat, cursing Nathaniel Cameron Garrett under her breath.

Sarah wriggled again, searching for a more comfortable spot. The movement dragged, and the stuffiness of the concert hall irritated her. Perhaps she shouldn't have come out after all. Indecent, Rachel would have called it, out in public so pregnant.

A contraction came so hard it made her gasp, and Clarke, quickly took in what was happening.

"Sarah!" he whispered harshly, placing a spread hand across her abdomen. It was tight. He knew the chances a premature baby had. Perhaps it was a false alarm? But he saw the truth in Sarah's pinched mouth. The music lover to their rear shushed them again, and Clarke whispered "Let's get her out of here, Nat! Can you walk, darling?"

"I think so." She was terribly pale. They moved instantly, Sarah rigidly straight. With Clarke at one elbow and Nathaniel at the other, so efficient, so composed, Sarah knew she could last the seconds of ripping pain.

Early! Why was it coming so early, tearing itself from the safeness of her womb? Was her baby to die, after all this? Welcoming Nathaniel's arms as they swept her up, Sarah clung to his neck. Clarke opened the door.

How many contractions came while they were waiting for the carriage, making the tortuous journey to the town house? She didn't know, but it seemed there was no time to rest between them.

Their baby, having decided to make an early appearance, apparently figured an immediate one was even better. Once home, Nathaniel sat by her, never leaving, never taking his hands from hers, though she nearly crushed his bones. She didn't think she could stand many hours of this.

But it wasn't to be hours, announced Clarke, frowning at his silent brother. "Are you sure you want to be here?" he asked. "We can manage. It looks as if it will be a hard, fast delivery. Sarah is doing everything right, not fighting it, and I really don't think it will go on long."

Sarah moaned.

"I don't want to leave," mumbled Nathaniel, but he looked terrified. Sarah smiled at him.

Eleanor and Tabby kept vigil in the hall. Sarah felt water gush to her legs and grabbed for her abdomen as Nathaniel in turn grabbed for her hands. Never had he loved her more, and never had she seemed such a part of him as she did now.

"Nathaniel?"

"Yes, my sweet girl."

"What you said," she gasped, "about wanting to rape me once?"

Clarke's eyebrows rose. "Oh hell, Sarah. Must you now?"

"I want to know." Another contraction stopped her. Finally she whispered, "Tell me."

"Woman, your audacity never fails to flabbergast me," complained Nathaniel. "One night up in the Cumberland you sat outside that cave in the moonlight. I think I was in love with you then."

Sarah smiled.

"Nathaniel, I think you'd better leave. Sarah is due for a good loud yell, and she won't with you there. Out with you. This won't be but a few more minutes."

Clarke's eyes met his brother's. Hadn't he felt this way, too? Women bore the pain of childbirth, but didn't men bear the guilt?

Sarah screamed, just as Nathaniel closed the door. It was an abrupt cry. The eldest Garrett slumped against the wall as Eleanor went to him. Trembling, face drawn, he looked terrible. Eleanor knew just what to say.

"Sometimes it helps to yell a bit. You big men are all the same, you know. You're giants until the baby comes, and that little baby brings you all to your knees."

"Mother, if I could, I'd bear it all. I did this to her."

Eleanor pursed her mouth. "I give you two weeks before you and Sarah are squaring off as usual."

"More like one," corrected Tabby lazily. Nathaniel grinned.

"Sarah, girl," cautioned Clarke, standing at her feet, his hand on her bent knees, "the head is about to come. I know you've had a baby, but each is different. Now, you should feel tremendous pressure. If you don't fight it, then that's *all* it will be—like you were going to burst. Remember? Give me some time. Just don't push."

Sarah nodded, bathed in sweat. It happened as he said, and Clarke kept talking, telling her everything that was happening, encouraging her.

"That's a love. There's lots of beautiful black hair! No, don't push. You're doing just beautifully. Now the shoulder. Easy does it."

"Can I push?"

"No, not yet. The shoulders—must be a boy with shoulders like this. Easy, easy, just let Nature do her work. That's fine. Now, Sarah Catherine Garrett, you have just been delivered of a son. Tiny little beggar. Isn't he pretty?"

The tiny little beggar didn't want to catch his breath as quickly as Clarke would have liked, but the doctor kept this to himself. One large factor in Sarah's favor had been her control. She hadn't prolonged the labor by fighting herself.

"He's premature, yes, but you're in good shape. I don't think your illness hurt him at all. Now, he's going to require close feedings and a lot of love. Nathaniel!" he called. "Come see your son!"

"Kiss your wife, Nathaniel," commanded Eleanor as she entered with her son. "Then shoo! You can come back when we have her all cleaned up."

Sarah was so happy she could have wept. Nathaniel kissed the smooth moist brow.

"Thank you, sweetheart. I love you—very, very

much. I do think he's kind of homely, though. Must take after your side of the family."

"I can slap you, if she can't," exclaimed Eleanor. "He's small, but he looks exactly like you did when you were born."

When Sarah was missing, Nathaniel had prayed often, passionately. Now, he did so again. For no matter what else they had, Peter's absence was breaking both their hearts. Thank God for Matthew, for Nathaniel could not leave his wife and new baby, not now.

And so he and Matthew got messages to one another nearly every day. Each lead turned into another lead—all false, or else good leads but happened upon too late. Would Sarah and Christopher and Nathaniel have to celebrate Christmas without that dear little face?

Nobody was allowed to see the baby until Christmas. He was a little weak, and Clarke wasn't taking any chances with Christopher Samuel Garrett.

Patty came by to see Sarah, however, making a supreme sacrifice by stitching a patchwork clown for Christopher. They wept together over Vance. Thankful that Patty wanted to talk about her twin, Sarah sat with her for quite a long time by the fireplace, remembering, neither of them trying to hide the grief. It did them both good. Patty had grown up into a woman nearly overnight, and Sarah knew Vance's death had hurt her terribly.

Sarah wouldn't allow anyone to help her at night with Christopher, for she had had no help with Peter. But as Christmas approached, the longing for Peter lay heavily on both Sarah and Nathaniel. Nathaniel hadn't dreamed it would take so long to find Rachel, and though he never voiced his grief, Sarah would often catch him brooding, with a bitter set to his mouth. What could they do but wait, and thank God for Matthew?

Christmas afternoon found everyone terribly subdued, what with Rick occupying Vance's usual place at the Garrett dinner table. The Herschell courage was evident, though, and Sarah vowed the bereft parents were a source of encouragement to her in her own grief.

"Do you think Nathaniel will spoil his son, Sarah?" inquired the bearded senator as he settled himself in a comfortable chair for a game of chess.

Sarah laughed. "I might, sir, but I hardly think Nathaniel will. He has that child's life planned, right up to college, and I don't see him settling for any detours."

"I personally think you're a tyrant, Nathaniel Garrett," Patty teased, her adoration of Nathaniel obvious. Sweeping lavender skirts, Patty made to leave the room. Amused, Sarah glanced up from her needlework to see her pass Rick, standing lazily in the doorway.

"You, daughter, have much to learn," commented George, setting up chess pieces and toying with his beard.

"Yes, doesn't she?" agreed the lean Rick, a crooked smile creasing his face as he stretched a determined arm across the doorway. Some new quality in his voice drew more than one pair of eyes to Rick. Patty halted in her tracks.

"Are you trying to tell me something, Rick?" she challenged, matching his manner with her usual bold coquettishness. But Sarah thought she noted a curious dent in Patty's usual resistance to Rick.

"Only that you ought to become a parent before you advise one, pretty girl," murmured the young man in a possessive tone that shocked everyone in the room. Margaret Herschell gave a small gasp of trepidation as she watched the boy she had known as an infant draw her daughter deliberately under a large clump of mistletoe.

"Say 'yes'," he demanded softly, glancing quickly up at the mistletoe for only a second. Patty's composure faltered, and the room sat hypnotized. Without any hesitation, holding his audience enthralled, Rick pulled Patty into his arms and bent to kiss her. He held her for so long that even Nathaniel began to fidget.

After several moments Patty twisted away from her persistent lover, dumbstruck and speechless.

"Say you'll marry me, or I'll do it again," he assured her. Margaret made a move to rise, then checked herself. Knowing she had turned scarlet, Patty struggled to free herself.

"Oh—yes! Yes!" Patty cried, wrenching herself free with a laugh. "To save my virtue, I agree. Dear me! How long have you been planning this!" she laughed.

Rick shrugged, clasping his hands to her waist. "Nearly twenty years now," he replied honestly.

"I swear, you're the most willful man I ever knew!" Everyone burst into excited laughter.

With no warning, Nathaniel jumped, sprinting for the door. Jerking open the front door so that it crashed back against the wall, he cleared the steps in one great leap.

"What the dev—" began Samuel, but Sarah was already at the window, snatching open the drape, sweat beading her forehead. A carriage clattered up and Sarah craned to see it, her heart pounding in her throat. She didn't even know tears were streaming down her cheeks. She could just barely see the huge form of Matthew ducking his head to step from the coach, his arms full with his blanket-wrapped gift.

"Peter!" she cried, stumbling from the room.

"Clarke," sobbed Eleanor, "help her! She'll fall on the steps! Oh, Samuel! The child is home!" The Garretts watched as chubby arms reached for Sarah. Both holding Peter, Sarah and Nathaniel wept without restraint.

Margaret held her breath as she watched Nathaniel and Sarah enter the room, everyone talking at once, laughing, crying, and hugging. But the knot in her throat was too hard, and it just wouldn't go away. As she bent her head, Margaret felt those fingers squeeze hers as they had so often over the years, and she lifted her head to smile through her tears, leaning on the strength of her magnificent husband.

The room was utter chaos for the next hour, Matthew telling and retelling the story. Surely there had never been a more suitable hero than Matthew!

"The old woman was too tired to run anymore. It was wearing her out. She didn't even put up a fuss when I told her I was bringing him home." Matthew smoothed his moustache and sipped Irish whiskey. "Couldn't help but pity the old lady. Sad, sad indeed."

"I don't pity her," snapped Patty.

"That's because you haven't lived long enough to look back and see your own life cluttered with mistakes, my dear," admonished her father. "People alone grow afraid of becoming old, of dying all alone." George fingered the ivory bishop in his hand, then shook his head.

"Nat, are you going to charge her with kidnapping?" Clarke smiled at Peter squatting beside the cradle of his new brother, rocking it gently back and forth with one finger.

Sarah was sitting on the rug at Nathaniel's feet, dreaming.

"No!" Her abruptness drew curious glances. Nathaniel's hands rested on her shoulders. "There's been enough misery in this family. Peter's home. That's all that matters. I don't want to think about Rachel Bradley or Channing-Adrien again. I have everything I want. Everything."

Darkness drew in, and George Herschell rose, gathering his family about him. "And I have everything I want," he said to Sarah, reaching down to draw her to her feet. "I have a new son, and some precious memories of one I loved very much. Thank you, Sarah. I shall never forget what your friendship meant to Vance. Never."

Sarah blinked hard. Standing on tiptoe she kissed his cheek. "He loved you very much."

"I know that."

If there had been any more words, Sarah would have said them. But there were none. Her new family and friends knew what was in her heart, and as good-nights were said, the Christmas of 1865 slipped away. Presently Nathaniel hefted his elder son to his shoulders and led the way, opening the bedroom door for Sarah and Christopher.

Peter was nearly asleep anyway, and dozed off before Nathaniel had finished dressing him for bed. Standing above their sleeping children, Sarah and Nathaniel slowly reached out their hands to one another.

This was the start of a new life—their lives together, really together, as a family. There would be time for endless love-making later on, all the time to explore one another the way Nathaniel had always wanted to explore Sarah, time for the tender reaching out that Sarah now permitted herself.

But neither wanted to move. Not now. For just this moment, at the end of Christmas Day, touching hands and breathing as one, and watching over their children was enough.

Nathaniel and Sarah stood there for a long, long time.

About the Author

LINDA SHAW received her Bachelor of Music Degree from North Texas State University. She lives near Ft. Worth, Texas, with her husband and three children. She has taught music for a number of years and gives performances at the piano and organ and on the viola. *Ballad in Blue* is her first novel.

Popular Romances
from
BALLANTINE

Bestsellers from BALLANTINE